STORIES OF PEOPLE & CIVILIZATION

AFRICAN

ANCIENT ORIGINS

FLAME TREE PUBLISHING
6 Melbray Mews, Fulham,
London SW6 3NS, United Kingdom
www.flametreepublishing.com

25 27 29 28 26
1 3 5 7 9 10 8 6 4 2

ISBN: ISBN: 978-1-83562-270-4

Cover and pattern art was created by Flame Tree Studio, with elements courtesy of Shutterstock.com/svekloid/MotionGrapix by stockeefy/ Irina Sevostyanova. Additional interior decoration courtesy of Shutterstock.com/Viktorija Reuta.

Judith John (lists of Ancient Kings & Leaders) is a writer and editor specializing in literature and history. A former secondary school English Language and Literature teacher, she has subsequently worked as an editor on major educational projects, including *English A: Literature* for the Pearson International Baccalaureate series. Judith's major research interests include Romantic and Gothic literature, and Renaissance drama.

A copy of the CIP data for this book is available
from the British Library.

Designed and created in the UK | Printed and bound in China

COLLECTOR'S EDITIONS

STORIES OF PEOPLE & CIVILIZATION

AFRICAN

ANCIENT ORIGINS

ROBIN WALKER

Foreword by
PROFESSOR MANU AMPIM

Further Reading and
Lists of Ancient Kings & Leaders

FLAME TREE PUBLISHING

CONTENTS

Series Foreword **12**

Foreword by Professor Manu Ampim **15**

Introduction to African Ancient Origins **21**

Origins of the Modern Countries in Africa 22

Beginning the Conquest of Southern Africa 23

African Resistance Battles 24

European Colonialism 27

The Pan-African Movement 31

Ethiopia: The only non-colonized country in Africa 36

The Independence Period 39

Decolonial Theory and Practice 41

The Southern African Freedom Struggle 42

Angola 44

Mozambique 48

Zimbabwe 49

South Africa and Namibia 51

Further Reading **54**

CONTENTS

Africa & Human Origins....61

Origin and Global Migrations of Homo Sapiens....61

Ancestors of Homo Sapiens....68

The Evolution of Africa's Prehistoric Cultures....77

Nilo-Saharan Culture....79

From Niger Kordofanian to Niger-Congo Culture....81

Afroasiatic Culture....83

Khoisan Culture....88

Batwa Culture....90

Bantu Culture....91

The Early History of Sudan & Egypt....95

The Riddle of the Sphinx....101

The Kingdom of Ta-Seti....103

The Old Kingdom Period of Egypt....107

First Kingdom of Kush....114

The Middle Kingdom Period of Egypt....116

Later Chapters in the History of Sudan & Egypt....122

The New Kingdom Period of Egypt....122

Second Empire of Kush....127

The Greek Era of Egypt....135

The Roman and Byzantine Era of Egypt....138

The Arab conquest of North Africa and Classical Egypt... 139
Medieval Nubia ... 141
The Turkish Empire in the Nile ... 149

The Early History of Tunisia ... 152
The Empire of Carthage ... 153
Conflict with the Greeks ... 155
Conflict with the Romans ... 156
The End of Carthage ... 159

The Early History of French West Africa ... 162
Timbuktu Scholars Preserve the History ... 165
Oldest Pottery in Africa ... 167
Early Copper Working ... 168
Birth of Stone Villages ... 169
Birth of West African Cities along the Niger ... 170
The Empire of Ghana ... 171
The Empire of Mali ... 180
The Songhai Empire ... 188
The Mossi Kingdoms ... 196

The Early History of Nigeria ... 202
The Dufuna Canoe ... 206
Oldest Iron-Smelting Site in the World ... 208
Nok and Igbo Cultures ... 208
The Yoruba City-States and Eredo ... 212

Great Benin 217
The Oyo Empire 224
The Hausa Confederation 228

The Slave Trade & West Africa.. 237
A British Government Select Committee on
the Slave Trade.. 238
West Africa and Transatlantic Enslavement 240
Transatlantic Enslavement Impacts More Countries...... 242
Impact and Repercussions in Africa.. 243
Consequences for the Ghana Region.. 245
The Ashanti Union 248
The Dahomey Kingdom and the Amazons.. 251

The Early History of Central Africa.. 261
The Bamoun Kingdom 264
Introducing Kanem Borno.. 266
Prehistoric Giraffe Etching.. 268
The Sao Culture 269
The Kanem-Borno Empire.. 271

The Early History of Ethiopia & Eritrea.. 281
The Da'amat Kingdom.. 283
The Axumite Empire.. 286
The City of Lalibela.. 294
From Moving Capitals to Addis Ababa 298

The Early History of Congo & Angola 307
The Mangbetu Kingdom 308
The Luba Kingdom 311
The Lunda Kingdom 315
The Kuba Kingdom 317
The Kongo Kingdom 322

The Early History of Southern Africa 332
In the Land of the Zulu 335
Birth of Mining in Eswatini 344
Evolution of Southern African Culture 345
Gold Working in Southern Africa 347
The Great Zimbabwe 348
The Muhumutapa Empire 351

The Early History of East Africa 362
The Bunyoro-Kitara Kingdom 365
Birth of Animal Husbandry 372
The Haya Iron smelters 372
Birth of East African Shipping 373
The Swahili Confederation 374

A Final Word 383

Ancient Kings & Leaders 388

STORIES OF PEOPLE & CIVILIZATION

STORIES OF PEOPLE & CIVILIZATION AFRICAN ANCIENT ORIGINS

SERIES FOREWORD

Stretching back to the oral traditions of thousands of years ago, tales of heroes and disaster, creation and conquest have been told by many different civilizations, in ways unique to their landscape and language. Their impact sits deep within our own culture even though the details in the stories themselves are a loose mix of historical record, the latest archaeological evidence, transformed narrative and the unwitting distortions of generations of storytellers.

Today the language of mythology lives around us: our mood is jovial, our countenance is saturnine, we are narcissistic and our modern life is hermetically sealed from others. The nuances of the ancient world form part of our daily routines and help us navigate the information overload of our interconnected lives.

The nature of a myth is that its stories are already known by most of those who hear or read them. Every era brings a new emphasis, but the fundamentals remain the same: a desire to understand and describe the events and relationships of the world. Many of the great stories are archetypes that help us find our own place, equipping us with tools for self-understanding, both individually and as part of a broader culture.

For Western societies it is Greek mythology that speaks to us most clearly. It greatly influenced the mythological heritage of the ancient Roman civilization and is the lens through which we still see the Celts, the Norse and many of the other great peoples and religions.

The Greeks themselves inherited much from their neighbours, the Egyptians, an older culture that became weary with the mantle of civilization.

Of course, what we perceive now as mythology had its own origins in perceptions of the divine and the rituals of the sacred. The earliest civilizations, in the crucible of the Middle East, in the Sumer of the third millennium BCE, are the source to which many of the mythical archetypes can be traced. Over five thousand years ago, as humankind collected together in cities for the first time, developed writing and industrial-scale agriculture, started to irrigate the rivers and attempted to control rather than be at the mercy of its environment, humanity began to write down its tentative explanations of natural events, of floods and plagues, of disease.

Early stories tell of gods or god-like animals who are crafty and use their wits to survive, and it is not unreasonable to suggest that these were the first rulers of the gathering peoples of the earth, later elevated to god-like status with the distance of time. Such tales became more political as cities vied with each other for supremacy, creating new gods, new hierarchies for their pantheons. The older gods took on primordial roles and became the preserve of creation and destruction, leaving the new gods to deal with more current, everyday affairs. Empires rose and fell, with Babylon assuming the mantle from Sumeria in the 1800s BCE, in turn to be swept away by the Assyrians of the 1200s BCE; then the Assyrians and the Egyptians were subjugated by the Greeks, the Greeks by the Romans and so on, leading to the spread and assimilation of common themes, ideas and stories throughout the world.

The survival of history is dependent on the telling of good tales, but each one must have the 'feeling' of truth, otherwise it will be ignored. Around firesides, or embedded in a book or a computer, the myths and legends of the past are still the living materials of retold myth, not restricted to an exploration of historical origins. Now we have devices and global communications that give us unparalleled access to a diversity of traditions. We can find out about Indigenous American, Indian, Chinese and tribal African mythology in a way that was denied to our ancestors, we can find connections, plot the archaeology, religion and the mythologies of the world to build a comprehensive image of the human experience that is both humbling and fascinating.

The books in this series introduce the many cultures of ancient humankind to the modern reader. From the earliest migrations across the globe to settlements along rivers, from mountainous landscapes to vast steppes, from woodlands to deserts, humanity has adapted to its environments, nurturing languages and observations and expressing itself through records, mythmaking stories and living traditions. There is still so much to explore, but this is a great place to start.

Jake Jackson
General Editor

FOREWORD

In historical studies, when we speak of 'African origins' two broad categories have emerged over the past 50 years: the African origin of *humanity*, and the African origin of civilization.

In this first category, after generations of fierce debate, the African origin of anatomically modern humans (i.e. *Homo sapiens sapiens*) has been proven by the mitochondrial DNA research of geneticist Dr. Rebecca Cann *et. al.* in 1987. The African origin of humanity is now a demonstrable fact and is referred to by scholars as the *monogenetic theory of human origins*, or more commonly known as the 'Out of Africa Model'. The scientific evidence supporting this model has thoroughly dismissed the opposing 'Multi-Regional Model' and its premise that distinct racial types evolved independently in the separate regions of Africa, Asia and Europe. This latter model was advanced to 'prove' an independent European origin as an explanation for the superior position of Europeans in the modern world. However, in the absence of scientific evidence to support this multi-regional claim the great Piltdown Man forgery was created in 1912 in England, and exposed in 1953 as the greatest scientific hoax in the twentieth century. The Piltdown Man skull was considered proof of the 'missing link' connecting modern Europeans to their pre-human hominid ancestors. However, the skull was an elaborate scientific hoax that misrepresented human origins and fooled laypeople and scholars alike in the Western world for nearly half a century.

The second great area of 'African origins' concerns civilizations (or advanced cultures), and this too is an area where old colonial myths are fading, but not without vigorous academic and political resistance. In the twentieth century, there was a cadre of Black scholars and writers, aided by the scholarship of other groups, who led the way and produced pivotal works that have greatly changed the public view on the African contributions to civilizations and the advancement of humanity. These works effectively exposed the colonial propaganda and the systematic misrepresentation of African history by suppressing evidence when needed, falsifying artefacts when convenient, and using the *diffusion theory* as a clever tool to explain that advanced civilizations in Africa were merely a result of "foreign influence". The hall of fame Black scholars in the twentieth century who exposed this fraudulent agenda are too numerous to name here, but the Senegalese scholar and scientist Dr. Cheikh Anta Diop (1923–1986), considered the 'Pharaoh of African Studies', had the greatest global impact in changing the world's view of Africa in recognizing its unique and formidable contributions to the world.

This scholarly work continues in the first quarter of the twenty-first century as more students and scholars are eager to publish on the advanced African civilizations and high-level cultures. Since the 1981 publication of UNESCO's *General History of Africa* series (projected eleven volumes), the influence of the old colonial history books on Africa has been in accelerated decline. Today, authors from various regions have joined the effort to rewrite the history of Africa, and Robin Walker is among this group of contributors.

FOREWORD

Robin Walker's *African Ancient Origins* covers the Black experience in Africa from human origins, through golden ages, and up to colonization and modern independence in the late twentieth century. This work solidifies Walker's role as a significant scholar from the United Kingdom who has been contributing to the rewriting of Africa's history for the past twenty years. This publication will help inspire additional authors to extensively document Africa's scientific achievements in fields such as iron smelting and agriculture. These and other lost sciences of Africa are often overlooked, yet they can fill many books and documentaries. Walker's book will help point the direction in the preservation of African scientific history and the documentation of its influential civilizations.

Prof. Manu Ampim
Professor of History & Africana Studies
Contra Costa College

STORIES OF PEOPLE & CIVILIZATION AFRICAN ANCIENT ORIGINS

INTRODUCTION
& FURTHER READING

INTRODUCTION TO AFRICAN ANCIENT ORIGINS

ORIGINS OF THE MODERN COUNTRIES IN AFRICA

The map of Africa that we have today is an artificial creation. It is a direct result of the European colonization of Africa in the nineteenth and twentieth centuries. It is also the result of different African peoples achieving independence from European rule from the mid-twentieth century onwards. Consequently, the political groupings that we call African countries today, for example Ghana, Nigeria, Somalia and Tanzania, bear *no resemblance* to the political boundaries of the African civilizations described in this book. Moreover, the colonial powers of Europe dismissed and then suppressed the history of Africans before the Colonial Period. Through propaganda, they created the lie that before European colonial rule African culture was all unknown prehistory, hidden in the African jungles.

However, in this book we will use phrases such as: 'archaeologists discovered artefacts in Kenya, near Nairobi, dating to the sixteenth century', and so on. The reader is advised that Kenya did not exist in current form before the Colonial Period. Nor did Nairobi, its capital. There was no such reality as a Kenyan at the time. However, for reasons of simplicity and geographical convenience, we will use these place names. Please bear this in mind throughout the book.

The Berlin Conference was held between 1884 and 1885. Called by the German ruler Otto von Bismark, the countries represented were Britain, Austria-Hungary, France, Russia, Germany, the US, Portugal, Denmark, Spain, Italy, Holland, Sweden, Belgium and Turkey. At this conference the representatives discussed how the African continent was to be seized, conquered and shared between them. Like cutting up a cake, the countries of Europe sought to divide the whole of Africa between them, taking control over their allocated territories. *The Times* newspaper at the time described it as the 'scramble for Africa'. Of course, no Africans were represented at these discussions. Yet it was at the Berlin Conference that the political map of modern Africa began to be drawn. In formal terms, three doctrines were expounded at the conference: (i) Doctrine of Spheres of Influence, (ii) Doctrine of Effective Occupation and (iii) Doctrine of European Protection of its Agents.

BEGINNING THE CONQUEST OF SOUTHERN AFRICA

However, the story of European seizure of African lands long predates the Berlin Conference. What the conference did was formalize this process. Jan van Rieebeck of the Dutch East India Company began the seizure of African land in the southern tip of Africa in 1652. Introducing the idea of private land ownership, the Dutch progressively appropriated land belonging to the Khoi and the San peoples. Dutch penetration inspired African resistance, leading to three Xhosa Wars between 1779 and 1803. Discontented Khoi joined with the Xhosa in this third revolt, in attacking European-appropriated farms. British penetration caused six Xhosa Wars against the British between 1811 and 1879.

In the Anglo-Zulu War of 1879, the Zulu forces had a stunning victory. During the Battle of Isandlwana, it initially appeared that the British invaders could win. The Martini Henry Rifles pinned the Zulu troops down, halting their advance. However, from the ridge, an old Zulu chief strode onto the battlefield in front of the crouched troops and ordered them to move forward. Said he: 'Your king never ordered you to lie down. He ordered you to fight!' The Zulus moved forward in the 'horns of a bull' formation. When the horns closed, the British line broke. Meanwhile the Zulu general, from a vantage point up on the ridge, watched his plan work. In two hours his troops had finished off the British force.

However, the celebrations were short-lived. The British did ultimately win against the Zulus at the Battle of Ulundi, but it took the use of the Gatlin gun – the first rapid-fire gun – to do so. With this technology, the British completed the colonization of southern Africa.

AFRICAN RESISTANCE BATTLES

There were several important battles in which Africans resisted having their lands colonized by Europe. The most celebrated examples are the resistance of the Wassoulou Empire in West Africa against the French, the Mahdist Rebellion in Sudan against the British and the Battle of Adwa in Ethiopia against the Italians.

Samori Touré founded the Wassoulou Empire in 1878. It extended through present-day Guinea, Mali and Sierra Leone to the northern Ivory Coast. Touré battled French colonial rule in West Africa from 1881 until his capture in 1898. His infantry and cavalry used weapons imported through Sierra Leone, or had them forged by Mandinka blacksmiths. Touré was a strategist; he tried to build an anti-colonial alliance with the Ashanti Empire of Ghana, failing only when Ashanti was defeated by the British. Yves Person, a French colonial administrator, wrote:

> *Samori arouses the highest passions because more than any other leader in pre-colonial Africa he symbolizes heroic and determined resistance to the European conqueror. Over seventeen years separate his first contact with the French and his arrest in 1898...but no other confrontation between colonized and colonizer had ever lasted so long without the former surrendering his liberty.*
>
> **Bruce Vandervort, *Wars of Imperial Conquest in Africa, 1830–1914*, 1998**

Even his adversary, Captain Albert Baratier, noted that:

> *He was the one who gave proof of those qualities characteristic of a chief of a people, a strategist and even a politician... an outstanding leader of men, possessing audacity, energy, the ability to follow up an advantage and plan in advance, and above all an irrepressible tenacity which could not be destroyed.*
>
> **Bruce Vandervort, *Wars of Imperial Conquest in Africa, 1830–1914*, 1998**

The Mahdist Rebellion against British colonialism in Sudan was led by a mystical figure called the Mahdi. According to Islamic tradition, the Mahdi or Messiah will bring the world to Islam in the End of Days. Muhammad Ahmad of Sudan proclaimed himself the Mahdi. He aimed to unify the whole Islamic Nile Valley, North Africa and the desert zone of West Africa under his rule. At first the Mahdi met with success. In 1882 he occupied Kordofan, defeating an Egyptian column and killing 10,000 troops commanded by the British; in 1884 his forces defeated the British governor of Darfur. On 26 January 1885 the Mahdi's troops engaged the British at their stronghold in Khartoum and defeated them. One of his soldiers killed General 'Chinese' Gordon with a javelin. In Sudan today the Tomb of the Mahdi in Khartoum remains a venerated building, with an opulent silver dome.

The Battle of Adwa in Ethiopia, unlike the previous valiant examples, was not a temporary victory. Led by Emperor Menelik II, this battle secured Ethiopian sovereignty for another 40 years. On 1 March 1896 the Italian Army met its Ethiopian counterparts at Adwa. Ethiopian forces quickly surrounded and destroyed the first battalion of the Italian general Albertone. The remaining Italian forces were crushed by other Ethiopian troops. They fired rifles, hurled javelins, swirled swords and fought hand to hand. Captured Italian soldiers were released by Ethiopia in exchange for payment of a 10 million lira reparation by the Italian government. In October 1896 Italy was forced to sign a peace treaty with Ethiopia, although they did keep control of a slightly reduced Eritrea. Nevertheless, as the only African nation successfully to resist European conquest during the scramble for Africa, Ethiopia became an enduring symbol of the pan-African movement. *The Manchester Guardian* wrote in

1901 that Ras Alula, the Ethiopian commander, was 'the best general and strategist that Africa has perhaps produced in modern times'.

EUROPEAN COLONIALISM

King Leopold II of Belgium ordered the colonization of the Congo between 1885 and 1908. The king personally acquired the Congo as his private colony through a series of treaties with local leaders, with the territory becoming known as the Congo Free State. Rubber was the main commodity that Leopold sought to obtain; it was in high demand globally, and he set high quotas for production. This led to the brutal exploitation and forced labour of the African population. The king created a private army, the Force Publique, to intimidate the population, and they used mass killings, torture and rape on a massive scale. Scholars estimate that between 10 and 15 million people died because of these policies – about half of the population of the Congo at the time. An official Belgian commission, reporting in 1919, concluded the population of the Belgian Congo had been 'reduced by half' since the beginning of the European occupation in the 1880s.

Germany colonized Guinea and Togo in West Africa, Tanzania, Burundi and Rwanda in East Africa, as well as Namibia in southwest Africa. However, German colonial rule in Africa proved relatively short, lasting from the 1880s until the end of the First World War.

In southwest Africa, Germans battled the indigenous people, the Nama and the Herero, for control of their land, resources and assets. This conflict was known as the Nama and Herero Wars of 1904 to 1907. Before declaring war in January 1904, the Herero leader, Samuel Maherero, wrote to the leader of the Nama, declaring:

> *All our obedience and patience with the Germans is of little avail for each day they shoot someone dead for no reason at all. Hence, I appeal to you, my brother, not to hold aloof from the uprising but to make your voice heard so that all Africa may take up arms against the Germans. Let us die fighting rather than die as a result of maltreatment, imprisonment or some other calamity. Tell all the Captains down there to rise and do battle.*
> **Bruce Vandervort, *Wars of Imperial Conquest in Africa, 1830–1914*, 1998**

However, the letter did not reach the Nama; it was passed to the Germans instead. Elsewhere the German general, Lothar von Trotha, had noted: 'They are all the same. They respect nothing but force. To exercise this force with brute terror and even ferocity was and is my policy.' (Basil Davidson, *Africa in History*, 1991). He issued his infamous 'extermination' proclamation later in the year. In October 1904 the Captain of the Nama, Hendrik Witbooi, also declared war.

The Herero and Nama peoples fought as mounted infantry. They were generally as well armed as the Europeans. Moreover, their proficiency as marksmen was well attested by the Germans who fought them in the war. Initially it seemed as though the Nama, with their mastery of guerrilla warfare, might be victorious. The German occupiers in Namaland were killed, and German soldiers invariably failed to catch the Nama fighters. When the numbers of German soldiers became too great to cope with, the trails were blocked and the scarce water holes put under surveillance. At this point Witbooi and his mounted men disappeared with their families into the Kalahari Desert, where no German soldiers could follow them. General von Trotha's failure to bring the Nama to heel eventually discredited him, with the authorities ordering his return to Germany.

In the end, the Hereros and Namas were defeated, rounded up and exterminated; others were put into 'concentration camps'. In 1904 there were 80,000 Herero and 20,000 Nama. By 1911 these numbers had been reduced by more than half to 15,130 Herero and 9,871 Nama.

The Maji-Maji Rebellion took place in Tanzania between 1905 and 1906. Germans in Tanzania forced the peasants to stop subsistence agriculture and instead to grow cotton as a cash crop. Forced labour was imposed on the indigenous people to construct roads and railways. The Germans also imposed harsh taxation policies and land seizures, as well as instituting physical punishment, torture and murder. However, in 1905 a spirit medium, Kinjikitile Ngwale, emerged as a prophet. With the help of other spirit mediums, he used a magical potion called 'maji' to inspire the people to fight. This is why the historians call it the Maji-Maji Rebellion. Although the prophet was captured and executed by the Germans, the rebellion spread to all southern Tanzania. However, the rebels failed to capture German outposts. In October 1905 three German columns marched south, to the main centres of resistance; en route they burned villages and destroyed crops. German forces caught the leaders of the rebellion and hanged them. By June 1906 the Maji-Maji Rebellion was over, with the starvation strategy proving remarkably effective. The famine created by the authorities killed between 250,000 and 300,000 Africans.

Britain built a vast empire in Africa that stretched across the continent, from the northern deserts to the southern tip. They conquered Egypt and Sudan in northeast Africa, Sierra Leone, Ghana and Nigeria in West Africa, Uganda, Kenya and Somalia in

East Africa, and finally Zambia, Zimbabwe, Malawi, Botswana and South Africa in southern Africa.

Like the Germans, they confined some of their colonial subjects to concentration and internment camps. Professor Bruce Vandervort, a military historian, gave an example from South Africa in 1899 to 1902:

> *In order to crush the Boer guerrillas, the British confined some 154,000 Boer men, women and children and 107,000 'black' Boers – African labourers and servants in Boer employ – in what soon became known as 'concentration camps'. The high death rates among the camp inmates, the vast majority of whom were civilians, shocked public opinion in many parts of the world.*
>
> **Bruce Vandervort, *Wars of Imperial Conquest in Africa, 1830–1914*, 1998**

The French conquered a massive colonial empire in Africa. They conquered Morocco, Algeria and Tunisia in North Africa, Senegal, Mali, Ivory Coast, Burkina Faso and Niger in West Africa, Chad, Central African Republic, the Congo and Gabon in Central Africa and Djibouti in East Africa, as well as islands in the Indian Ocean.

In Central Africa the French colonial authorities constructed a railway called the Congo-Océan railway. Designed to provide a vital connection between the Atlantic coast and the interior of Congo, it was completed in 1934. The 320-mile train line began at the coastal city of Pointe-Noire and ended in Brazzaville, Congo's capital city. However, behind the feat of construction lay a major tragedy. Between 1921 and 1934 the French conscripted 127,250 local men as forced labourers. As many as 20,000 of them died during the railway's construction.

THE PAN-AFRICAN MOVEMENT

By 1900 Europe had colonized nearly all of Africa. Blacks in the US were Jim Crowed, Blacks in South America were second-class citizens, Blacks in the Caribbean were colonial subjects and Blacks in Britain faced the colour bar. Only Ethiopia in Africa and Haiti in the Caribbean were free, while Black people were historically in the worst position they had ever experienced. With London as the centre of the British Empire, it also became the centre of pan-African ideas. Some pan-Africanists aimed for the liberation and unity of the African continent; others had a bigger perspective. Yet other pan-Africanists aimed at the mutual support, unity and liberation of all African peoples anywhere on the globe.

In 1900 Henry Sylvester Williams, a lawyer from Trinidad, organized a three-day Pan-African Conference in central London. There were 30 delegates. Ordinary Black people attended but so did some celebrities, such as the legendary classical composer Samuel Coleridge Taylor. Among those attending was Bishop Alexander Walters from the United States, who represented the African Methodist Episcopal Zion Church. Another African American attendee was the legendary academic Dr W.E.B. DuBois. He delivered his famous speech at the conference, predicting that the main problem of the twentieth century was going to be 'the problem of the colour line'. The Conference managed to obtain a promise from Queen Victoria, delivered through Joseph Chamberlain, not to overlook the interests or welfare of the native races.

Before pan-Africanism entered the vocabulary, there was an earlier ideology called 'Ethiopianism'. In the Bible there is a passage in Psalm 68:31 which says: 'Princes shall come out of Egypt. Ethiopia shall stretch forth her hands unto God'. Historically the name 'Ethiopia' had two meanings: firstly, an East African country and secondly, the whole of Africa. The biblical passage was thus adopted by African Christians as a prophetic declaration of future liberation from European oppression. As a global Black nationalist movement, it reached its zenith in the late nineteenth and early twentieth centuries. Centred in an African Christian liberation ideology, its biblically inspired ideas travelled on an African revolutionary wave from the United States to Africa to the Caribbean, and on to Black people in Europe. The first churchmen to create this radical Christian theology were the African American radicals who created the African Methodist Episcopal Church and the African Methodist Episcopal Zion Church.

Henry Sylvester Williams enrolled at Grays Inn in Central London in 1896. Here, while qualifying as a barrister, he met students from West Africa. Alice Kinloch was born in Cape Town in 1863. She attended mission school and became an activist in the Kimberley Diamond mine, the biggest in South Africa. Kinloch organized protests against the implementation of a de facto apartheid mining system that had a devastating effect on mining communities. Following a meeting between Kinloch and Williams, the idea for creating the African Association was born.

Williams wrote to a colleague stating that, 'The Association is the result of Mrs Kinloch's work in England and the feeling that as British subjects we ought to be heard in our own affairs'. (Danny Thompson, *Ethiopianism: The Forgotten Movement*, 2022) The African Association became a landmark Black organization in Britain. Its membership consisted of West Indians and Africans and it was heavily supported by the West African press. *The Lagos Standard* implored 'our countrymen to rally around the standard of the Association', while *The Lagos*

Weekly Record urged 'our people throughout Africa' to 'give unqualified support'.

The collaboration between Henry Williams and Alice Kinloch exemplifies Ethiopianism in Britain: a Trinidadian and a South African sharing a Pan-African vision rooted in an African Christianity. Initially dependent on white liberals, they reached their ultimate Ethiopianist vision of an independent African Association, which led in turn to the Pan-African Conference of 1900. We can then trace the story from here to the five Pan-African congresses, to African independence, to African American civil rights and finally to the African Union.

Dr W.E.B. DuBois, the African American intellectual, called the First Pan-African Congress in 1919. Held in Paris, its aim was to embrace Negro leaders from the US, Ethiopia, Liberia, Haiti, the French and British colonies, and other parts of the Black world. In the event, 57 delegates attended from 15 countries. The upshot of the congress was a call to the colonial powers to institute policies that protect 'the natives'. In particular, policies were sought to prevent exploitation, to abolish slave labour and to stop capital punishment in the countries under colonial control. Participants also called for colonial governments to educate the colonized people. Finally, they called for 'the natives' to participate in the running of their own countries. However, this congress, like all the others, lacked any real power to change the repression under which Black people lived. Nevertheless, they represented a movement of ideas in which Black people could protest and develop strategies, from where something of value could eventually emerge.

From 1919 to 1945 Dr DuBois presided over five congresses before independence. He acknowledged and defended the struggle, common goals and unity of all Africans, and also advocated for the world historical importance of the continent. In his later years DuBois went to live in Africa. He died in 1963 at the age of 95, working in Ghana on the *Encyclopaedia Africana*.

Another important Pan-Africanist, although he never used the term, was Marcus Garvey. A Jamaican by origin, he used nation and race interchangeably, aiming to build a global Pan-Africanism that sought to free Africa for the Africans 'at home and abroad'. In 1914 Garvey founded the Universal Negro Improvement Association and the African Communities League. In 1920 the organization held its first convention in New York. Soon the Association boasted 1,100 branches in more than 40 countries, including Cuba, Panama, Costa Rica, Ecuador, Venezuela, Ghana, Sierra Leone, Liberia, Namibia and South Africa. Aimed at independence from European domination, Garvey was an institution builder. His movement had their own militias, the Black Cross nurses, barbershops, bakeries, tailors, newspapers, steamships and, most impressive of all, six million paid-up members. Moreover, the movement had an uncompromising ideology to address economic, cultural and religious transformation and reconstruction, in addition to its political and military programme.

Garvey and DuBois clashed openly in their struggle for pre-eminence. Garvey criticized DuBois for a whole year in his newspaper, *The Negro World*, before DuBois finally responded. Garvey claimed that DuBois's criticism of imperialism was inconsistent. In December 1920 DuBois issued a response to Garvey in his newspaper, *The Crisis*. He referred to Garvey as a remarkable leader of men, adding that he believed him to be fundamentally a sincere and honest individual who possessed tremendous vision, dynamic force and tenacity, along with a selfless desire to serve. However, he also said that Garvey was dictatorial, arrogant and lacking in business sense. He accused

Garvey of introducing the Jamaican Black vs. Mulatto divide into America. In addition, Garvey had alienated the Liberians, where he hoped to build a base, and had caused unnecessary animosity between the other Black leaders.

DuBois led the Second Pan-African Congress in 1921. Held in London and Brussels, there were 113 delegates with 41 from Africa, 34 from the United States, 24 from Europe and 7 from the West Indies. They issued a call for local self-government in the colonized countries. DuBois led the Third Pan-African Congress, held in London and Lisbon, in 1923; one influential European to attend was the celebrated writer, H.G. Wells. As before, the call was weak: we ask the world 'that Black folk be treated as men'.

Lapido Solanke, a Nigerian activist, established the West African Students Union, or WASU, in London in 1924. He wished his organization to have practical functions as a hostel, a bureau of information on African history and research and an institution to promote self-help, unity and co-operation among the various persons of African descent. Moreover, it aimed to foster a spirit of national consciousness and racial pride among all African peoples, to publish a monthly magazine and to raise funds. At one time the legendary African American Paul Robeson served as honorary president of WASU.

The Fourth Pan-African Congress was held in New York in 1927. While Dr DuBois led the Congress, he credited American Negro women for reviving the idea of holding the events. There were 280 delegates, but Africa was sparsely represented. The Africans who attended came from the Gold Coast, Sierra Leone, Liberia and Nigeria.

Ethiopia, also called Abyssinia, faced a major crisis in 1935 when they were attacked by the Italians under the Fascist leader Benito

Mussolini. However, this invasion became a galvanizing force that affected Black people all over the world. For the first time in history Black people from many different countries were on the same page. Jomo Kenyatta, the legendary Kenyan leader and author of *Facing Mount Kenya*, mentions the crisis and reveals his anger at the Italian invasion. An Abyssinian Association was formed, consisting of many prominent Nigerians who supported the Ethiopian cause. In London Africans formed the International African Friends of Abyssinia. The Ethiopian crisis united African Americans, 'West Indians' and Africans resident in Britain.

DuBois led the Fifth Pan-African Congress in 1945. Among the people who supported his decision to go ahead with the congress was Amy Jacques Garvey, Marcus Garvey's widow. Held in Manchester, England, there were around 200 delegates, including serious representation from East Africa, South Africa and the West Indies. In attendance were Africans Kwame Nkrumah, J.C. DeGraft-Johnson, Nnamdi Azikiwe, Jomo Kenyatta and others. Trinidadians George Padmore and C.L.R. James also attended. For the first time ever, delegates called for African independence. And at a later date…*they get it*! The Africans in attendance became the movers and shakers of an independent Africa.

ETHIOPIA: THE ONLY NON-COLONIZED COUNTRY IN AFRICA

After the Ethiopian Crisis of 1935–41, the Italian Fascist regime lost control of Ethiopia. Emperor Haile Selassie I, who had been the ruler since 1930, returned from exile to rule the country. He aimed to modernize Ethiopia, including its military, education system and economy, but despite his efforts Ethiopia remained largely agrarian. Many people continued to live in rural poverty, while the monarchy and the elite held significant power. By the late 1960s and early 1970s Ethiopia's economy was in decline, exacerbated by droughts and famine. Many felt that the imperial government was out of touch with their needs. Students led protests and political unrest spread across the country, especially in the cities.

However, on the African stage Haile Selassie commanded respect. Ethiopia played a key role in creating the Organization of African Unity, or OAU, on 25 May 1963. Haile Selassie himself was a leading advocate for African unity and independence. His government influenced the establishment of the organization in Addis Ababa, the Ethiopian capital, and Selassie himself became the movement's first chairman. Thirty-two independent African states joined up. The OAU Charter aimed to eliminate European colonial control of Africa, prevent conflicts between African nations and promote economic and social development on the continent.

Ethiopia played a significant role in the anti-apartheid movement that fought against the White supremacist South African regime. They assisted the African National Congress, or ANC, in its struggle, helping to train and support ANC members in exile. They also helped its armed wing, the *Umkhonto we Sizwe*, led by Nelson Mandela and Oliver Tambo. Nelson Mandela was granted Ethiopian citizenship, which allowed him an Ethiopian passport with which to travel. Oliver Tambo was granted asylum in Ethiopia, where he lived for several years, co-ordinating efforts to build international support for the anti-apartheid movement. Moreover, Ethiopia hosted several OAU conferences at which apartheid was a key agenda item. The OAU supported the economic isolation of South Africa, with member states agreeing to boycott South African goods. Finally

Ethiopia played a role in creating the Frontline States Alliance – a coalition of Southern African countries that supported the ANC and other liberation movements in the region.

In 1974 the Ethiopian military overthrew Haile Selassie and instituted a military government known as the Derg. Led by Haile Mariam Mengistu, the Derg introduced a Marxist-Leninist government. They promised socialist economic reforms by confiscating land from the nobility and redistributing it to the peasants; they also nationalized industries and large estates. The Derg expanded access to education too, especially for girls, rural and other marginalized populations, and worked to close the educational gap between urban and rural populations. Adult education programmes were introduced to address the high illiteracy rates. However, the policies to deliver improvements in agricultural productivity failed. Other policies were also unsuccessful due to mismanagement and corruption. Moreover, the human rights record of the Derg was abysmal; they arrested, tortured and executed thousands of opponents.

During 1984 and 1985 Ethiopia faced severe famine, widely reported across the world as one of the worst humanitarian crises in modern history. A BBC journalist, Michael Buerk, famously described it as a famine of biblical proportions. In response a group of British and Irish musicians, led by Bob Geldof and Midge Ure, organized the Live Aid event on 13 July 1985. This fundraising event was broadcast around the world and raised millions for famine relief. Yet a consequence of the publicity was that televized images of starvation did much to destroy the international reputation of Ethiopia, in particular, and of Africa in general. Many non-Africans came to see Ethiopia as a poor, hopeless country, in constant need of foreign aid.

A coalition of rebel groups overthrew the Derg in 1991. A rebel leader, Meles Zenawi, became Prime Minister and introduced reforms that focused on creating a more federal state. Regional autonomy allowed groups such as the Tigray, Oromo, Amhara and others to assert more control over the affairs of their respective regions. Zenawi pursued state-led development that emphasized the building of infrastructure projects. In 2011 he launched the Grand Ethiopian Renaissance Dam. It aimed to create a reliable and sustainable supply of electricity, drive industrialization and bring job opportunities. These policies created significant economic growth. Between 2000 and 2015 Ethiopia's economy grew at an average annual rate of around 10 per cent – a major achievement.

THE INDEPENDENCE PERIOD

Independence from European rule initially took placc in the North African countries: Libya (1951), Egypt (1951) and Morocco (1956). 'The Winds of Change' then hit Ghana (1957), Nigeria (1960), Somalia (1960), Tanganyika (1961), Uganda (1962), Kenya (1963), Malawi (1964) and Zambia (1964). The story began for the Caribbean countries with Jamaica (1962), Trinidad and Tobago (1962), Barbados (1966) and so on. Along with the African Americans, they received the vote and other civil rights reforms (1964 to 1968). Southern Africa remained in bondage, however, and thus refused to join the 'Winds of Change'.

After 1957 Pan-Africanism stopped being a theoretical idea promoted by the African diaspora and started to become a practical reality in Africa. There were now attempts to bring together African countries, mostly led by Dr Kwame Nkrumah, the first president of modern Ghana. These alliances were short-lived, but they did exist.

Kwame Nkrumah was born in Ghana in 1909, but educated in the United States. His ideas on Pan-Africanism were partly influenced by Marcus Garvey and by Dr W.E.B. DuBois. In the US he was a friend and colleague of C.L.R. James, George Padmore and John Henrik Clarke.

However, the newly independent nations faced serious challenges. Colonial powers had forced European languages, especially English, French and Portuguese, on huge numbers of ordinary people, undermining local languages and cultures.

Secondly, colonial boundaries created by the Europeans caused major problems in Africa. These new boundaries bore no relationship to the ancient African states. They divided people who belonged to the same culture across different modern boundaries, separating people physically from their heritage. For example, the Mozambique people, whose heritage includes the Empire of Munhumutapa, must cross a border to visit the neighbouring country of Zimbabwe if they wish to see the Great Zimbabwe, their former capital.

Thirdly, the colonial boundaries grouped together people with historically separate cultural histories. For example, the colonial boundaries of Nigeria include five or more historically separate cultures: the Benin Empire, the Yoruba cities, Igboland, the Hausa Confederation, the capital city of Kanem Borno and many others.

Fourthly, Africa had largely been stripped of its wealth. The process of wealth-stripping had begun during enslavement; in 1502, for example, the Portuguese sailed off from West Africa with fifteen shiploads of gold. The wealth-stripping increased exponentially during the Colonial Period.

Wealth causes a chain of consequences. Businesses make products and create jobs that employ people. Employed people can afford to feed, clothe and house their families. Employed people pay their taxes to the government. Governments can use the tax revenue to build roads, infrastructure, schools and hospitals. These building projects create jobs. This means even more people can afford to pay their taxes. In addition, more people can afford to buy the products made by the businesses. They in turn make more money. Consequently, businesspeople have more resources to build more businesses, which creates more jobs, and so on. So the cycle of wealth continues.

On the other hand, poverty causes a chain of negative consequences: poor people everywhere have the least resources to create businesses. Fewer businesses mean high levels of unemployment. High unemployment means fewer people can afford to feed, clothe and house their families. In addition, fewer people can afford to pay their taxes to the government. Consequently, governments have little revenue to build roads, infrastructure, schools and hospitals. The cycle of poverty thus continues. This explains why poor countries often have dirt roads, crumbling infrastructure, few schools and shabby hospitals.

DECOLONIAL THEORY AND PRACTICE

Frantz Fanon (1925–1961) was a psychologist from Martinique. His first major book was *Black Skins, White Masks*. With this book he became the first psychologist to show how the conquering powers of Europe manipulated the thinking and emotions of the people over whom they ruled. Through control of education and the mass media, colonial powers instilled the following into their subjects: European culture is superior and universal while African culture is primitive and marginal. European languages and received pronunciation represent global standards, but African languages are the dialects of the uneducated. The European beauty standard of whiteness represents perfection while African beauty standards of blackness represent sin. Moreover, Fanon showed how books, films, comics and advertisements from the Colonial Period all reinforced these messages. He began the discussion on why we need to have more balanced media representations of groups that have since been marginalized.

In his follow-up book, *The Wretched of the Earth*, Fanon taught colonized people the techniques of how to free themselves mentally from the manipulations imposed by the conquering people. This was a necessary step in breaking free from European rule.

Fanon was also an intellectual giant in the theories of 'decolonization'. These theories relate to how to prevent one's country from slipping back into being a puppet, once again controlled by outside powers. It was important for a colonized country to reclaim its indigenous language as the language of government, promote its culture as the standard culture, and adopt its own religions, myths and legends as its cultural standards. Fanon's theories helped most of the Third World countries to escape from European colonial rule.

THE SOUTHERN AFRICAN FREEDOM STRUGGLE

Many African nations became independent in the years between 1957 and 1964. However, freedom and independence bypassed southern Africa. This part of the continent remained in bondage and had to fight for its freedom. Dr Nkrumah himself described all southern Africa as 'slave states'.

In 1912 the South African Native National Congress began under the leadership of John Dube. It represented Africans across the country – mine workers, farmers, urban and rural people – and protested at the treatment they received at the hands of the whites. The South African Native National Congress sent a delegation to London to protest against a proposed Land Act, in which Africans were to receive just 13 per cent of their country's total land area. The British government refused to hear the delegation, telling them to go back to South Africa and work with the whites; it eventually passed the Land Act in 1913. The Africans concluded that they had to prosecute their own cause, and by 1923, the organization had a new name: the African National Congress (ANC).

The ANC created a Youth League in 1944. Among its founders were Nelson Mandela, Walter Sisulu and Oliver Tambo. In 1947 the ANC built alliances that broadened its base with the Natal Indian Congress and the Transvaal Indian Congress. In 1948 the Afrikaners, the Dutch-speaking whites, voted overwhelmingly for the National Party, which went on to create a stricter policy called 'apartheid'. One consequence of the policy was that Africans and Indians were removed from electoral rolls. Residential and mobility laws were also tightened.

In the 1950s branches of the ANC spread throughout English-speaking Central Africa. Zambia's Kenneth Kaunda influenced the creation of 116 branches of this organization. In 1953 he was elected Secretary General of the party. When the white power structures eventually banned this organization in South Africa, it affected the other branches too. Their leaders across southern and Central Africa were imprisoned.

The Freedom Charter was drawn up by the Congress of the People in Kliptown, South Africa, led by the ANC and other anti-apartheid groups. Adopted in 1956, the Freedom Charter called for popular government, equal rights, sharing of the country's wealth, fair use of land, equality before the law, access to work and security, access to higher education and peace and friendship. However, the South African government struck back and arrested 156 members of the ANC.

Members of the Pan-Africanist Congress split from the ANC in 1958 to create an exclusively African organization. The PAC protested against the Pass Laws and Influx Control Act on 21 March 1960. They called for 'African males in every city and village…to leave their passes at home, join demonstrations and, if arrested, offer no bail, no defence, and no fine'. However, the non-violent protesters were attacked by government forces, resulting in 69 protestors being killed and 180 injured. The Sharpeville Massacre, as it was known, became an iconic moment in the struggle, with Africans reminding each other to 'Never Forget Sharpeville!' The government banned the ANC and the PAC from all political activity. Both movements went underground.

ANGOLA

The Portuguese rejected the idea of independence for their African colonies, which they saw as indispensable to Portugal'slife and economy. Angola, for example, was a major prize due to its massive size, location, natural wealth and proximity to Europe. Portugal was also ruled by the Fascist dictator Antonio de Oliveira Salazar, who had been in power since before the Second World War. In addition, Portugal had the backing of NATO.

However, three independence movements emerged to fight the Portuguese, all regionally based groups built on strong ethnic orientations. The Popular Movement for the Liberation of Angola, or MPLA, formed in 1956. Initially it led by Viriato da Cruz, followed later by Agostinho Neto. The National Front for the Liberation of Angola, or FNLA, formed in 1961 and was led by Holden Roberto. In 1966 the National Union for the Total Independence of Angola or UNITA was formed, led by Jonas Savimbi, a former member of the FNLA. All three movements had support from outside Angola itself. MPLA had backing from the socialist world while the FNLA, opposed to communist rule, received support from the United States and Congo Kinshasa. Holden Roberto also had personal ties to Mobutu, the ruler of Congo Kinshasa. The third organization, UNITA, had backing from white South Africa and China; it went on to receive backing from right-wing Western supporters for many years. Readers will have noticed that the names of each liberation movement and their acronyms do not seem to correspond. This is true when the names are translated into English, but they do match up in the original Portuguese.

In 1961 protesters allied with the MPLA attacked police stations and prisons to free African political prisoners, arrested by the Portuguese authorities. Elsewhere cotton workers attacked colonial officials, public buildings and the Catholic mission. In the northwest, Africans associated with the FNLA attacked isolated white farms and towns in 40 co-ordinated raids, killing hundreds of Portuguese occupiers. Further sporadic attacks took place in other parts of the country. The insurgents also battled the *assimilados*: Africans who had adopted Portuguese culture and sided with their officials. Many of them worked as overseers, managers and administrators. Rich Portuguese farmers and officials fled to Portugal, fearing for their lives, while poorer whites formed groups to defend their privileges.

However, the Portuguese rulers responded with brutality and reprisals. Some organized vigilante groups to terrorize African villagers, isolating and killing leaders and their followers. The Portuguese army led a campaign of wholesale bombings from the air that were, from their perspective, successful. The United Nations Resolution 163, issued in June 1961, criticized the bombing campaign. Strangely enough, the indiscriminate nature of the bombings caused further mobilization of the Angolan masses and helped the liberation groups to find new recruits. More than 40,000 Africans were uprooted during the rebellion of 1961. Many fled to Congo across the border. Others were killed, many dying from starvation and disease brought about by the disruptions of the rebellion. One source put the refugee numbers as high as 400,000 to 500,000.

After the uprising, the Portuguese made popular reforms in an attempt to hold on to Angola. They increased the number of paved roads by a factor of six in a few years and developed domestic air routes. They also sought to stimulate economic growth among Angolan farmers, for example by supporting coffee producers. Moreover, compulsory cotton cultivation, i.e. forced labour, was abolished. However, none of this satisfied the liberation groups. The Portuguese did too little, too late.

However, the balance of power changed. A newly independent Zambia allowed the MPLA to establish bases in their country in 1965, a decision that was to prove crucial. They were able to build up their strength and establish themselves in eastern Angola. Moreover, Agostinho Neto, the new leader of the MPLA, met Che Guevara. His organization began to receive Cuban instructors, along with Soviet and East German help. By late 1966 the MPLA and FNLA had brought ever larger areas of the country under their control, even if they frequently fought each other. By early 1967 the Portuguese were left in control of only the areas around larger towns and along the most important communications. The Portuguese then made dramatic gains and came close to winning by late 1973, having defeated or chased out most of the guerrilla fighters.

In Portugal in 1974, however, a left-wing coup overthrew the fascists. The new government was tired of war in Africa and handed over power to the three liberation movements. Armed conflict then broke out between them. The white regime in South Africa sent troops into southern Angola to support UNITA while Congo sent forces to support FNLA. Cuba, meanwhile, sent troops to support MPLA. On 11 November 1975 the MPLA declared independence for Angola. Agostinho Neto was elected the first president of Angola and ruled until his death in 1979.

Following him in the MPLA, Jose Eduardo dos Santos became the next ruler. Civil war raged for many years before the ultimate victory of the MPLA over their rivals to stabilize the country. Cuba sent 50,000 mostly Black troops to the battlefield. Their support was definitive in defeating the Western and South African backed forces that attempted to keep the civil war going. In 1992 MPLA won Angola's first multi-party elections. However, Jonas Savimbi of UNITA rejected the outcome and resumed the guerrilla war. He was finally killed by government troops in 2002, bringing peace to the country.

MOZAMBIQUE

In 1962 three regionally based nationalist organizations combined as FRELIMO to fight Portuguese colonialism. Eduardo Mondlane was selected to be its first president. He founded the headquarters at Dar es Salaam, in newly independent Tanzania, and started to build the organization's military wing. In 1964 FRELIMO began the military campaign against the Portuguese regime, but in 1969 Mondlane was assassinated. One story claims that a bomb was planted under his desk at the FRELIMO headquarters in Dar es Salaam, another that a bomb was planted in a book sent to him, which exploded when he opened the package. Mondlane's death galvanized many Mozambicans, who saw him as a martyr for independence.

Samora Machel became the new leader of the resistance. FRELIMO's military wing proved effective; by the 1970s they had seized control of Mozambique's northern and central regions from the Portuguese. Their 7,000 guerrilla fighters outmanoeuvred the 60,000 Portuguese troops. By 1975 the Portuguese were defeated and willing to negotiate independence.

Samora Machel became the first president of independent Mozambique, withe FRELIMO ruling as a semi-socialist one-party state. They supported Robert Mugabe's ZANU party and the guerrilla campaign against the Rhodesians. They also supported the ANC against the Afrikaners and the British. However, white farming interests, drawing on support from white regimes in Rhodesia and South Africa, created chaos by arming a terrorist group known as the Mozambique Resistance Movement (RENAMO). Its members – presented as 'freedom fighters' by some of the Western media – burned granaries, bombed communication facilities and killed many professional people.

Samora Machel battled to hold the country together against RENAMO, but was killed in a suspicious air crash in 1986. His widow Graça became the last wife of Nelson Mandela in 1998. His successor as president was Joaquim Chissano, who led Mozambique to stability, growth and a multi-party system. Eventually FRELIMO subdued the rebels and negotiated a peace treaty in 1992.

ZIMBABWE

In 1953 British imperialists created the Central African Federation. They also called it the Federation of Rhodesia and Nyasaland out of the colonies that they ruled: Northern Rhodesia, Southern Rhodesia and Nyasaland. Eventually, after independence, Northern Rhodesia became Zambia, Southern Rhodesia became Zimbabwe and Nyasaland became Malawi.

However, two nationalist groups emerged in Southern Rhodesia. The Zimbabwe African People's Union (ZAPU) was founded in 1962 by Joshua Nkomo, with mainly Ndebele support. The Zimbabwe African National Union (ZANU) was a breakaway group, founded in 1963 by Ndabaningi Sithole and Robert Mugabe; it had mainly Shona support. The Ndebele and the Shona were the main African ethnic groups in the country. The British banned both movements and imprisoned their leaders.

In time the Central African Federation collapsed, with Zambia and Malawi becoming independent under Black rule in 1964. The Zambian president, Kenneth Kaunda, supported the Zimbabwean and the South African struggle.

In Southern Rhodesia, however, the white occupiers wanted to remain in power. Consequently, on 11 November 1965, Ian Smith, leader of the white Rhodesia Front Party, unilaterally declared independence from Britain. Although this act was illegal, the British took little action. Economic sanctions were put in place against Rhodesia, but the white South African government ignored the sanctions and continued to trade with Rhodesia. Rhodesia, in turn, were thus able to continue white supremacy rule.

From 1966 until 1979 ZANU, and later ZAPU, engaged in guerrilla warfare against white rule. ZANU received help and support from Mozambique. Rhodesia, on the other hand, created the terrorist organization in Mozambique called RENAMO. In 1967 the ANC forged an alliance with ZAPU, while the South African Defence Force supported the Rhodesian regime. However, by 1979 both ZANU and ZAPU had seized much of the country outside of the cities and the Smith government was ultimately defeated.

Rhodesia became independent in 1980 and was renamed Zimbabwe. Robert Mugabe won the first elections and became president, where he remained for the next 30 years. However, he ordered reprisal killings against Ndebele 'dissidents'. In 1987 a deal was agreed to merge the two rival parties, in order to form the Zimbabwe African National Union Patriotic Front or ZANU-PF. This political party carried out a dramatic land distribution programme, designed to reclaim stolen farmland from white occupation. This policy was unpopular with the West and has resulted in most of the anti-Mugabe propaganda in the media to date. The free and liberated Zimbabwe supported the South African freedom struggle.

SOUTH AFRICA AND NAMIBIA

After Sharpeville, Nelson Mandela argued for the setting up of the military wing, the *Umkhonto we Sizwe* (literally, 'the Spear of the Nation'). In June 1961 the ANC executive considered his proposal on the use of violence and agreed that those who wished to support Mandela's campaign would not be prevented. They used sabotage to fight the regime, targeting government resources and equipment, but avoided bloodshed at all costs.

However, Nelson Mandela was arrested in 1962, alongside several other members of the ANC. On 12 June 1964 Mandela and seven others were sentenced to life imprisonment. He was incarcerated at Robben Island prison and later moved to Pollsmoor prison.

In Namibia in 1960, a land colonized by South Africa, a liberation movement arose called SWAPO – in English meaning South West African People's Organization. By 1962 this movement had swallowed up all the other liberation groups. In 1966 they began the 24-year Namibian War of Independence against the South African Defence Force. The military wing of SWAPO, called the People's Liberation Army of Namibia, launched a guerrilla war, with backing from Tanzania, Ghana and Algeria. International support came from the USSR, North Korea and China. Later in the conflict logistical support came from independent Angola, while additional troops came from Cuba.

In South Africa Stephen Biko became the leader of the Black Consciousness Movement – an organization that sought to undermine the tribalistic thinking that divided Sotho from Zulu, Xhosa from Venda and so on. One of the founders of the Black People's Convention in 1972, Biko was later elected president, but was banned by the government in 1973. The BPC brought together nearly 75 different black consciousness groups and associations, including the South African Students Movement.

The South African Students Movement led a demonstration on 16 June 1976, demanding an end to a discriminatory education system. Specifically, they demanded to be taught in the language of their choice, not in Afrikaans. The march of 15,000 students started off peacefully, but the police intervened and ordered the young protestors to disperse. They started singing *Nkosi Sikelel'iAfrika*, the anthem used by Black radicals in the liberation movement. Before the crowds could disperse, the police opened fire. Officially, they killed 176 young men and women, but according to Wikipedia the figure could have been as high as 700. Hector Pieterson, only 13 years old, was martyred. The following year, Biko was detained by the East Cape security police on 21 August. His captors beat him to death in prison, where he died on 12 September 1977.

Nelson Mandela's reputation continued to grow while he was in prison. By 1982 several thousand guerrilla fighters were active in the country who were not being suffocated by the regime. His wife Winnie Mandela kept his name and story alive in the world media and through the 1980s public opinion in Western countries turned against apartheid South Africa. She was the visible power inside the country for the ANC.

In 1986 the South African government declared a state of emergency and arrested 40,000 people in a four-month period. However, in 1988 the Cubans defeated the South African Defence Force in Angola, forcing their withdrawal. By 1990 SWAPO won their 24-year War of Independence and declared Namibia independent of South Africa under Black rule. SWAPO thus ended 75 years of South African rule, with Sam Nujoma becoming Namibia's first Black president.

Public opinion on South Africa was a delicate balancing act in Britain, Israel and United States. As examples, Margaret Thatcher denounced the ANC as terrorists. David Cameron joined a student society that printed a leaflet entitled 'Hang Mandela'. In 1990 F.W. de Klerk, the president of South Africa, unbanned the African National Congress and the Pan-Africanist Congress. Nelson Mandela was released on 18 February 1990 and was elected president of the ANC the following year. Oliver Tambo became the ANC's National Chairman. In April 1994 a coalition of the South African Communist Party, the Congress of South African Trade Unions and the ANC won a landslide victory. Nelson Mandela became the first Black president of South Africa.

On 10 May 1994, President Mandela declared:

> *We have, at last, achieved our political emancipation. We pledge ourselves to liberate all our people from the continuing bondage of poverty, deprivation, suffering, gender and other discrimination. We succeeded to take our last steps to freedom in conditions of relative peace. We commit ourselves to the construction of a complete, just and lasting peace. We have triumphed in the effort to implant hope in the breasts of the millions of our people. We enter into a covenant that we shall build the society in which all South Africans, both black and white, will be able to walk tall, without any fear in their hearts, assured of their inalienable right to human dignity – a rainbow nation at peace with itself and the world.*
>
> **Statement of the President of the African National Congress, Nelson R. Mandela, at his inauguration as President of the democratic Republic of South Africa, Nelson Mandela Foundation, Johannesburg**

FURTHER READING

William Y. Adams, '*The 'Library' of Qasr Ibrim*', in *The Kentucky Review*: Vol. 1: No. 1, Article 2, 1979

Molefi Kete Asante, *The History of Africa*, US, Routledge, 2007

J.A. Atanda, *An Introduction to Yoruba History*, UK, Ibadan University Press, 1980

Georges Balandier, *Daily Life in the Kingdom of the Kongo*, UK, George Allen & Unwin Ltd., 1968

John Beattie, *Bunyoro: An African Kingdom*, US, Holt, Rinehart and Winston, Inc., 1960

Hilary McD. Beckles & Verene A. Shepherd, *Trading Souls*, Jamaica, Ian Randal Publishers, 2007

Ayele Bekerie, *Ethiopic: An African Writing System*, US, Red Sea Press, 1997

Suzanne Preston Blier, *Royal Arts of Africa*, UK, Lawrence King, 1998

Saburi O. Biobaku ed. *The Living Culture of Nigeria*, Nigeria, Thomas Nelson & Sons, 1976

James Henry Breasted, *Ancient Records of Egypt*, Vol. I, US, University of Chicago Press, 1906

A.T. Bryant, *The Zulu People*, US, Negro Universities Press, 1970 reprint

E.A. Wallis Budge, *A History of Ethiopia, Nubia & Abyssinia*, Vol. I, UK, Methuen & Co, 1928

Gilbert and Colette Charles-Picard, *Daily Life in Carthage*, UK, George Allen and Unwin, 1961

Daniel Chu and Elliott Skinner, *A Glorious Age in Africa*, US, Africa World Press, 1990

Ronald Cohen, *The Kanuri of Bornu*, US, Holt, Rinehart and Winston, 1967

Basil Davidson, *Africa in History*, UK, Macmillan, 1991

Basil Davidson, *Old Africa Rediscovered*, UK, Victor Gollancz, 1959

Basil Davidson, *The African Slave Trade*, US, Little, Brown and Company, 1980

Vivian Davies and Renée Friedman, *Egypt*, UK, British Museum Press, 1998

Gavin de Beer, *Hannibal: The Struggle for Power in the Mediterranean*, UK, Thames and Hudson, 1969

Bernard de Grunne, *The Birth of Art in Black Africa*, France and Luxembourg, Adam Biro & Banque Generale du Luxembourg, 1998

Wolfgang Decker, *Sports and Games of Ancient Egypt*, US, Yale University, 1992

Cheikh Anta Diop, *Precolonial Black Africa*, US, Lawrence Hill Books, 1987

Sergio Domian, *Architecture Soudanaise: Vitalite d'une tradition urbaine et monumentale*, France, Éditions L'Harmattan, 1989

W.E.B. DuBois, *The World and Africa*, US, The Viking Press, 1947

Jacob Egharevba, *A Short History of Benin*, Nigeria, Ibadan University Press, 1968

Christopher Ehret, *Ancient Africa: A Global History to 300 CE*, US, Princeton University Press, 2023

Christopher Ehret, *The Civilizations of Africa*, 2nd Ed., US, University of Virginia Press, 2016

Nnamdi Elleh, *African Architecture: Evolution and Transformation*, US, McGraw-Hill, 1997

Ekpo Eyo, *Two Thousand Years of Nigerian Art*, UK & Nigeria, Ethnographica, Federal Department of Antiquities, 1977

Ekpo Eyo and Frank Willett, *Treasures of Ancient Nigeria*, UK, William Collins & Sons, 1980

V. Tarikhu Farrar, *Precolonial African Material Culture*, US, Lexington Books, 2020

M. Al Fasi ed. *General History of Africa*, Vol. 3, UK, Heinemann, 1988

Charles S. Finch, *The Star of Deep Beginnings*, US, Khenti, 1998

Peter Garlake, *Early Art and Architecture of Africa*, UK, Oxford University Press, 2002

Belai Giday, *Ethiopian Civilization*, Ethiopia, self-published, 1991

Werner Gillon, *A Short History of African Art*, UK, Penguin, 1984

Roderick Grierson editor, *African Zion*, US, InterCultura, 1993

Kevin Hart, '*On Hannibal and Elephants*, in *Amphora*', US, American Philological Association, Vol. 2, Issue 2, Fall 2003

Erik Hornung, *History of Ancient Egypt*, UK, Edinburgh University Press, 1999

John O. Hunwick, *Timbuktu and the Songhay Empire: Al-Sadi's Tarikh al-Sudan down to 1613 and other Contemporary Documents*, Netherlands, Brill, 1999

Shamil Jeppie and Souleymane Bachir Diagne eds. *The Meanings of Timbuktu*, South Africa, HSRC Press, 2008

F. George Kay, *The Shameful Trade*, UK, Frederick Muller, 1967

Herman O. Kiriama, *The Swahili of the Kenyan Coast*, Kenya, Eight Publishers, 2005

Philip Koslow, *Hausaland: The Fortress Kingdoms*, US, Chelsea House, 1995

Philip Koslow, *Kanem-Borno: 1,000 Years of Splendor*, US, Chelsea House, 1995

Alisa LaGamma, *Heroic Africans: Legendary Leaders, Iconic Sculptures*, US, The Metropolitan Museum of Art, New York, 2011

Serge Lancel, *Carthage: A History*, UK, Basil Blackwell, 1995

Duncan MacNaughton, *A Scheme of Egyptian Chronology*, UK, Luzac & Co., 1932

Saki Mafundikwa, *Afrikan Alphabets*, US, Mark Batty Publisher, 2004

Rachel Mariembe, '*Museum of the Bamoun Kings: ancient treasures from Cameroon find a spectacular new home*', on *The Conversation* (website), 20 December 2024

S.I.G. Mudenge, *A Political History of Munhumutapa c 1400--1902*, Zimbabwe, Zimbabwe Publishing House, 1988

Gert Muller, *The African Origin of Modern Humanity*, UK, Pomegranate Publishing, 2016

David Northrup, '*The Growth of Trade among the Igbo before 1800*', in *Journal of African History*, Vol. 13: No. 2, ed. J.D. Fage *et al*, UK, Cambridge University Press, 1972

Roland Oliver and Anthony Atmore, *Medieval Africa: 1250–1800*, UK, Cambridge University Press, 2001

Roland Oliver and Brian Fagan, *Africa in the Iron Age*, UK, Cambridge University Press, 1975

Sir Richmond Palmer, *The Bornu Sahara and Sudan*, UK, John Murray, 1936

Michael Rice, *Egypt's Making*, UK, Routledge, 1991

J.A. Rogers, *World's Great Men of Color*, Vol. I, US, Macmillan, 1972

H. Ling Roth, *Great Benin: Its Customs, Art and Horrors*, UK, F. King and Sons, 1903

G.T. Stride & Caroline Ifeka, *Peoples and Empires of West Africa*, UK, Thomas Nelson and Sons, 1971

John E.G. Sutton, *A Thousand Years of East Africa*, Kenya, British Institute in Eastern Africa, 1990

J. Spencer Trimingham, *A History of Islam in West Africa*, UK, Oxford University Press, 1962

Bruce Vandervort, *Wars of Imperial Conquest in Africa 1830-1914*, US, Indiana University Press, 1998

Ivan Van Sertima ed. *African Presence in Early America*, US, Transaction Publishers, 1992

Ivan Van Sertima ed. *Blacks in Science: Ancient and Modern*, US, Transaction Publishers, 1983

Ivan Van Sertima ed. *Black Women in Antiquity*, US, Transaction Publishers, 1988

Ivan Van Sertima ed. *Egypt Revisited*, US, Transaction Publishers, 1989

Jan Vansina, *Kingdoms of the Savanna*, US, University of Wisconsin Press, 1966

Barbara Watterson, *The Egyptians*, UK, Blackwell Publishers, 1997

Derek A. Welsby, *The Kingdom of Kush*, US, Marcus Wiener, 1996

Derek A. Welsby, *The Medieval Kingdoms of Nubia*, UK, The British Museum Press, 2002

Freda Wolfson ed. *Pageant of Ghana*, ed UK, Oxford University Press, 1958

Dietrich Wildung ed. *Sudan: Ancient Kingdoms of the Nile*, France, The Institut du Monde Arabe, 1997

Bruce Beyer Williams, *The A-Group Royal Cemetery at Qustul: Cemetery L*, US, The Oriental Institute of the University of Chicago, 1986

Chancellor Williams, *The Destruction of Black Civilization*, US, Third World Press, 1987

Robin Walker (Author), 'The Black History Man', was born in London but has also lived in Jamaica. He is an entrepreneur, publisher, educator and author. He read Economics at the London School of Economics; then studied African World Studies with Dr Femi Biko and Mr Kenny Baikie; and later trained as a secondary school teacher. In 2006 Walker wrote the seminal *When We Ruled*, the most advanced synthesis of ancient and medieval African history ever written by a single author. Subsequent books include *Blacks and Science* Volumes I, II and III, *Blacks and Religion* Volumes I and II, *A History of Africa* and the ALCS-award-winning *Black History Matters*, as well as books in collaboration with others such as *Everyday Life in an Early West African Empire*. In 2022 he co-founded the online adult education business, The Black Secret, which teaches Black History and African Heritage to adults. He has delivered classes and lectures for many organizations, from the Department for Education to the Victoria & Albert Museum.

Prof. Manu Ampim (Foreword) is a noted scholar and tenured professor of History and Africana Studies at Contra Costa College in San Pablo, California (USA). He has conducted primary research on classical African civilizations in two dozen countries for the past 36 years, and is an author of several influential books, namely *Towards Black Community Development* (2nd ed. 1996), *Death of the Willie Lynch Speech: Exposing the Myth* (2013), and *A History of African Civilizations* (2nd ed. 2023). Ampim is also the Director of Advancing The Research (Oakland, Calif., USA).

AFRICA & HUMAN ORIGINS

In late 1924 a surprising discovery occurred at a limestone quarry in Taung, Botswana. A skull, unearthed by accident, was brought to Professor Raymond Dart, an Australian anatomist. His analysis led to the publication of his article on 7 February 1925 in the science journal *Nature*, titled '*Australopithecus africanus*: The Man-Ape of South Africa'. In this piece Dart concluded that the fossil represented an extinct species of apes, intermediate between today's anthropoids and modern humans.

This discovery was revolutionary and influential, shifting scientific focus in the search for human origins from Asia to Africa. Professor Robert Broom, a Scottish geologist, zoologist and medical doctor, joined the search after reading Professor Dart's paper. Many others followed, including Mary Leakey, and her husband Louis. In 1960 Mary Leakey discovered a skeletal type called *Homo habilis* (i.e. man with ability) at the Olduvai Gorge site, now in the East African nation of Tanzania. In response to these finds, the anthropological fraternity began to look to Africa as the cradle of the human species.

ORIGIN AND GLOBAL MIGRATIONS OF HOMO SAPIENS

The oldest known anatomically modern humans excavated were from five African sites: Omo in Ethiopia, Herto in Ethiopia,

Laetoli in Tanzania, Klasies River Mouth in South Africa and Border Cave in South Africa. Of these, the Omo evidence is the oldest. Anatomically modern humans were found there and called Omo I and II. They had respective cranial capacities of 85⅜ and 87¼ cubic inches, well within the modern range, yet the remains dated back 195,000 years. In Herto fossilized skulls were found that dated back 160,000 years. The other African sites produced anatomically modern humans, dated back more than 110,000 years. In comparison, the oldest anatomically modern human fossil found outside Africa, discovered at Jabal Qafzeh in Israel, is only 100,000 years old.

In 2007 an article appeared in the online site *Science Daily* titled 'Earliest Evidence of Modern Humans Detected'. The archaeological evidence it revealed gave proof of modern human behaviour. On the coast of South Africa humans harvested food from the sea, employing complex bladelet tools. Bladelet tools were made from tiny pieces of quartzite and quartz. They could be attached to the end of the stick to form a spear, lined up like barbs on a dart or used like a pen knife. The evidence dated back an astonishing 164,000 years.

Professor Ashley Montagu of Rutgers University was an eminent post-war anthropologist who helped to draft the UNESCO Statement on Race. Concerning the origin of the human species, the evidence of the fossil discoveries in Africa led him in 1957 to draw the following conclusion:

> *It is quite probable that man's immediate ancestors as a group had already lost a considerable part of the hairy coat which is characteristic of all anthropoids, indeed, of all primates. What the skin color was we cannot be sure, but since the ancestors of*

man were almost certainly tropical animals of African origin, they were almost equally certainly black-skinned.
Ashley Montague, *Man: His First Million Years*, 1957

The scientific work of Charles Darwin is important to the teaching of biology in schools and universities. As the father of natural selection theory, he wrote *The Descent of Man* in 1871. This radical work contained the first-ever attempt to apply theories of natural selection to the origin of humanity. One of the topics Darwin discussed was *On the Birthplace and Antiquity of Man*. This section begins as follows:

We are naturally led to enquire, where was the birthplace of man… In each great region of the world the living mammals are closely related to the extinct species of the same region. It is therefore probable that Africa was formerly inhabited by extinct apes closely related to the gorilla and chimpanzee; and as these two species are now man's nearest allies, it is somewhat more probable that our early progenitors lived on the African continent than elsewhere.
Charles Darwin, *The Descent of Man*, 1871

Christopher Ehret, a professor of history at the University of California, is the author of a recent book, *Ancient Africa: A Global History to 300 CE* (2023). The book received a positive review in *The Telegraph*, the Conservative British broadsheet. In it Ehret presents the mainstream perspective on Africa's role in human origins, noting: 'Barely more than 50,000 years ago, the primary ancestors of every single human being alive today lived in eastern Africa. World history to that point was African history.'

Scholars at the University of Berkeley, California, have pioneered the use of mitochondrial DNA as a tool for tracing human origins. Studying people from Africa, Asia, Europe, Australia and New Guinea, they found that all non-African populations possess anatomically modern African DNA. Moreover, everyone could be traced back to a female ancestor from around 200,000 years ago. Originally published in 1987 in *Nature*, the mitochondrial DNA evidence has since found global acceptance. The evidence formed the basis of *The Incredible Human Journey*, a 300-minute, five-part BBC documentary. Filmed across five continents, the series was broadcast in 2009.

Andrew Marr brilliantly summarized the implications of this discovery in his television series, *Andrew Marr's History of the World*:

> *But after studying the evolution of human DNA, scientists have concluded that only one tribe lasted long enough outside Africa to leave a lasting legacy... And amazing as it sounds, almost all of us alive today are related to one woman in this tribe. Of course we don't know her name, but she was a survivor, and we could call her simply 'Mother'. Because there is a tiny genetic mutation in every single person alive today who isn't from sub-Saharan Africa. And scientists have tracked it back to one migration out of Africa, one tribe, one woman. It seems impossible but whether you're from Aberdeen or Islamabad, Tokyo or New York, Scandinavia or the Pacific Islands, she is your universal African mother.*
>
> **Andrew Marr's History of the World, Episode 1, 2012**

Early Modern Humans Outside Africa

Fossilized remains of anatomically modern humans with early dates have also been found outside Africa. Forensic anthropologists have reconstructed their craniofacial appearances. Among those published were human fossils from 100,000 years ago in Israel (known as Qafzeh 9), 40,000 years ago in Romania (from Pestera cu Oase), 36,000 years ago in Russia (known as Kostenki 14), 11,500 years ago in Brazil (known as Luzia) and 10,000 years ago in England (known as Cheddar Man). In each case, the fossils represented the oldest anatomically modern human evidence in the region. All the published reconstructions show people of African or Australian aborigine appearance.

What is surprising, however, is that although this evidence has emerged relatively recently, earlier scholars had long theorized along the same lines. Dr James Cowles Prichard (1786–1848), a scholar from Oxford University, was one of the founders of physical anthropology. In 1813 he issued a highly influential and much quoted volume entitled *Researches into the Physical History of Man*. In this work Prichard wrote the following: 'On the whole there are many reasons which lead us to adopt the conclusion that the primitive stock of men were probably Negroes, and I know of no argument to be set on the other side.'

Consequently, the early people left Africa with their rich dark complexions intact and maintained these complexions at least as late as 10,000 years ago. The non-African appearance of modern Europeans, modern Asians, Polynesians and the indigenous Americans must therefore be a relatively recent evolution. Geneticists have in fact dated these alterations in physical appearance to within the last 10,000 years. One of the reasons why these facts are not as well-known as they should be is that biology textbooks continue to misrepresent the appearance of early humans. They give the false impression that early humans were Europeans.

From African to Non-African Appearance

What route did these intrepid people take to leave Africa and settle in the rest of the world? One theory is that they crossed from North Africa, perhaps Morocco, into Spain. Another theory is that they crossed from Egypt into the Middle East. A third theory suggests that they crossed from Ethiopia into Yemen. Scholars are not sure whether some, or indeed all, of these theories are correct. There could have been many such migrations out of Africa between 120,000 and 30,000 years ago. Obviously, humans continued to migrate from Spain to elsewhere in Europe, while others travelled from the Middle East to elsewhere in Asia and Europe. Yet others moved from Asia to Australia.

What is known about the peopling of the earliest Americas? A 2014 article entitled '*Homo sapiens* in the Americas: An overview of the earliest human expansion in the New World', written by Aurelio Marangoni, David Caramelli and Giorgio Manzi and published in the *Journal of Anthropological Sciences*, responds as follows to this interesting question:

> *The crania of the earliest Americans…have been referred to as the 'Paleoamericans'. These tend to be similar to those of extant Australians, Melanesians and Sub Saharan Africans… Indeed, they exhibit a dolichocephalic morphology, prognathic and low faces, with relatively low, broad orbits and noses. By contrast, late prehistoric and recent Native Americans, also known as 'Amerindians', tend to exhibit a cranial morphology similar to later and modern East Asian populations…with a*

brachymorphic cranial vault, orthognathic high, broad faces, and relatively high and narrow orbits and noses.

Geneticists have long known that the closer to the regional origin of any species, the greater within-species diversity one encounters. Nikolai Vavilov, the pioneering Russian scientist, botanist and geneticist, demonstrated this in the 1930s through his work on plants. Consequently, indigenous Africans have the widest genetic variation of any group of people. Africans have the largest total number of alleles, as well as the largest number of unique alleles. This is more than the populations of Europe or Asia. Indigenous Africans have the largest height differences of any group of people, from the Khoisan at the shortest to the Nilotic speakers at the tallest. Indigenous Africans also possess the greatest linguistic diversity of any group of people. African languages contain the highest number of phonemes, which are the distinct units of sound that differentiate words. Finally, indigenous Africans have the widest range of craniofacial features: from broad faces to long narrow faces (that have become typical of Europeans) and to flat faces with epicanthic folds (that have become typical of East Asians).

Since the variety in craniofacial shapes already evolved in Africa, the key difference between African and non-African appearances is skin depigmentation. Geneticists have identified the two genes responsible: SLC24A5 and SLC45A2. Both probably originated in Central Asia and spread to northern Europe and to East Asia. Around 9,000 years ago, SLC24A5 emerged. It depigmented its bearer by 32.5 per cent of its skin colouring. Populations with this gene would have been darker than individuals with one African and one European parent. Around 8,000 years ago SLC45A2 emerged. It depigmented its bearer by 60 per cent of its skin colouring. The modern European complexion range emerged when populations began to carry both genes.

ANCESTORS OF HOMO SAPIENS

In 2016 the Ministry of Tourism in Ethiopia came up with a bold new marketing slogan. Ditching the old slogan 'Thirteen Months of Sunshine', they decreed that Ethiopia would now be known as 'Land of Origins'. The National Museum of Ethiopia in Addis Ababa has exhibits that substantiate this bold marketing rebranding. There is a wall display called 'Early Hominids in Africa'. Hominids are a primate family that includes all human and premodern human forms, going back millions of years. However, in very recent times some scholars have widened the definition to include the Great Apes as well: chimpanzees, gorillas and orang-utans. These same scholars include humans as the fourth branch of the Great Ape family. The museum wall display has the following information:

> *Africa is the cradle of humanity. Indeed, from the earliest known fossil hominids... are known only in Africa and nowhere else on Earth. These early hominids have been found in several African countries. Out of them, Ethiopia has the richest and most complete record. Yet early hominids from other countries are important.*

Outside of Omo in Ethiopia, older human fossils have been found elsewhere in Africa. These did contain some archaic as well as modern physiological traits, but could broadly be classified as *Homo sapiens*. One fossil, from Jebel Irhoud, Morocco, dated back 300,000 years. Another, from Florisbad, South Africa, dated back 260,000 years. Adrie and Alfons Kennis sculpted a life-size reconstruction of the Jebel Irhoud fossil. It shows an African appearance with some facial traits resembling 50 Cent.

Africa is the richest source of earlier hominin fossils considered ancestral to anatomically modern humans: *Homo erectus*, *Homo habilis* and the *Australopithecines*. The older these hominins are, the less they resemble modern humans. *Homo erectus* was found in Africa and has been dated to 1.8 million years old. However, *Homo erectus* fossils have also been found elsewhere on the planet. Famous examples of these are Peking Man and Java Man. *Homo habilis* dates back 2.5 million years. Archaeologists have found even earlier hominin forms in Africa called the *Australopithecines*, which date back more than 4 million years. Another set of remains, the *Ardipithecus*, are even older than the *Australopithecines*, dating back 5.8 million years. In Chad remains of an even older hominin have been found, dating back 7 million years.

Ethiopia is particularly rich in early hominin remains. Fossils found there include *Ardipithecus kadabba*, dated back between 5.8 and 5.2 million years, *Ardipithecus ramidus*, dated back 4.4 million years, *Australopithecus anamensis*, dated back 4.1 million years, *Australopithecus afarensis*, dated back between 3.7 and 2.9 million years, *Australopithecus ethiopicus*, dated back between 2.7 and 2.3 million years, *Australopithecus garhi*, dated back 2.5 million years and finally the relatively youthful *Australopithecus bosei*, dated back between 2.3 and 1.4 million years.

On display in the museum is a famous skeleton called 'Lucy'. The information surrounding this skeleton is given as follows:

Internationally renowned, Lucy, also called Dinkinesh in Ethiopia ('You are wonderful'), was discovered in 1974. Lucy stood about 105 cm tall, shorter and much less heavy than Ardi. Even for her species, Australopithecus afarensis, Lucy was short and petite. This and the shape of her pelvis indicate she was a female. She was a young adult when she died: her wisdom teeth were in place but not worn. Lucy was probably more at ease on the ground than Ardi, as evidenced by her pelvis morphology. Still, she may have been more prone to tree climbing than modern humans.

The oldest known possible ancestral type of humanity dates back 7 million years. The species, called *Sahelanthropus tchadensis*, was discovered in Chad on 19 July 2001 by Ahounta Djimdoumalbaye from the University of N'Djamena. The almost complete fragments of the skull indicate a brain size of between 21⅜ and 22⅝ cubic inches, resembling that of modern chimpanzees. However, other aspects of its skull structure suggest that *Sahelanthropus tchadensis* had some human-like traits. In 2002 Professor Michel Brunet from the University of Poitiers, the director of the Franco-Chadian paleoanthropological mission, published on this find, concluding that the characteristics of the skull are not those of a great ape. He wrote: 'Its anatomy clearly indicates that it belongs to the human branch and is separate from gorillas and chimpanzees.' The face of the skull is flat, like that of the hominins; it also possessed smaller teeth than is typical for a monkey. Moreover, the orifice through which the spinal cord passed is not unlike the other ancestral forms of humanity. This suggests that the hominin was bipedal, i.e. walked upright on two legs.

Ardipithecus is a genus of early ancestral types of humanity that dated back between 5.8 and 4.4 million years. This genus includes *Ardipithecus kadabba* and *Ardipithecus ramidus*, both of which were discovered in Ethiopia. Their brain sizes were like those of modern apes, roughly around 18¼–21⅜ cubic inches. Their teeth appear to be intermediate, between those of apes and later hominins, with the canine teeth smaller than those of most other apes. Unable to make stone tools, they probably used sticks and branches instead. Their diet was mainly fruit, seeds and other plants, though they may have scavenged for meat and eaten small animals. From analysis of an almost complete skeleton called 'Ardi', discovered in 1994, these types were not only bipedal but also arboreal, i.e. tree-dwelling. Scholars believe they lived in a forested or woodland environment, as opposed to the open savannah favoured by later hominins.

The *Australopithecines* are a group of early ancestral types of humanity that dated back to between 4 and 1.4 million years ago. This genus includes *Australopithecus anamensis*, *Australopithecus afarensis*, *Australopithecus ethiopicus*, *Australopithecus africanus*, *Australopithecus garhi*, *Australopithecus bosei* and *Australopithecus sediba*. They lived primarily in East, Central and southern Africa. The most famous example, of course, is Lucy, mentioned above. Their brain sizes were around 24⅜–30½ cubic inches and they had relatively large, protruding jaws. Their teeth were adapted to a mixed diet that included fruits, leaves and tubers. The shape of the teeth arrangement was more human-like, featuring molars with thicker enamel; this may indicate a diet that included harder foods. Body heights ranged from 3 feet 6 to 5 feet and males were generally larger than females, indicating sexual dimorphism. These early forms of humanity were forager-scavengers and used sticks and stones as tools. However, scholars believe they managed to live in a range of environments, from forests to open savannahs – a flexibility that helped them to survive during times of climatic changes. By one million years ago, the *Australopithecines* had died out entirely.

The *Homo* family succeeded the *Australopithecines*, possibly originating around 2.5 million years ago. *Homo habilis*, the first of the pre-humans to *make* tools, existed for over a million years in East Africa alongside the later *Australopithecines*. Moreover, like the *Australopithecines*, there is no evidence that this species had ever left Africa. *Homo habilis* finally died out around 1.6 million years ago. Their brain sizes ranged from 36⅝ to 48.8 cubic inches and the protrusion of their lower jaws (prognathism) was less than in earlier species. Their teeth were also smaller and more modern-looking, suited to their omnivorous diet of fruits, seeds, nuts and meat. They may also have scavenged from larger predators or hunted small animals. *Homo habilis* had an estimated height of between 3 feet 6 and 4 feet 6, and typically weighed between 70 or 80 pounds. They were consequently shorter and smaller than later species of *Homo*. Scholars remain deeply divided over whether *Homo habilis* is an ancestor of later humans or whether they in fact represent a side branch that went extinct without directly contributing to later human evolution.

Homo habilis created a culture known to scholars as the Oldowan industry. The evidence for this was found in the sites of Ledi-Geraru in Ethiopia, Koobi Fora in Kenya and the Olduvai Gorge in Tanzania. Here the earliest known stone tool traditions was discovered, representing a significant milestone in the evolution of human culture. It suggests a hitherto unprecedented level of problem-solving, planning and manual dexterity. The tools themselves were comparatively simple, unrefined implements, consisting of choppers, flakes, hammerstones and scrapers. They were made from basalt, flint and quartzite. The choppers, made from rounded stones or cobbles, were used for breaking animal bones to access the marrow. The flakes were sharp pieces of stone, used for cutting and slicing plants or thick-skinned animals. The hammerstones were hard stones, used to strike flakes from other stones, while scrapers served to scrape or process animal hides, wood or other materials. Construction using wood may therefore have begun in this period. Another cultural milestone is that the standardized creation of tools suggests that the *Homo habilis* pre-humans were passing on knowledge about how to make and use tools, indicating some form of social learning.

Homo erectus became the next species to emerge, about 1.9 million years ago. This was the first of the early ancestral types of humanity to travel away from Africa. *Homo erectus* skeletons were found in Asia, such as Java Man and Peking Man. Java Man is 1.6 million years old and Peking Man is 750,000 years old. *Homo erectus* fossils dating back 1.8 million years have also been discovered in Dmanisi, Georgia – a discovery that suggests *Homo erectus* may have migrated out of Africa earlier than previously thought. They lived in a wide range of habitats, from Africa to Asia, before dying out around 110,000 years ago. Their brain sizes ranged from 48⅞ to 73⅛ cubic inches and, although not as large as modern human skulls, there is some overlap in size with smaller modern ones. The main difference was that *Homo erectus* skulls were lower and flatter, with more pronounced brow-ridges. The tallest of them stood six feet tall; they also had longer legs than earlier hominin forms, adapted for efficient walking and running over long distances. This trait would become crucial for successful migration and hunting. Scholars speculate that *Homo erectus* lived in small groups and may have used language to communicate, although evidence for this is lacking.

Building on the Oldowan tool tradition, *Homo erectus* also developed the Acheulean industry. The tools of this industry had evolved to be more refined and specialized than the earlier stone tools. Among them was the bifacial handaxe, a teardrop-shaped stone tool worked on both sides to create a sharp edge. Such handaxes were primarily used for cutting, butchering animals and hacking plants. Other tools were refinements of Oldowan tools, but with various improvements. The Acheulean tools were more symmetrical, indicating that the fashioner had an image of the desired shape and worked to produce a tool conforming to this image. In addition, the shape and size of tools were consistent, which suggests that they were designed for specific functions. Moreover, *Homo erectus* domesticated fire. In archaeological sites such as Koobi Fora and Olduvai Gorge archaeologists have found remains of constructed fire pits, along with charred animal bones and plant materials. This indicates that fires were deliberately used for cooking, warmth and possibly protection. The cooking of food using fire would also have made food easier to digest and safer to eat. All this evidence paints a picture of social co-operation encompassing the hunting of larger animals, the use of fire and the sharing of food within groups, all of which would have been essential for survival.

Homo Heidelbergensis became the next to emerge. Originally a jawbone belonging to this species was discovered in Heidelberg in Germany in 1907, hence the name; a complete skull was later found in Kabwe, Zambia. Found to be 600,000 years old, it had a cranial capacity of 75 cubic inches – at the lower range of what one would expect from a modern human skull. In addition, it had a less prominent and smaller jaw. These prehumans are thus likely to have had better language skills than previous species. Hafted stone tips, probably tips of spears, have been found in South Africa and are associated with *Homo Heidelbergensis* culture. In addition, they made use of coloured pigments: another first. Some members of these species are believed to have migrated into Europe, where they evolved into *Homo neanderthalensis*. However, the ones that remained in Africa are believed to have evolved into anatomically modern humans.

THE EVOLUTION OF AFRICA'S PREHISTORIC CULTURES

Humans as we are today have been around for 200,000 years. However, the earliest humans probably did not speak any of the languages we have today. According to Professor Ehret, a leading authority on African prehistory and whose book *The Civilizations of Africa* (Second Edition, 2016) we refer to in this chapter, the ancestral forms of languages spoken today in Africa date back perhaps 22,000 years. Early humans, concerned where their next meal was coming from, adopted progressive technologies that increased their access to subsistence. Ehret traces the languages spoken in Africa today to a handful of subsistence strategies. These were used in different parts of Africa by the ancestors of the people known to academics as Nilo-Saharan speakers, Niger-Kordofanian speakers, Afroasiatic speakers, Khoisan speakers and the Batwa cultural complex.

The Nilo-Saharan speakers built the civilizations of Nubia, Kush, Kanem-Borno, Songhai and Mangbetu. They spoke the following languages: Meroitic, Kanembu, Kanuri, Songhai and Nemangbetu. During the Colonial Period, when Europeans conquered Africa, these civilizations would form the basis of the modern countries Sudan, Chad, Niger, Mali, Congo, etc.

One group of Niger-Kordofanian speakers became the Niger-Congo speakers. They built the civilizations of ancient Ghana, Mali, Mossi, Igbo, Yoruba, Benin, Ashanti and Dahomey. They spoke the following Niger-Congo languages: Soninke, Manding, Mooré, Igbo, Yoruba, Edo, Twi and Fon. During the Colonial Period these civilizations formed the basis of the modern countries Senegal, Gambia, Mauritania, Guinea, Burkina Faso, Nigeria, Ghana, Togo, Benin, etc.

Moreover, one group of Niger-Congo speakers became the Bantu speakers. They built the civilizations of Kongo, Ndongo, Kuba, Luba, Lunda, Bamoun, Bunyoro, Swahili, Munhumutapa and the Zulu Empire. They spoke the following Bantu languages: Kikongo, Ndonga, Bushong, KiLuba, Chilunda, Bamoun, Runyoro, Swahili, Shona and IsiZulu. During the Colonial Period these civilizations would form the basis of the modern countries Congo, Angola, Cameroon, Uganda, Somaliland, Kenya, Tanzania, Mozambique, Zimbabwe, South Africa, etc.

The Afroasiatic speakers built the civilizations of ancient Egypt, Carthage, Da'amat, Axum, Abyssinia, Hausaland and Borno. They spoke the following Afroasiatic languages: ancient Egyptian, Punic, Proto-Ethiopic, Ethiopic, Amharic, Hausa and various Chadic languages. During the Colonial Period, these civilizations would form the basis of the modern countries of Egypt, Tunisia, Ethiopia, Eritrea, Nigeria, etc.

Finally, the Khoisan and the Batwa form significant populations within the modern colonially created countries of Uganda, Rwanda, Democratic Republic of Congo, Namibia, Botswana and South Africa. The Batwa have long adopted the languages of the neighbours, but the Khoisan use the language families of Khoekhoe, Sandawe and the !Kung language.

NILO-SAHARAN CULTURE

Between 22000 and 9500 BCE, two distinctive groupings inhabited the middle and southern parts of the Middle Nile Basin. One of these groups spoke languages of the Nilo-Saharan family; the other group spoke languages of the Niger-Kordofanian family.

The Nilo-Saharans occupied the eastern parts of the basin along the Nile, plus the areas between the Nile and the Ethiopian Highlands. Their environments consisted of extensive plains and isolated ranges of hills. Antelopes and other large herbivores preferred these terrains. Consequently, the Nilo-Saharans primarily hunted large game. Among the tools they made were stone blades, which they used as points in their hunting spears. As well as the use of spears, a study of their early vocabulary shows that they had words for bows and arrows – linguistic evidence that confirms their use by this culture. Additionally, they engaged in fishing where the environment permitted it.

The Nilo-Saharans probably had a monotheistic religion. They believed that the divine expressed itself as a force that animated animals and humans. This force is the source of human anger, fears and affections. However, human beings could restrain it through their receptive consciousness. Furthermore, the animating forces of the dead, both humans and animals, could become a danger to the living when not properly dealt with through correct burial rituals and religious observances. This is where evil comes from.

Some Nilo-Saharans migrated to the eastern Sahara about 8500 BCE, where they encountered Afroasiatic speakers. What followed was thousands of years of mutual interactions which shaped African history. The Nilo-Saharans adopted wild grain collection and used grindstones in their toolkits, all skills adopted from the Afroasiatic speakers. Moreover, they added wild sorghum and pearl millet to their diets.

However, they also created something new and important: their own pottery. This was the second independent invention of pottery in Africa 8500 BCE, making this the fourth time that pottery was independently created in world history. Using ceramics, the Nilo-Saharans cooked their grains in new ways by adding flour mixed with water to create porridge. It became a staple in their diets from which other foods such as gravy, meat, vegetables and cooking oils could be added. Cattle became an important part of their way of life. Since it was important to move herds about, in order not to exhaust the scattered and limited pastures available, their homes were mere transient settlements.

Before 7000 BCE, the Nilo-Saharans began to cultivate sorghum. In doing so, they created an indigenous agriculture different to the wild grass collections of earlier periods. These radical subsistence practices multiplied what could be grown and thus enabled the support of a growing population. Nor was it just sorghum. Over the next millennia, they added the cultivation of melons. By 6000 BCE, the Nilo-Saharans were cultivating yet another crop: cotton. Near Khartoum in Sudan, archaeologists have discovered spindle whorls of baked clay, made in the heart of the Middle Nile Basin and used to turn cotton into thread. This represents a key step in making cotton into textiles. Cotton has had far-reaching effects in Africa and in world history. The evidence from Khartoum is the oldest cotton technology in the world.

In the sixth millennium BCE, Nilo-Saharans built round houses with conical roofs. The technique spread rapidly, with Niger-Congo speakers of the savanna zones of West Africa also building these house forms. In addition, we know a little about the musical instruments that the Nilo-Saharans played. Horns existed, used as trumpets or as instruments of announcement. Some were side blown. Originally fashioned from the horns of animals, such as antelopes and cows, even metal trumpets were later curved into horn-like shapes. Some trumpets, curving and carved of wood, were 9⅞ feet in length.

Ultimately, the Nilo-Saharan people were the ancestors of the civilization builders of Nubia, Kush, Kanem-Borno and Songhai. In later chapters we detail their histories.

FROM NIGER KORDOFANIAN TO NIGER-CONGO CULTURE

The Niger-Kordofanian speakers inhabited regions to the west of the Nilo-Saharans. They lived west of the Nile, in the Nuba Mountains and areas to the south and west, reaching to the Middle Nile Basin. However, they split into two linguistic groups. One branch, the Niger-Congo people, migrated far away from this region, moving to West Africa between 12000 and 9500 BCE. The other branch, the Kordofanians, remained in and around the Nuba Mountains. According to Professor Ehret, there is no information about where the Kordofanians fit into history. No archaeology of any value has been done: there is a blank. However, more is known about the Niger-Congo speakers.

In the sixth or fifth millennium BCE, one branch of the Niger-Congo speakers became a separate group called the proto-Benue-Kwa. They are the direct ancestors of the Yoruba, Igbo and Akan, who have done much to shape more recent pages of African history. For the first time hereditary clan chief priests came into existence.

Presiding over communal ceremonial observances, they acted as the ritual intermediary between the people of the clan and the spirits of ancestors. The priests settled disputes within the community and may have allocated land to newly joined members of the clan.

In addition, the proto-Benue-Kwa created a West African agricultural tradition distinct from collecting wild grasses. Cultivating yams and oil palms, the proto-Benue-Kwa speakers planted shoots back into the ground, not seeds. With the creation of a new type of stone axe, they were able to clear deep forests. This enabled exposure to the sunlight necessary for raising crops. The new stone axe broadened the range of West African tool technology from microliths alone.

Between 5000 and 3500 BCE, the proto-Benue-Kwa spread through the woodland savannah and rainforests from Ivory Coast to Cameroon. This movement of people also brought some of the crops they previously cultivated elsewhere: black-eyed peas and groundnuts. The proto-Benue-Kwa migrants absorbed the already existing hunter-gatherer inhabitants of those regions into their communities. This ultimately created more proto-Benue-Kwa speakers.

In the fourth millennium BCE, the proto-Benue-Kwa culture created a new technology of historical magnitude. They created the broad loom, weaving raffia fibres into textiles. The cloth initially served local demands, but later became articles of long-distance trade. These textiles were in demand in different parts of West and Central Africa.

At this time, the Niger-Congo speakers lived in relatively compact villages containing 100 or 200 people. Most of them belonged to one clan, but men were also attached who had joined after marrying local women. They built village houses on both sides of a single street. If the village was near a river, they built a single row of houses on one side. In those villages skilled craft activities took place. Weavers created articles for everyday use: mats for sleeping on, mats for preparing food and woven baskets. Others fashioned bark cloth. They removed sheets of bark from trees and produced textiles. Woodcarvers carved canoes from single large logs of trees. Others carved figurative sculptures. This represents the beginnings of the Niger-Congo wooden art tradition. Others carved drums of different pictures. Since Niger-Congo speakers were targeted during the period of transatlantic enslavement and shipped to the Americas, scholars believe there is an unbroken tradition of drum-based music from prehistoric times to modern-day African American genres of ragtime, jazz, and rhythm and blues.

The Niger-Congo culture were the ancestors of the civilization builders of ancient Ghana, Mali, Mossi, Igbo, Yoruba, Benin, Ashanti and Dahomey. One branch of Niger-Congo speakers became the Bantu. The Bantu created the civilizations of Kongo, Ndongo, Kuba, Luba, Lunda, Bamoun, Bunyoro, Swahili, Munhumutapa and the Zulu Empire. In later chapters we detail their histories.

AFROASIATIC CULTURE

In 19000 BCE an unknown people speaking an unknown language in northern Nubia and southern Egypt began using sedges as a food source. These nut grasses produced underground tubers which they ground into flour. Archaeological excavations have found numerous grindstones, showing that sedges were ground to produce a source of carbohydrates. Stone blades of medium size were also found and probably used for spears. Smaller points discovered there were probably used for bows and arrows.

However, at some moment before 15000 BCE, other communities also began to harvest the seeds of wild grasses. Living in the Horn of Africa, these people spoke Afroasiatic. However, as Professor Ehret points out, this is an unfortunate name for scholars to use for this language family. Originating in the Horn of Africa, there is nothing Asiatic about its origin. Nevertheless, from an analysis of the vocabulary used by the ancient speakers, we learn the wild grain collectors ground the grains into flour on grindstones, made dough from that flour and baked the dough into flatbreads.

The Afroasiatic speakers lived in numerous clan-based communities. Clans were social groupings that claimed common descent from a founding ancestor. However, in practice things were never so clear cut. Many clans included people who came from another background but had been adopted into the group. Professor Ehret believes that each clan also had a hereditary priest. They did not have the political power of later kings or priests, since decision-making affecting the whole clan involved extended discussions in communal meetings. Yet this hereditary ritual priest did derive power from religious authority. Each of the different communities centred their ritual observances around a clan deity to whom the clan members owed allegiance. The priest presided over the community rituals and acted as intercessor and interpreter of the deity. Boys were probably circumcised. It is possible this practice was brought to the Levant from Africa by the earliest Afroasiatic grain collectors.

By harvesting the seeds of wild grasses, Afroasiatic communities were able to obtain a greater quantity of food from the same amount of land. This revolutionary concept gave them a long-term demographic advantage over neighbouring societies who persisted with older methods. Consequently, population sizes grew among Afroasiatic speakers. Their communities probably consisted of several hundred people, outnumbering by several times their hunter-gatherer neighbours. Professor Ehret suspects typical Afroasiatic houses had rectangular plans with flat thatched roofs supported by wooden pillars. As Afroasiatic settlements grew, they impacted on the resources available to their neighbours, creating crises in food supply for those neighbours. Undoubtedly these caused localized conflicts. However, the neighbouring communities may also have responded by assimilating into Afroasiatic societies. They would absorb Afroasiatic agricultural techniques, absorb the vocabulary associated with it and thus become Afroasiatic speakers themselves. In this way the Afroasiatic populations increased.

Afroasiatic Divides into Branches

Professor Ehret distinguishes two groups of Afroasiatic speakers who emerged before 15000 BCE. One group established themselves in the central and southern parts of the Ethiopian Highlands. A second group began to relocate to areas along the Egyptian Nile. Archaeological excavations in Egypt has found small, crescent-shaped stone blades for harvesting grain. Over the next 2,000 years this second group spread wild grain-based practices north towards the Nile Delta. As before, they absorbed and assimilated local pre-existing communities into this culture, who then copied these agricultural techniques.

In the thirteenth millennium BCE an offshoot Afroasiatic group spread these technologies from the Sinai region into the Levant. Scholars called these people the Mushabian culture. These migrant communities became neighbours to the Kebaran culture, which already existed in the region. Eventually these two cultures fused to create a mixed culture called the Natufian culture. Between 11000 and 10000 BCE the Natufians began to practise wild grain collection.

The ancient Egyptian language evolved from the Afroasiatic communities who brought wild grain collecting into the Nile Valley. They built a civilization that will be explored in later chapters. Semitic may have been spoken by the Mushabian people who brought these technologies from Africa into the Levant. Other Semitic speakers built civilizations in Ethiopia and Eritrea, also to be considered in later chapters. Berber and Chadic languages evolved from the Afroasiatic people who moved westward from Egypt after 9000 BCE across the North Central Sahara and North Africa. The Berber languages were spoken by the Africans of the desert and the indigenous North Africans. Some would be joined by Semitic-speaking newcomers from the Middle East, who claimed distant East African origins. Out of this arose a civilization in Tunisia called Carthage. The Chadic speakers went on to build the Hausa civilization in Nigeria. Hausa has now become the second most widely spoken indigenous language in Africa.

The domestication of sheep and goats took place in the Middle East. From there they made their appearance around 7000 to 6500 BCE in the Capsian culture, then spread south into different parts of Africa. The domestication of wheat and barley also took place in the Middle East, with the cereals also entering Africa at this time. The domestication of the donkey by the Cushitic people (see below), in around the sixth millennium BCE, took place in the Red Sea coastal regions. Before 4000 BCE the keeping of donkeys spread from Africa into southwestern Asia, where donkeys became important beasts of burden. The Chadic people introduced domesticated donkeys into the central Sahara in the sixth millennium BCE.

After 3500 BCE speakers of a branch of Afroasiatic called Cushitic moved south into modern-day Kenya, adapting their ways of life to a very different, much hotter environment. There the newcomers encountered Khoisan-speaking communities. From them, the Cushitic speakers received honey, from which they made mead, their fermented drink. After 1800 BCE the Cushitic speakers spread into northern Tanzania. As they spread their subsistence techniques among the Khoisan speakers, many of the latter chose to adopt Cushitic. Today, only two Khoisan languages are still spoken in East Africa: Hadza and Sandawe.

Sometime in the fourth or very early third millennium BCE a new group of crops of Middle Eastern origin entered Ethiopia. Wheat, barley, chickpeas and lentils became part of the way of life of Ethiopian farmers. In addition, a new piece of technology entered the region: the plough. Plough technology spread from Egypt to the Red Sea hills.

In the late second millennium BCE the Cushitic speakers began to build irrigation works in the Rift Valley areas of southern Ethiopia. Many small streams flow down to the plains from higher elevations, making it it possible to turn water from the streams into irrigation furrows, able to bring the water to nearby fields. Another important development happened in the centuries before 1000 BCE, when highland Cushitic farmers began to build stonewall terraces to stave off erosion of their lands. They also used stone as building materials for houses, walls of community meeting areas and the foundation for flat roof houses, otherwise built of wood. In some areas people laid stone pavements on pathways between settlements, or even between settlements and fields. Stone was used in other ways, too, with megaliths taking on a ritual and artistic significance. One practice was to place free-standing tall stones on the burial grounds of clan priest chiefs.

Ultimately the people of the Afroasiatic culture were the ancestors of those who built the civilizations of ancient Egypt, Carthage, Dama'at, Axum, Abyssinia, Hausaland and Borno.

KHOISAN CULTURE

Before 16000 BCE the Khoisans had a culture belonging to the eastern African microlithic or Wilton complex. Before the Ice Age came to an end, varieties of this culture complex existed much further south, with evidence being found in regions of modern-day Zimbabwe and southern Zambia. In the seventh millennium BCE the southern African Wilton variety of this culture complex spread across the rest of southern Africa. With it came the spread of the Khoisan language family.

The Khoisans had used several stringed instruments over several millennia. The single-string musical bow may have been the earliest such instrument, but four- and five-stringed instruments, with hollow gourd resonators, were also played. These too were of great antiquity.

The Khoisan created an ancient and distinctive tradition of rock art, painting on the bare walls of rock shelters or caves. Evidence of their work survives today in Tanzania, Zimbabwe and Namibia. Where there were no rock surfaces, the artists made rock engravings. Religion formed the basis of the paintings' subject matter; they represented the kinds of scenes encountered in trance states. It may thus be assumed that trance healers probably made these art pieces. The Khoisan believed in spirit as a force that existed outside human beings, as well as in some animals. They believed that it was possible to tap into this force by means of a trance dance. In this procedure, a shaman danced until he or she went into a state of trance, which might last for many hours. In this state they could heal sickness and relieve social and individual stresses, even conflicts. Such healers were not full-time specialists, however, and so did not become priests. As a result they held no special elite hierarchical position in the society.

Khoisan culture flourished in dry savannah, steppe or desert climates. When Khoisan communities spread across southern Africa in the eighth and seventh millennia BCE, they chose these same types of climes. They used subsistence strategies that allowed them to cope better than their neighbours in these environments. The men hunted a great variety of game, large and small, with bows and arrows. Using poisoned arrows, it was possible to kill large animals; a weakened animal could be tracked as the poison worked its way through the animal's bloodstream. Meanwhile, women collected a great variety of wild plant food, with wild honey becoming part of the diet.

Using poison arrows for hunting in arid lands gave the Khoisan a subsistence advantage over their neighbours. These arid conditions meant that it was advantageous to live in small bands of between 25 and 30 men, women and children. These bands were mobile, able to resettle in different locations two or three times a year. They thus built small, hemispherical houses, easy to build and of no great loss if one had to move and build elsewhere. Each Khoisan band claimed a territory in which it had primary rights for hunting and gathering. Since the climate was arid, this territory could range from 154 or 193 square miles. They could even go up to – or exceed – 1,544 square miles. Different bands would meet up at agreed times of year at places with reliable food resources and dependable water. They held dances and traded surpluses from their hunting and gathering. At these meetings the younger people would find marriage partners, since it was important to marry outside of your band. Kings and elites did not exist in these early cultures. Conflicts and differences could be solved by individuals starting their own band, joining another band or moving away from the area.

Rock paintings also existed in southern Africa, dating back 30,000 years. Since the Khoisan speakers only spread into these regions from around the eighth millennium BCE, however, they could not have been responsible for the earlier art. Some other group of Africans, speaking unknown languages, must have created these.

Finally, in the second millennium BCE, the Khoisan people built stone dams. Archaeologists have discovered them along the coasts of modern-day KwaZulu Natal and the Transkei regions. They were built to make fishing more productive. During a high tide, rising sea water would fill in the areas behind the small dams. As the tide receded, water would filter out between the stones, stranding the fish in the shrinking pools of water, where they were easy to catch.

BATWA CULTURE

During the last glacial maximum, and for thousands of years after 9500 BCE, the Batwa created a long-lived and distinctive cultural tradition. They lived across the Congo basin, spreading southward into modern-day Angola and eastward into the African Great Lakes region. Some of their distinctive rock art has even been found in Zambia. The Batwa are often known for their distinctive short stature, but in fact there are significant differences in people's height and appearance.

The Batwa have historically preferred wooded savannah or rainforest environments, and in some of these places they created geometric art. Many of the figures are weather signs, suggesting that the pieces have practical implications for religious observances. These rock sites were probably places where religious experts among the Batwa carried out rainmaking rituals. Certainly the non-Batwa inhabitants continue to use the sites for this purpose.

The Batwa may also have invented a particular African type of crossbow called the arbolet. This was an important technology for hunting in the forests.

However, scholars investigating the Batwa have been hampered by the fact that the Batwa adopted the languages of the neighbours long ago. Since they no longer speak their own languages, an entire body of potential historical information has been lost.

BANTU CULTURE

By 3000 BCE, the Proto Bantu, a branch of Niger-Congo speakers, lived in the region of the Sanaga and Nyong rivers in southern Cameroon. Using stone axes to clear woodland for their crops, they built boats, made sculptures in wood and carved masks for public festivals and dances. They also lived in villages, in rectangular houses with gabled roofs of sewn palm thatch.

Living in these areas were the hunter-gatherers of the Batwa cultural tradition. However, the early Bantu migrants, rather than challenge the Batwa in the forests, sought out open areas along the streams and areas of savannah where there was little heavy tree growth. As a result, much of the rainforest remained available for the Batwa, even down to recent times. Trade took place between the two groups of people. The Batwa acquired property and polished stone axes from their Bantu neighbours. The Bantu gained new knowledge of the rainforests' environment, along with honey, meat and the skins of wild game.

During the fourth millennium BCE, some Bantu speakers extended their settlement southward to the Ogowe River. Later, other Bantu migrants passed eastward, out of the Nyong River, towards the confluence of the Sangha with the Congo River. Other communities also moved progressively eastwards, as far as the confluence of the Aruwimi, the Lomami and the Congo rivers. By 1000 BCE, the eastern outliers of this Bantu expansion had reached the west side of the great Western Rift. Moreover, they brought their agricultural techniques, fishing techniques and tool technologies into these new territories, previously occupied by the Batwa hunter-gatherers.

In the late second millennium BCE, cultural practices came into being as rites of passage that turned boys into men and girls into women. Boys were circumcised and initiated into age sets during adolescence. Age sets were social groups of people of similar age who almost become brothers for life, passing together through the same set of age-related statuses. These observances, which lasted several weeks, included secluding the boys in a circumcision camp, masked dancing and the ritual marking of the boys with white clay. Girls were individually initiated at puberty into the status of young women. After a woman gave birth to a child, a second rite was performed.

Despite the movements of the Bantu speakers, some as late as 1000 BCE, the Batwa tradition continued to flourish from present-day Angola to Zambia and along the western side of East Africa. Meanwhile the Khoisan tradition continued to flourish in south-central East Africa and across most of Africa south of the Zambezi.

These populations were to become part of many of the Bantu civilizations: Kongo, Ndongo, Kuba, Luba, Lunda, Bamoun, Bunyoro, Swahili, Munhumutapa and the Zulu Empire.

THE EARLY HISTORY OF SUDAN & EGYPT

The maps of Egypt and Sudan as we have them today are Colonial Period creations. From 1852 Britain kept an increased presence in northern Egypt to maintain the overland trade route to India and to oversee the construction of the Cairo–Alexandria railway, a piece of British technology on foreign soil. In 1882 Britain conquered Egypt and eventually placed it under a protectorate, while maintaining the facade of Ottoman sovereignty. Meanwhile, in Sudan to the south, Britain conquered the land by defeating the Sudanese at the Battle of Omdurman in 1898. In the following year the region became known as Anglo-Egyptian Sudan, governed jointly by Britain and Egypt. Although Egypt nominally shared power, it was in practice under British control.

However, people from the British Isles had entered the land well before then to document its logistics. One such scholar was Richard Robert Madden, an Irish doctor. An area that attracted his attention was identifying which populations in modern Egypt might have the greatest affinity with the ancient Egyptians. In his book *Travels in Turkey, Egypt, Nubia and Palestine in 1824, 1825, 1826 and 1827*, published in 1829, Madden described his research techniques:

> *I employed five hours a day in examining the tombs... I had a strong hope that the accurate examination of mummy heads, on craniological principles, and the comparing them with those of the Copts and Nubians, might throw much light on the question of the descendants of the Egyptians. I have made a collection of the skulls of the various inhabitants of Egypt, Turks, Jews, Copts, Arabs and Greeks, and each has its decided national peculiarities.*

This work may well be the first anthropological study ever conducted on the ancient Egyptians. In it Madden concluded:

> *[I]t is evident that there is no affinity between the head of the Egyptian mummy and that of the Copt; but allowing, in all the measurements, three-quarters of an inch for the difference of the scalp on the Nubian head, it follows that the measurement of the latter corresponds with that of the mummy head in every particular. But the great distinction between the mummy and Copt, in a line drawn right across the orbits, from one external angle of the eye to that of the other, is in the greater space of the Copt across the eyes, in every skull that I measured, the line across the orbits of the Copt being half an inch longer than in the same line of the mummy. In this respect, likewise, the Nubian skull differed nothing from the latter. The old Egyptian head is of so peculiar a form that it would be impossible to confound it with the Turkish, Grecian or Arabic head... The old Egyptian skull is extremely narrow across the forehead, and of an oblong shape anteriorly. I suppose I must have seen several thousands of mummy heads, but I never found one with a broad expanded forehead... Herodotus, whose own observations are deemed veracious, describes the old Egyptians, among whom he was*

residing, as a people of black skins and short woolly hair; the Copts have neither one nor the other; and above all, what, in my opinion, is the strongest of all evidence on the subject, is the utter dissimilarity in the form of the heads of both people… It is among the Nubians we are to search for the true descendants of the Egyptians; a swarthy race with wiry hair; surpassing, in the beauty of their slender forms, all the people of the East; living on the confines of Egypt, where, probably, their ancestors had been driven by the Persians; and possessing a dialect somewhat mixed with Arabic, but which, I have observed, no Arab understands.

Recent physical anthropology supports this view. In 2005 two German scholars, A-M, Mekota and M. Vermehren, wrote a scientific article on ancient Egyptian elite mummy skin. In this work, titled 'Determination of optimal rehydration, fixation and staining methods for histological and immunohistochemical analysis of mummified soft tissues' and published in the journal *Biotechnic & Histochemistry*, they noted that:

Skin sections showed particularly good tissue preservation, although cellular outlines were never distinct. Although much of the epidermis had already separated from the dermis, the remaining epidermis often was preserved well… The basal epithelial cells were packed with melanin, as expected for specimens of Negroid origin.

DNA Tribes was an American personal genomics and biotechnology company that offered individuals the opportunity to trace their ancestry based on autosomal STR genetic markers, developed by the FBI for individual identification in a forensic context. On 1 January 2012 the company announced that 'geographical analysis of the Amarna mummies' had been performed. The Amarna mummies are royals dating from the Eighteenth Dynasty (fourteenth century BCE). In a table, they presented the average MLI, that is Match Likelihood Index, of STR, or Short Tandem Repeats, occurring in an individual's genome. Among their findings, published in *DNA Tribes® Digest* on 1 January 2012, was the discovery that:

> *Average MLI scores…indicate the STR profiles of the Amarna mummies would be most frequent in present day populations of several African regions: including the Southern African (average MLI 326.94), African Great Lakes (average MLI 323.76) and Tropical West African (average MLI 83.74) regions.*

Professor Jean-Philippe Gourdine and his team conducted this research into the genetic make-up of ancient Egyptian elite remains, seeking to identify their origins. The Amana and Ramesside mummies used included Thuya, Yuya, Amenhotep III, Tutankhamen and Ramesses III. In August 2018 the scientists published their results in a journal article called 'Ancient Egyptian Genomes from northern Egypt: Further discussion'. These revealed that on average the sample group were found to have 3.3 per cent ancestry from Asia, 15.4 per cent ancestry from Eurasia and 81.3 per cent ancestry from sub-Saharan Africa. To sum up the genetic evidence, one of the studies suggest a majority sub-Saharan origin for the ancient Egyptian royals. The other study suggests the Egyptian royals had genetic material most similar to contemporary indigenous South Africans.

The landscape and buildings of the Sudan have also caught the interest of foreigners. George Bethune English, an American adventurer, diplomat and soldier, took part in a Turkish Egyptian military campaign of 1821 to attack 'brigands' in the Sudan region. Through these attacks, the Turkish Egyptians conquered Sudan and made it part of their empire. English published an account of what he had seen travelling along the Nile through the Sudanese lands. In *A Narrative of the Expedition to Dongola and Sennaar*, published in 1822, English described the landmarks of his journey: on one day, 'All the villages we have passed to-day have in their centre a fort or castle, fortified with towers at the corners'. On another day, he noticed a 'continued succession of villages and castles which occupied both banks of the river'. He mentions castles in Sudan at least 15 times and is careful to distinguish the more recent ones built by the Mamelukes from the others of a great age. In one case gives the following details:

> *In walking along the shore, saw at a distance a large castle, lately occupied by the brigands; on visiting it, found it capable of accommodating at least a thousand men. The walls and towers very thick and pierced with loopholes: it had been taken by the aid of the Pasha's artillery, and almost everything combustible in it had been burned by the troops.*

English was also aware of the agricultural potential of the Sudanese lands. He commented in his *Narrative* that:

> *The country of Shageia, possessed by the brigands, was the best cultivated we had seen this side of Assuan; the water-wheels, so far as we have passed their country, being frequently within half a stone's throw of each other.*

English mentioned water-wheels in Sudan seven times – yet, amazingly, this is not common knowledge. Even today many people repeat false ideas about African cultures not having the wheel! Whatever the case may be, the castles, some able to accommodate 1,000 people, the agricultural water-wheels and the fortifications belong to a medieval age in Sudan. Three kingdoms flourished in the region: Nobadia, Makuria and Alwa, whose stories and achievements we will explore below. Moreover, on his journey English saw evidence of ancient heritage:

> *I found before this rock the ruins of a very large temple, which covered a great space of ground. Some columns, almost consumed by time, were standing nearly buried in the rubbish. The bases of others were visible, which, from their position, evidently once supported an avenue of pillars… Among the ruins saw two large lions of red granite, one broken and the other little injured, and a small headless statue, about two feet high, in a sitting posture… The pyramids were close by these ruins. I counted seventeen, some of them in ruins, and others perfect.*

These temples, statues and pyramids belonged to an ancient age in Sudan. Ancient kingdoms flourished there at this time: Ta-Seti, Sai and Kush, also discussed below. Finally, English arrived at Sennar where he was greeted by the ruler, Sultan Badi IV:

> *On approaching the city, the army saluted this long wished-for town, where they imagined that their toils and privations would cease, at least for a time, with repeated and continued volleys of cannon and musquetry,*

accompanied with shouts of exultation. But these shouts subsided on a nearer approach, on finding this once powerful city of Sennaar to be almost nothing but heaps of ruins, containing in some of its quarters some few hundreds of habitable but almost deserted houses. After the camp was pitched, and I had refreshed myself with a little food, I took a walk about the town. At almost every step I trod upon fragments of burnt bricks, among which are frequently to be found fragments of porcelain, and sometimes marble. The most conspicuous buildings in Sennaar are a mosque and a large brick palace adjoining it. The mosque, which is of brick, is in good preservation; its windows are covered with well-wrought bronze gratings, and the doors are handsomely and curiously carved… The palace is large, but in ruins, except for the centre building, which is six storeys high, having five rows of windows. By mounting upon its roof you have the best possible view of the city, the river and the environs that the place can afford. I judged that Sennaar was about three miles in circumference. The greater part of this space is now covered with the ruins of houses, built of bricks either burnt or dried in the sun.

THE RIDDLE OF THE SPHINX

The Great Sphinx of Giza is the oldest known colossal statue in art history. Carved in the shape of a lion, it has an African head wearing the pharaonic headdress. What do we know about it? Nearly all historians and archaeologists think that a pharaoh from the Fourth Dynasty commissioned it to be carved. Egyptian records name that pharaoh as 'Khafra' or 'Suphis II', while Greek records call him 'Kephren'. Historians are agreed that Khafra, Suphis II and Kephren are in fact different names for the same ruler.

However, a minority of historians take a very different view. They believe that the Great Sphinx of Giza was carved in pre-dynastic times. This means it was carved before the time of the pharaohs. However, Manetho, an ancient Egyptian historian, wrote a *History of Egypt* in 241 BCE in which he dated the Fourth Dynasty to between 4938 and 4654 BCE. Most historians today disagree with him. Using the 'Short Chronology', they believe that the Fourth Dynasty existed between 2613 and 2494 BCE, and that the Sphinx of Giza was built around 2550 BCE. However, Professor Robert Schoch, a geologist from the University of Boston, is of the opinion that the Sphinx dates from 5000 BCE, or even longer ago. Nobody has been able to disprove him. Manetho's dates for the Fourth Dynasty seem closer to Professor Schoch's dating of 5000 BCE than do the dates used by others.

There are three possibilities for how this could be interpreted. The first is that the Great Sphinx of Giza was built before the time of the pharaohs; historians are thus wrong to say it was commissioned by Khafra. The second is that the Great Sphinx of Giza was built during the time of Khafra, in around 2550 BCE, but Professor Schoch's findings are still not accurate and should be disregarded. The third possibility is that the Great Sphinx of Giza was built during the time of Khafra, but historians should use the Manetho dating for Khafra rather than the 'Short Chronology'.

THE KINGDOM OF TA-SETI

Archaeologists discovered the remains of the Kingdom of Ta-Seti in 1962. There they found the royal tombs of a dynasty of 10 to 12 kings of Nubia, who even then were using regalia later adopted by Egyptian pharaohs. Moreover, the cemeteries and their layouts indicated that the society was stratified into social classes, with royal and religious elites. Writers of classical antiquity wrote admiringly about an 'ancient Ethiopia', located immediately south of ancient Egypt. Stephanus of Byzantium, for example, wrote: 'Ethiopia was the first established country on earth and the Ethiopians were the first to set up the worship of the gods, and [the first] who established laws'. Yet before this archaeological discovery there had been no proof of its existence.

Centralized at Qustul near the modern Egyptian–Sudanese border, this ancient kingdom exercised power over a wide expanse of land. To the north, they controlled land beyond the first cataract of southern Egypt. Significantly, there is a Nubian tomb in Hierakonpolis of royal size and design. To the south, their power extended into Sudan. In addition, they controlled land 124¼ miles west of the River Nile, along with an unknown expanse of territory to the east of the Nile.

The megalithic astronomical site of Nabta Playa was within its territory. The people of this kingdom, like the people of Nabta Playa, were Nilo-Saharan speakers. In a work on astrology attributed to the ancient Greek satirist Lucian, we get another glimpse of classical praise for the 'ancient Ethiopians' just south of Egypt. Lucian declared:

The first inventors of astrology were the Ethiopians; of which two probable causes may be assigned, one, the eminent sagacity of that people, for which and many other particulars, they were peculiarly remarkable above other nations: the other is their fortunate situation; for they are always surrounded by a serene sky[...] What first attracted their attention in the sky were the changes of the moon, which, instead of remaining always the same, shewed itself under different aspects, and alternately transformed itself from one into the other. The fact seemed to them surprising, and deserving of stricter investigation. They observed and examined therefore so long, till they found out that the cause of it was that the moon has no light of its own, but is illumined by the sun. They discovered also the motion and the course of some other stars, which we call planets [...] they searched into their nature, their power, their sphere of action, and their diverse influences; they invented names for them, serving not, as most names do, merely to distinguish, but at the same time as symbols of their properties and effects.

After the Ethiopians had made these preliminary observations on the sky, they handed over the crude and uncultivated science to their neighbours the Egyptians, who much improved it[...]

Lucian, *Of Astrology*, trans. William Tooke, *Lucian of Samosata. From the Greek*, Vol. 2, 1820

Before the archaeological discovery of Nabta Playa, there was no proof to confirm Lucian's assertions. Some of the megaliths were aligned to the three stars of Orion's Belt: Alnitak, Alnilam and Mintaka. Others were aligned to different stars in Orion: Betelgeuse, Bellatrix and Meissa.

Archaeologists discovered Ta-Seti in 1962. With the building of the Aswan Dam in Egypt, Nubian artefacts were placed at great risk of being flooded forever. A group of archaeologists led by Professor Keith C. Seele saw the need to excavate and remove as many artefacts as possible from the area before the flood waters buried them. He led the Great Archaeological Rescue Campaign and discovered the royal tombs, but the artefacts were removed to the University of Chicago's Oriental Institute. Fortunately, in 1979, a researcher at the institute publicized the importance of this evidence. A news story appeared in the *New York Times* under the headline 'Ancient Nubian Artifacts Yield Evidence of Earliest Monarchy'. The article contained the information that:

> *Evidence of the oldest visible monarchy in human history, preceding the rise of the earliest Egyptian kings by several generations, has been discovered in artifacts from ancient Nubia in Africa.*

If the 'Short Chronology' is used, this may date the beginning of this kingdom to 3500 BCE.

The tombs contained 5,000 artefacts, most of which were locally made. However, others were acquired by trade with their neighbours on the Red Sea, central Sudan, Egypt and the Middle East. Boats appear in their art, revealing how they travelled to trade. Five styles of pottery were also discovered, helping archaeologists to date the site by comparing the Nubian pottery to ancient Egyptian pottery. They found that the first 9 or 11 pharaohs ruled here 200 or 300 years before the first pharaoh of Egypt. Some ceramics even bore fragments of hieroglyphic writing.

The golden artefacts included a golden bracelet and a necklace; the latter consisted of a golden pendant shaped like a fly, connected to gold-sheet beads. In later Egyptian times, this same design evolved into the Egyptian military decoration: the Order of the Fly. The copper artefacts included maceheads, spearheads, rings, a copper tray and a copper cap for a furniture leg. The ivory artefacts included spoons and gaming pieces (accompanied by wooden gaming boards). There were artistic pieces of terracotta and limestone hippopotami as well as mortars, pestles and palettes. Highly polished, and made of coloured quartz, these were used to grind malachite for application as eye paint. The jewellery items were made of amethyst, carnelian and rock crystal. There were also around a hundred vessels made of stone. Finally, more than 4,000 other objects made from seashells were discovered. In an article titled 'The Lost Pharaohs of Nubia', published in *Archaeology Magazine* in 1980, Professor Bruce Williams of the Oriental Institute observed that:

> *The range of these and other fragments from the plundered cemetery began to indicate a wealth and complexity that could only be called royal.*

In addition, some of the artefacts record victories over the Egyptians and Libyans. A storage jar at Qustul attests to a Ta-Seti military campaign against Hierakonpolis in Egypt. Another bowl from Qustul records Nubian campaigns waged against Ta-Shemau (Upper Egypt) and against Ta-Tjemeh (Libya). The Gebel Sheikh Suleiman monument, a well-known historical monument, boasts of other Nubian military victories over the Egyptians. However, with the rise of the Egyptian First Dynasty, Pharaoh Hor-Aha, its second ruler, campaigned against Ta-Seti's ninth or eleventh generation pharaoh. Hor-Aha's ill-fated campaign destroyed the Nubian kingdom.

THE OLD KINGDOM PERIOD OF EGYPT

The ancient Egyptians were Afroasiatic speakers. Geographers divide their land into two. The southern three quarters were called Upper Egypt. The northern quarter was called Lower Egypt. Each of the two lands had their own capital cities, heraldic flowers, crowns and protective goddesses. Upper Egypt, which had its capital at Nekhen, the land of the lotus flower. Its rulers wore the White Crown. The people of Upper Egypt believed that Nekhbet, the vulture goddess, protected their land. The capital of Lower Egypt was at Buto, the land of the papyrus plant. Its rulers wore the Red Crown. The people of Lower Egypt believed that Wadjet, the snake goddess, protected their land.

Archaeologists have discovered a pictorial stone document called 'Narmer's Tablet' that shows how the two lands were unified. Narmer is portrayed wearing the White Crown of Upper Egypt. A mace is in his hand and he stands with his arm raised, as if about to strike an enemy. The other side of the document depicts Narmer wearing the Red Crown of Lower Egypt; high-ranking officials in royal garb walk before him. Historians interpret this as meaning that Narmer, ruler of Upper Egypt, defeated the people of Lower Egypt and took their crown. Narmer thus became the first king of a unified Egypt. All the later rulers of unified Egypt also wore the double crown, representing their authority over Egypt's northern and southern regions.

Other information on the first king comes from much later sources. The ancient Greek historian Herodotus visited Egypt around

450 BCE. After speaking to some ancient Egyptian priests, he noted that, 'The priests said that Menes was the first king of Egypt, and that it was he who raised the dike which protects Memphis from the flooding of the Nile', adding, 'in addition to these works, he also… built the Temple of Vulcan, which stands within the city'. Vulcan is a European name for the Egyptian God Ptah. We can also infer that the city of Memphis, built on the border between Upper and Lower Egypt, was built during the reign of the first king.

Another source of information comes from an ancient Egyptian historian called Manetho, who wrote a *History of Egypt* around 241 BCE. He recorded that:

> *The First Dynasty consisted of eight kings. The first was Menes the Thinite; he reigned for 62 years and perished from a wound made by a hippopotamus.*

This tells us that Menes came from an Upper Egyptian city called Thinis, that he was the first king of a dynasty of eight rulers, ruled for 62 years and died from a hippopotamus wound. However, archaeologists have also found details of an extra ruler of this dynasty, bringing the total up to nine rulers. Elsewhere in his writings Manetho placed the date when Menes ruled as between 5717 and 5655 BCE, but most modern authorities on ancient Egypt believe he ruled c. 3200 BCE. For simplicity, we shall use this 'Short Chronology' for ancient Egyptian dates. However, readers should be aware that all these early dates are the subject of debate.

Other information comes from a later king of the Nineteenth Dynasty. In 1864 archaeologists found the tablet known as the Tablet of Abydos, commissioned by the ruler Seti I to pay homage to 75 royal ancestors. The first king in this list of ancestors is Mena, which may be the correct Egyptian pronunciation of Menes. Most writers believe that Mena, or Menes, and Narmer are the same person.

King Hor-Aha was the next ruler of the dynasty, who overthrew the rulers of Ta-Seti. His successor, Djer, is said by Manetho to have written books on anatomy and medicine that were still being read thousands of years later. Mer-Neith was the next ruler, the first woman to lead a nation in history. Djet, the next ruler of the line, is best known for the artistic merits of his tomb stela, now in the Louvre Museum in Paris. Den followed him onto the throne. *The Edwin Smith Papyrus* is a much later Egyptian medical record that contains research on bone fractures conducted during his time. We know very little about the last three members of this dynasty, as later kings erased their names from inscriptions: we do not know why.

The Second Dynasty consisted of 12 rulers who reigned between 2980 and 2686 BCE. They were from the Upper Egyptian city of Thinis, like the rulers of the First Dynasty. However, beyond knowing the names of these kings, we do not know much; very little material has survived. However, in the nineteenth century, archaeologists discovered an interesting Second Dynasty monument near Memphis. The people of modern Egypt call it 'The Enclosure of the Boss', but this is probably not its real name. The structure's walls were 49 feet thick and measured a staggering 1,150 feet wide by 2,130 feet long. It may be the world's very first building made of stone. Unfortunately, no one knows what it was called or what it was used for.

During the first two dynasties, agriculture formed the basis of the economy. Farmers paid their taxes to the government in grain and foodstuffs, which the government stored in warehouses. If there was a food shortage, the government would give the grain to those who needed it. If there was a surplus of grain, they sold it into the Middle East. The Egyptians could afford to buy wood from Lebanon and Syria, olive oil from Palestine and lapis lazuli from Afghanistan. From the Red Sea area, they acquired flint, gold, lead and tin. The government also spent huge amounts on lavish monuments for the dead. According to their religious beliefs, buildings for deceased relatives were more important than buildings for living people.

The Egyptian court had a Court Chamberlain, the Commander of the Nile Flood, the Commander of the Elders, the King's Chief Butler, the Royal Seal Bearer, the Royal Architect, the Keeper of the King's Vineyards, the Leader of the Peers and the Master of Ceremonies. The country had two treasuries: the Red House (for Lower Egypt) and the White House (for Upper Egypt).

The Third Dynasty consisted of six rulers (2686 to 2613 BCE) from the city of Memphis. However, the structure of government underwent a shift, with the prime minister becoming important for the first time. The first person to hold this post was Imhotep, prime minister during the time of King Djoser, second ruler of the dynasty. Imhotep was the first great individual in history who was neither a king nor a queen. He was an architect, astronomer, physician, poet and philosopher. His titles included High Priest of Heliopolis, Administrator of the Great Palace, Chancellor of the King of Lower Egypt and First after the King of Upper Egypt.

For Djoser, Imhotep designed the Funerary Complex of Saqqara, a complex that contains Egypt's very first pyramid: the Step Pyramid. Built of six steps, its form is symbolic of the primordial creation mound. Inside was a superb life-size statue of the pharaoh. The whole complex marked a major leap forward in both Egyptian technology and artistic skills. Several thousand years later tourists still flock to see this structure.

The Fourth Dynasty (2613 to 2494 BCE) consisted of seven rulers from the capital city of Memphis. Six extraordinary pyramids were the greatest achievement of this dynasty. Its first king was Sneferu, whose armies battled the Nubians to the south, seizing 7,000 prisoners and 200,000 heads of cattle. To the west Sneferu's armies battled the Libyans, seizing 11,000 prisoners and 13,100 heads of cattle. He commissioned the Pyramid at Meidum, the Bent Pyramid of Dashur and the Red Pyramid. Great wealth was buried with his queen. In her tomb archaeologists have discovered a magnificent alabaster sarcophagus, a carrying chair inlaid with gold, a gold encased bed, golden implements and silver bracelets inlaid with butterflies. The Egyptians of later times remembered Sneferu as a beneficent ruler who ruled over a time of great prosperity.

Egypt in the Pyramid Age was an urban civilization. Cities, towns and ports were dotted along the Nile. Cities were constructed around temples, craft specialities, graveyards and government buildings. Statisticians believe the population of this period to have been around eight million people. As only 11,500 square miles of Egypt were habitable, this meant that an average of 695 people lived per square mile in Egypt – a higher figure than modern Belgium, the most densely populated part of Europe. Egypt was therefore as urbanized then as modern industrial societies are today. Their houses consisted of one or two storeys with courtyards in front. One-storey houses had three rooms and a veranda; two-storey houses had six rooms and an outside staircase. The walls were of sun-dried brick and floors were of beaten earth; columns, ceiling beams and stair supports were of wood. Surrounding these houses were pools and gardens with flowerbeds. The furniture consisted of couches, stalls and chests. The beds were single beds with wooden frames, strung with leather or string webbing. Bed legs were designed to resemble the legs and feet of animals. Lamps burning castor oil or animal fat lit the insides at night.

Khufu was the second king of the dynasty. He commissioned the Great Pyramid of Giza, the first of the Seven Wonders of the World. This is the single most important piece of architecture in world history. Its great size and the accuracy and orientation of its construction have impressed mathematicians, astronomers, architects and surveyors for centuries. Khafra, the fourth ruler of the dynasty, commissioned the Second Great Pyramid of Giza. Some historians believe that his face was the model used for the Great Sphinx, next to his pyramid. Menkaura, the fifth ruler of the dynasty, commissioned the Third Great Pyramid of Giza. However, during his reign a problem emerged that would ultimately undermine the Old Kingdom period. Egypt was made up of 42 different districts called nomes. The head of each district, a nomarch, held the belief that their rights to govern came from the protection of the local god of that district, and that they could pass on their positions of power to their children. The pharaoh's power was reduced as a result. He could not appoint the officeholders of his choice because the nomarchs appointed their own children.

The Fifth Dynasty (2494 to 2345 BCE) consisted of nine kings. Their origins lay in the Egyptian Nubian border city of Elephantine. Sahura was the second ruler of the dynasty. He sent a fully documented expedition to Punt, a region which bore the status of a holy land or a land of the ancestors to the Egyptians. It was probably where Ethiopia is today. The pyramid of the last king of the dynasty, Unas, features some wonderful wall inscriptions known as the Pyramid Texts. This is the oldest surviving religious literature in the world, containing spells, religious sayings and hymns. They represented an ancient Egyptian idea that when the king died, his soul would go on a difficult and challenging journey to meet the god Ra. The spells, religious sayings and hymns were necessary for the king to make his spiritual journey successfully and to stay righteous before Ra. (Originally, this applied to just Unas but later it applied to other rulers, before applying to everyone.)

The Sixth Dynasty (2345 to 2181 BCE) consisted of seven rulers from Memphis. Pepi II, the fifth ruler of this dynasty, inherited the throne as a child. Ultimately, he ruled for 94 years, the longest of any king in history. While Pepi was still a child, one of his subjects, known as Harkhuf, made four important voyages into Central Africa. He returned with foreign goods including ebony, incense, ivory, oils and panther skins. He also returned with a pygmy. The child king wrote a letter to Harkhuf saying how keen he was to meet him. The letter also says:

> *Hurry and bring with you this Pygmy whom you brought from the Land of the Horizon Dwellers who does the dances of the Gods.*
>
> **Pepi II's letter to Harkhuf, in the Autobiography of Harkhuf, trans. Miriam Lichtheim, *Ancient Egyptian Literature: A Book of Readings*, Vol. I, 1973**

Years later, as an adult, Pepi II became a great conqueror. He seized control of countries to the south of Egypt such as Wawat, Irthet and Punt. However, in his most senior years things fell apart. The central administration was weakened as the nomarchs gained more and more power, using the king's advanced age as leverage to push for more power and concessions. When Egypt faced economic problems such as famine, the central government was unable to help. Merernre II succeeded to the throne and remained in place for a year. The queen Nitocris, who died in 2181 BCE, was the last of the 50 rulers of the Old Kingdom period, ruling for 12 years. During the reign of the next few dynasties, the country fell into a period of chaos. This lasted for 740 years according to Manetho, and for 141 years according to the Short Chronologists.

FIRST KINGDOM OF KUSH

Following the destruction of the Kingdom of Ta-Seti, several small sacral kingdoms speaking Nilo-Saharan existed in the south. By the late third millennium BCE, two large states emerged that absorbed the others: Kush and Sai. The city of Kerma was at the heart of Kush. Its authority reached from the Second Cataract of the Nile down to the Fourth Cataract. Chosen for security reasons, the capital lay at the northern end of the Dongola Reach, just south of the Third Cataract. From here the city could control river-borne traffic and prevent movement up and down the river if required.

Charles Bonnet, a Swiss archaeologist, has dated Kush using the research of historian Brigitte Gratien. She divides Kushite history into the Ancient Period (between 2500/2400 and 2050 BCE), the Middle Period (between 2050 and 1750 BCE) and the Classic Period (between 1750 and 1500 BCE). It is unfortunate, however, that Gratien has dated the Kerma artefacts in conformity to the Short Chronology, when that is debatable.

By around 2400 BCE, Kerma had emerged as the capital of a unified state. Bonnet believes (according to his *The Kingdom of Kerma, in Sudan: Ancient Kingdoms of the Nile*, 1997) that it lasted intact for nearly one thousand years. By the Middle Period, beginning in 2050 BCE, Kush had become a powerful state; its rulers wore the long White Crown of Ta-Seti. The burial practices of Kush suggest their main deity was Amen, as in Egypt of the same period. The kings were buried in huge tombs, over 262 feet in diameter. Luxury items such as jewellery, weapons, pottery and inlaid furniture lined these tombs. Some of the products, for example vessels and stone sculptures, were of Egyptian manufacture.

During the Classic Period (1750–1500 BCE) Kush became a powerful and very large state. Its rulers gained control of the Sai kingdom to the north in the eighteenth century BCE, thus dominating the entire Nubian Nile from the First Cataract. Archaeological evidence indicates that its territories stretched almost to the confluence of the Blue Nile. An Egyptian inscription in the city of Waset lists 242 Kush and Punt towns, cities and districts. Kerma became the largest city in Africa outside Egyptian territory.

At its peak Kerma covered 65 acres. Surrounding the central parts of the city was a wall of massive size with a ditch in front of it. Built of mud bricks, the wall stood 30 feet high with projecting rectangular towers and four fortified gates. The gardens, the king's palace, the nobility's homes and the *deffufa* – a massive white temple – were located within the city. There was also a second religious complex separated by a wall 16 feet in height. This complex consisted of bronze workshops, storerooms, housing for the priests and chapels. Archaeologists have discovered a large audience hall that probably dates from the Middle Period (2050–1750 BCE). This building was circular and may have been thatched. Also found there were thousands of mud blanks, used for making official seals; these are evidence that business transactions took place on the site. Another building was the palace, which had an audience hall and a throne on a raised platform. The king sat here and received delegations.

Large columns supported the roof. The palace is believed to have been 25 feet high.

Kush controlled gold mines and major trade routes between Egypt and the rest of Africa. The goods sold into Egypt were incense, ebony, ivory, ostrich eggs, animal skins and slaves. Kush itself produced high-quality pottery that was eggshell thin – the finest ceramics industry in the ancient world. The city also produced bronze implements of exceptional quality.

The decline of Kush was linked to the drying up of its water supply. The city of Kerma went into decline because of the closure of the two Nile channels that had supplied it with water. The final blow came with the rise of Egypt's Eighteenth Dynasty, whose destructive campaigns destroyed the city.

However, archaeologists have found another city around a mile away called Doukki Gel. Said to have been built by the Egyptian conqueror Thutmose I to administrate the conquered lands, it possesses decidedly un-Egyptian architecture. One of the most striking features are rounded floor designs, organic forms and forests of columns built suffocatingly close to one another. All were constructed with perfectly regular and vigorously repeated patterns. At best, all that Thutmose I could have done was to rebuild this Kushite city.

THE MIDDLE KINGDOM PERIOD OF EGYPT

The Eleventh Dynasty (2130 to 1991 BCE) consisted of seven rulers from the southern city of Waset. When these Eleventh Dynasty kings came to power, the Tenth Dynasty still ruled the majority of Egypt from their capital at Herakleopolis. Mentuhotep I and Antef I, the first two kings of the Eleventh Dynasty, only had power over a very small part of Upper Egypt. That changed under Antef II, the third king of the Eleventh Dynasty. His armies conquered lands north towards Tefibi and south towards Elephantine, the former Egyptian Nubian border. Mentuhotep II, the fifth king of the dynasty, made his conquests much further north, defeating the Tenth Dynasty rulers of Herakleopolis and bringing all of Egypt under his rule. This marks the beginning of the Middle Kingdom Period, or Second Golden Age, which lasted from 2040 to 1786 BCE. Waset became the new capital of the unified Egypt. Mentuhotep II commissioned a great monument in Deir-el-Bahri, in the necropolis near the capital Waset (near modern Luxor), called the Mortuary Temple – a structure which, at a later period, inspired Hatshepsut to build her temple. The Hatshepsut Temple is currently one of Egypt's most celebrated monuments.

The Twelfth Dynasty (1991 to 1786 BCE) consisted of eight rulers. Amenemhet I, the founder of the dynasty, was of the nomarchy of Elephantine. Originally he was the prime minister of Mentuhotep IV, but he overthrew the king to become the next ruler himself. Amenemhet I sent his forces into Wawat, the country to the south of Egypt. He guarded control over Wawat by building a chain of powerful fortresses. He relocated the royal residence to a location near Memphis. Sheet copper was laid over the palace's doors, silver inlay decorated the floors and gold leaf adorned the walls. The palace's ceilings were adorned with lapis lazuli.

The Middle Kingdom was a very different period to the Old Kingdom. Its pharaohs spent less on grand monuments that reached to heaven and more instead on practical things: wells, reservoirs, agriculture, roads and business. Moreover, they guarded their power by building strong fortresses over territories they controlled. In many ways the Middle Kingdom rulers behaved more like the way in which governments act today.

Middle Kingdom ships were large. Diodorus Siculus, an ancient Greek historian, wrote that the largest ship in the fleet of King 'Sesostris' was 480 feet in length. However, when the Greeks mentioned 'Sesostris', they sometimes referred to the Twelfth Dynasty rulers Senwosret I, II, or III; on other occasions they meant Rameses II of the Nineteenth Dynasty. Whichever is the case, one of the Twelfth (or Nineteenth) Dynasty ships was four times the length of the *Santa Maria*, the ship in which Columbus sailed to America.

Mathematical documents from this period exist today. There is the *Rhind Mathematical Papyrus*, the *Moscow Mathematical Papyrus*, the *Egyptian Leather Roll*, the *Berlin Mathematical Papyrus*, the *Reisner Papyri* and the *Kahun Papyrus*. The numerical problems in these documents resemble the senior school mathematics that students learn today. Among the topics covered were multiplication, division, algebra, simultaneous equations, area, volume, fractions, square roots, geometric series and trigonometry.

Senwosret I was the second king of the Twelfth Dynasty. He completed the Egyptian occupation of Wawat, the country immediately to the south of Egypt, and commissioned the building of castles at Quban and Aniba to secure his power. The armies of Senwosret III, the fifth king of this dynasty, continued the colonization of Wawat. He commissioned castles to be built over a distance of 30 miles.

Senwosret II was the fourth king of this dynasty, and he also commissioned the building of dams and canals. In order to irrigate the Fayum region, he constructed them around Lake

Moeris. Another of his constructions was the city of Kahun. Archaeologists have discovered it was a planned city with straight roads that crossed each other at right angles; a stone gutter ran down the centre of each street. The smallest homes of the poorest people contained four to six rooms – larger than most modern flats. In the area for the wealthy inhabitants, archaeologists found five mansions, each with 70 rooms.

Amenemhet III was the sixth king of this dynasty. At Hawara, he commissioned the Labyrinth, the largest building ever built in antiquity, with an astonishing 3,000 rooms and 12 palaces. About half of the rooms were above ground, with the other 1,500 underground. Herodotus, the ancient Greek historian, saw the Labyrinth in ruins thousands of years later. He wrote:

> *I visited this place, and found it to surpass description; for if all the walls and other great works of the Greeks could be put together in one, they would not equal, either for labour or expense, this Labyrinth; and yet the temple of Ephesus is a building worthy of note, and so is the temple of Samos. The pyramids likewise surpass description, and are equal to a number of the greatest works of the Greeks; but the Labyrinth surpasses the pyramids.*
>
> **Herodotus, *History of Herodotus*,**
> **trans. George Rawlinson, 1910**

Amenemhet IV, the next king, ruled for nine years. Sebekneferura, the leader of the last dynasty, succeeded him on the throne. The queen's reign of three years and 10 months was the end of the Middle Kingdom. During the period ruled by the next few dynasties, the country descended into chaos for a second time, with some of the new rulers being outsiders from Asia. Manetho suggested that this period of chaos lasted for 1,439 years, but most modern writers believe that the period lasted for 226 years.

LATER CHAPTERS IN THE HISTORY OF SUDAN & EGYPT

THE NEW KINGDOM PERIOD OF EGYPT

Pharaoh Ahmose I was the first of the 15 rulers of the Eighteenth Dynasty (1560–1295 BCE). Moreover, he started the New Kingdom period, the Third Golden Age of Egypt, which lasted from 1560 to 1080 BCE. Yet this was also a time of change. Egypt now had large Asian and Afro Asian populations who had entered Egypt during the years of chaos. The political landscape was different too. Civilizations had emerged all over western and southern Asia, some of which would later fight – and even defeat – the Egyptians.

Amenhotep I was the second king of this dynasty. He brought together scientists, artists, architects, poets and theologians, who combined to create the greatest cultural flowering since the Twelfth Dynasty. An Egyptian astronomer invented a water clock. Egyptian scholars wrote a medical encyclopaedia, known to historians as the *Ebers Papyrus*. It contained chapters on intestinal disease, ophthalmology, dermatology, gynaecology, obstetrics, pregnancy diagnosis, contraception, dentistry, and a range of other conditions. Egyptian priests also wrote a religious book, the *Book of the Hidden Chamber*, that depicted the idea of Hell for the first time.

The military conquests of Thutmose I, the third king of this dynasty, extended Egyptian power further. Kush, the empire to the south of Wawat, was conquered by the king's forces; its capital city was sacked and then burned. His armies moved into the Middle East and conquered as far as Syria. Thutmose chose the ancient city of Memphis to be the military headquarters of the empire while Waset remained its cultural and religious centre.

Hatshepsut succeeded Thutmose as the next ruler. She commissioned the building of a temple, cut out of the rock at Deir-el-Bahri, which she dedicated to the gods Amen, Anubis and Hathor. On the temple walls are records of voyages that the queen ordered to be made, from Egypt to Punt – still viewed by Egyptians as a land of distant ancestors. The Egyptian sailors sold weapons and jewellery to the people of Punt, and the Puntites traded incense, animals, animal skins, gum, gold, ivory and ebony in return. The king and queen of Punt are also depicted on the temple walls. Tourists continue to admire this remarkable monument today. Other important constructions were the two obelisks at Karnak. Gigantic in size, they rose to almost a hundred feet, their tops encased in an alloy of silver and gold. The obelisk barges to move these monuments are thought to have been 312 feet long and 105 feet wide with a deadweight of 2,500 tons. For comparison, such barges were larger than HMS *Victory*, Lord Nelson's flagship from the Battle of Trafalgar.

Egypt became wealthy and powerful during the fourteenth century BCE, in the reign of Amenhotep III. Trade was plentiful and the Egyptians sold grain, papyrus, linen and leather to the outside world. Meanwhile goods entered Egypt from Asia Minor, Crete, Cyprus and elsewhere in Africa. Coniferous woods came from Asia Minor and wine, oils, resins and metal weapons from Syria. Vases came from Crete, copper from Cyprus and silver came from the region of the Aegean Sea. Nubia and the lands to the south supplied ebony, elephant ivory, gum, leopard and panther skins, ostrich plumes and eggs, resins and a variety of animals. Donkey, mules and asses travelled the caravan trails to and from Egypt to transport these goods.

One million people lived in the city of Waset, which spread out for six square miles on both sides of the Nile. On the edge of the city, along tree-shaded avenues, lay the mansions of the nobles, typically containing around 50 and 60 rooms, with grounds containing lakes and flower gardens. Inside were beautifully painted walls, exquisite furniture, gorgeous vases and fine sculptures, made of gold, bronze, ebony, ivory and glass. Towards the centre of the city stood the royal palace, the House of Rejoicing. Along the Nile, in the centre of the city, the great temples of Karnak and Luxor towered over everything. Students and priests worked in the temples, while horse-drawn chariots were driven along the sphinx-lined avenues. On the river lay quays where the merchant ships of the Nile mingled with those from the Mediterranean. Other equally magnificent temples were visible on the western plain across the river. A route from there led to the Valley of the Kings, the royal graveyard.

Akhenaten, the tenth member of this dynasty, commissioned a new capital north of Waset which he called Akhetaten. This was a planned city on a horizontal vertical grid, landscaped with flowers and beautiful gardens. Cleanliness was important here; Akhetaten had sewerage systems and toilets, soap was used for washing the body and perfumes kept away bodily smells. Natron kept insects away from houses. Moreover, Akhenaten changed his country's religion. He avoided the influence of the Amen priests, accusing them of corruption, and instead spread his new ideas of peace, perfect love, brotherhood and truth. He created Aten, a new god, and made him the only god in Egypt.

Tutankhamen, the twelfth member of the dynasty, inherited the throne as a boy. Because of his young age, his chief priest made the decisions, and swiftly reversed the radical religious ideas of Amenhotep IV. Amenism was back and Waset restored as the religious capital. Tutankhamen died as a teenager. *New Scientist* (25 June 2010) reported research on his mummy that indicated he died from sickle cell. Unlike most of the other pharaohs, Tutankhamen's tomb was discovered intact in 1922. Extraordinary items were buried with him.

The Nineteenth Dynasty (1295 to 1187 BCE) consisted of six rulers. Seti I was the first king of the dynasty. He led military campaigns into Asia and Nubia, and also fought against the Libyans, but his greatest legacy was in architecture. Seti commissioned the Hypostyle Hall at Karnak, which had 134 columns and covered 5,000 square feet. One architectural scholar described it thus:

> *The mass of its central piers, illumined by a flood of light from the clerestory, and the smaller pillars of the wings gradually fading into obscurity, are so arranged and lighted as to convey an idea of infinite space; at the same time, the beauty and massiveness of the forms, and the brilliancy of their coloured decorations, all combine to stamp this as the greatest of man's architectural works.*
>
> **James Ferguson, *A History of Architecture in All Countries*, 3rd Ed., Vol. I, 1893**

The second king of this dynasty, Rameses II, faced political problems in the Middle East. A new military power had formed in the

Turkish region called the Hittites, and they posed a threat to Egyptian power in the Middle East. Things came to a head at a great battle called the Battle of Qadesh. The outcome of this battle is disputed: the Egyptians claimed they won, but other evidence indicates the reverse. Over the next 100 years, the Egyptians lost all their power in the Middle East. Nevertheless, Rameses II's architectural legacy was significant. In the swamplands of Lower Egypt he built the new capital city called Pi-Rameses; he also commissioned major buildings in Waset. However, his most famous monuments, still visited today, were in Kush. Rameses commissioned the carving of two rock-cut temples at Abu Simbel, which contain four colossal statues of himself. Some historians believe that the Lincoln Memorial in Washington, D.C. was inspired by this ancient structure.

Merneptah was the third king of the dynasty. He relocated the capital from Pi-Rameses back to the most ancient capital of Memphis, bringing it a new prestige during his time. He also commissioned the building of his palace complex there. However, Merneptah faced new political threats. The Libyans had joined forces with Europeans, referred to as 'Sea Peoples' by scholars, who came from across the Mediterranean. Many of them settled in Libya, but this 'invasion party' was crushed by Merneptah's forces.

The Twentieth Dynasty (1187 to 1080 BCE) consisted of 10 kings. Rameses III, the second king of the dynasty, faced problems from the Libyans and the Europeans. His armies repelled invasions from both groups of people and his forces enslaved 30,000 people from among the Europeans and Asiatics. However, government corruption caused great discontent among the general population: workers went on strike when their payments were over two months in arrears. They organized a protest march, only returning to work after the prime minister of Upper Egypt and the High Priest of Amen gave the strikers 50 sacks of wheat to divide between them. More problems quickly emerged. Grave robbery became a problem, with some of the strikers implicated in it. There were crime waves and famine, with all the kings from Rameses IV to Rameses XI proving weak. The value of copper and bronze fell. When the Twentieth Dynasty ended, central authority in Egypt collapsed. The country became split into two powers, the north and the south. The death of Rameses XI in 1080 BCE brought about the end of the New Kingdom period, a point on which the Manetho chronology and the 'Short Chronology' agree. During the period of the next few dynasties, the country fell apart for a third time. Most of the new rulers came from Libya or Sudan.

SECOND EMPIRE OF KUSH

In 1918 archaeologists discovered the burial of an important Kushite ruler, known as Lord A because his name has unfortunately not survived in any records. He reigned from approximately 860 BCE and was followed by three equally shadowy rulers, Lords B, C and D.

Alara is regarded as the first king of a new dynasty in 785 BCE. He was succeeded by Kashta, who extended Kushite power into Egypt, taking control of Waset in 760 BCE. Kashta named his daughter the next High Priestess of Amen and appointed her as such. After his death, the king was buried in a gilded wooden anthropoid coffin of gold foil, lapis lazuli and coloured glass. It became a standard practice for Kushite pharaohs to place their female relatives in position as rulers of Egypt. For example, Amenirdas I, Kashta's daughter, had her own prime minister. She undertook public works and restoration programmes in Waset and elsewhere, with titles such as 'Chief Prophetess of Amen', 'Queen of Thebes' and the 'Mistress of Egypt'.

King Piye was also an important builder. He refurbished and enlarged the old Egyptian temple of Amen at Gebel Barkal, making it the single most important religious building in Kush. The nearby city of Napata became the Kushite capital city. Piye was buried in 716 BCE in Nuri, which became a royal burial site of pyramids.

Shabaqo, Piye's son, retook Egypt and established the Twenty-Fifth Dynasty. Before becoming king, he had served in the army and been stationed in the Delta for some years. After ascending the throne, Shabaqo built a huge empire. Memphis became a royal residence of the Kushite pharaohs and Waset the capital of the empire. Inscriptions inform us that Kush was divided into nomes, as was Egypt, each with its own capital. As ruler, Shabaqo abolished the death penalty and replaced it with hard labour, according to Herodotus, writing around 450 BCE:

> *When an Egyptian was guilty of an offence, his plan was not to punish him with death: instead of so doing, he sentenced him according to the nature of his crime.*
>
> **Herodotus, trans. George Rawlinson, *History of Herodotus*, Vol. II, 3rd Ed., 1875**

Taharqo ruled from 690 until 664 BCE. He inherited a huge empire from Syria in Asia to Sudan. Eratosthenes claimed that the king conquered a vast territory in North Africa and 'penetrated into Europe as far as the "Pillars of Hercules"' (quoted in Phaon Goldman, *Egypt Revisited*, 1989). Florian de Ocampo, a Spanish historian, wrote *Coronica General de España* in 1553. Its chapter on Taharqo's Spanish exploits began as follows:

> *A few years after the events and upheavals in Sicily, the like also increased in Spain, where a large army of upstart people passed through with many ships, causing tumult on those shores and ports that fall on our Mediterranean Sea, whose lord and master they called Taracus, whom Strabo also called Taracus, but whom other chroniclers call Tearco. Sacred Scripture calls him Taraca. They brought their great armies of valiant and warlike black men, and he himself, naturally, was black, born in the land called Ethiopia, which has always been a very great region, surrounded by the African provinces, of which it is hottest and most zealous.*
>
> **Florian de Ocampo, *Coronica General de España*, trans. Dr Şizen Yiacoup, 2023**

On a different topic, there is an inscription from December 685 or January 684 BCE which describes the athleticism of Taharqo's troops. Entitled 'Stela Reporting the Running of the Army of the Son of Re Taharqa May He Live Eternally', the text declares: 'His Majesty ordered that his army, which had been levied for him, had to run every day in his five companies'. It continues:

> *The king himself was on the horse to observe the running of his army. He was running with them on the back of the desert of Memphis in the hour of Sehetepnes (= 9th hour of night). They reached the 'Great Green' (= the Fayum) in the hour Weben (= first hour of day), and they returned to the capital in the hour 'Meketnebes' (= third hour of day).*
>
> **Trans. Ahmed Mahmoud Moussa, 'A Stela of Taharqa [sic] from the Desert Road at Dahschur', *Mitteilungen des Deutschen Archäologischen Instituts Kairo*, Vol. 37, 1981**

This run was from Memphis to Fayum and back, places that are 31 miles apart. Moreover, the inscription reveals that the pharaoh gave the runners different prizes to indicate the one who came first and the runners-up:

> *He awarded the winners and arranged for them to eat and drink with his body guards; he awarded also the losers and rewarded them with everything, for his majesty liked the struggle performed for him.*
> **Trans. Moussa, 'A Stela of Taharqa...'**

This feat of endurance should be as well known to the general public as the Greek marathon is today.

However, the Kushites eventually lost their colonies. In 671 BCE the Assyrians launched the first of three invasions of Kushite-controlled Egypt. On the third campaign, mounted in 663 BCE, they devastated Waset. They placed a vassal king, Psammetik I, on the throne; he in turn installed his daughter as High Priestess of Amen in 654 BCE, replacing the Kushite Priestess, Shepenoupet II, who had previously held that position. The destruction of the city of Waset proved a turning point. Egypt had fallen under the foreign rule of the Assyrians. From then until modern times, the country was repeatedly occupied and looted by different Middle-Eastern and European peoples.

Having lost its European, Middle Eastern and Egyptian colonies, for the next few hundred years Kush became simply a country. What do we know about it at this time? Herodotus reported what was witnessed by a Persian spy:

> *He led them to a fountain, wherein when they had washed, they found their flesh all glossy and sleek, as if they had bathed*

in oil – and a scent came from the spring like that of violets… When they quitted the fountain the king led them to a prison, where the prisoners were all of them bound with fetters of gold. Among these Ethiopians copper is of all metals the most scarce and valuable. After they had seen the prison, they were likewise shown what is called 'the table of the Sun'. Also, last of all, they were allowed to behold the coffins of the Ethiopians, which are made (according to report) of crystal.

Herodotus, trans. George Rawlinson, *History of Herodotus*, Vol. II, 3rd Ed., 1875

According to Professor Hansberry, a pioneering historian of African antiquities, the fountain was a bath house, sharing affinities with those of the Romans that were discovered in Meroë in 1912. The violet scent was the smell of incense, brought into Kush from the Red Sea coast. The Table of the Sun has also been identified as a particular Meroë temple. Finally, the coffins of crystal were actually found to have been made of glass, as well as gilt.

The economy of Kush was built on animal husbandry and agriculture. They reared sheep, goats and cattle, while vines, cotton, sorghum, date palms, wheat, barley, beans, lentils and vegetables were among their crops. Civil engineering harnessed the water for irrigation and animal husbandry. In addition, a national system of reservoirs had been constructed, located at Musawarat, Naqa, Hordan, Umm and Usuda in the Gezira region, as well as at Duanib, Basa and others. The ruins of these water tanks still exist today.

The working of both iron and gold were important economic mainstays. Steel tools have been discovered that date from the time of the Twenty-Fifth Dynasty. Meroë became the centre of an iron-working industry that produced superior metal. The archaeologist A.J. Arkell said of the site:

> *Here at Meroe, where both iron-stone and wood fuel were available, the Cushites about this time set about manufacturing iron weapons and tools on such a scale that, after examining the slag heaps through which the railway now runs on its way to Khartoum, one archaeologist described Meroe as having been the Birmingham of Africa. I have seen them myself and I think this is a fair description.*
>
> **A.J. Arkell, *The Valley of the Nile*, in *The Dawn of African History*, ed. Roland Oliver, 1961**

Housing complexes have been found in Gaminarti, near the Second Cataract, that consisted of two-room apartments. The entire village at Abu Geili consisted of a two- or more-storey complex of interconnected houses, while houses near Abu Simbel had both internal and external staircases. At Karanog, the rooms of an excavated castle were arranged around a central internal courtyard on three levels. At Qasr Ibrim, archaeologists have discovered a tavern – a rectangular building with six interconnecting rooms.

The period that began with Pharaoh Natasen (r. 328–308 BCE) was to be highly remarkable. In it the Meroïtic script was developed, in which 900-year-old texts have survived. It had 23 letters, four of which were vowels; there was also a word divider. A mathematical numerical system was also created. Writing was generally done on purposefully designed wood and skins, but examples are also found on walls, vases, etc. Diodorus Siculus, the ancient Greek historian, noted in his *Library of History* (Vol.

III, first century BCE) that, unlike in Egypt, universal literacy was achieved in Kush.

Some of the rulers at Meroë were women. They held the title Kentake, meaning Queen Mother, a title that when Latinized became Candace. Pseudo-Callisthenes' *Alexander Romance* of the fourth century BCE mentions that Alexander the Great visited 'Candace, the black Queen of Meroe'; she was apparently a 'wondrous beauty' (quoted in Larry Williams and Charles S. Finch, *The Great Queens of Ethiopia*, in *Black Women in Antiquity*, ed. Ivan Van Sertima, 1988). On the outskirts of the city are the Meroitic Pyramids, the ruins of at least 84 of them visible. Unlike the Pyramids of Egypt, people are buried in these buildings. Kentake Amanishakheto, a ruler of the first century BCE, was buried in one of them. On the chapel walls in front of the pyramid are victorious depictions of the queen striking her enemies. Her pyramid contained treasures made of gold, silver, gemstones, wood and copper alloy. In 1834 an Italian grave robber, Giuseppe Ferlini, dynamited her pyramid and stole these treasures.

At Musawarat another curious structure is located. Called the Great Enclosure, and originally thought to date from between 235 and 221 BCE, its foundation may have been in the sixth century BCE. Covering an area of 10⅞ square feet is a complex consisting of three temples, some of them built on artificial terraces with connecting ramps, corridors and passages, and surrounded by huge walled courtyards. Originally, the walls were covered in gold leaf. Some authorities believe that the Great Enclosure was a national Kushite shrine where pilgrims worshipped Apedemak, the lion deity. Others think that it was a place of investiture for the Kushite rulers. Another view, which has gained traction in modern Sudan, is that the structure was a university.

In Gebel Barkal there are pyramids in a good state of preservation. Some authorities date these to around 100 BCE. In total, Kush had a total of 223 or more pyramids in the sites of Nuri, Gebel Barkal and Meroë.

The Roman conquest of Egypt in 30 BCE brought a new challenge to Kush. Augustus Caesar threatened an invasion, following his Egyptian campaign. Queen Mother Amanirenas gave the order to march into Egypt and attack the invaders. The Kushites sacked Aswan with an army of 30,000 men, going on to destroy the statues of Caesar in Elephantine. The Romans then counterattacked Kush, capturing Qasr Ibrim and invading as far south as the capital city Napata, which they sacked. Amanirenas evaded their clutches and ordered her armies to march a second time, with the aim of seizing the Roman garrison. This time, however, a standoff with the Romans was reached without fighting. *Pax Romana* (a form of peace) was declared when the Roman army retreated to Egypt and dismantled their fort. Because the Meroïtic account of this encounter still cannot be read in full, the extent of the Roman humiliation has not yet been revealed.

Pharaoh Netakamani and Queen Amanitore were the last great builders of Kush, between 1 and 20 CE. Their buildings were raised in Keraba, an area between the Nile and the Atbara rivers, and they also built in Naqa. In this city, the Temple of Apedemak, one of their best-known monuments, remains in a good state of preservation. Naqa also contains a famous Kiosk – a temple that mixes architectural motifs from the Nile Valley, with Roman and Greek influences. Finally, they authorized the digging of reservoirs around Meroë, restoration of its huge Temple of Amen and the rebuilding of the Amen Temple of Napata.

The period of decline dates from 200 CE. Nomads from the desert obstructed vital trade routes and also infiltrated the country.

The Kingdom of Axum, now part of Ethiopia and Eritrea, posed a significant threat; their armies marched on Kush in 350 CE, bringing about its eventual collapse after a history of 1,000 years.

THE GREEK ERA OF EGYPT

The Persians were the next Middle Eastern power to conquer Egypt, seizing control of the country in 525 BCE. Egypt became part of the Persian Empire where eight Persian kings ruled as the Twenty-Seventh Dynasty (525–404 BCE). The Persian conquerors then allowed Greek scholars to enter Egypt, starting a practice of Greeks studying there that lasted for several centuries. Among these scholars were Solon, Thales, Hecataeus, Herodotus, Plato, Pythagoras, Eudoxus and Democritus. The academics rose to prominence among Greek intellectuals and some became great philosophers.

Until 332 BCE, the Persians had only intermittent control over Egypt. The three subsequent dynasties attempted to challenge Persian rule, with one king, Amyrtaeus, ruling as the Twenty-Eighth Dynasty. Of Libyan descent, Amyrtaeus led a five-year uprising against the Persians. There were four kings in the Twenty-Ninth Dynasty, which lasted from 399 to 380 BCE. They achieved some freedom from Persia, not least because the Persians had their hands tied by internal civil wars. Egypt minted its first coins during this period, copying Greek models. The Thirtieth Dynasty (380343 BCE) consisted of three kings who were probably indigenous Egyptians. Nectanebo II, the last ruler of the dynasty, was defeated by the Persians in battle and fled to Kush.

In 332 BCE Egypt was conquered by the Greeks under Alexander the Great. However, Alexander was regarded by some Egyptians as a hero who defeated the Persians and put an end to their cruelty. He established Alexandria, a city on Egypt's Mediterranean coast, which became the intellectual capital of the Greek Empire. Eventually a Greek general was crowned Ptolemy I. He began a new dynasty of foreign rulers in Egypt: 11 to 15 Ptolemies, and seven Cleopatras (305 to 30 BCE). Ptolemy I started the Museum and Library at Alexandria, which became the chief institution of learning in the world. Ptolemy II commissioned the Pharos Lighthouse, later one of the Seven Wonders of the Ancient World, but unfortunately this building no longer exists. Ptolemy V commissioned major rebuilding works of temples in the far south of Egypt: at Denderah, Edfu and Kom Ombo. However, later members of the Greek dynasty had power struggles with each other, murdering rivals and driving others into exile. However, two important pieces of literature emerged during this period. First, the Jewish Bible's first five books were translated from Hebrew into Greek. Second, Manetho wrote a *History of Egypt* for a Greek-speaking audience.

An important piece of Roman art from the second century BCE depicts Egypt from this period. Known as the *Nile Mosaic of Palestrina*, it depicts the Nile flowing from Kush, towards the back of the mosaic, through Egypt, and overflowing into the Mediterranean, towards the front of the mosaic. Greeks are shown towards the front of the image. Kushites are shown towards the back of the image, hunting with bows and arrows. Significantly, indigenous Egyptians are also depicted. They are shown near to their capital city, highlighted by its iconic structure: Karnak Temple. Unlike the Kushites, the Egyptians carry shields. The Roman artist emphasized the difference between the appearance of the Greeks and that of the Egyptians and Kushites.

Cleopatra VII, the last ruler of this dynasty, attempted to keep Egypt free from direct Roman rule. In 146 BCE the Romans began their conquest of North Africa, conquering Egypt in 48 BCE under Julius Caesar. However, Cleopatra persuaded Caesar to marry her and with his help she became a co-ruler of Egypt. Caesar returned to Rome, promising to send for Cleopatra. She later joined him in Rome where they lived together. She brought with her books, scientists and scholars, who reformed both the Roman calendar and their accounting system. However, in 44 BCE Caesar's enemies in Rome had him killed and Cleopatra returned to Egypt.

Mark Anthony was one of the candidates for the position of Roman emperor. Eventually he too met Cleopatra and they married, hatching a plan to defeat his rivals in Rome. If successful, they planned to join the power of Egypt to the power of Rome as equals. However, Mark Anthony was defeated in this attempt. Cleopatra sailed back to Egypt and Mark Anthony followed her; the victorious Roman forces pursued them both. Mark Anthony committed suicide in the Egyptian city of Alexandria. Octavian, the Roman rival, conquered Egypt in 30 BCE. Cleopatra also committed suicide, leaving the Romans to rule North Africa for the next 600 years. Farmers in Lower Egypt produced the grain that fed the Roman Empire. During the Roman period of dominance, Christianity became an important part of Egyptian culture.

The different conquests of Egypt changed the Egyptian population. Various European and Middle Eastern peoples have repeatedly occupied the land from that time until the present, meaning that the Egyptian population was altered by occupation. Many conquerors stayed on due to the fertility of the Egyptian soil, which made it an excellent place to grow food crops. Prior to the Second Intermediate period, Egypt consisted almost exclusively of Africans, but after that it became African and Asian; many of the Asians were white. Egypt eventually evolved into the Arab-dominated, Afro-Eurasian mix that it is today. In 639 CE the Arabs conquered Egypt from the Middle East, going on to seize the whole of North Africa by 708 CE. They are still the ruling population today.

Most modern Egyptians therefore no longer resemble the Egyptian mummies, skulls or sculptures. Only in the far south of the country, among the Saidis and the Nubians, do the populations begin to resemble the Egyptians of old.

THE ROMAN AND BYZANTINE ERA OF EGYPT

In 30 BCE Egypt became a part of the Roman Empire, following the defeat of Cleopatra VII and Mark Antony by the forces of Octavian. Octavian became Emperor Augustus. Egypt's strategic location and its wealth, derived from its grain production, made it an essential province for Rome. The Roman emperors thus controlled Egypt directly, with a prefect appointed to oversee the province.

Archaeologists have excavated many burials of the Roman ruling classes in Egypt. The Fayum portraits, for example, were discovered in the Fayum Oasis, located southwest of Cairo – a centre for burial practices during the Roman period. These portraits were placed over the faces of mummies in the form of lifelike images to represent the deceased for the afterlife. The art shows Greek aesthetic influences and Graeco-Roman modes of dress.

In 395 CE, following the division of the Roman Empire, Egypt became part of the Eastern Roman Empire, known as the Byzantine Empire. The transition was marked by growing tensions between the local Egyptian and Greek populations, as well as between the

Christian and traditional religious communities. Christianity, which had gained momentum during the Roman period, became the dominant religion. Egypt, previously a centre of traditional religion and Graeco-Roman traditions, slowly saw the decline of its ancient temples, including the famous Temple of Serapis. Alexandria emerged as an important centre of Christian thought. In the far south of the country St Anthony and St Pachomius, both indigenous Egyptians, founded monastic communities in the Egyptian desert. Their monastic traditions would later influence Christian practices across the world.

THE ARAB CONQUEST OF NORTH AFRICA AND CLASSICAL EGYPT

In **639 CE** a new conquering force swept into Africa. The Arabians seized Egypt, Cyrenaica and Tripoli, then pushed on to Carthage and Numidia, sweeping away 600 years of Roman occupation. Many Africans fled south from North Africa to lands south of the Sahara to escape Arabian domination. Those that remained were converted to Islam. The Arabs occupied Tripoli in 643, and south west Morocco by 681. The historian El-Maqrizi (1364–1442) recorded who the Arabians encountered on entering Egypt:

> *Know the land of Egypt when the Mussulmans entered it was full of Christians, but divided among themselves in two sects, both as to race and religion. The one part was made up of men about court and public affairs, all Greek, from among the soldiers of Constantinople…their views as well as their religion were, for*

all of them, Melkite; and their number was above three hundred thousand, all Greeks. The other portion was the whole people of Egypt, who were called Qibt, and were of mixed descent; among whom one could not distinguish Copt from Abyssinian, [or] Nubian.

Taqi-ed-Din El-Maqrīzi, *A Short History of the Copts and of Their Church*, trans. the Rev. S.C. Malan, 1873

When writers use the term 'Copt' in an Egyptian context today, they mean 'Christians'. Consequently, there were both Egyptian Christians descended from the European conquests as the ruling class, and also the mass of Egyptian Christians of indigenous origins, indistinguishable from Ethiopians and Nubians. Famous Egyptian Christians who were descended from largely European heritage includee Pope Shenouda III, who in 1971 became the 118th Pope of the Coptic Orthodox Church. Another example is Professor Michel Habib, a distinguished medical expert known for his pioneering work on Parkinson's disease and other neurological disorders.

The conquering Arabs established Fustat as their administrative and military capital. Founded in 641 CE by the Arab general Amr ibn al-As, the city was located near Egypt's ancient capital Memphis. It became the first centre of Islamic governance in the country as well as the site of Egypt's first mosque, named after Amr ibn al-As. Not only did he encourage the spread of Islam into Egypt, but he also allowed Christians to practise their faith freely. In time, Fustat would become absorbed into Cairo.

The Fatimid Caliphate was founded in 909 CE in North Africa, Their initial stronghold was in Tunisia, and by the middle of the tenth century they had conquered large parts of North Africa. Before long they set their sights on Egypt. In 969 CE the Fatimids, led by General Jawhar al-Siqilli, successfully captured Egypt. They established Cairo, slightly south of Fustat, as their new capital and transformed it into one of the most important centres of politics, culture and trade in the Islamic world. Meticulously planned and a hub of religious scholarship and cultural exchange, Cairo grew rapidly into a thriving metropolis. Among the most important of the capital's building projects was the Al-Azhar Mosque; founded in 970 CE, it was to become one of the world's oldest and most prestigious universities. Scholars from across the Islamic world gathered there to study theology, philosophy, science and law. In addition, Egypt became a key centre for the preservation and translation of classical Greek, Roman and Persian texts.

Most Egyptians today are of Arab descent and the country's official name is the Arab Republic of Egypt. They celebrate this period as their Classical Age.

MEDIEVAL NUBIA

From at least the sixth century CE three Nubian kingdoms existed: Nobadia to the north, whose capital was at Faras; Makuria in the middle, whose capital was at Old Dongola; and Alwa to the south, whose capital was at Soba. Throughout these kingdoms cultural continuities from Kush were of great significance. The Nubians continued to venerate the goddess Isis; they also continued to build Kushite-style temples at Qasr Ibrim, Jebel Adda and Soba. However, Christianity spread into the region in the sixth century CE. In 531 Emperor Justinian of Byzantium apparently got the idea of making the Nubians his allies, with the aim of damaging the Persians. Byzantine missionaries went on to spread Christianity there.

Professor W.Y. Adams led an archaelogical team, in campaigns between 1972 and 1978, that discovered a Nubian library on the site of Qasr Ibrim. It contained thousands of legal texts and documents in Meroïtic, Latin, Greek, Coptic, Old Nubian, Arabic and Turkish, with the majority being in Greek, Coptic and Old Nubian. This demonstrates that educated medieval Nubians could read at least Old Nubian, Coptic and Greek – as well as, at a later date, Greek Creole: a synthesis of Greek and Nubian. Furthermore, some scholars had facilities in Meroïtic, Latin, Arabic and Turkish.

Islam stimulated the meteoric rise of the Arabians as a military force. Their armies marched into Egypt in December 639, ending over 600 years of Roman occupation. However, the Arabians attempted to invade Nubia. In 641 or 642 the Arabs sent an army of 20,000 men into Nubia, killing and plundering as they went. The Nubians amassed a large army of 100,000 men and struck back at the Arabs with such force that, according to the tenth-century writer Ahmad al-Kufi, 'the Muslims had never suffered a loss like the one they had in Nubia' (trans. Fr. Giovanni Fantini, *Oriental Sources Concerning Nubia*, 1975). Hostilities were ended without significant Arab gains. Then a king of Nobadia raided the Arabs in Upper Egypt, leading to a second Arab campaign against Nubia in 652. This time the Arabs marched further south to the Makurian capital of Old Dongola. They laid siege to the walled city and battered away at it with catapults, in the process destroying the Church of the Stone Pavement. However, not everything appears to have gone to plan. An Arab sheikh who participated in these invasions reportedly said:

I never saw a people who were sharper in warfare than they. I heard one of them say to the Muslims: 'Where do you want me to hit you with my arrows?' and in case the Muslim would disdainfully say: 'In such a spot', the Nubian would never miss it. They were fond of fighting with arrows: but their arrows would scarcely ever hit on the ground. One day they arrayed themselves against us and we were desirous to carry the conflict with the sword: but they were too quick for us and shot their arrows, putting out our eyes.

Reported by ninth-century Egyptian court historian Al-Baladhuri, trans. Fr. Giovanni Fantini, *Oriental Sources Concerning Nubia*, 1975

The Makurians put up a determined resistance under King Qalidurut and fought the Arabs to a stalemate. Eventually a *Baqt* or peace treaty was drawn up. According to Al-Masudi, the *Baqt* stipulated that the Makurians should supply annually to the Arab rulers of Egypt: 365 slaves to the treasury of the Muslims, 40 slaves to the emir of Egypt and 38 slaves to dignitaries in Aswan, who supervised the delivery of the *Baqt*. In return, the Arabs agreed to provide Makuria with the following: 1,000 ardeb of wheat (an 'ardeb' is an old measure of volume – no one knows what it meant a thousand years ago, but in nineteenth-century Sudan one ardeb is roughly 40 gallons), 300 ardeb of wheat to the delegates of the Makurian king, 1,000 ardeb of barley, 1,000 jugs of wine for the king, 300 jugs for the king's delegates, two horses of the breed used by the emir, four pieces of qabati cloth for the king, three pieces of qabati cloth for his delegates, eight pieces of buqturiyyah cloth, five pieces of mu'lama cloth, a mantle of mukhmala silk (velvet or wool), ten pieces of Abu Buqtor cloth, and ten pieces of Ahasi cloth.

Opinions vary on the *Baqt*. While it may have caused 600 years of relative peace between Nubia and the Arabs, delivering 400 slaves a year to Egypt caused great social dislocation in Nubia. However, during this period Nobadia disappeared from historical records, becoming incorporated into the northern part of Makuria. Three original Nubian kingdoms now became two: Makuria and Alwa. Makuria is the better known because of the large quantity of Arab sources and the archaeology, but Alwa was even more important. In the tenth century Ibn Selim Al-Aswani, a tenth-century Egyptian diplomat of indigenous non-Arab origins, recorded that, 'The King of Alwa is more powerful than the king of Maqurra, has a larger army and more horses than the Maqurran: his country is more fertile and larger' (quoted in Derek A. Welsby, *The Medieval Kingdoms of Nubia*, 2002). Another eyewitness, Ibn Haukal, a geographer from what is today's Turkey, believed that Alwa was the most prosperous region in Nubia (cited in Fantini). Abu Salih, a late-twelfth- and early-thirteenth-century Egyptian scholar of Armenian origin, tells us that Alwa had 400 churches (B.T.A. Evetts, *The Churches and Monasteries of Egypt and Some Neighbouring Countries*, attr. Abu Salih, the Armenian, 1895).

Agriculture was the mainstay of the Nubian economy, supplemented by animal husbandry, hunting and fishing. In the northern region cotton was grown and at Soba, the capital of the southerly kingdom of Alwa, several crops were cultivated, including bulrush millet, foxtail millet, cowpea, cucumber seeds, dates, dom palm, fig seeds, hulled barley, lentils, nuts, peas, pulses, sesame and termis bean. Other products grown were bananas, barley, big citrus, dhurra/sorghum, palm trees, vines and wheat. Agriculture was enhanced using *saqias*, a wooden wheels that carried two parallel ropes to which pots were attached. They were rotated through a series of gears by a donkey or other draught animal. As this happened, the pots filled with water as they were submerged and emptied that water at a higher level into an aqueduct. In 951 Ibn Haukal recorded that:

> *The most prosperous part of the country is the territory of Alwa, which has a continuous chain of villages and a continuous strip of cultivated lands, so that a traveller may in one day pass through many villages, one joining the next, supplied with waters drawn from the Nile by means of* saqias.
>
> **Ibn Haukal, cited by and trans. Fr. Giovanni Fantini, *Oriental Sources Concerning Nubia*, 1975**

Nubia's most important international trade commodity was gold. Though available in northern Nubia, Ibn Selim tells us that gold was plentiful in Alwa. Ibn Haukal concurs, observing that the 'Alwans control the gold mines'. Goods from the Islamic world certainly reached as far south as Soba. Excavations have recovered fine glassware from there, including tableware and containers for perfume and other products. Chinese porcelain has also been recovered, dating from the twelfth to thirteenth centuries. Iron was used extensively for weaponry and large numbers of arrows have been found, while tools made of iron – including adzes, axes and hammerheads, blades from a bow saw, chisels, knives, hoes, metal cutters and tongs – were discovered in the royal tombs at Ballana. Iron also used to make bindings for strengthening boxes and chests. Copper alloy was widely used for needles, vessels of various types and weaponry.

Archaeologists have also found large lumps of glass from Debeira West and Soba. Glass was the material of choice for the majority of beads at Ibrim, while glass windows were discovered at the Makurian cities of Old Dongola and Hambukol. The Cathedral of the Granite Columns at Old Dongola had glass windows in the seventh century.

Cloth manufacture was conducted on a large scale at Qasr Ibrim, and archaeologists have found a large collection of equipment associated with sewing, spinning and weaving. Numerous textiles made of cotton, wool, silk and linen were also discovered. Silk was imported from Egypt, the Middle East or China. The four dyes of madder, indigo, weld and Persian berries were used to colour other locally produced textiles, which produced a wide range of colours. Exquisite clothing has also been recovered from Soba. Individuals were buried wearing flax fibres interwoven with gold thread. The church and cathedral paintings depict the nobility of Makurian society wearing rich robes. Nubian shoes were of light construction, like modern slippers. A woman buried at Soba East had exceptionally fine leather sandals on her feet. At Ibrim a knee-length riding boot, made of fine leather or pigskin, was discovered. Moreover, superlative examples of shoes with patterns in gilt can be seen on the walls of Faras Cathedral.

River trade was conducted at Philae between the Nubians and Arabs. Qasr Ibrim was connected to the Red Sea port of Aidhab by a significant trade route; other routes connected the kingdom of Alwa to the Red Sea ports of Badi, Dahlak and Sawakin. Land trade from Nubia to West Africa took place along the camel caravan routes.

Faras was originally the capital of Nobadia before it was swallowed up by Makuria during the *Baqt*. Its defensive walls were 38 feet in height and nearly 13 feet thick, with substantial square external towers at the angles. Within the defensive circuit were the cathedral, three churches, two palatial structures, a monastery and an industrial complex that produced pottery. The two palaces date back to the seventh century and were at least two storeys in height.

Old Dongola was the capital of Makuria. Abu Salih described it as follows:

> *It is a large city on the banks of the blessed Nile, and contains many churches and large houses and wide streets. The king's house is lofty, with several domes of red brick.*
>
> ***The Churches and Monasteries of Egypt and Some Neighbouring Countries*, attributed to Abu Salih, the Armenian, trans. B.T.A. Evetts, 1895**

The city was encircled by seven walls, with high-status houses built to the north of the ecclesiastical complex. In his work *Christian* 'Nubia at the height of its civilization', published in volume III of the *General History of Africa* (1988), the Polish archaeologist and historian Stefan Jakobielski reveals more about these houses:

> *Further northwards extend a[n]...eighth- to...ninth-century housing complex. The houses discovered here differ in their hitherto unencountered spatial layout as well as their functional programme (water supply installation, bathroom with heating system) and interiors decorated with murals.*

The Monasteries were also important. They were the largest building complexes in Nubia and contained a church, a refectory and accommodation for the monks. Ruins of other houses still survive, reaching to a height of two storeys or more; the upper storeys had large, arched windows. A common feature of these houses is the presence of a narrow toilet unit.

Between the eighth and the twelfth centuries several battles occurred between Arab- and Turkish-ruled Egypt and Makuria.

Both sides were the aggressors on occasion. These were mere skirmishes, however, and should be considered as such. By the middle of the eighth century the balance of power had swung in favour of Makuria. Nubia became a rich and great civilization during this period, as shown by its glass, textiles, leather goods and metals. However, by the thirteenth century Nubia was starting to decline.

At this time Makuria faced grave challenges from Egypt. In 1265 the ruler of Qoz (from Egypt) attacked Makuria, where, according to El-Maqrizi, his forces 'killed many people, took prisoners and then returned' (Fantini). Moreover, the northern parts of the Empire had become arabicized – a process that began in the ninth century when Arabs were able to acquire land in Maris, a province in northern Makuria. Makurian law decreed that all land was the property of the emperor (i.e. the state), but a number of Muslim residents of Aswan successfully challenged this in Egyptian courts. As a result Arabs were able to own their own land in Maris, and to pass it on to descendants through the generations.

In 1276 Shekanda, a Makurian prince, visited Cairo. He sought the Sultan's help against the Makurian emperor in a plan to secure the Makurian throne for himself. The plot worked and Shekanda was installed as the puppet ruler on the Makurian throne. As a result, the Sultan of Egypt now owned half of Makuria's revenue; Shekanda was also obliged to provide him with three elephants, three giraffes, five female panthers, 100 camels and 400 oxen each year. Other Makurian rulers attempted to make equally foolish deals with Egypt in 1314 and 1316. More problems followed in 1365, and on 8 December the Egyptians assembled an army of 3,000 cavalry and marched on Makuria. The Makurian Empire was no more.

The Kingdom of Alwa held on, but ultimately collapsed in the late fifteenth century. The desert Arabs from the east occupied the country, seizing Soba, its capital, and reducing it to ruins.

THE TURKISH EMPIRE IN THE NILE

Turkish people originated in Central Asia – specifically from the Altai Mountains, which are located where modern-day Mongolia, Kazakhstan, China and Russia meet. Most of the figurative art in Islam that depicts humans is Turkish in origin. Consequently, the people depicted have Mongolian appearance. A significant number of Islamic rulers of Egypt were of Turkish heritage, for example the Tulunid Dynasty that ruled Egypt (and Syria) between 868 and 905. They built the Mosque of Ibn Tulun, on the edge of Fustat, one of the glories of Islamic architecture. People of Turkish heritage ruled again in Egypt between 1250 and 1382, creating the Mamluk Sultanate. The complex of Sultan Hasan in Cairo, built between 1356 and 1364, is another superb piece of architecture.

The Ottoman Turks conquered Egypt and made it a part of the Ottoman Empire. In 1516, led by Sultan Selim the Grim, the Turkish forces defeated the Mameluke army in Aleppo in Syria. In 1519 they seized control of Mameluke-governed Egypt. Now a province of the vast Ottoman Empire, Egypt retained a degree of local autonomy under Ottoman-appointed governors known as pashas, but the quality of life and culture in Egypt went into decline. Poverty engulfed the country and it rapidly faded into obscurity. Local power struggles took place between various military and political factions, including the powerful Mameluke, who gradually regained some control. Despite the weakening of central Ottoman power, the Turkish rulers continued to control the region until the late eighteenth century. In 1798 the French invasion, under Napoleon Bonaparte, brought this period to an abrupt end.

Mehmet Ali, also called Muhammad Ali, arrived in Egypt in 1801, as part of an Ottoman army sent to fight with and remove the French. After this successful campaign, he fought off rivals to become the Pasha of Egypt in 1807. In this position, Mehmet Ali transformed the country; Crete was also transferred over to his rule by the Ottomans.

The era of modern Egypt began with Mehmet Ali's rule. In 1820 his forces conquered Sudan, integrating it into the Ottoman Empire's administrative structure. Exploiting Sudan's resources, he used slaves, ivory and gold to boost Egypt's economy. In 1831 he ordered an attack on Ottoman-controlled Syria and occupied it. However, in 1841 the Ottoman Sultan agreed to offer Muhammad Ali hereditary rulership of Egypt, provided he gave up Crete and Syria. He died in 1849 and is buried in the splendid Muhammad Ali Mosque in Cairo.

Many famous twentieth-century Egyptians were of Turkish heritage. Egypt's last monarch, King Farouk I, was part of Muhammad Ali's dynasty. Hosni Mubarak, the former president of Egypt, is said to have had Turkish roots through his paternal line.

LATER CHAPTERS IN THE HISTORY OF SUDAN & EGYPT

THE EARLY HISTORY OF TUNISIA

At the end of the nineteenth century France began colonizing Tunisia due to growing imperial ambitions to control important North African territories. By the 1880s Tunisia, which had been a part of the Ottoman Empire since the sixteenth century, was politically weak. In 1881 France, under the pretext of protecting its interests and stabilizing the country, imposed a treaty called the Bardo Treaty with the ruling Husainid Dynasty. Even though Tunisia technically remained under the Bey of Tunis's sovereignty, in effect it became a French protectorate.

As well as having Ottoman rule, Tunisia was subject to the Arab rule of the Fatimids in the Middle Ages and the rule of the Roman Empire in ancient times. It is consequently an Arab-dominated country today. Much of its population is also descended from Roman colonists, and from Vandal colonists too for that matter. The Vandals were German speakers who captured Tunisia in CE 439; they went on to establish a kingdom along the North African coast. The oldest civilization in the region was written about learnedly by two French scholars, Gilbert and Colette Charles-Picard, in their book *Daily Life in Carthage*, published in 1958 (1961 ed. quoted below). The culture was called the Empire of Carthage.

The anthropological examination of skeletons found in tombs proves there was no racial unity; the so-called Semitic type, characterised by the long, perfectly oval face, the thin aquiline nose, and the lengthened cranium, enlarged over the nape of the neck, has not been found in Carthage, nor for that matter in Sidon. On the other hand, another cranial form, with a fairly short face, prominent parietal bumps, farther forward and lower down than usual, is common in Lebanese burial-grounds and in those of the new Tyre; Perhaps it belonged to the real Phoenicians. But most of the Punic population seemed to have had African, and even Negro, ancestors.

THE EMPIRE OF CARTHAGE

The city-state of Carthage was founded in the ninth century BCE. Situated on the North African coast of modern Tunisia, it was founded by the incoming Phœnicians, the early Palestinians, and given the name Qart Hadasht or Carthage. Other influences in the culture came from different sources. The native Libyans of North Africa played a significant and ultimately dominant role. They were a Berber-speaking branch of Afroasiatic. Other cultural practices originated in the Nile Valley. Some derived from Afroasiatic speakers, others from Nilo-Saharan speakers.

Herodotus, the ancient Greek historian, discussed the origin of the Phœnicians. 'This nation,' he observed, 'according to their own account, dwelt anciently upon the Erythræan sea; but, crossing thence, fixed themselves on the seacoast of Syria, where they still inhabit' (*History of Herodotus*, Vol. IV, trans. George Rawlinson, 1875). The Phœnicians are thus believed to have migrated from Erythrea, on the coast of the Red Sea, about the year 2000 BCE; they travelled to the Mediterranean, where they were first established on the Palestinian strip. A Semitic-speaking branch of Afroasiatic, the Phœnicians were of distant Horn of Africa heritage.

Carthage was founded by a Phœnician exile called Elissa in 814 BCE. She fled Tyre, in the Levant, with some of its leading citizens and loyal followers. Her fleet landed on the island of Cyprus, where she earned the name of Dido. There she successfully rescued 80 virgins from the bondage of sacred prostitution in the island's Temple of Venus. On arriving on the North African coast of modern Tunisia, envoys from nearby Utica gave their blessings and brought gifts. From Tyre, Elissa brought liturgical artefacts for the worship of Melqart.

By the seventh century BCE Carthage had become a modest city of mud-brick walling and beaten-clay floors. It already occupied a sizeable part of the littoral plain, with most of its inhabitants being indigenous Libyans. However, many artefacts showed Nile Valley influences. Archaeologists have found statues and tombs in a vaguely Egyptian style along with locally made jewellery, also in Egyptian style; ivory was discovered in an area where Egyptian iconography is clearly visible. Moreover, thousands of scarabs and amulets were recovered. Among these were wadjet eyes, uraei (representations of sacred serpents) and images of Nile Valley deities. There were images of Ptah, Bes, Anubis, Ma'at, Bastet and Amen. Images of Khnum, a specific Nubian deity, proved more intriguing. Finally there is evidence that the great Kushite ruler Taharqo conquered as far as Spain, so bringing Carthage into his sphere of influence. Skeletons have been found in a Carthaginian cemetery by archaeologists. Eugène Pittard, a distinguished Swiss anthropologist, describes the sarcophagus of the highly venerated Priestess of Tanit as 'the most highly decorated and artistic of those found'. The 'woman it contained exhibited Negroid characters. She was an African by race!' (Eugène Pittard, *Race and History*, 1926).

CONFLICT WITH THE GREEKS

By the end of the seventh century BCE, Carthage faced the first of many challenges from Europe when the Greeks began to dispute mastery of the western Mediterranean. As early as the eighth century BCE the Greeks had colonies on Campania and the island of Ischia; now they also sought to establish trade routes and dominate markets. In addition, they desired the island of Elba and the mineral wealth of Etruria. Greek forces took control of the entrance to the Tyrrhenian Sea and occupied the Straits of Messina. They soon established colonies on the east coast of Sicily, most notably in the towns of Gela and Syracuse.

In 654 BCE Carthage established a colony on Ibiza. From the sixth century BCE the city was in control of a variety of territories – some colonies that Carthage had established, others that had originally belonged to the Phœnicians. When the city of Tyre fell in 573 BCE, Carthage became the region's leading city, having lost its Phœnician parent. Carthage controlled Malta from the sixth century BCE, as well as overseeing Lampedusa and Gozo; Sardinia had already been colonized by the Phœnicians in the ninth century BCE. From the sixth century onwards Carthage extended its boundaries into Africa, creating a Libyphœnician culture. To lease the land, Carthage stopped paying the Libyans annual tribute by the second quarter of the fifth century BCE. At that time the city controlled Majorca, Minorca, Sardinia, western Sicily, the smaller Mediterranean islands, a portion of Spain and finally North Africa, in one way or another. Skulls identified as Phœnician have been discovered west of Syracuse in Sicily. They were prognathous, dolichocephalic (having a relatively long skull), and distinctly Negroid in appearance.

Rivalry with the Greeks quickly turned into conflict, with Sicily as the combat zone. In 480 BCE the Carthaginians were completely defeated in a battle. In 410 BCE war broke out once more in Sicily, this time with more victories. Hannibal of the House of Mago oversaw the conquest of Selinus, Himera and Syracuse, brutally destroying these Greek colonial cities. He returned in 407 BCE and destroyed Agrigentum, Gela and Camarina. After much bloodshed, a peace treaty was agreed between Carthage and the Greeks in 383 BCE. Sicily was divided between them with an agreed boundary.

CONFLICT WITH THE ROMANS

Such empire building had implications, especially for merchant shipping. In effect, the western Mediterranean had become the Carthaginian lake; with the real threat of severe penalties for foreign sailors, they controlled who could or could not sail there. From Carthage gold, precious stones, locally manufactured goods and slaves were transported to Italy. Malta, another of their colonies, had an industry in beautiful cotton textiles, known for their fineness and softness. These were transported to African markets. Wax and honey were produced and slaves were exported from Corsica. One of the islands mined and smelted an unending supply of iron. Majorca and Minorca produced fruit and bred mules. Carthage discovered a new market for its manufactured goods in Spain. Additionally, Carthage engaged in a thriving land trade with other African nations, purchasing dates, gold, salt and slaves. Herodotus specifically mentions that dumb barter was used to acquire some of the gold, which came from 'a Libyan country' later identified as Guinea. This same method of trade continued to be used for 2,000 years.

By the third century BCE the city of Carthage had become opulent and impressive. It was home to at least 700,000 people, possibly as many as a million. A 23-mile circuit of towering walls contained numerous magnificent buildings, a fortress and imposing temples. Barracks for 20,000 soldiers, magazines for war supplies, stalls for 300 elephants and stables for 4,000 horses were all contained within the city's extraordinarily thick walls. Tall houses, six storeys in height, lined both sides of three streets. Harbours could be reached via the streets, and to the north and the west of the city lay the great suburb of Megara; full of gardens and villas, it was associated with the idle rich. The forum was probably situated in the lower town close to the two ports. Docks for ships were sited all around the circular war harbour. Before each dock stood columns, decorated with Ionic capitals; these formed part of a colonnade that surrounded the entire harbour. In the centre of the island stood the Admiralty buildings and palace, from which trumpeters would convey orders to the warships. The Carthaginian temples were ornate, lavishly decorated with metals, wood and marble. Herodotus described pillars of gold and lapis lazuli standing before them and 60 steps led up to the city's richest Temple of Eshmun. Last but not least, Carthage had public baths, theatres, libraries and restaurants.

Carthaginian control over Mediterranean trade routes soon brought them into conflict with the newly rising power of Rome from the other side of the Mediterranean. The rivalry once again turned to conflict with the first of the Punic Wars. The confrontation began in 264 BCE on the island of Sicily. Despite conducting a series of campaigns between 246 and 242 BCE that almost drove the Romans off the island, Carthage suffered an unexpected naval defeat in 241 BCE. As a result the Carthaginians granted Hamilcar full authority to negotiate with Rome and pursue peace. Carthage was forced to give up its claim to the colony of Sicily by the Romans, who emerged victorious.

The Second Punic War

Hannibal of the House of Barca seized Saguntum in Spain in 219 BCE. The Romans interpreted this breach of the 241 BCE treaty as a declaration of war; a year later the Second Punic War commenced. Hannibal is the famous general of antiquity who most people have heard of. Superb coins survive that show his personal Indian elephant, Surus, on one side and Hannibal's face on the other. In May of that year Hannibal raised an armed force of 90,000 men on foot and 12,000 men on horseback. They reached the River Rhône by the summer. However, they were now a much smaller force consisting of 37 elephants, 9,000 horses, and 50,000 soldiers.

Hannibal's forces crossed the Alpine passes at the end of the year. It proved a difficult and costly crossing in the winter, and numerous animals and people perished. The survivors attacked Italy in a march from the north. In 216 BCE they broke deep into Italian territory and took Cannae, killing 70,000 Roman soldiers in the process. By contrast, during the same campaign, Carthage lost 5,500 soldiers and 200 horses. They marched on Rome next, but were unable to get through the city walls. Hannibal's forces camped there for years. As Sir James Frazer wrote in *The Golden Bough*, published in 1890: 'Hannibal hung with his dusky army like a storm-cloud about to break, within sight of the sentinels of Rome.' In the end the land's gold and silver mines, the foundation of Carthage's wealth, were taken over by the Romans. Around 206 BCE, as Carthage began to lose, the King of Numidia, an African state to the west of Carthage, switched allegiance. He persuaded the Roman commander Scipio to bring the war to Africa by aligning himself with Rome. Scipio then invaded Africa in 204 BCE, causing Hannibal and Mago, his brother, to leave Italy and go back to their homeland. At the Battle of Zama in 202 BCE the Romans engaged them and won. Scipio had anticipated and hampered Hannibal's use of elephants, his secret weapon.

THE END OF CARTHAGE

The terms of the peace treaty of 201 BCE were harsh. Carthage was compelled to return lands that once belonged to Numidia. They were forbidden to make war on any people without the consent of Rome. They had to hand over their elephants and were not allowed to acquire others. They had to abandon all their ships except ten. Finally, they had to pay a reparation of 10,000 talents over 50 years. Following the treaty, Scipio burned the Carthaginian fleet.

Carthage did nevertheless make some sort of recovery during this period, with Hannibal still at the helm. The city's business was once again as successful as ever, with Carthage even making a proposal to repay Rome's reparation in ten years. The Carthaginians eventually agreed to hand over Hannibal to the Romans, but in 196 BCE he fled into exile. The Romans continued to have misgivings about Carthage's rapid progress towards recovery. Concerns were voiced in public by a Roman senator. Cato the Elder is reported to have ended every speech in the Senate between 152 and 150 BCE with the phrase: 'In any case I am of the opinion that Carthage must be destroyed.' Moreover, in 151 BCE the last of the 50 payments from Carthage was delivered. Rome was now looking for a reason to humiliate Carthage further.

They got their chance in 150 BCE. Carthage counterattacked Numidia, who had abused Carthage for years while the Romans turned a blind eye. This allowed the Romans to claim that the treaty of 201 BCE had been breached. In the following year Carthage sent an embassy to Rome to discuss the matter. All war engines, catapults, cannonballs and weapons were taken from Carthage by the Romans. Carthage gave in. The Carthaginians then received the final terms of agreement from the Romans. They wanted the people of Carthage to leave their city and move 9¼ miles inland from the sea. When the news of the Roman terms was made public, Carthage went mad. People were torn to pieces in the streets, and Italians found there were tortured. The Carthaginians then reached the pinnacle of their power after the torrent was contained. They locked the gates and made the decision to fight to the death. But how was this to be done? There were no ships of war in the ports; the arsenals were empty; the stalls where the elephants and horses were stabled were also empty. Without weapons, without any means of defence but the strong walls, the Senate of Carthage declared war on Rome. Within a very short time the city was transformed into a huge factory.

Rome attacked in 149 BCE and besieged the city for three years. Eventually they breached the walls and began the genocide. At least 250,000 people were slaughtered in the atrocity and 50,000 more were sold into slavery. Some 500,000 volumes of the Carthaginian library disappeared. The smouldering fires in Carthage were relit, the marbles were hacked, the temples destroyed; so thorough was the work of destruction that hardly one stone remained on another. Then the plough was passed over the blackened soil, and the final curse was pronounced which dedicated the place to the Infernal Gods. The site on which Carthage had stood for 700 years was cursed; the land was never to yield a harvest; no human habitation was to be raised on ground given over to the spirits of darkness.

THE EARLY HISTORY OF FRENCH WEST AFRICA

The map of West Africa today is the result of French colonialism and the decolonization that followed, which explains why some of the borders are straight lines. France began its colonial conquests in West Africa in the nineteenth century, although they had gained a toehold in Senegal as early as 1659. France came to control lands today called Senegal, Mauritania, Mali, Niger and Burkina Faso (formerly Upper Volta), all acquired during the so-called 'Scramble for Africa'.

Captain Louis Binger was a French agent known for his reconnaissance mission into nineteenth-century West Africa. He entered the Land of Mossi, in what is now Burkina Faso, to spy out the land. His book *Du Niger au golfe de Guinée par le pays de Kong et le Mossi*, published in 1892, provides intriguing insights into the area, including his interactions with the various kingdoms there, such as the Mossi kingdoms and the Land of Kong. His writings detail the customs, politics and landscapes of the Mossi and Kong regions, providing the French government with the information it would need to conquer those kingdoms.

However, the book also contains other information, of great interest to those concerned with Africa's history. As well as a written narrative, the book features etchings of Mossi and Kong culture rarely spoken of today: castles, walled cities, household utensils, cavalry on horseback, mounted royal bodyguards with chainmail, roads and paths with individual symbols giving name to them, mosques built in distinctive West African architectural aesthetics, buildings consisting of two, possibly three storeys, scenes of collective Islamic prayer and a metals factory.

Professor Vincent Tarikhu Farrar, an African American historian of African technological history, drew upon Binger's narrative in writing the technological history of Mossi metallurgy. Farrar found that in the fifteenth century iron and cotton cloth were the two most important trading products from the Mossi kingdoms. In the second half of the eighteenth century the Mossi Kingdom of Yatenga created a new type of furnace up to 21¼ feet in height, capable of smelting one ton of ore with a resulting bloom (the initial product of smelting, still containing slag) of 23 stone 8 lbs. The slow combustion reduction processes lasted from three to seven days and produced more iron with less waste. The iron was cheap and high-quality material, dictated by the needs of the marketplace: ingots, knives, hoes and axes. At the time of the French conquest 1,000 of these furnaces were in operation, with these smelters producing over 500 metric tonnes of iron per year. This is, of course, on an industrial scale.

Major Felix Dubois, a French journalist and explorer, wrote *Timbuctoo the Mysterious*, published in 1896. His book is in part about his travels in West Africa, but it is also the pioneering work on the history of Songhai. The Songhai Empire at its height covered Mali and several surrounding countries: Gambia,

Senegal, Guinea, Mauritania, Niger and Nigeria. The book contains a variety of delicate, black and white images of scenes from the cities of Djenné and Timbuktu: two-storey town houses with terraces of fifteenth- and sixteenth-century dates, Koran schools, city scenes of all types and more.

Dubois based the historical sections of his book on a manuscript by a seventeenth-century West African scholar called Abdurrahman Al-Sadi, an academic from an indigenous African university at Timbuktu in Mali. Al-Sadi's manuscript was called *History of the Sudan*. The term 'Sudan' is from the Arabic and means 'black' or 'blacks'; scholars of Al-Sadi's time used the term 'Sudan' (or 'Soudan') rather as we use 'Black Africa' today. Dubois explained why he was so impressed by Al-Sadi's book and why he relied on it so heavily:

> *Its style is very simple and clear, entirely lacking those literary artifices so much in vogue among the Arabs; and the author displays an unusual conscientiousness, never hesitating to give both versions of a doubtful event. His biography of the great infidel Sunni Ali shows him to be sufficiently impartial, and his book is above everything remarkable for the admirable philosophy (Islamic, be it understood) pervading it. It is a work of elevated morals, and is particularly adapted to exercise a happy influence upon the negraic mind; for Abderrahman is not content with a mere narration of events – he explains them, and that without having recourse to the convenient fatalism of the Mussulman who says of a calamitous event, 'It was written'.*
>
> **Felix Dubois, *Timbuctoo the Mysterious*,**
> **trans. Diana White, 1896**

TIMBUKTU SCHOLARS PRESERVE THE HISTORY

Towards the end of the sixteenth century, a large portion of West Africa, especially the part known in colonial times as French West Africa, was under the rule of the Arma, a Moroccan military regime. The Arma confiscated the libraries of West African scholars; Professor Ahmed Baba, a famous sixteenth-century West African scholar, lost 1,600 books in this way. Despite this plunder, Mali in West Africa, as well as surrounding countries such as Mauritania, are rich in monuments, ruins and manuscripts. West Africa certainly had universities in medieval times.

However, West African historians attempted to preserve the history of their region. One key source is *History of the Sudan*, a work completed in 1656 by Abdurrahman Al-Sadi, mentioned above. It was he who led the University Mosque in the Malian city of Timbuktu and was also employed by the government as a high-ranking civil servant, responsible for writing important documents. Al-Sadi stated that he was inspired to write on Songhai history for the following reasons:

> *I saw the ruin and collapse of the science of history, and I observed that its gold pieces and small change were both disappearing. This science is rich in gems and can give many lessons because it gives people knowledge of their country, their ancestors, their records, the names of heroes and their biographies. With the help of God, I undertook to record all that I had been able to glean about the princes of the Songhai people, telling their adventures, history, exploits and battles. Then I added the history of Timbuktu from the foundation of*

that city, of the princes that ruled there, and of the scholars and saints who lived there.

Abdurrahman Al-Sadi, *History of the Sudan*, trans. O. Houdas, *Tarikh es-Soudan*, 1900, English translation adapted by Robin Walker

The second source is *History for the Truth Seeker* by Mahmud Kati, written between 1519 and his death in 1593; his grandson, Ibn al-Mukhtar, added other information after his death. Kati was a professor, a civil servant and a close friend of Askiya the Great, a Songhai ruler. In giving his reasons for writing his book, Kati also linked the pursuance of history with moral betterment:

It is customary for philosophers and learned doctors to recount the sovereign acts of princes and other great ones of the earth. In doing so, they act in accordance with the teachings of the Holy Koran, for to recall events that have been eroded from memory – to return to a time that has fallen into oblivion through human negligence – is to strive to make men of good will better citizens.

Mahmud Kati and Ibn al-Mukhtar, trans. and ed. Christopher Wise, *Ta'rikh al fattash: The Timbuktu Chronicles 1493–1599*, 2011

These two manuscripts tell us about the rise and fall of three empires in this region: ancient Ghana, Mali and Songhai. These three gold-based empires did not exist at the same time; in fact they spanned many centuries. Ghana was the dominant force in West Africa from around 300 until 1240. Mali dominated from 1240 to 1433, followed by Songhai from 1469 to 1591. The manuscripts also describe the raids and attacks by the enemies of these empires, such as the Mossi. In addition, this region has a distinguished archaeological record.

OLDEST POTTERY IN AFRICA

Pottery of an extremely old age has been discovered at Ounjougou, close to the Bandiagara Cliffs in Mali. Between 2002 and 2005 an international team of archaeologists discovered six ceramic fragments of great importance. The pieces were found to be at least 11,400 years old, making them the oldest pottery in Africa. They are also the oldest artefacts belonging to speakers of the Niger Congo family. Only pottery from the Far Eastern cultures of Siberia, Japan and China is older than these.

Professor Eric Huysecom of the University of Geneva led the international team of 50 interdisciplinary workers, who came from Germany, Mali, Switzerland, France and Britain. Beginning in 1997, this team conducted a project called 'Human population and paleo environment in West Africa'. Over the course of the project they made numerous discoveries about ancient stone-cutting techniques and tools, but unearthing the ancient fragments of burnt clay is one of the most significant so far.

Huysecom believed that pottery was invented in West Africa to enable humans to adapt to climate change. Quoted in a 2007 piece by Simon Bradley, called 'Swiss archaeologist digs up West Africa's past' and published online at www.swissinfo.ch, he commented that, "'Apart from finding the oldest ceramic in Africa, the interesting thing is that it gives us information about when and under what circumstances man can invent new things, such as pottery'". In addition, Huysecom noted that '...the invention of ceramic is linked to specific environmental conditions – the transformation of the region from a desert into grassland'". It is a shame that Huyescom used the term 'man' in the context of this invention, especially as Professor Christopher Ehret (*Ancient Africa: A Global History to 300 CE*, 2023) believes it far more likely that the inventors were women. The people of the region intensively collected African wild grains such as fonio, developing in the process a new foraging system for the region. Women invented the ceramic pots to boil fonio in its whole-grain form, which transformed it into something edible.

The invention of ceramics coincided too with that of small arrowheads, also discovered by the team. These arrowheads were probably used to hunt hares, pheasants and other small game. Professor Huysecom regards the date of 11,400 years old for the pottery as conservative; Bradley quotes him as remarking that "'We know...that they are at least 11,400 years old, but they could be 50 or even 1,000 years older'".

EARLY COPPER WORKING

Copper and its alloys were worked in prehistoric Egyptian times. However, copper working appeared for the second time in Africa in the Aïr Mountains in 2500 BCE. Believed to have been an independent invention in the region, the inventors are thought to have spoken a language of Songhai ancestry, a Nilo-Saharan language. Archaeological evidence shows that the copper-working did not develop there fully fledged. If the technology had been fully fledged, it could be argued that the techniques developed somewhere else and were brought to this region. Since the techniques were not fully fledged, this makes them more probably a local invention. The culture that produced this copper buried its dead in cemeteries marked by megaliths: both rectangles and circles of large stones.

BIRTH OF STONE VILLAGES

Archaeologists found impressive villages in stone at Dhar-Tichitt, near Walata in Mauritania, that have survived in ruined form to this day. They date back to around 2000 BCE. The report by American archaeologist Patrick Munson, titled 'Archaeology and the Prehistoric Origins of the Ghana Empire' and published in 1980 in the *Journal of African History*, claims that these villages were built apparently 'without major external influences'. The villages consisted of roughly circular compounds connected by 'well defined streets'. They were built near lakes for the accessibility of water, making fishing a viable economic activity. Archaeological evidence of herding and agriculture has also been found.

According to Munson, archaeological evidence indicates that between 1000 and 800 BCE four times as many villages flourished, accompanied by a greater development of agriculture. As before the villages were large and of stone, but they were also walled. Each village was 'encircled by a masonry wall over 6⅝ feet high and 3¼ feet thick'. Together with the fact that they were built on hills, this implies that the walled enclosures were constructed for defensive reasons. There is speculation, derived from the writings of the Greek historian Herodotus, that the Soninkes were seeking to protect themselves from sustained hostility from the Garamantes of the desert.

BIRTH OF WEST AFRICAN CITIES ALONG THE NIGER

Professor Roderick McIntosh has reported evidence ('Before Timbuktu: Cities of the Elder World', Shamil Jeppie and Souleymane Bachir Diagne eds., *The Meanings of Timbuktu*, 2008) that Mali's Middle Niger region had an indigenous urbanism as dense and expansive as those of ancient Egypt and ancient Iraq. This urban culture dated back to the first millennium BCE. Archaeologists have found evidence of mounds that were remains of melted clay brick houses, spread over 50 hectares or more, which gives some idea of each city's size. In a BBC television documentary, *The Lost Libraries of Timbuktu*, Aminatta Forma and archaeologist Douglas Park emphasize that some of these cities were as large as Ur or Uruk in ancient Mesopotamia, with areas of between 70 and 100 hectares. Moreover, at least one of these pre-Islamic cities was twice as large as Timbuktu at its height.

Professor McIntosh tells us that the Méma region (southwest of Timbuktu) contained cities dating from at least the end of the first millennium BCE. These were occupied until the thirteenth and fourteenth centuries CE. Cities from the Djenné region dated from at least the third century BCE and lasted to around the fourteenth century CE, while those of the Dia region of Masina dated to before Djenné (others say as early as 800 BCE). Villages and urban sites in the Timbuktu region date from 500 CE and were abandoned by 1500 CE. One of them, Wadi-el-Ahmar, was an enormous town of 5⅜ square feet, surrounded by a ring of satellites; it was probably abandoned between 900 and 1200 CE. McIntosh thinks that this site may have been the parent city of Timbuktu. He also believes that the other sites may well be the cities mentioned in early sources, but which have not yet been identified: Awqham, Safanku, Tirekka and Bughrat.

Old Djenné was one of these early cities, dating back to 250 BCE. By 500 CE it had a significant population of 20,000 people – London, for example, took another 700 years to reach this figure. Old Djenné was a centre of long-distance trade in which they were the middlemen. Ceramics, copper, foodstuffs and iron exchanged hands here and a trade also existed in gold and salt, two very important products in the ancient world. Encircling this early metropolis by the year 800 was a clay brick wall, with a thickness of 9 feet. Before long settlements and workshops grew up around the city, associated with craft specialities such as smiths, potters, sculptors, jewellers, brickmakers and builders, shipwrights, traders, fishermen and farmers. In addition, Old Djenné was a trans-shipment point where goods were transferred from boat to donkey. It was located near several channels of the Niger River, which gave it a natural moated defence. Copper entered Old Djenné from the east and gold from the west, having been mined in the Bambuk and Boré regions, 372⅞–497 miles to the southwest. Less than 62 miles to the east was a major iron-producing area. Finally, the city of Old Djenné lay between waterways, moist soils and dry savannah country.

THE EMPIRE OF GHANA

Ancient Ghana was a kingdom situated in today's Mali and southern Mauritania region, between the Senegal and Niger rivers. By the eleventh century, at the height of its power, the empire also ruled parts of today's Senegal and Guinea, holding sway over the lands to the Atlantic Ocean. The capital was located at the archaeological site of Kumbi-Saleh, but Nema, Walata and Audoghast were also important cities.

The Soninkes were the main ethnicity, dominating this culture for most of its history. They were a Niger-Congo people, but scholars are unsure of the ethnicity of its earliest kings. Modern historians present them also as Soninke, but two history books from the medieval university culture of Timbuktu take a different view.

Both of these suggest that a dynasty of 20, or perhaps 22, kings ruled in ancient Ghana before the time of the Muhammad. This indicates that the first of these kings came to power around the year 300, if not earlier. These kings were Berbers, and possibly Sanhaja Berbers. By African standards, some of these were of a lighter complexion – sometimes significantly so. One of the Timbuktu histories says the early kings took the dynastic title Kayamaga, meaning 'king of gold'; interestingly, gold mines were opened in the region of Boré during this early period. Moreover, one of these kings ruled at the same time as the Prophet. The only early ruler mentioned by name, he was called Kanissa'ay and ruled from the capital city of Kunbi. Scholars believe this to be the same place as the archaeological site of Kumbi-Saleh. Kanissa'ay's mother had a residence in the town of Kurunka. At this residence were 1,000 horses, tied up with silken ropes and looked after by 3,000 attendants.

However, this dynasty was to come to a sticky end. In the seventh century a violent revolution took place, described in a chronicle as follows:

Then Allah brought their rule to an end. He gave the most ignoble of their people power over their nobles. They killed all the children of their kings, even ripping open the women to kill those in the womb.

Mahmud Kati, History for the Truth Seeker, quoted in Nehemia Levtzion, *Ancient Ghana and Mali*, 1973

What was this revolution? If the earliest kings were Sanhaja Berbers…was it the overthrow of the Sanhaja Berbers by the Soninkes? Or if the earliest kings were Soninke…was it the overthrow of one Soninke family by another? No one can yet give satisfactory answers to these questions.

Ancient Ghana began as a city-state in the fourth century. By the eighth century, through territorial conquests and the building of alliances, it had developed into an empire, able to dominate its neighbours by a pre-eminence in iron technology. Exploiting this advantage for warfare, Soninke military supremacy was assured. They fought with lances and swords of iron against opponents equipped with bars of ebony. Iron also assisted in the development of agriculture, producing farming tools that were superior to alternatives. An Arab writer of the eighth century, Ibn Fazari, called Ghana the land of gold; he described its size as being equal to that of the Idrisid state of Morocco (*Kitab as-Sindhind al-Kabir*, cited in J. Spencer Trimingham, *A History of Islam in West Africa*, 1962). Ghana first appears on a map drawn by Al-Kwarizmi before 833 CE.

Ghana's wealth was based on an extensive trade network. Kumbi-Saleh was the centre of major trade caravans which brought salt from the Sahara and gold from the Wangara region. Camel caravans came from the north, trekking across the Sahara and laden with salt.

Donkey caravans were the most popular throughout the kingdom, while goods from the south were carried on the heads of porters. The waterways were also important, especially in later periods. Barges laden with goods sailed along the Senegal and Niger rivers, with Ghanaian authorities imposing a series of import and export taxes on the traffic. Each merchant, for example, typically paid one dinar of gold (a golden coin) in taxes before being allowed to bring one donkey-load of salt into Kumbi. Moreover, each merchant had to pay another two dinars in gold for the privilege of taking that same donkey-load of salt out of Kumbi. Thus, every time a donkey-load of salt passed through the capital, the Ghanaian treasury became three dinars richer. A dinar was equal to 72 grains of barley.

Ibn Khaldun, the celebrated historian of the fourteenth century, discussed the pre-eminence of the Ghanaian capital as follows:

> *At the time of the conquest of Northern Africa [that is, by the Arabs and between 639 and 708] some merchants penetrated into the western part of the land of the Blacks and found among them no king more powerful than the king of Ghana. His states extended westwards to the shores of the Atlantic Ocean.*
>
> **Ibn Khaldun, *Histoire des Berbères et des dynasties musulmanes de l'Afrique Septentrionale* (trans. Baron de Slane), 1856/1954, quoted in Cheikh Anta Diop, *Precolonial Black Africa*, trans. Harold J. Salemson, 1987**

He adds that its capital city:

> *was made up of two towns…and formed one of the greatest and best populated cities in the world.*

Early in the ninth century, the Sanhaja Berbers challenged Ghanaian power. They inhabited the northern frontier of Ghana and therefore controlled much of the Saharan trade between Ghana and North Africa. Audoghast was a key city in their possession. The Berbers raided Ghana's northern provinces, drawing on some 10,000 camel-mounted soldiers as they sought to disrupt the salt trade to Kumbi-Saleh. However, the Soninkes managed to re-establish control over their frontier areas. A century later they seized Audoghast from the Berbers.

In the tenth century an Arab geographer, Ibn Haukal, who was born in today's Turkey and wrote a book called *Surat al-Ard* in 977, visited this region and saw for himself the scale of the trans-Saharan trade. He was amazed at the enormous transactions of merchants in the region, describing a cheque for 42,000 golden dinars written to a merchant in Audoghast by his partner in Sidjilmessa. Ibn Haukal also informs us that the King of Ghana was 'the richest king on the face of the earth' (*Surat al-Ard*, cited in J. Spencer Trimingham, *A History of Islam in West Africa*, 1962). His pre-eminence was due to the quantity of gold nuggets amassed by himself and by his predecessors.

In Spain, another geographer called Al-Bakri wrote *The Book of the Roads and Kingdoms*. Written in 1067, a year after the Battle of Hastings, it contains a vivid narrative on ancient Ghana. Kumbi-Saleh had a royal town known to Muslims as Al-Ghaba, meaning 'forest' or 'grove'. Encircled by a wall was the king's castle and domed buildings, along with a Royal Court of Justice. Close to the court stood a mosque, built for visiting Muslims. Outside Al-Ghaba itself was a guarded area of cottages, groves and coverts where the traditional priests kept their icons. Prisons and royal cemeteries were also on this site. The second town, originally six miles away from Al-Ghaba, was a Muslim quarter that included 12 mosques. Each institution had its own imams, muezzins and recitors, with one mosque functioning as the Friday congregational mosque. Eventually the space between the two towns became filled with suburbs, creating a large city. Stone houses graced suburbia, standing in gardens. Other buildings were of stone with beams of acacia wood.

Al-Bakri also alludes to the city's intellectual activity, driven by lawyers and scholars. So enduring was this academic reputation that Al-Sadi, the distinguished seventeenth-century chronicler, referred to Kumbi in retrospect as not only a centre of trade caravans, but also 'the resort of the learned, the rich, and the pious of all nations' (according to Lady Lugard's *A Tropical Dependency* where Lugard says the passage was 'according to the author of the *Tarikh-es-Soudan*'). Of metropolitan colour and fashions, Al-Bakri described wrappers of cotton, silk or brocade worn by the populace, their incomes determining who could afford to wear what.

Emperor Tunka Menin was the ruler at the time. His court showed an opulent level of wealth, as Al-Bakri observed:

> *When he gives audience to his people he sits in a pavilion around which stand his horses caparisoned in cloth of gold: behind him stand ten pages holding shields and gold-mounted swords: and on his right hand are the sons of the princes of his empire, splendidly clad and with gold plaited into their hair. The governor of the city is seated on the ground in front of the king, and all around him are his ministers in the same position. The gate of the chamber is guarded by dogs of an excellent breed, who never leave the king's seat: they wear collars of gold and silver.*
>
> **Al-Bakri, quoted in Basil Davidson,**
> ***Old Africa Rediscovered*, 1959**

The city of Audoghast was originally independent of Ghana, but it was captured in 990. Al-Bakri informs us that it was a prosperous caravan centre, large and densely populated, with some of its people coming from far-off Spain. A place of wealth and comfort, it had very elegant houses, fine public buildings and several mosques. Meat was plentiful, the pastures surrounding the city being well stocked with meat and cattle. The rich cultivated wheat as a garden crop, but everybody else grew dhurra, a rice-like substance. At its markets, and also at Kumbi-Saleh, it was possible to buy wheat imported from the north, along with cattle, sheep and honey from the south and various food products from elsewhere. Merchants imported robes from Morocco and red and blue blouses from Moorish Spain. Goods changed hands on the receipt of gold dust, gold coins, cowrie shells or salt.

Further west, in the region of the Senegal River, were the city-states of Tekrur and Silla. The relationship of these cities to the Ghanaian Empire is unclear, but these cities appear to have enjoyed a semi-independent status. Tekrur probably dates to around the first century BCE. By the time written records become available, it ruled over a sizeable portion of the Senegal River region. According to Al Bakri, these city-states

> *like the rest of the Negroes, were once pagan…until the reign of War-Jabi, son of Rabis. This king joined Islam and introduced Islamic law. He enforced the religion upon his subjects… He died in…A.D. 1040/1.*
>
> **Al-Bakri, quoted in J. Spencer Trimingham,**
> ***A History of Islam in West Africa,* 1962**

Concerning Silla, he noted that 'its people are Muslims, having been converted by War-Jabi'. Moreover, 'it is an extensive and populous kingdom, almost equal to that of Ghana. The means of exchange of the inhabitants of Silla are dura, salt, brass rings and fine cotton strips'.

The Almoravides, a veil-wearing, hard-line Islamic movement, posed the first serious threat to the power of Ghana. The Ghanaian Emperor, after all, had a standing army of 200,000 soldiers with 40,000 cavalry at his disposal (by contrast England, in 1066, had only 15,000 soldiers at its disposal). However, Ghanaian rule over Tekrur and the city of Audoghast made enemies for the empire in these dependencies, and this would later rebound on Ghana.

Sometime around 1020, a Berber ruler of Audoghast converted to Islam. Yahya, his successor, made a pilgrimage to Mecca where he met the Islamic cleric Ibn Yasin. Yahya invited the cleric to return to Africa with him to evangelize among the Berbers. It didn't work. The Berbers exiled Ibn Yasin, who was forced to flee to Tekrur. There he founded his Islamic movement: the Almoravids. Berber and Tekrur converts flocked to his standard, fired up both by Islam and revenge. The Berbers wanted Audoghast to be independent of the non-Islamic rule of Ghana. On the other hand, the Tekrur wanted their independence from Ghana. A match had been made. By 1055 the Almoravides wrested Audoghast from Ghanaian rule. By 1062 they had founded the city of Marrakesh in Morocco. In 1076 they declared Holy War on Ghana and sacked Kumbi-Saleh. Finally, the Almoravides conquered Spain and established a ruling dynasty there.

However, Almoravid rule over the empire of Ghana collapsed in 1087. Ghana returned to Soninke leadership which sparked a brief renaissance, though some of the Empire's dependencies had become independent. Al-Idrissi, a Moorish geographer who worked at the court of Sicily, described this period in *The Book of Roger*, written in 1153. At this time the residence of the Ghanaian emperor was a well-built castle; constructed in 1116, it was thoroughly fortified, decorated inside with sculptures and pictures, and adorned with glass windows. Moreover, Al-Idrissi gave a picture of the Wangara region of Ghana:

> *In the country of Wangara there are flourishing cities and renowned fortresses, its inhabitants are wealthy; they possess gold in abundance, and receive the products brought to them from the other remotest portions of the earth. They attire themselves in robes and other kinds of raiment.*
>
> **Al-Idrissi, *The Book of Roger* (*Idrissi géographe*, trans. Amédée Jaubert, 1836), quoted in Cheikh Anta Diop, *Precolonial Black Africa*, trans. Harold J. Salemson, 1987**

However, the attempted Islamicization by the Almoravides left a major mark on Ghanaian culture which became – and remains – a feature of West African politics. Traditional and Islamic cultures were not always compatible, and by the twelfth century the empire had broken up. Some kingdoms, such as Mali and the city-state of Tekrur, became independent of the empire. In 1180 some Soninkes established a rival kingdom to Ghana, ruling from the city of Sosso. In the early thirteenth century the Sosso launched raids on Kumbi-Saleh, but both were soon faced with a more menacing rival in the newly rising power of Mali. By 1240 the Malians had destroyed both the Sosso kingdom and the Ghanaian capital. The fall of Kumbi-Saleh ended an era in history; the old capital, later abandoned, became a lost city.

However, in 1914, during the French colonial era, one Bonnel de Mezières, a French district officer, dug into a site suggested to him by locals. There he found sarcophagi, tombs of great dimensions, metallurgical workshops and ruins of towers. Subsequent excavations revealed a public square and ruined houses of excellent masonry with basements, upper floors, staircases and connecting halls. One house had nine rooms. Also excavated was The Great Mosque, which could comfortably have held 2,000 people.

THE EMPIRE OF MALI

Medieval Mali was the second major empire in West Africa. It began as a kingdom under ancient Ghanaian rule in 800 CE, with its rulers taking the title of Mansa. However, Mali turned the tables on Ghana. In 1240, led by Sundiata Keita, they seized Ghana's capital Kumbi-Saleh and destroyed it. After these military actions, Sundiata returned to the ruins of Djeriba, his capital city, and received the sworn loyalty of the rulers of the conquered people. The ceremony was triumphant and impressive; the Emperor of Ghana was allowed to retain the title of king, with the other former rulers receiving new titles. The Malians became the new masters of the gold and salt trade and their language and culture, Mandinka – another Niger-Congo culture – came to dominate the region.

Later, the Malians opened the copper mines of Takedda to provide an additional source of revenue. Chroniclers of the time attested to the importance of the trade. Ibn Khaldun, the most important of the medieval historians, wrote that camel caravans trekked across the Sahara by way of the Hoggar mountains, one of half a dozen well-used trade roads. Each year no fewer than 12,000 camels were counted on one of the routes. At its height in the fourteenth century, Mali included the lands now called Senegal, Gambia, Mauretania and Niger. It was, in short, the second largest empire in the world of the fourteenth century, comparable in size to all of Western Europe combined.

Ibn Battuta, the famous Muslim travel writer of the Middle Ages, described the Malians favourably. In his work, he noted that they

> *are seldom unjust, and have a greater abhorrence of injustice than any other people. Their sultan shows no mercy to anyone who is guilty of the least act of it. There is complete security in their country. Neither traveller nor inhabitant in it has anything to fear from robbers or men of violence.*
>
> **Ibn Battuta, *Travels in Asia and Africa*, trans. H.A.R. Gibb, 1929**

Sundiata never took to the battlefield again. Devoting his time instead to economic and social development of the empire, he turned his armies into farmers and encouraged a programme of agricultural expansion. The soldiers grew cotton, peanuts and grains, and were also encouraged to raise poultry and cattle. Sundiata also founded a new capital city called Niani, located on the confluence of the Upper Niger and Sankarini rivers. There were other military actions, but Sundiata's generals led them. The Malians conquered lands to the east, the southern forest belt and the northern desert regions, marching as far as the Atlantic. These conquests led to Malian control of the goldfields of Wangara and created the trade route from these to the new capital of Niani.

In 1285 a freed slave declared himself Mansa of Mali, Mansa Sakura. His armies fought against Tekrur and raided the Gao area; they may also have pacified Takedda, a centre famous for copper production. The empire became prosperous under his reign, attracting merchants from the Middle East and elsewhere in Africa to trade. However, in 1300 Sakura was assassinated in Somalia after returning from a religious pilgrimage. In 1999 the BBC produced an outstanding television series entitled *Millennium*, based around the historical scholarship of the Oxford historian Dr Felipe Fernandez-Armesto. The programme devoted to the fourteenth century opens with the following observation:

> *In the fourteenth century, the century of the scythe, natural disasters threaten civilizations with extinction. The Black Death kills more people in Europe, Asia and North Africa than any catastrophe has before. Civilizations which avoid the plague thrive. In West Africa the Empire of Mali becomes the richest in the world.*

A Syrian scholar, Ibn Fadl Al-Umari, published *Masalik ab Absar fi Mamalik al Amsar* (a book on how Egypt and Syria were administrated during the Mamluke period of Egypt) in Cairo around 1342. The tenth chapter of his work includes an account of two significant maritime expeditions, ordered in 1312 by the king who proceeded Mansa Musa to the Malian throne. This mariner king is not named by Al-Umari, but modern writers have identified him as Mansa Abubakari II. According to Al-Umari, this king sent 200 ships filled with men and a further 200 ships amply stocked with enough food, gold and water to last for two years. The king despatched them on a mission to explore the extremity of the Atlantic Ocean. Eventually, just one ship returned. Its captain told the Malian king of his adventures.

'"Prince", he replied, "we sailed for a long time, up to the moment when we encountered in mid-ocean something like a river with a violent current. My ship was last. The others sailed on, and gradually as each of them entered this place, they disappeared and did not come back. We did not know what had happened to them. As for me, I returned to where I was and did not enter that current."'

Recorded by Al-Umari in *Masalik ab Absar fi Mamalik al Amsar*, quoted by Davidson, cited by John Jackson, *Introduction to African Civilizations*, 1994

The Mansa decided to see for himself. He had 2,000 prepared, of which 1,000 were equipped with provisions. They set sail across the Atlantic with a large party – but never returned. Abubakari II left Mansa Musa I in charge of the empire.

Does this account imply that the Malians visited the Americas in 1311? This was 181 years before Christopher Columbus reached the continent. We shall never know.

However, it is well known that Columbus himself believed this. Columbus, to give just one example, reported that he acquired metal goods of West African manufacture from the Native Americans. Other evidence of this possible African voyage comes from an analysis of maps. Old maps of the Mexico region, drawn by Europeans, show that the Malians renamed places in the region after themselves. Names such as Mandinga Port, Mandinga Bay and Sierre de Mali exist as place names. Moreover, two skeletons of Negro males have been recovered from a grave in Hull Bay, close to the Danish Virgin Islands. Dated at 1250, this is only 61 years away from the period of the proposed Malian visit.

In addition, an old inscription was discovered at the bottom of a waterfall in the Reef Bay Valley, not too far from where the African skeletons were found. This inscription was written in an old African script called Tifinagh. Originally of ancient Libyan origin, a Berber group in Mali used this script. The text translates as: 'Plunge in to cleanse yourself. This is water for purification before prayer'. Finally, the scholarly art historian, Count Alexander von Wuthenau, directed attention to fourteenth-century carvings that were found in the Americas. These sculptures, made by Native Americans, show men, clearly African; some have tattoo marks cut into their cheeks. This art may well depict people from Mali.

Mansa Musa I, who ascended the throne in 1312, was perhaps the most colourful personality in West African history. Of this monarch, the Ghanaian economist and historian Dr DeGraft-Johnson wrote that:

> *It was in 1324...that the world awoke to the splendour and grandeur of Mali. There across the African desert, and making its way to Mecca, was a caravan of a size which had never before been seen, a caravan consisting of 60,000 men. They were Mansa Musa's men, and Mansa Musa was with them. He was not going to war: he was merely going to worship at Mecca.*
> **Dr DeGraft-Johnson, *African Glory*, 1954**

The caravan included a personal retinue of 12,000 slaves, all dressed in brocade and Persian silk. Musa himself rode on horseback, directly preceded by 500 slaves, each carrying a staff of gold. Then came Mansa Musa's baggage-train of 80 camels, each carrying 300 pounds weight of gold dust. The caravan made its way from Niani on the Upper Niger to Walata. From there it went to Tuat, and then on to Cairo. Mansa Musa's piety and open-handed generosity, the fine clothes and good behaviour of his followers combined quickly to make a good impression. However, in Egypt Musa spent so much money in gold that he devastated that nation's economy. Gold lost its value in the Middle Eastern nations for several years due to Musa I's spending.

In 2000 Cynthia Crossen, senior editor of the prestigious financial newspaper *The Wall Street Journal*, wrote in her book *The Rich and How They Got That Way*:

> *You've heard about the extraordinary wealth of Bill Gates, J.P. Morgan, and the Sultan of Brunei, but have you heard of Mansa Musa, one of the richest men who ever lived?*

She adds that:

> *Neither producer nor inventor, Mansa Musa was an early broker, greasing the wheels of intercultural trade. He created wealth by making it possible for others to buy and sell.*

In October 2012 newspapers reported new research that estimated the net worth of the 25 richest people in all human history. They ranked Musa I top of the list, with a net worth equal to $400 billion. He was famously depicted on a 1375 Spanish map, holding a golden coin in one hand and a Fleur de Lys sceptre in the other.

Ferbers (a type of government official) oversaw the provinces that made up Mali. The chief municipalities were ruled by inspectors, known as mocrifs. In the provinces, merchants and their caravans could move around freely with little to fear from banditry. There were also vassal kingdoms not under direct imperial rule, such as

Djenné. During the time of Musa I, between 13 and 24 of these semi-independent kingdoms existed, all in alliance with the empire. The Mansa maintained a standing army of 100,000 men, of whom ten per cent were cavalry, mounted on camels and horses.

Musa I hired a Spanish architect to build the Hall of Audience in Niani, which had an interior door leading to the royal palace. It was an admirable monument surmounted by a dome, adorned with arabesques of striking colours. The windows of an upper floor were plated with wood and framed in silver foil, while those of a lower floor were plated with wood, framed in gold. In Timbuktu, the great university city, Musa I commissioned indigenous architects to build the Djinguerebere Mosque; this is still a city landmark, and still in use today. During this period there was an extraordinary level of urban living. In his 1989 work *Architecture Soudanaise*, Sergio Domian, an Italian art and architecture scholar, commented:

Thus was laid the foundation of an urban civilization. At the height of its power Mali had at least 400 cities, and the interior of the Niger Delta was very densely populated.

According to UNESCO, Mali in the fourteenth century had a population of 50 million people.

In 1351, during the reign of Mansa Suleiman, Ibn Battuta, the most acclaimed traveller of the age, visited Mali. His account of this visit, *Travels in Asia and Africa*, is not only a classic, but it also contains the best eyewitness details of life in Mali at this time. On Fridays the Mansa held festivals after the late afternoon prayers, as Ibn Battuta observed:

The men-at-arms come with wonderful weaponry: quivers of silver and gold, swords covered with gold, their sheaths of the same, spears of silver and gold and wands of crystal. Four of

> *the* amirs *stand behind him to drive off flies, with ornaments of silver in their hands which look like riding stirrups. The commanders, the judge and the preacher sit according to custom, the interpreter Dugha brings in his [i.e. the Mansa's] four wives and his concubines, who are about one hundred in number. On them are fine clothes and on their heads they have bands of silver and gold with silver and gold apples as pendants. A chair is set there for Dugha to sit on and he beats an instrument which is made of reeds with tiny calabashes below it, praising the Sultan, recalling in his song his expeditions and deeds. The wives and the concubines sing with him and they play with bows. There are with them about thirty of his pages wearing red woollen robes and white caps on their heads. Each one of them has a drum tied to him and he beats it. Then come his retinue of young men who play and turn in the air, as they do in India. They have a wonderful gracefulness and lightness in this. They juggle with swords beautifully and Dugha performs a marvellous game with a sword. At that point the Sultan orders that a gift be given him, and they bring him a purse of two hundred* mithqals *of gold dust.*
>
> **Ibn Battuta, *Travels in Asia and Africa*, quoted in Said Hamdun and Noël King, *Ibn Battuta in Black Africa*, 1994**

Civil war broke out on the death of Mansa Suleiman, lasting nine months. Mari Jata II became king in 1360 after defeating Qasa, his rival. Mari Jata II cultivated the friendship of the court of Morocco. He sent them a giraffe, which created a stir after making a precarious journey across the Sahara. Mari Jata II also maintained friendly relations with Egypt. However, severe economic problems emerged during his reign. The king sold the largest golden nugget in the government's possession to Egyptian merchants for a knock-down price, a sale that bankrupted the treasury. Interestingly, the world-famous nugget in question had come from the Ghanaian emperor's treasure chest hundreds of years before. In 1374 Mansa Musa II succeeded him on paper, but in practice played very little political role. Keeping the Mansa in seclusion, the prime minister, yet another Mari Jata, ruled the empire. He suppressed a Tuareg rebellion in Takedda and commanded raids on Gao. Mari Jata was the last great ruler of Mali, and after him things fell apart.

With Magan III's accession in 1390, Mali began to fragment. First the Soninke state of Diara threw off the Mali yoke, then, in about 1400, the Mossi of Burkina Faso plundered deep into Masina while the Songhai began to occupy Mali territory. The Tuareg seized the commercial centres of Arawan, Walata and Timbuktu in about 1433, ruining what remained of Mali's control of the trans-Saharan trade.

THE SONGHAI EMPIRE

S**onghai was the** third major empire in West Africa, taking over from that of Mali. At its height in the sixteenth century, the empire controlled West Africa's two major waterways: the Senegal and the Niger rivers. Barges able to carry up to 80 people sailed these waterways. Ultimately, Songhai ruled over a vast area comprising today's Senegal, Gambia, Guinea, Mauritania, Mali, Niger and Northern Nigeria.

However, the Songhai people had a documented history before the sixteenth century. During the time when ancient Ghana dominated West Africa, a line of Songhai dynasts ruled from the city of Kukiya. This line of kings, known as the Zuwa Dynasty, held power from 690 to 1335, avoiding the clutches of ancient Ghana, but succumbing to conquest by the Mali Empire. Furthermore, we can name the 31 rulers of this dynasty. Gao, another Songhai-speaking city, was very important. One Arab chronicler in the ninth century called it 'the greatest sovereignty of the Negroes, the most important and influential, to whom the other kingdoms pay allegiance'. Tim Insoll, an archaeologist from St John's College, Cambridge, carried out important excavations in Gao in 1993. A particularly intriguing find was an artefact entitled 'Fragments of alabaster window surrounds and a piece of pink window glass, Gao, 10th–14th century'.

During the Second Dynasty period in Songhai, known as the Sonni Dynasty, the Songhai made themselves independent of Malian imperial rule. Sonni Ali, the eighteenth ruler of this dynasty, assumed power over the Songhai kingdom in 1464. His armies captured Timbuktu, with its famous University of Sankore Mosque, in 1469. Djenné was the next city to fall, after a siege that lasted over seven years. This city was an even greater prize, offering links to international commerce, a university and the most outstanding architecture of the region. It was conquered by Sonni Ali's forces in around 1473. To the south lay the kingdoms of the Mossi, an enemy of the Songhai. In 1480 they launched a raid on the Songhai city of Walata, besieging the city for a month and forcing it to capitulate. The victorious Mossi seized people and booty from Walata. Soon afterwards, in 1483, Sonni Ali's army successfully drove this threat out of the kingdom. Sonni Ali himself established the Songhai state as the third great West African empire in this region. After conquering most of the old Malian Empire, he became a famous ruler around the world. In November 1492 he was killed in a military campaign. He was mummified after his death, thus following very ancient African traditions.

Sonni Baru Dao, the son of Sonni Ali, was also a follower of traditional African religion. He rejected all attempts to convert him to Islam by Muslims in his empire. After several weeks of negotiations, with no conversion achieved, the Muslims overthrew him in April 1493. This brought Mohammed Touré, a former general, to lead the empire. He adopted the dynastic title 'Askiya', and everyone who followed him did the same. A devout Muslim, Askiya Mohammed I made a pilgrimage to Mecca in 1496, accompanied by 1,000 infantry and a cavalry detachment of 500 horsemen; he also took 300,000 gold pieces. In Mecca, Askiya met the Caliph of Egypt, the Pope of the Islamic Church. Askiya requested that the Caliph appoint him as his religious representative in West Africa, and the Caliph agreed. So it was that Askiya Mohammed returned to Gao in 1497 with a new title. He was now the Caliph of the Western Sudan, spiritual ruler of all West African Muslims.

The empire that Askiya had inherited from the Sonni Dynasty was already massive, yet he expanded it north, east and west by conquest. Ultimately the empire would cover an area about the same size as all of Europe. By 1514 Askiya's armies had captured the Hausa Confederation of Northern Nigeria. Next to capitulate was the city of Agadès in Niger, and finally the regions to the far west of the empire around the Atlantic. As the kingdom grew into an empire, Askiya Mohammed came up with new methods of government, establishing a strongly centralized administration. Among the most important posts were the Minister of the Treasury, the Minister of Tax Collection, the Minister of the Army and Navy and the Minister of Trade and Industry. In some territories the Askiya allowed the regional kings to rule as they had before, as long as they paid tribute. In other territories, the Askiya created a parallel post to the local governor called the *mondyo* (inspector), who formed the official link to the imperial Songhai government. Askiya Mohammed died in 1538 and was buried in a Step Pyramid at Gao. He is also known as Askiya the Great.

At this point, there were as many as 100,000 people living in Gao. According to Leo Africanus, a Moorish diplomat and author born in Granada, Spain, it was unwalled. Its houses were generally ugly, although a few, such as the royal buildings, were impressive. Most of the residents were wealthy merchants who frequently travelled between locations to trade goods and gold. Rice, meat and bread were abundant, as were cucumbers, melons and fine pumpkins; wells of fresh water were also plentiful. On market days, a busy slave market flourished.

Timbuktu had spacious houses, built of clay bricks, wood and plaster. The city also contained three famous mosques. The Djinguerebere Mosque, a strange, nine-storey structure with the appearance of a fortress, was built in the fourteenth century by the great Malian king, Mansa Musa I. There was also the University Mosque in which 25,000 students studied, and the Oratory of Sidi Yayia. In addition Timbuktu possessed around 165 Koran schools, in which 30,000 children received instruction. Factories also flourished, especially in the textile industry, which made goods of cotton cloth and linen. Some of these institutions employed up to 100 apprentices, working under the guidance of a master tailor. Leo Africanus provides the following information about life in the city:

> *In Timbuctoo there are numerous judges, doctors of letters and clerics, all receiving good salaries from the king. He pays great respect to men of learning. There is a big demand for books in*

manuscript, imported from North Africa. More profit is made from the book trade than any other line of business.
Leo Africanus, *A History and Description of Africa*, 1526, quoted in Walter Rodney, *The Groundings with my Brothers*, 1975

According to Mahmud Kati:

Timbuktu has no equal among the cities of the Blacks...and was known for its solid institutions, political liberties, purity of morals, security of its people and their goods, compassion towards the poor and strangers, as well as courtesy and generosity towards students and scholars.

Djenné was an eight-gated city, encircled by a rampart that could be approached only by crossing narrow streams and canals. Its buildings were attractive, consisting of houses of two storeys, indoor drainage systems and toilets. The Grand Mosque was outstanding. It was renovated in 1204 as a mosque, but began life as a palace in the eleventh century. The most iconic architectural piece in West Africa, replicas of it exist in Torremolinos, Spain; Jeju-do, South Korea; and Fréjus, France. Trade also flourished in Djenné, with gold and salt being brought to its markets. Following his visit there, Leo Africanus noted that golden coins were still used in the area:

The coinage used by these Blacks is unstamped gold.
Leo Africanus, as quoted in John O. Hunwick, *Timbuktu and the Songhay Empire: Al-Sadi's Tarikh al-Sudan down to 1613 and other Contemporary Documents*, 2003

They also used pieces of iron for the purchase of items of low value, such as milk, bread and honey.

In 1529 Askiya the Great was deposed by his son Musa, causing 20 years of instability. Askiya Daud became emperor in 1549, and his military victories restored Songhai control over trade routes to the north. Fighting broke out with the Mossi, the Fulani, the Malians, Kebbi and Katsina. Daud was so sure of the bravery and fighting ability of his soldiers that he sent a raiding party of just 24 horsemen to attack the Hausa city of Katsina. These resolute men hurled themselves at the 400 Katsina cavalrymen who had come out to engage them. Not surprisingly they were defeated. The struggle resulted in 15 of the horsemen being killed and the remaining nine were wounded and captured. However, the ruler of Katsina sent the nine men back to Daud with the message:

Men of such incomparable bravery do not deserve to die.
Cited in J.C. DeGraft-Johnson, *African Glory*, 1954

In 1556 the Moroccans attacked Taghaza. They killed the Songhai governor of the city, along with a number of Tuaregs working in the salt caravans. The surviving traders petitioned Daud to abandon Taghaza for safer pastures. In 1557 the Askiya opened a new salt mine in which the old salt traders found work.

In Morocco there were several sinister developments. In 1577 Al Mansur was the sultan, having deposed the Black ruler Sultan Mohammed XI. Al Mansur was seeking alliances to help build his kingdom even as Elizabeth I, the ruler of England, was looking for alliances to expand England into an empire. She secretly negotiated the supply of British timber to help build Morocco's navy, hoping in return that Morocco would help her to attack Spain. Al Mansur just wasn't interested; he wanted to fight in the south. His gaze landed on the prosperous Songhai Empire.

In Songhai, Askiya Daud ruled until his death in 1582. Civil wars followed his death, during which the Moroccans sent a spying mission to the country. In *Timbuctoo the Mysterious*, published in 1896, Major Dubois tells us that:

> *He [Al Mansur] sent an embassy in 1583, ostensibly charged with magnificent gifts, but in reality commissioned to reconnoitre the roads and principal towns [of Songhai] and to make a study of its army.*

Meanwhile Askiya El Hadj II received the embassy at Gao, but 'returned it laden with gifts of still greater splendour than those it had brought'. This proved to be a red rag to a bull.

Askiya Al-Hajj Mohammed II, victor of the civil war, ruled for four years. Mohammed Bano succeeded him and ruled for two years. Stability only returned in 1588, when Askiya Ishak II became emperor. West Africa's Golden Age was severely interrupted by an invasion from Morocco in 1591.

A Moroccan source informs us that Al Mansur spent many years convincing his Council of War of this massive project. Their main fear was the death toll involved in crossing the Sahara. After persuading the Council of War and engaging in further planning, he wrote to Elizabeth I on 23 June 1590, requesting England's assistance. The Queen was more than happy to supply soldiers and weapons, including artillery, cannonballs and guns. The possible rewards of looting the Songhai Empire for its gold seemed too great an opportunity to miss.

In October 1590 an army staffed with many Europeans left Morocco under Judar Pasha to invade Songhai. The army consisted of 2,000 soldiers, 1,500 lancers, 500 cavalry, 1,000 camel-men, 8,000 camels, 1,000 packhorses and 600 scouts. Presumably the other 7,000 camels were laden with artillery and supplies. Guarding Judar Pasha was a personal unit of 70 trained bodyguards. Numerous lives were lost on the journey across the desert. One-third of the army did not survive, but the remainder continued their surge towards Songhai. In February 1591 they reached the River Niger. Songhai scouts soon learned of the nature of the expedition and immediately raised the alarm. The Songhai War Council quickly assembled 18,000 cavalrymen and 9,700 soldiers, led by Askiya Ishak II. Songhai prepared to do battle. Despite being vastly outnumbered, Judar Pasha had the advantage, possessing guns, cannons and ammunition. Songhai had none of these weapons. As the war commenced, vast numbers were brutally slain.

After his initial victory, Judar Pasha pressed on. He sacked, pillaged and burned the cities of Djenné, Gao and Timbuktu to the ground. His army filled in water wells and destroyed fields of crops. Al-Sadi tells us that after the invasion:

> *The high cost of food...was excessive; a great number of people died from hunger and the famine was such that people ate the corpses of draught animals and of human beings. The exchange rate fell to 500 cowries. Then the plague came in turn to decimate the population and killed many that the famine had spared. This high cost of food, which lasted two years, ruined the inhabitants, who were reduced to selling their furniture and utensils. All the elders were unanimous in saying that they*

had never seen such a calamity and that not one of the elders before then had ever told them about anything like it.

Abdurrahman Al-Sadi, *History of the Sudan*, trans. O. Houdas, *Tarikh es-Soudan*, 1900, English translation adapted by Robin Walker

The troops from Morocco seized the professors from Sankore University in arrests that occurred towards the end of October 1593. The captured scholars were deported to Morocco in chains. Some of them were killed in a massacre along the way; many of those that survived were forced to serve the Moroccans, while others were imprisoned. The army also confiscated the libraries of the scholars. Professor Ahmed Baba, the head of the university, lost 1,600 books in this way, while other scholars with even larger libraries lost even more. In her book *A Tropical Dependency*, published in 1905, Lady Lugard commented that 'while other forms of wealth were greedily appropriated, the contents of the libraries were destroyed'. She went on to declare that the sack of Timbuktu 'was the signal for the letting loose of all the evils of lawless tyranny upon the country', after which the history of the region 'becomes a mere record of riot, robbery and decadence'.

THE MOSSI KINGDOMS

Mossi history may well date back to the eleventh century CE. Oral traditions identify a princess called Yennenga as the mother of the Mossi kingdoms. She was not indigenous to the region, but instead came from the Kingdom of Dambon, in present-day Ghana, as a royal exile. In her homeland Yennenga had a military background and had seen active service from the age of 14. Skilled with javelins and bows, she was a distinguished horsewoman and commander of her own battalion. Following a disagreement with her father, she escaped on horseback to the territory of the Mossi. En route she met a young hunter, Rialé, with whom she later had a child called Ouedraogo. He ultimately became the first Mossi king and the founder of Wagadugu in about 1050. However, Yennenga later returned with Rialé as the prodigal daughter to her homeland, the Kingdom of Dagbon. The elites in Dagbon supported and trained Ouedraogo. They also gave him cavalry, cattle and other goods which he used to found Wagadugu.

Wagadugu became the largest and most powerful of the Mossi kingdoms. Its king, known as the Mogho Naba, or King of All the World, served as the emperor of all the Mossi. Beneath the king of Wagadugu were 16 ministers and an imposing court. His morning audiences took the place of councils of state while his evening audiences became courts of law. Wagadugu is still important today; it is the capital of Burkina Faso and contains a famous statue of Yennenga. The princess is depicted in a dramatic attitude, wielding a javelin and a bow.

There were four other Mossi kingdoms of historic importance. These were Yatenga, to the north of Wagadugu, Fada-n-Gurma, to the east, Mamprusi, to the south, and Dagomba, even further south. Yatenga was founded in around 1170, and the three other kingdoms came into existence some time before 1500. All the kingdoms were independent, but each claimed descent from Ouedraogo, their common ancestor. All the Mossi kingdoms were ruled by kings known as Naba, supported by a council of dignitaries and military leaders who helped to centralize power. They remained suspicious of all external ideological influences and followed traditional religions. The kingdoms had large, well-trained armies, mounted on horseback. These armed forces were powerful enough to do battle with their neighbours to the north and west, the empires of Mali and Songhai. Mali and Songhai were the superpowers of the region.

The Mossi led an incursion into Songhai in the middle of the thirteenth century. They attempted to seize the city of Timbuktu in a campaign that lasted four months before they finally withdrew. In 1338 the Mossi attacked Timbuktu a second time. The event was described by a Timbuktu chronicle:

> *The sultan of the Mossi entered the town, pillaged it, set fire to it, reduced it to ruins and, after putting to death everyone he could lay hands on and seizing all the wealth he could find, he returned to his country.*
>
> **Abdurrahman Al-Sadi, *History of the Sudan*, trans. O. Houdas, *Tarikh es-Soudan*, 1900, English translation adapted by Robin Walker**

Another Timbuktu chronicle mentions a third raid by the Mossi against Mali, which took place just before 1433. In 1480 Naséré, ruler of the Mossi, marched northwest into the desert, then launched a raid on the Malian city of Walata. They besieged the city for a month, forcing Walata to surrender. The Mossi seized women and children, along with a large quantity of spoil. The Mossi forces then attempted to return home to the Volta region, but they were pursued by Omar, the former governor of Timbuktu. He overtook the Mossi forces and managed to rescue most of the women and children who had been abducted.

Six established trade caravan routes crisscrossed the Mossi territories, connecting the Mossi to other countries in Africa and, ultimately, to the rest of the world. It was thus common to see products made in one African country appearing in the markets of other African countries. Traders used lines of donkeys as beasts of burden to move goods to markets in and out of the Mossi territories. The Mossi kingdoms raised revenue by levying taxes on the produce of their farmers, on trading transactions, on the trading caravans and on foreign traders. The Mossi had industries in the tanning of leather, fine leatherwork, cotton textiles, basketry, lead and antimony, copperware, mats, jars, pots, pans, soap and dried fish. In the nineteenth century the breeding of donkeys and ponies became a significant trade. The animals were exported to markets elsewhere in Africa using the donkey caravans. Meanwhile the Mossi imported salt, coffee, tea, perfumes, carpets, fine robes, even items such as needles. Once again the goods entered their territories by trade caravans.

Ultimately the Mossi kingdoms were conquered and swallowed up by European colonialism. In 1888 a German army advanced to the Mossi borders, where it met an overwhelming show of force by the Mossi. The Germans retreated, but French forces were more successful, following a detailed reconnaissance mission conducted by Captain Binger. They led an army into Wagadugu in July 1896, seizing territory which became part of French West Africa, a huge landmass controlled from Paris. However, after independence in 1960, the Mossi territories became a large part of the nation of Upper Volta. In August 1984 Upper Volta changed its name to Burkina Faso. In his work 'African Empires and Civilizations', published in 1934 as part of *Negro: An Anthology*, Raymond Michelet provided a good summary of the Mossi achievement:

Between Songhai and the southern forests lies one of the most interesting of all the African empires, a genuine unalloyed Negro empire which always held aloof from all outside Mussulman influence, which was firmly organised and always lived on its own resources. Smaller than the empires of Gao, Ghana or Mali, it has outlived them thanks to its homogeneity and the soundness of its institutions.

THE EARLY HISTORY OF FRENCH WEST AFRICA

THE EARLY HISTORY OF NIGERIA

The British colonization of Nigeria began in the early nineteenth century. Initially British interest in Nigeria was driven by the transatlantic slave trade, for which they established coastal trading posts such as Lagos and Calabar. The British established formal control over Lagos in 1861. Through military conquest and strategic alliances with local rulers, Britain extended its dominance over the different kingdoms. By 1914 the regions had been formally unified into the Colony and Protectorate of Nigeria.

Lieutenant General Augustus Pitt Rivers was an English military man and archaeologist whose international collection of 22,000 objects became the founding collection of the University of Oxford's Pitt Rivers Museum. In 1900 he wrote a book on the Renaissance-era art seized from the Empire of Benin, the principal culture in southern Nigeria. The pieces had now come into Pitt Rivers's possession and his catalogue was called *Antique Works of Art from Benin*:

> *Benin is situated on the Guinea Coast, near the mouth of the Niger, in latitude 6° 12 north, and longitude 5 to 6 east. It was discovered by the Portuguese at the end of the fourteenth or commencement of the fifteenth centuries. The Portuguese were followed by the Dutch and Swedes, and in 1553 the first English expedition arrived on the coast, and established a trade with the king, who received them willingly. Benin at that time*

appears by a Dutch narrative to have been quite a large city, surrounded by a high wall, and having a broad street through the centre. The people were comparatively civilized. The king possessed a number of horses which have long since disappeared and become unknown.

Lady Lugard was a British aristocrat married to Sir Frederick Lugard, the first Governor-General of Nigeria. She had an interest in the history of the region, particularly the desert belt, and wrote A *Tropical Dependency* in 1905. In it she described the Hausa Confederation, the principal culture in Northern Nigeria, as follows:

The territory covered by Haussaland to-day stretches roughly from about 9° to 14° N. lat., and from 4° to 11° E. long., and it contains a population estimated at perhaps ten millions of people. No accurate census has as yet been made, and this estimate, lower than that usually given, is only approximate. The Haussa language, which is classed with Coptic amongst the Hamitic languages, is said to be more widely spoken than any other single native language in West Africa... Within historic times they have been known as divided into seven independent Haussa states, upon which certain other states, also largely peopled by Haussas, have been dependent. The seven original states were Biram, Gober, Kano, Rano, Zaria, Katsena, and Daura. Some of these have now sunk into insignificance. Some form still the most important provinces of Northern Nigeria. Though within any period of which we have record – dating for about a thousand years – these states have been independent of and generally hostile to each other, their own traditions point to a more ancient period when they were united in some form of federal bond.

During the early Colonial Period, missionaries opened schools in Igboland, Nigeria, to teach the natives English. Conversely, one such teacher, the Rev J.K. Macgregor, himself ended up being schooled. He said:

In a class I was teaching, a pupil deeply resented the statement that the civilisation of the people in Nigeria was primitive because they had no writing. He declared that they had a writing called nsibidi*. This happened in April, 1905. As I was at the beginning of a new term, I set myself to find out all I could about* nsibidi*… The few specimens I got were grossly misinterpreted to me so as to tone down their meaning. Still from them it was possible to see that here we have a genuine product of the native civilisation the origin of which is so old as to have become the subject of a* Märchen.

The Rev J.K. Macgregor, *Some Notes on Nsibidi*, in *The Journal of the Royal Anthropological Institute of Great Britain and Ireland*, Vol. 39, 1909

The script, however, was pictorial not alphabetical. Macgregor reproduced 97 symbols, but the correct figure was probably thousands. The scholarly world is aware of more than 600. This raises the question: how accurate was it for recording details? The Rev Macgregor tells us that:

The use of nsibidi *is that of ordinary writing. I have in my possession a copy of the record of a court case from a town on the Enion Creek taken down in it, and every detail, except the evidence, is most graphically described, – the parties in the case, the witnesses, the dilemma of the chief who tried it, his sending out messengers to call other chiefs to help him, the finding of the court and the joy of the successful litigants and of their friends are all told by the use of a few strokes.*

Macgregor, *Some Notes on Nsibidi*

Nsibidi originated from the Ekoi people, neighbours of the Efik and Ibibio ethnic groups in Nigeria. However, it was later adopted by the Igbos. Originally, *nsibidi* was used by select secret groups of men of power. One such secret society was the Ekpe Leopard Secret Society, still found in present-day Abia. With the transatlantic slave trade, *nsibidi* was exported to the Caribbean islands such as Cuba, taken by African captives. In the Marvel blockbuster, *Black Panther*, the African script used in Wakanda is a derivative of *nsibidi*. A key question is: how old is this writing system? Christopher Slogar, professor of art history at California State University, suggested this writing system goes back to the fifth century CE. In his own words:

The Calabar ceramics, incorporating such a great variety of discrete motifs – including arcs, arrows, chevrons, concentric circles, crosses, lozenges, spirals, and stars – evidence an iconography readily comparable to nsibidi. *Moreover, the decoration found on the anthropomorphic figurines suggests that ancient people may have embellished their own bodies in a manner similar to the use of modern* nsibidi *and other motifs as body decoration. Hence, a close study of the archaeological ceramics, which span the period from the fifth to the fifteenth century* CE, *provides some historical depth to this important visual tradition.*

Christopher Slogar, *Early Ceramics from Calabar, Nigeria,* in *African Arts,* Spring 2007

THE DUFUNA CANOE

The Dufuna Canoe was the oldest boat discovered in Africa, dating to 6000 or 6500 BCE. A local man of Fulani origins discovered it by chance in 1987. Mallam Ya'u stumbled upon the canoe while digging a well on 4 May 1987. Digging near the village of Dufuna in Yobe State, North East Nigeria, Mr Ya'u came across a hard object, buried in the ground at 177⅛ inches deep. He reported the discovery to his village chief.

In 1989 and 1990 the University of Maiduguri, Nigeria, carried out a preliminary study. Professors Garba Abubakar and Peter Breunig returned to the location as part of a collaborative study, supported by the universities of Maiduguri and Frankfurt. In 1994 they excavated the site, involving two weeks of digging by 50 labourers. The canoe, made of African mahogany, was found to be 330¾ inches long, 19¾ inches wide and 2 inches thick.

Radiocarbon dating of a charcoal sample close to the site has dated the canoe to between 8,500 and 8,000 years ago. It is the third-oldest boat in the world ever discovered, with only the dugouts from Noyen-sur-Seine, France, and Pesse, in Holland, being older. At Iho-Eleeru Cave in Western Nigeria, evidence of flint cutting and carving tools that could have been used to make the boat was found. These tools date back to 9200 BCE. The bow and stern of the canoe had been skilfully worked to points, and the work was probably done with core axe-like and pick-axe bifacial tools of microlithic appearance.

The boat would have been used on Lake Mega Chad. As one commentator said: 'It equally gives concrete evidence of transportation by seas as well as providing evidence of some form of long distance commercial activities indicative of existing political and economic structures' (Afolasade A. Adewunmi, 'Dufuna Canoe Find: Birthing the Underwater Cultural Heritage in Nigeria', in *University of Ibadan Journal of Public and International Law*, Vol. 4, 2014). Research by an American science team in 2015 found that Lake Chad had shrunk by 95 per cent over the last 40 years. This implies that in the distant past the Dufuna region would have been part of the lake's flood plain.

Professor Breunig of the University of Frankfurt is reported in the above article as saying that the canoe's age 'forces a reconsideration of Africa's role in the history of water transport'. It shows, he observes, 'that the cultural history of Africa was not determined by Near Eastern and European influences but took its own, in many cases parallel, course'. Moreover, as he noted, 'The bow and stern are both carefully worked to points, giving the boat a notably more elegant form', compared to 'the dugout made of conifer wood from Pesse in the Netherlands, whose blunt ends and thick sides seem crude'.

Professor Breunig stated that the canoe's construction ability had evolved over time and that it was not a new design. He explained, 'It is highly probable that the Dufuna boat does not represent the beginning of a tradition, but had already undergone a long development, and that the origins of water transport in Africa lie even further back in time'. The canoe is currently housed in Damaturu, the Yobe State capital.

OLDEST IRON-SMELTING SITE IN THE WORLD

In Lejja, 9¼ miles south of Nsukka in South East Nigeria, archaeologists found the world's oldest iron-smelting site. Hundreds of smelting debris, recently radiocarbon dated to over 2000 BCE, were discovered by scholars from the universities of Nigeria, Nsukka and Oxford. However, this information upset the status quo as far as the global story of ironworking is concerned. For many years, conventional academic wisdom taught that the Iron Age started in Southwest Asia and spread to the rest of the world. However, the African evidence is older.

In an academic paper of 2023 titled 'Science, Not Black Magic: Metal and Glass Production in Africa', Foreman Bandama and Abidemi Babatunde Babalola addressed this issue. They found that the beginnings of iron production had multiple centres of origin in West, East and Central Africa. Discoveries of iron-smelting sites in Lejja, in the Nsukka region, were dated from between 2631 and 2458 BCE. Discoveries of ironworking in Obui in the Central African Republic were dated from between 2136 and 1921 BCE. Other early iron discoveries were made in Niger and Togo. Since none of these sites are near the African coasts, these must relate to indigenous technologies.

NOK AND IGBO CULTURES

In 1928 Lieutenant-Colonel J. Dent Young, an Englishman, led tin mining operations in the Nigerian village of Nok in the Jos region. As these were carried out, one of the miners found a small terracotta piece resembling a monkey's head. Other finds included a terracotta human head and a foot. Young subsequently arranged for these artefacts to be placed in a museum in Jos. In 1942 another artefact belonging to this culture was found – this time in Jemaa, 24 miles away. This find was brought to the attention of Bernard Fagg, an English cadet administrative officer who had a background as an archaeologist. Fagg wrote about his discovery, and about other finds in the region, in the mid-1940s. By that time the ancient culture was referred to as the Nok culture, named after the village in which the small terracotta monkey's head had been discovered. Since then around 400 pieces of Nok art have been recovered, mostly associated with elite burials widely distributed across the country. They had been sculpted between 1000 and 300 BCE.

Made of terracotta, the artefacts are mostly human statues. Ranging in height from a few inches high to almost life-size, they are shown wearing rows of bracelets, necklaces, skullcaps and, in at least one instance, a cape. The coiffeurs of the hair are inventive, featuring highly individual plaits, ridges, locks and buns. The sculptors of these figures experimented with geometric shapes including conical, spherical or cylindrical heads. Moreover, these are the oldest known art pieces sculpted in African proportions – an aesthetic in which the statue's head is one-quarter or one-third the size of the body. One authority distinguishes five styles of Nok art. These were the Jemaa style, the Kuchamfa style, the Katsina Ala style and two peripheral styles that may even suggest two new and separate civilizations – the Sokoto style and the Katsina style. Statues of elephants, monkeys, ticks and snakes were all made, as well as human-animal combinations.

The Nok culture was part of Niger-Congo heritage. Their artwork is significant, since this culture was the first to evolve terracotta art from the older Niger-Congo tradition of wooden sculptures.

Moreover, since terracotta ceramic-making and terracotta sculpture are perceived in this culture as a female preserve, most authorities believe that female artists were responsible for this art tradition. It was highly regarded, with kings and elite figures patronizing this art.

Agriculture laid the basis of the Nok culture. Grindstones were used to pound grain, and two statues depict a farmer carrying a tool, possibly an axe or a hoe slung over the shoulder. Oil-bearing seeds called atili were cultivated to extract oil from them; yams and millet were also cultivated. Iron technology dated at least as far back as 500 BCE. Archaeologists have found smelting tuyeres, pieces of furnace walls, iron slag and objects of wrought iron.

In 1938 a major discovery took place in Onitsha Province in Eastern Nigeria, when Isaiah Anozie discovered leaded bronze art and craft pieces. Once again, these pieces were discovered by accident. While attempting to dig a water cistern in his back yard, Mr Anozie discovered remnants of a long-lost Igbo civilization. Following this find, archaeological campaigns on his brother's lands yielded even more artefacts. The quality of the pieces discovered were astonishing. One archaeologist declared the jewellery to be as fine as that made by Carl Fabergé.

The Igbo themselves are part of the Benue-Kwa branch of Niger-Congo culture. In the ninth and tenth centuries CE they created a state ruled by a priest king called the Eze Nri. The priest's authority rested on his role as intermediary between the people and the ancestral and territorial spirits. It was not based on military force or earthly power.

The Nri patronized leaded bronze sculptors. The burials contained more than 700 artworks, exquisitely cast in bronze, copper and copper alloys. Among the finds were pendants, copper chains, wristlets, staff ornaments, vessels resembling seashells, drinking cups, cooking woks, sword scabbards, and a copper altar stand, all contributing to a picture of opulence. Also found were fly whisks, used by kings or high priests. Historians thus believe that these treasures belonged to elite burials.

Professor Ehret suggests (in *The Civilizations of Africa*, 2016) calling this culture 'the Nri state'. It flourished along the northern fringe of the rainforest belt, east of the middle parts of the lower Niger River. Igbo-Ukwu, the site of the burials, was the capital. Since the Igbo territories lacked a source of copper, trans-Saharan trade caravans could have brought the copper to this capital from the north. In return, the Nri state exported ivory, pepper, kola nuts and spices north to the Saharan states. Horses could well have been used to conduct this trade. However, some speculate that the source of the copper was the Katanga District in Congo, since there was no barrier to importing copper from there into the Nigeria region. Finally trade caravans connected Igbo Ukwu to lands farther afield. In the burials were 165,000 glass beads of foreign manufacture. Some were Indian-made, while others may have come from Venice in southern Europe.

In the thirteenth century the Igbos created a city-state called the Igala Kingdom. Located west of the confluence of the Niger and Benue rivers, in woodland savannah country, its capital was at Idah. The Nris continued to exercise spiritual power, but a new type of political system emerged. Kings emerged, able to muster armed forces, and cavalry became an important part of their power. This kingdom remained connected to that of the Nri state, with its rulers continuing to be crowned by Nri kingmakers – a practice that continued into the twentieth century. At some point before the mid-fifteenth century (we don't know exactly when), the Igala Kingdom conquered Nupe, to the northwest. The victors made the conquered people pay tribute of one male member per family, to be sent as a slave to the Igala rulers. However, in the fifteenth century King Tsoede of Nupe ended Igala dominance.

THE YORUBA CITY-STATES AND EREDO

On 23 May 1999 *The Sunday Times* carried an article entitled 'Jungle reveals traces of Sheba's fabled kingdom'. The article told of an archaeological campaign that a Bournemouth University archaeological team had been conducting since 1994. Led by Dr Patrick Darling, they mapped the remains of a Nigerian site previously covered by centuries of forest overgrowth. A BBC journalist described the discoveries as possibly 'Africa's largest single monument'. The team discovered a huge earthen wall with moated sections which encircled a city. From the base of the ditch to the summit of the rampart measured a towering 70 feet. The rampart was 100 miles long and formed a rough circle, enclosing a staggering 400 square miles. Within the walls a three-storey ruin with living quarters, shrines and courtyards was tentatively identified as the royal palace. Radiocarbon dating established that the buildings and walls dated back to 800 CE.

The builders shifted 3.5 million cubic metres of earth to build just the rampart alone. This is one million more man-hours than were required to build the Great Pyramid of Giza. Yoruba people who live near the ruined city say that a wealthy and childless queen, Bilikisu Sungbo, built the city. Some believe that she had it built as a religious offering.

The Yoruba themselves are part of the Benue-Kwa branch of Niger-Congo culture. Beginning in the eighth or ninth centuries CE, they created city-states ruled by kings titled *Oni* or *Oba*. Though Eredo was certainly the largest, Ife became the most influential.

Ife was a manufacturing centre for glass beads and the home of a vibrant brass sculptural tradition. It was also the city-state to which the other Yoruba looked as their culture's ancestral home. The centre of trade routes, the people of Ife imported horses, salt, copper and brass from the Saharan states, paid for by the export of large crops of kola nuts and cloth. Textiles were also an important industry. In the mid-nineteenth century William Clarke, an English visitor to the city, remarked that: 'As good an article of cloth can be woven by the Yoruba weavers as by any people, and for durability far excel the prints and homespuns of Manchester' (William H. Clarke, *Travels and Explorations in Yorubaland 1854–1858*, ed. J.A. Atanda, 1972). But how far back in time does this industry go? Mrs Euba of the University of Ife explains that:

> *By the time of the ancient Ifes, weaving on the vertical loom was more extensive in the cotton-growing areas. From the bronzes of Ife and Benin...we may picture a basic style of dress which makes use of draped cloths of various lengths, although even in earlier times the use of sewn garments was not unknown... Everywhere in Nigeria weaving had reached a highly advanced stage by at least the end of the fourteenth century. Cotton was the yarn most frequently used... A silk yarn...called* anaphe *was, and still is, used by the Yoruba to produce a cloth called* sanyan. *It was perhaps also used by the Hausa who today use the same silk...to embroider costly robes.*
>
> **Titi Euba, *Dress, in The Living Culture of Nigeria*, ed. Saburi O. Biobaku, 1976**

Professor Leo Frobenius, a German scholar, was one of the first to see value in African history, particularly the history of non-Islamic West and Central Africa. He was a pioneering authority on Yoruba civilization. When he first encountered this culture in the early twentieth century, he felt he had discovered remnants of the lost Greek civilization of Atlantis. Having unearthed beautiful statuary and old palaces, he came to hear, among the Yoruba, legends describing these ancient times. One story alluded to an ancient royal metropolis with a palace of golden walls that had sunk beneath the waters of the Atlantic. Moreover, Frobenius identified Olukun, the Yoruba sea god, with Poseidon, the ancient Greek deity (Leo Frobenius, *The Voice of Africa*: Vol. I, 1913). While this analysis is now considered incorrect, Professor Frobenius was not alone in claiming a European connection to the civilization of Yoruba. Captain Richard Burton visited the Nigeria region in 1862. He was deeply puzzled by the architecture he witnessed because:

> *It is impossible not to think that Yoruba in ancient times derived its architecture through the Romans, whose conquests in Northern Africa were as extensive as in the North of Europe. We find in every house a Tuscan atrium, with a cavædium or gangway running round the rectangular impluvium, the tank or piscine, which catches the rain and drippings falling through the compluvium or central opening in the roof. Sometimes the atrium is a tetrastyle in which pillars at the four corners of the impluvium support girders or main beams of the roof.*
>
> **An F.R.G.S. [Richard Burton], 'My Wanderings in West Africa' in *Fraser's Magazine*, March 1863**

What we can learn from the descriptions of Professor Leo Frobenius and Captain Richard Burton is that the quality of Yoruba civilization was such that some of its attributes could be compared to cultures in southern Europe.

At the centre of Ife stood the Afin, the walled royal palace. Professor Frobenius said it was an edifice 'built of bricks well burnt, brilliant with coloured tiles and sundry other ornament!' (Leo Frobenius, *The Voice of Africa*, trans. Rudolf Blind, Vol. I, 1913). Ife itself was walled and paved, with excavations showing that its walls were built in two concentric circles. As the population grew, or the direct influence exerted by the Oni increased, new walls were taken under royal protection.

Professor Ekpo Eyo, a highly distinguished Nigerian historian, narrates (in Ekpo Eyo and Frank Willett, *Treasures of Ancient Nigeria*, 1980) a curious oral tradition concerning Oni Oluwo, a ruler of Ife. Apparently, she was walking around the capital when her regalia got splashed with mud. Oluwo was so upset by this that she ordered the construction of pavements for all the public and religious places in Ife. Archaeology confirms the existence of pavements at the following Ife sites: Oduduwa College, Lafogido, Ita Yemoo, Obalara's Land and Woye Asiri Land. The pavements had regular and geometric patterns, emphasized by the incorporation of white quartz pebbles in their surface. Such pavements had also been found on prehistoric sites, from Chad in the northeast to Togo in the west.

One of the great achievements of the Yoruba is their urban culture of walled cities surrounded by farms. In the twelfth and thirteenth centuries the Yorubas established more city-states, each ruled by an Oni or Oba. Among them were Owu, Oyo, Ijebu, Ijesa, Ketu, Popo, Egba, Sabe, Dassa, Egbado, Igbomina, the 16 Ekiti principalities, Owo and Ondo. The ruling dynasties of most, if not all, of these cities traced their origins to Ife. As in Ife, female Obas were quite common. Moreover, women participated in trades on an equal basis with men. Married women did not become wards of their husbands, but instead maintained their own wealth and possessions.

Agriculture supported the populations of these city-states. Practising crop rotation, their farmers cultivated local crops of yam and oil palm. In later periods they grew potato, cotton, holchus sorgum, rice, cassava, melon, beans, groundnut, sugar cane, orange, okra and various vegetables. Professor Vincent Tarikhu Farrar, an African American expert on African technology, singles out (in *Precolonial African Material Culture*, 2020) the agricultural techniques in Yorubaland for their efficiency, productiveness, and their ability to intensify and scale. Their farmers could feed huge city-states and the surrounding areas.

Ife continued to exercise religious influence over the other walled cities, such as Owo. This religious influence was reflected by the beauty of Yoruba sculpture in wood, brass, clay and ivory. Ife yielded many artworks which honoured Yoruba beliefs and rulers. They evolved one of the greatest schools of sculpture the world has known. Professor Frank Willett believes that Yoruba art 'would stand comparison with anything which Ancient Egypt, Classical Greece and Rome, or Renaissance Europe had to offer' ('Ife and its Archaeology', *Papers in African Prehistory*, 1970). However, the development of Yoruba art is something of a puzzle because the artefacts found have all been masterpieces; no traces of early beginnings by less accomplished artists have ever been found. In March 2010 the British Museum in London hosted an exhibition called *Kingdom of Ife*. In a review of the exhibition for a British newspaper, the *Daily Telegraph*, Richard Dorment observed:

This is the first show ever devoted to the sculpture of Ife anywhere in the world. The quality of the full-length statues, portrait heads, ritual objects and vessels loaned by Nigeria's National Commission for Museums and Monuments is flabbergasting. What can I say? Shows like this come along once in a lifetime.

GREAT BENIN

Great Benin was an important state that flourished in southern Nigeria. In the fifteenth century it was an empire distinguished by the sumptuousness of its capital, Benin City, and the refinement of its royal art. Oba (King) Ewuare the Great, founder of the empire, reigned between *c.* 1440 and *c.* 1473. Noted as a brilliant ruler, he is remembered for strong leadership and military prowess. Ewuare the Great marched against 201 towns and villages over the southern Nigeria region, capturing their leaders and compelling their populations to pay tribute. Among the subdued regions were Eka, Ekiti, Ikare, Kukuruku and Igbo territories west of the Niger River. An able politician, he used religious authority and constitutional reforms to strengthen his hand.

The people belonged to the Benue-Kwa branch of the Niger-Congo culture. Their humble beginnings were associated with the Ogiso Dynasty. Igodo, the first of its 15 rulers, lived around 900 CE and enjoyed a long reign. Ogiso Ere, his son and successor, founded many villages such as Erua and Ego. The guilds of weavers, carvers and potters date back to his reign. Moreover, Ere established royal emblems and the ceremonies that accompanied them, which continued into later times. These included the throne, the stool, ritual swords, the fan, the anklets, the collars and the crown. The eighth ruler, Ogiso Orhorho, is remembered as a wicked queen who was eventually killed for her tyranny. The twelfth ruler, Ogiso Hennenden, oversaw a time of prosperity, with the population of the village of Benin growing as a result. Owodo, the last ruler of the Ogiso Dynasty, is mostly remembered for never convening a meeting except when things were going wrong or there was a crisis. He was later banished for incompetence as an ineffectual ruler. Two administrators, Evian and Ogiamve, ruled during the interregnum that followed his expulsion. However, the republican period proved to be short-lived. Evian attempted to install his son as the next Oba, but the people revolted. The Yorubas took advantage of this crisis to appoint Prince Oranmiyan as the next ruler.

After overcoming Ogiamve's resistance, Prince Oranmiyan founded the Second Dynasty in *c.* 1170 CE. Accompanying the Yoruba dynastic connection came the importation of state swords into Benin, along with stables of horses for ceremonial occasions and, later, a guild of royal brass casters. In the time of Oranmiyan's successor, Eweka I, developments in statecraft occurred. Eweka established the Uzama Nihinron, a body of seven Counsellors of State who ensured that each new Oba was installed according to precedent. Subsequent rulers built a palace inside Benin City that became the new royal residence. In the fifteenth century new reforms created a new tier of bureaucrats known as the Town Chiefs. They were appointed to undermine the control of the hereditary Palace Chiefs.

Benin City began as an unwalled village. The first population expansion, which turned the village into a thriving town, took place during the time of Ogiso Hennenden, around 1000 CE. Around 1283 Oba Oguola built the first walls. For security reasons, he also arranged for moats to be dug around the outskirts of the town and at other important towns and villages. Oba Ewuare raised new walls in *c.* 1460, building the great innermost walls and other ditches. He constructed good roads inside the city, including Akpakpava Street and Utantan Street. At that time Benin City had a walled and moated inner core of nine gates, which contained the Ogiso Dynasty and Second Dynasty palaces. The houses of functionaries and the wards for guilds – of ivory carvers, blacksmiths, weavers and embroiders, drummers and sculptors – were also located here. Ewuare popularized the impluvium architecture style of the Yorubas, creating for the first time in Benin a city with parts on a horizontal vertical grid. The main city walls and other earthworks have been excavated. They were parts of a 10,000-mile defensive wall system. *The Guinness Book of Records* describes this construction activity as the largest earthworks in world history that were carried out before the mechanical era.

Crafts, Trade and Industry

Arts and crafts were very important, with wood and ivory used by the carvers to fashion a range of artefacts. During the Ogiso period terracotta heads were made that surmounted the altars of the kings. There were also early manufactures in brass, making bracelets and bells. Over three centuries later a Yoruba sculptor founded the Benin guild of bronzesmiths. Later still Ewuare, the great Oba of the fifteenth century, was a patron of ivory carving. Some of the ivory was beautifully carved into condiment sets and tableware that graced none but the highest tables. For example, the pieces sold to European elites depict knights, sometimes on horseback, Portuguese coats of arms and Christian iconography. Portuguese royalty bought these works, as did the Medici, the Duke of Saxony and others. A later ruler, Oba Esigie, ascended the throne in *c.* 1504. He commissioned a highly improved metal art that has since achieved worldwide distinction. Among the best-known pieces are the famous Queen Mother Idia busts. Professor Felix von Luschan, a former official of the Berlin Museum für Völkerkunde, stated that:

> *These Benin works notably stand among the highest heights of European casting. Benvenuto Cellini could not have made a better cast himself, and no one has before or since, even to the present day. These bronzes stand even at the summit of what can be technically achieved.*
>
> **Felix von Luschan, *Die Altertümer von Benin*, Vol I, 1919, trans. Kathryn Wysocki Gunsch, 'Art and/or Ethnographica? The Reception of Benin Works from 1897–1935', *African Arts*, Winter 2013, Vol. 46, No. 4**

In 1485 or 1486 an ambassador from Portugal established diplomatic links with Benin, and commercial links between the two countries were soon forged. Prior to that Benin's trade links were primarily with the Saharan states to the north; they exported ivory, pepper and cotton goods in exchange for Saharan copper and Sudanese horses. Once trade links had been made with Portugal and elsewhere in Europe, Benin exported dyed cotton cloth, wool, jasper, leopard skins, soap and, later, palm oil, in addition to ivory tableware and pepper. The trade in soap was on such a scale that Portugal banned imports of West African soap to protect its own soap boiling industry.

The historic village of Ughoton was transformed into the seaport of Gwatto in the latter half of the sixteenth century. The Oba imposed a series of tolls and customs on goods that passed through here, some of which came via the Hausas from the Saharan trade. Benin prospered greatly at this time, with its markets typically held in large public squares every three or four days. D. R., an anonymous Dutch source of *c.* 1604 or earlier, tells us that 'These markets…are held and arranged in a very orderly manner'. The currency was cowrie shells. When James Welsh visited the location in 1588, he found the following items on sale: soap that 'smelleth like beaten violets'; ivory spoons, 'very curiously wrought' with decorations of 'foules and beasts made upon them'; cotton and woollen cloths, 'very curiously woven'; bark cloth, pepper, ivory, palm oil and mats that Welsh described as 'pretie' and 'fine' (James Welsh, 'A voyage to Benin beyond the Countrey of Guinea' collected in Richard Hakluyt, *The Principal Navigations, Voyages, Traffiques and Discoveries of the English Nation*, Vol. 6, 1589). Incidentally, Welsh presented the Oba with the gift of a telescope. Other goods included dishes, jugs, drinking cups and ironwork products, such as hoes. Dr Olfert Dapper, a Dutch geographer, listed (in his book discussed below) Dutch textiles and other goods that were on sale in Benin, including gold and silver cloth, linen, red velvet, fine cotton stuffs, woollen stuffs and Harlem stuffs with flower designs.

At the Height of Power

The empire achieved its maximum expansion in the sixteenth century, when it encompassed Ishan to the north, Isoko and Urhobo of the lower Niger Delta, Yoruba territories to the south and western Igboland. Administering this territory were three tiers of imperial government. At the top was the Oba, an increasingly austere and sacred figure. Then came the State Council of Benin City, and beneath that the tributary units. The units consisted of an overlord, royally appointed, who headed the unit and he in turn appointed a servant as his representative. Finally, there were the people of the village, town or dependency. Tradition dictated that the overlord lived in Benin City. His role was to transmit the interests of his constituents to the Oba. Moreover, he had to organize the yearly or twice-yearly collection of tribute in the form of yams, palm oil, meat, livestock and foodstuffs to be sent to the Oba's court. Tradition further dictated that his servant would live in the village, town or dependency to represent the overlord there.

In the early seventeenth century other envoys from Europe visited Benin. Some of these left eye-catching descriptions of what they saw. Samuel Blomert, a man who lived in Africa for several years, is one such example. In 1668 the Dutch scholar Dr Olfert Dapper paraphrased Blomert's rich and full account in a famous book entitled *Description of Africa*. Apparently, Benin City, including the Queen's Court, was 20 or 24 miles in circumference:

> *It is protected at one side by a wall ten feet high, made of double stockades of big trees, tied to each other by cross-beams fastened cross-wise, and stuffed up with red clay, solidly put together. This wall only surrounds the town on one side... The town possesses several gates, eight or nine feet in height and five in width, with doors made of a whole piece of wood, hanging or turning on a peg, like the peasants' fences here in this country [i.e. Holland]. The king's court is square, and stands at the right-hand side when entering the town by the gate of Gotton [i.e. Gwatto], and is certainly as large as the town of Harlem [in Holland], and entirely surrounded by a special wall, like that which encircles the town. It is divided into many magnificent palaces, houses and apartments of the courtiers, and comprises beautiful and long square galleries, about as large as the Exchange at Amsterdam,*

but one larger than another, resting on wooden pillars, from top to bottom covered with cast copper, on which are engraved the pictures of their war exploits and battles, and kept very clean. Most palaces and the houses of the king are covered in palm leaves instead of square pieces of wood, and every roof is decorated with a small turret ending in a point, on which birds are standing, birds cast in copper with outstretched wings, cleverly made after living models. The town has thirty very straight and broad streets, every one of them about one hundred and twenty feet wide…from which branch out many side streets…

Quoted in H. Ling Roth, *Great Benin: Its Customs, Art and Horrors*, 1903

This indicates a planned city, built on an enormous scale, with parts structured on a horizontal vertical grid. In colour, the buildings were terracotta red. Dapper compared the Exchange at Amsterdam with the palaces of the courtiers since it was the largest building in Holland. Captain Richard Burton visited the Nigeria region in 1862. He informed us that the royal palace 'is supposed to contain not less than fifteen thousand souls' (An F.R.G.S. [Richard Burton], 'My Wanderings in West Africa', *Fraser's Magazine*, April 1863). This data corroborates both Blomert, who suggested that the palace was the same size as the Dutch city of Harlem, and the description of another traveller, a German who worked as a military surgeon on Dutch ships, Andreas Josua Ultzheimer. Writing in 1603, Utzheimer suggested that the royal palace was 'about the size of the [German] city of Tubingen' (quoted in Basil Davidson ed., *African Civilization Revisited*, 1991).

However, Benin's later history in the eighteenth and nineteenth centuries demonstrates cultural stagnation rather than advancement.

The port of Gwatto silted up, leading to the merchants going elsewhere to trade. There were no great Obas after Orhogbua (*c.* 1550–*c.* 1578). In addition, the shortcomings of an overly centralized government began to manifest themselves in weak local representation and growing administrative corruption. Even its metal art began to show a stiffness of concept and execution, although the wood and ivory guild workers maintained an extremely high artistic and technical standard right to the end.

Benin history continued until 1897. In that year the British army invaded and plundered the country, exiling the Oba. The conquerors stole thousands of priceless artefacts that are still held by London institutions and in private collections. One of them, Lieutenant-General Augustus Pitt Rivers, even produced a catalogue of the stolen material. Others were sold to European institutions. Following this outrage, they burned the city. Benin became a part of the colonially created country that the British ruled: Nigeria.

THE OYO EMPIRE

Herbert Wendt, a German science writer, painted the following picture of Yorubaland during the Ife and Oyo periods:

> *Modern ethnologists have found the art of the Yorubas so astonishingly high in quality that they did not [at first] ascribe it to a Negro race… It was Leo Frobenius who first ranked the culture of the Yorubas with that of the Mediterranean… The Yoruba empire consisted of city-states similar to those of ancient Greece…some of these states had a hundred and fifty to two hundred and fifty thousand inhabitants.*

> *Art objects of the highest quality were found in their ruins – glazed urns, tiles with pictures of animals and gods on them, bronze implements, gigantic granite figures. The Yorubas introduced the cultivation of yams, the preparation of cheese and the breeding of horses into West Africa. They had outstanding artists in metal, gold-casters, cotton-weavers, wood-carvers and potters. Their professions formed themselves into guilds with their own laws, their children were brought up in educational camps, their public affairs were directed by a courtly aristocracy and an exuberantly expanding bureaucracy.*
>
> **Herbert Wendt, *It Began in Babel*, 1963**

In the fifteenth century Oyo was just another of the numerous Yoruba city-states. It had ceramic tiled pavements laid in the thirteenth or fourteenth centuries and was surrounded by walls and ditches. However, it was strategically located at the northern edge of the Yoruba world in the savannah fringe of the rainforest. It therefore benefitted from trade caravans coming south into the forest area and from goods carried north to the desert belt. Through these commercial relations the Alafins, or rulers of Oyo, possessed unhindered access to horses. For environmental reasons, they were one of the few Yoruba city-states that couldn't breed horses. At some point between 1578 and 1608 (we cannot be more specific) Benin fought off a major attack from Yoruba. Negotiations at the end of the war established Otun as a frontier boundary town between the two countries.

Through a series of wars between 1600 and the early 1700s, Oyo brought most of the Yoruba city-states under its control. We have no details of who battled who, or when, as Yoruba record-keeping has not been good. While the conquered cities remained self-governing, they had to pay tribute to Oyo. In addition, Oyo seized control of the Fon and Ewe region to the west, and subjugating the kingdoms and princely states in Dahomey and elsewhere. This meant that Oyo ruled parts of the countries we know today as Benin and Togo. Again, we do not have the details of the conflicts that enabled Oyo to rule all these territories. From 1682 to 1683 Oyo cavalries put down rebellions in these territories; they did so again in 1698. The Alafin of Oyo had access to 100,000 horsemen who may have worn chainmail. What we do know is that Oyo slave-traded people captured in these wars to Europeans as part of the transatlantic system of enslavement. The captives ended up being deported to the Americas by European slave traders.

Oyo came to dominate the trade caravans. Two such caravan routes linked Yorubaland with the outside world. The first traversed the region in a north to southwest direction. Passing through Hausaland, it linked the Yorubas at Oyo to the trans-Saharan trade. From Oyo the route passed through Kisi, Saki, Iseyin and so on, eventually reaching the coast at Ajase, the modern Porto Novo. The second caravan route traversed the region in a north to southeast direction. Again it centred on Oyo, but this time it passed through Ilesa, Ekitiland and Owo to the Kingdom of Benin, where it eventually reached the coast. Feeder routes linked these caravans from all directions within the Yoruba territories. Goods moved by head porterage, or sometimes by ferry if the routes crossed rivers. Nominal tolls were imposed on the movement of goods. In addition, taxing their dependencies, such as Dahomey, brought in massive revenues.

In 1775 Alafin Abiodun became ruler of the Oyo empire. He assumed power in a very bloody coup, in which he killed off the previous prime minister and all his extended family. Trusting few people, Abiodun replaced the personal royal bodyguard of tradition with 4,000 warriors commanded by one of his sons. A 200-mile stretch of the empire was known as the Egbado Corridor; in the southwest, this was Oyo's trade route with the coast. Abiodun successfully colonized the whole area along the trade route through building Yoruba towns, to be governed by relatives he trusted. Moreover, Abiodun had a royal official stationed tasked with administering the highway and tolls. Incidentally *Esusu*, a type of rotating savings and credit association, was recorded to have been practised in Oyo during his reign. Black Britons continued to use this credit system from the *Windrush* days until the 1980s.

At the Height of Power

In the eighteenth century Oyo reached the height of its political power. At the head of the empire was the Alafin of Oyo, the supreme overlord of all his people. He claimed descent from Oranyan, a mythical founder ancestor of Oyo, but was legitimated by his family ties to the city of Ife. There was the Oyo Mesi, the Supreme Council of State whose seven members were the kingmakers. The Bashorun was the head of the Oyo Mesi; he functioned as the prime minister, but was also a powerful figure in traditional Yoruba religion. The Ogboni was a powerful secret society composed of freemen noted for their age, wisdom and importance in political and religious affairs. Together with the prime minister, they provided checks on the power of the Alafin. Finally there was the Eso, the Society of War Chiefs, with the Are-Ona-Kakanfo, the Imperial Army's supreme commander, at its head. He was required to live by a code that demanded suicide rather than accept defeat.

During this period the city of Oyo covered 5⅜ square feet and had around 100,000 inhabitants. Its Afin, or palace, evolved over many generations into a great walled complex that enclosed buildings, courtyards and large areas of forestland. Susan Denyer, an architectural authority, writing in *Traditional Architecture* (1978), suggests that it may well have had over 100 courtyards, each of an astonishing size, and so was far larger than a private house. One of the courtyards was as large as two football pitches. Each courtyard was used for a special function such as public assemblies, dancing at festivals or reserved for the Alafin's private use. Denyer further suggests that the courtyards may well have been paved with quartz pebbles and potsherds. Seven of the doors in the private complexes were covered in silver. She notes that when Captain Clapperton, the English traveller, visited it in the 1820s, he reported that the palace complex covered an area of 642½ acres.

However, the Oyo Empire collapsed in the nineteenth century. They came under attack from the north to Fulani invaders, who went on to raid, burn and pillage villages in Oyo. The Fulani eventually destroyed the Oyo capital in 1835. Six decades later British colonialists overthrew the fragmented remains of Oyo. This territory became a part of modern Nigeria.

THE HAUSA CONFEDERATION

Northern Nigeria contained seven autonomous cities, and the areas around them, which comprised the Hausa Confederation. These cities – Gobir, Biram, Katsina, Kano, Daura, Rano and Zazzau – were referred to as the Hausa Bakwai, or 'pure' Hausa states. Zazzau was the furthest to the south and Gobir the furthest to the north.

They flourished from between the eleventh or twelfth centuries to the early twentieth century. Despite having a common language, the Hausa never established a single territory for most of their history. As a result, scholars refer to them as a confederacy of sovereign states. The Hausa speakers are the Chadic branch of Afroasiatic culture. According to Hausa historians, the Banzai Bakwai, or 'impure' Hausa States, are also a part of Hausa history: Nupe, Gwari, Kebbi, Zamfara and Kwararafa.

Each state was initially based on a walled village, or *birni*. The walls enclosed a sizeable, self-sufficient community in which trade, industry and agriculture occurred, setting it apart from a typical village or hamlet. Additionally, in times of emergency brought on by threats from enemy armies, villagers from the nearby rural areas could enter the *birni*. Every *birni* was made to resist blockades. There was trade between farmers and artisans living inside the walls. The most significant became capital cities after the Hausas united the various *birni* and hamlets into towns. The capital cities served as both seats of government and the rulers over hundreds of other walled villages. Each capital developed a complex administrative structure. To give an idea of scale, Lord Lugard estimated in 1904 that there were still 170 walled towns in existence in the entire Kano province alone.

The Rise of Kano

Bagauda became the first Hausa Sarki (king). Ruling Kano from 999 to 1063, the *Kano Chronicle* portrays him as a conqueror who seized power over the settlement of Dala. At this settlement, a culture flourished among the Abagayawa; archaeologists have discovered their rock paintings and ironworks. The Abagayawa were part of the Sao culture. The third Sarki of this line, Gijimasu, raised the first great walls of Kano City in the late eleventh or early twelfth century.

During the reign of Tsaraki, the fifth Sarki, the first walls of Kano were completed. Tsaraki also armed his soldiers with shields made of sturdy hides, enabling Kano both to govern and protect the people of the surrounding rural communities. In the fourteenth century Islam began to make its presence felt; it was introduced by Wangarans from Mali. Sarki Yaji (1349–1385) was a Muslim ruler who constructed Kano's first mosque.

The fifteenth century was eventful with brilliant reforms. Abdullah Burja, the eighteenth ruler of Kano, was the architect of great prosperity. He was the first to encourage the use of camels as beasts of burden. Previously Kano businessmen and traders had waited on camel caravans, controlled by the Tuaregs, to arrive from the north. Under Burja's new policy, however, Kano merchants could transport their own goods across the desert. In the footsteps of these merchants followed the Hausa language and culture. Hausa became the most widely spoken indigenous language in Africa after Swahili.

Rumfa became ruler of Kano in 1463. He built the Gidan Rumfa, an impressive new palace with courtly attendants dressed in Borno fashions. They wore extravagant sandals of ostrich feathers and sported fans made from the same bird. Each of Rumfa's highest officers constructed their own palaces. Reforming the government, he appointed a nine-member council of advisors and promoted slaves to important positions. Slaves managed the treasury, staffed the palace, attended to the harem and policed the city. Rumfa also enforced Islamic law. Humiliating the Abagayawa, he compelled their leading citizens to become Muslims and built a Friday Mosque on their sacred Shamuz site. Moreover, Id al-Fir, the great Islamic festival after Ramadan, was celebrated in Kano for the first time. Rumfa also offered active support to scholars. Sheikh Muhammad

Al-Maghili, a well-known scholar from North Africa, taught Koranic studies in Katsina and law in Kano. He wrote a treatise on government called *On the Obligations of Princes* (before 1502). In addition, Rumfa is described in the *Kano Chronicle* as 'he who can have no equal in might, from the time of the founding of Kano, until it shall end'.

The Rise of Zazzau

Zazzau in the fifteenth century had various fortified places, such as Turunku and Kufena. Zaria city, on the other hand, was founded in 1536 by Bakwa Turunku. Her previous capital, Turunku, lacked sufficient water sources to meet the expanding requirements of its commercial centre. Karama, a soldier, assumed power when Bakwa Turunku passed away around 1566. His campaigns were accompanied by Turunku's daughter, Princess Amina, who in 1576 became the undisputed ruler of Zazzau. She led campaigns and became distinguished as an empire builder. Some of the walled forts Amina had constructed, which served as area garrisons to consolidate the conquered territory, still stand today. Amina subdued the whole area between Zazzau and the Niger and Benue rivers, absorbing the Nupe and Kwararafa states. According to the *Kano Chronicle*, 'Every town paid her tribute. The Sarkin Nupe sent her forty eunuchs and ten thousand kolas… In her time all the products of the west came to Hausaland'. Slaves were available in abundance because of the southern expansion. In addition, Zazzau came to control the trade route from Gwanja, and so began to benefit from trade previously enjoyed only by Kano and Katsina.

The Hausa and the Nupe, to the south, shared some distant cultural ties. Well known for the excellence of their craftsmanship in the production of glass, silver and brass, they also proved adept at building boats for trade and warfare. After defeating the Igala

Kingdom's hold on his people, Sarki Tsoede united the Nupe peoples into a state at the beginning of the fifteenth century. He led the Nupe on a programme of territorial expansion, amassing sizeable cavalry forces in the process. On the lower Kaduna River Tsoede established the city of Gbara. On the opposite bank he founded the city of Dokomba. Originally a stable for his 1,000 horses, Dokomba became the main city after Gbara outgrew itself. Unique among the 'Hausa' states, there are nine surviving bronze masterpieces – of controversial origins, they are associated with Sarki Tsoede. The works are comparable in style and quality to the brilliant metal art of the Yoruba and Benin. Moreover, both the Grassi Museum of Ethnology in Leipzig and the British Museum continue to house elaborate brass vessels, urns, daggers, hilts and other items etc. of Nupe manufacture. They are several centuries old, with some dating back to the fifteenth century.

Kano and Katsina were bustling industrial centres of cotton goods, leather manufacture, agriculture, iron smelting, weaving and dyeing. Nupe specialized in brass, silver and glass manufacture. The royalty of Nupe and Kebbi boasted copper-sheathed boats of local manufacture. The Hausa Confederation traded with the Yoruba to the south, bought Akan gold from the west and traded with Egypt and the rest of North Africa. The fall of Songhai in 1591 brought a new impetus to some of these commercial activities. 'It has been estimated that in 1851, the City of Kano exported 10 million pairs of sandals, 5 million hides and sheepskins, each year to North Africa,' a modern scholar has noted, despite referring to a later period (Benaebi Benatari, 'The Document of African Civilisation', unpublished paper, 1999). Another scholar has observed that 'for several centuries the best bindings for European books came from Nigeria; for Morocco leather (so-called because Europe imported it via Morocco) is made from Nigerian goat skin' (S. Irein Wangboje, 'Art and Crafts', *The Living Culture of Nigeria*, 1976).

The Kano market was the most important place for the buying and selling of these products. Canon Charles Robinson, a Cambridge University authority on Hausa Studies, described this institution with respect. Writing in 1900, he declared:

> *Kano may claim to possess the largest market place, not merely in Africa, but in the world. The French traveller Colonel Monteuil estimated its average daily attendance at thirty thousand; and though I should not have ventured on quite so large as one myself, I do not think that his estimate is very extravagant. Size, moreover, is the least interesting feature of the Kano market. In the first place its antiquity is deserving of notice. The market has probably been held on the exact site where we now find it for at least a thousand years. At the time of the Norman conquest of England trade was being conducted in the Kano market amidst surroundings closely resembling those that we now see. Kano would then have furnished better-made cloth than any to be found in England at that time.*
>
> **Charles Henry Robinson, *Nigeria: Our Latest Protectorate*, 1900**

After Timbuktu fell in 1591, Katsina became the dominant intellectual hub of West Africa. It 'seems to have been regarded as a sort of university town,' commented Lady Lugard, and its most renowned scholar was Abu Abdullah Mohammed ibn Mohammed (1595–1667). Also known as Dan Masani, he wrote works on politics, poetry, theology, law and even on the wonders of Yorubaland. In addition, he authored a 500-page commentary on the 'Ishiriniya of al-Fazazi', which was a thirteenth-century praise poem originally written by a Moroccan poet dedicated to Prophet Muhammad; a treatise on rebellion; and a treatise on Maliki law.

The Rise of Gobir

During the eighteenth and nineteenth centuries, Gobir emerged as the most powerful state in the Hausa Confederation. Under Sarki Barbari (r. 1742–1770) Gobir started taking advantage of the power void created by a failing Kebbi in the early eighteenth century. Sarki Barbari's armies marched against Zamfara, Maradi, Katsina, Yauri and Nupe; they also extracted tribute from Kano.

However, the Fulanis, a people of the desert, posed a much greater threat to Gobir itself. Austere and fervent in their faith, they could no longer tolerate the Hausa rulers' corruption and laxity. In 1804 they overthrew these governments, declaring jihad against the ruling class. Ordinary Hausas joined the Fulani campaigns in large numbers, sympathizing with the Fulanis' criticism of the high taxes exacted by the Hausa rulers. Moreover, Hausa officials were not above confiscating livestock from ordinary people – or abducting young women to serve in the harem.

Uthman Dan Fodio, a Shehu (meaning 'teacher'), defeated the Hausa kings in 1812. He renamed the captured city of Gobir 'Sokoto' and instituted a centralized government, thus bringing stability to the area. This in turn sparked an economic boom, unlike anything Hausaland had seen since the fifteenth and sixteenth centuries; half of West Africa, for example, was clothed with Kano cotton. Consequently, the kings and elites of Dahomey, Bamoun, Mossi and West Africa wore Hausa textiles.

In addition, the Shehu and his offspring were brilliant scholars. About 258 books and essays on a range of theoretical and practical topics are credited to Uthman, his brother Abdullah and his son Muhammad Bello. Two English explorers, Dixon Denham and Hugh Clapperton, travelled to the Caliphate between 1822 and 1830. They recorded that the palace of Kano possessed a mosque and 'several towers three or four storeys high' (Bovill, E.W. ed., *Missions to the Niger*, Vol. 4, *The Bornu Mission*, 1822–25, 1966). Dr Barth visited there in 1854, when he estimated the population of Hausaland to be around 50 million people.

The best concise description of the Caliphate, however, comes from the pen of William Winwood Reade. He wrote a splendid summary of what the Englishmen witnessed on their travels: Denham and Clapperton 'were astonished to find…magnificent courts; regiments of cavalry, the horses caparisoned in silk for gala days and clad in coats of mail for war'. Moreover, they 'attended with wonder the gigantic fairs at which the cotton goods of Manchester, the red cloth of Saxony, double-barrelled guns, razors, tea and sugar, Nuremberg ware and writing-paper were exhibited for sale'. Finally, the men were impressed to find a banking and an intellectual culture: 'They also found merchants who offered to cash their bills upon houses at Tripoli; and scholars acquainted with Avicenna, Averroes, and the Greek philosophers' (*The Martyrdom of Man*, 1872).

The fall of this culture is associated with the military activities of the British, whose armies overthrew the Sokoto Caliphate in 1903. They incorporated the captured territory with the conquered lands of Benin, Igbo, Yoruba and other territories to form the modern state of Nigeria.

THE SLAVE TRADE & WEST AFRICA

The 'scramble for Africa' was the driving force behind European colonization of Senegal, Gambia, Ghana, Togo and Benin in the late nineteenth and early twentieth centuries. The French had a toehold over Senegal as early as 1659, but only came to rule Senegal as an official French colony in 1895. A small British colony was established in Gambia in 1815, but their reach over the land expanded in the late nineteenth century. Beginning in 1821, the British came to dominate Ghana, originally known as the Gold Coast. By 1896 they were the undisputed rulers of the land. From 1884 until the First World War Togo was a German colony; in 1922 the League of Nations mandated that France and Britain should assume control of the country. Dahomey, situated to the east of Togo, was initially a French protectorate in the 1890s, but by 1904 had been formally incorporated into French West Africa. Confusingly, this country changed its name to 'Benin' in 1975. This is *not* the same place as Great Benin, which is in Nigeria.

However, European involvement in the region predated all this. It went back to the fifteenth century, to the time of the mass capture and transatlantic enslavement of Africans. This part of world history affected Africa, the Americas and Europe. This was the period that Europe came to dominate the globe – and also the period when Africans outside Africa came to be seen as inferiors, no more than slaves. Another group of people who lost their status were the Native Americans, but that is another story.

A BRITISH GOVERNMENT SELECT COMMITTEE ON THE SLAVE TRADE

In April 1790 a British Government Select Committee summoned Charles Berns Wadstrom to testify in front of them. They published his testimony on 11 May 1790 in a report entitled *Minutes of the evidence taken before the Select Committee on the Slave Trade*. The Select Committee cross-examined several of these expert witnesses, chosen for their first-hand knowledge of the kidnapping and mass enslavement of Africans. For instance, Mr Wadstrom had a particularly thorough understanding of its effects on the West African regions of Senegal, Gambia and Gorée Island. The quotation below is taken from the testimony that he gave on 29 April 1790.

Keen to know about the quality of culture in that part of Africa, they asked Wadstrom: 'Have they any manufactures amongst them?' Mr Wadstrom's reply, quoted in Robert Norris et al., *Minutes of the evidence taken before the Select Committee on the Slave Trade*, Abstract of Evidence 1790, proved edifying:

> *I have been surprised to see with what industry they manufacture their cottons, their indigo, and other dyeing articles, as well as several sorts of manufacture in wood; they make soap; they tan leather, and work it exceedingly well, and even with good taste…they work bar iron…into several articles, as for instance, lances, instruments for tillage, poniards, &c.; they work in gold very ingeniously, and so well, that I never have seen better made*

> *articles of that kind in Europe; a great number of articles for ornaments of gold, silver, brass, leather, &c.*

Wadstrom further stated that:

> *Their cloth and their leather they manufacture with uncommon neatness; and I have samples with me to shew in case it should be desired." (Ibid).*

From the Wadstrom testimony, additional facts emerged. The region's king was called Dalmanny. A well-educated man, he had held the position of Grand Marabout before his election as king. His subjects were very honest and hospitable; they had shown Wadstrom 'all civility and kindness'. In addition, he observed, they had 'an extraordinary genius for commerce'. Interestingly, they had a 'Materia Medica' consisting of 'about 2,000 or nearer 3,000' plants. King Dalmanny 'had entirely prohibited the Slave trade throughout his whole Kingdom' and had also banned the sale of alcohol. The Senegal Company, a French concern, had initially attempted to bribe the king to change his policy on the trade in people, but he refused their overtures. The Senegal Company then resorted to bribing the lighter-skinned Moors to attack and kidnap Dalmanny's subjects, supplying them with the necessary equipment (arms, gunpowder and ammunition) to carry out the raids. The result of this aggression, according to Wadstrom, was 'the chief hindrance to the improvement of the cultivation; in so far as the Negroes never venture to go out into the fields unless very well armed'.

Significantly, the Select Committee asked: 'Do you mean to say, that if the Slave Trade was abolished, they would extend their cultivation and manufactures?' Wadstrom's response was clear:

Yes; particularly if some good European people had enterprising spirit enough to settle among them in another way than is the case at present. (Ibid).

WEST AFRICA AND TRANSATLANTIC ENSLAVEMENT

Historians usually begin the story of the European mass enslavement of Africans in 1441. In that year young Portuguese mariner, Antam Gonçalves, set sail for Rio de Oro in southern Morocco. Gonçalves reportedly exclaimed to his crew, 'O how fair it would be if we, who have come to this land for a cargo of such petty merchandise, were to meet with the good luck to bring the first captives before the face of our Prince'. Later joined on the coast by Nuño Tristão, 'a youthful knight, very valiant and ardent', they did indeed kidnap 12 Africans and duly gave them to Prince Henry of Portugal as a gift. One of the captives, of noble birth, revealed to the Portuguese the specifics of the country from which he travelled. The African noble offered five or six more Africans in exchange for his release. Gonçalves returned to the south and ransomed the one captive in exchange for 10 more.

In 1482, on the coast of Ghana, the Portuguese built Elmina Castle. The local ruler Kwame Ansa initially opposed the construction of the first of many fortified dungeons. He turned down the Portuguese request to build there, arguing that friends who only see each other occasionally are better friends than those who live close together. However, Diogo de Azambuja, the Portuguese agent, refused to take 'no' for an answer. Although he appeared to concede, Kwame Ansa issued a warning that truth and peace must be maintained. The following day, as the Portuguese began to build, 'the Negroes…briskly attacked the men at work'. In response, the Negroes were bribed with Portuguese gifts. The Africans were still dissatisfied. Diogo de Azambuja decided to burn their village because they allegedly 'committed so many thefts and evil deeds' against the Portuguese. The voyage of Christopher Columbus to the American continent in 1492 opened this part of the world to European predatory activities. Millions of indigenous people were gradually killed off, with Africans enslaved and sent to the Americas to replace them. Previously all such captives had been sent to Europe or the islands off the coast of Africa such as Madeira. Now the Spanish conquerors found great demand for labour in the West Indies and the mines of Central America. Native Americans were initially enslaved, but the high mortality rates made this an unreliable labour force. As a result, indentured labour from other sources became necessary.

The first shipment to Europe of West Indian sugar produced by enslaved Africans arrived in 1515. Three years later the first Africans were transported directly to the Americas and the Caribbean, marking the beginning of the Triangular Trade. The credit for this system was partly due to Las Casas, a Spanish humanitarian priest. He wanted to stop the genocide of the Native Americans and held the administrative position 'Protector of the Indians'. In 1517 Las Casas suggested that each Spanish gentleman should be allowed to import 12 slaves of African descent out of good will and in the interest of the indigenous people of the Americas. His advice was followed. One of his favourites received a patent from the Spanish ruler allowing him to import 4,000 Africans annually to Hispaniola, Cuba, Jamaica and Puerto Rico. The Genoese later acquired this patent and shared it among the Portuguese. Soon other nations of Europe became involved in the traffic.

TRANSATLANTIC ENSLAVEMENT IMPACTS MORE COUNTRIES

By the end of the sixteenth century the Portuguese and the Spaniards did most of the enslavement activities. By the beginning of the seventeenth century other European nations had become involved, including Holland, England, France, Denmark, Sweden and Prussia. The European powers conquered land in the Americas and the Caribbean to send their captives to, as well as enslaving Africans in Africa. For instance, the Dutch set up the Dutch West India Company in 1621. Controlling 27 lists of slave buyers, the company linked the enslavement of Africans to the colonizations in the Western Hemisphere. The English colonized Bermuda in 1609 and Barbados in 1625; they also conquered territories in New England, Maryland and Virginia. The French began the colonization of Guadeloupe in 1626 and Martinique in 1635; they also possessed Nova Scotia and St Lawrence on the mainland. The Danes began the colonization of St Thomas in 1671. The Black people of the United States, Canada, Mexico, Columbia, Brazil and the Caribbean islands are the direct descendants of peoples captured in Africa and deported to these places. These Afro descendants would mostly have been Niger-Congo speakers and their Bantu descendants. Also in the mix would have been Nilo-Saharan and Afroasiatic speakers.

Transatlantic enslavement affected all the countries of West Africa. It also affected most of the countries of Central Africa, including those usually left out of the picture, such as Libya. In the face of this onslaught, rulers of African kingdoms faced depopulation through mass murder, social disruption, migration and forced population transfers. They had to contend with refugees fleeing into their countries. Technological progress stalled as young and skilled individuals were killed or taken into custody. The rulers were forced to make their economies subservient to constant warfare, damaging both industries and markets. Finally, mass enslavement and the conflict attached to it destroyed economic activity due to violence and uncertainty.

European kidnapping began the mass capture and enslavement of Africans. These activities continued for decades, arguably accounting for 40 per cent of the total number of Africans captured in transatlantic enslavement. However, since the building of Elmina Castle and other slave dungeons, even more Africans were captured by African states fighting one another in wars – which may have accounted for 45 per cent of the total number of Africans captured. The remaining 15 per cent involved sales of prisoners by African kingdoms.

Within Africa, transatlantic slavery created huge divisions. Many rulers thought it was better to betray their neighbours than to be enslaved themselves, so nations raided each other in horrific wars. They sold captured rivals to Europeans on the coast to buy weapons, with which they hoped to protect themselves from being raided in turn. This created a vicious cycle of constant warfare between African kingdoms, complemented by European gun-running. The kingdoms reduced economic activity for security reasons, focusing instead upon either attacking other kingdoms or defending themselves from other raids. The economies of African countries became increasingly dependent on selling captives to Europe to buy more arms.

IMPACT AND REPERCUSSIONS IN AFRICA

The challenges that ordinary people faced were distinct. People retreating before the slave traders often fled to some of the most inhospitable places they could find: some took to the hills, others to the swamps and yet others to the caves. Their cultures deteriorated, frequently to the point of savagery. If organized enslavement and violence continued over generations, whole communities came to know no other life other than the hills, the caves or the swamps. This also means that modern African ethnic groups in areas affected, particularly West and Central Africa, are likely to include ancestors from other ethnic groups, who had fled to their regions as refugees over the last 600 years. As a result, no African ethnic group in these regions is of pure lineage.

There were additional repercussions. Small communities, cut off from all others for generations, soon developed their own dialects and languages. This is the root cause of the hundreds of dialects spoken today, even over small geographical areas. Moreover, a mentality of distrust of others developed among these fragmented and isolated communities – often caused by invaders' use of Africans and people of mixed ancestry to conduct the slave raids. Communities increasingly saw other Black groups as 'traditional enemies', to be blamed and mistrusted for generations. The so-called 'tribalism' of modern Africa is rooted in a combination of migrations, raids by rival groups, the emergence of new languages and dialects and a mentality of suspicion and exclusivity.

The trade had a wide range of effects on each region. It largely destroyed Kongo and Ndongo, as we shall see in Chapter 11. Although Great Benin did occasionally engage in the sale of captives, a policy was enacted to prevent the trade from monopolizing its interactions with outsiders. Between the sixteenth and seventeenth centuries it continued to export mostly textiles. When the Benin kingdom resisted the growing demand for slaves, Oyo responded to it. The Oyo military leaders embarked upon a series of wars, with their fast-moving cavalry forces bringing most Yoruba city-states under its control between 1600 and 1750. These wars produced captives, leading to Oyo's conquests generating new wealth in the form of duties and tribute. Dahomey, a second important state, became even more closely associated with the slave trade than Oyo. A third state closely associated with the slave trade was the Ashanti.

CONSEQUENCES FOR THE GHANA REGION

In Ghana the Portuguese built Elmina Castle in 1482, although not without opposition. In 1556 William Towerson, an English merchant and navigator, visited the area. In his book *First Voyage to Guinea, 1555–6* (edited and reprinted in 1942), Towerson documented the difficulties the Portuguese presence had on the lives of local people:

> *We judged that the Portugals had spoiled their boats, because we saw half of their towne destroyed… A young fellow… tolde us that the Portugales were bad men, and that they made them slaves if they could take them, and would put yrons upon their legges.*

Moreover, some locals put up resistance to the Portuguese actions. Towerson wrote that 'Don John [a chief] had warres with the Portugals'. He also noted in the same work:

> *This town of John de Viso standeth upon an hill, like the towne of don John, but it hath been burned, so that there are not passing sixe houses in it; the most part of the golde that comes thither*

> *comes out of the countrey, and no doubt if the people durst for feare of the Portugals bring forth their gold, there would be had good store; but they dare not sell anything, their subjection is so great to the Portugales.*

In 1683 a French slaver named John Barbot went to the area. In his book *A Description of the Coasts of North and South Guinea*, translated in London, 1732, Barbot paints a mixed and complicated picture of life, but he shows that the Dutch were now in control. They had overthrown Portuguese dominance:

> *The better to curb the blacks along the coast, and to engross the whole trade, [the Dutch] erected small forts at Butri, Shama, Cape Coast, Anomabu, Koromantin and Accra, pretending to the blacks they did it to protect and defend them against the outrages and insults of their neighbouring enemies of the inland country, who used often to attack them. Being thus grown powerful, the more to keep down the blacks and prevent their attempting anything against them, they laid duties on their fishery at Axim, Elmina and Mori, forbidding them, under severe penalties, to hold any correspondence, or trade with other Europeans, as has been observ'd before.*

Clearly life had not improved very much for the dwellers of this unhappy region. The Dutch were clearly ruling, since only a government could levy taxes on the locals. However, Barbot informs us that the European settlements 'increased the plenty of goods, and consequently lessened their prices'. Thus some Africans would have approved of the European presence and been keen to trade with them. On the other hand, Barbot also reveals in his book the wars that occurred between the Akwamus and the Akim. The Africans sold their war captives to the Europeans residing at Nungwa and Accra, meaning that 'a ship is often furnish'd with four or five hundred blacks in a fortnight or three weeks'.

William Bosman, of the Dutch West India Company, described the story in 1700. Like Barbot, his account (*A New and Accurate Description of Guinea*, London, translation 1705) presents a complex and mixed picture. For example, Axim flourished exceedingly under European influence. It is not difficult to see why they would have encouraged trade with the Europeans:

> *This country called Axim, is cultivated, and abounds with numerous large and beautiful villages, all extraordinary populous; some of which are situated on the sea-shore, and others farther on the main land; the most considerable amongst the former lie under the Brandenburgian and Dutch forts, of which the latter is by much the best. The Negro inhabitants are generally very rich, driving a great trade with the Europeans for gold...[and] industriously employ'd either in trade, fishing or agriculture, and that is chiefly exercised in the culture of rice, which grows here above all other places in an incredible abundance and is transported hence all the Gold Coast over.*

Unfortunately, there were other consequences, as Bosman revealed:

> *But the last fatal war betwixt the Ahantas and the Adomians hath reduced [Sekondi] to a miserable condition and stript it of most of its inhabitants... 'Tis indeed deplorable to see it at present and reflect on its former flourishing condition in the years 1690 and 1691.*

In addition:

> *The English fortress [at Secondi] was burnt and destroy'd by the Ahanta Negroes; its chief commander and some of the English being killed, and the rest being plunder'd of all their own and the company's goods...Sekondi was one of the finest and richest villages, as well in money as in people, upon the whole coast. But the Adomese conquerors entirely burnt and destroy'd it... The village or town of Takoradi...'tis now so ruined, that no visible remnants of it are left... The town of Sharma is moderately large and well peopled, but its inhabitants so miserably poor that I do not believe they have any like them on the Gold Coast... About 15 or 16 years past [Elmina] was very populous...but about 15 years past the smallpox swept away so many, and since by the Komenda wars together with the tyrannical government of some of their generals, they have been so miserably depopulated and impoverished, that 'tis hardly to be believed how weak it is at present... Under the English fort [at Cape Coast, the town]... was formerly well-peopled; but this, as well as all the other[s], has suffered very much in the Komenda war; besides that the multiplicity of English interlopers hath continually stript it of its inhabitants.*

THE ASHANTI UNION

Inland from the coast, the Ashanti Union was established after the year 1700. Part of the Benue-Kwa branch of Niger-Congo speakers, they came to rule over most of the modern Ghana region for the next 200 years. The union was founded by Osei-Tutu, who advocated for a common citizenship based on devotion to the Golden Stool, the nation's emblem. According to tradition, the stool fell from heaven and landed gently into the lap of Osei-Tutu.

The basis of the empire was trade: agriculture, textiles, gold and captives. Crops of transatlantic maize, sweet potatoes and pineapples were grown. Gold remained an important mainstay; some was obtained by panning in streams, but much of it was mined. Deep shafts were common and such mines could reach 100 feet deep; they were connected by tunnels several hundred feet long. Finally, trading the conquered enemies of Ashanti as slaves proved profitable. Muskets made in Birmingham, England, provided the Ashanti army with their weapons. In addition to the Dutch at Elmina and the English at Cape Coast, the Ashanti traded with other West African states.

During the time of Opoko Ware, 1720–50, the Ashanti Union expanded across the central forestlands. Creating the Ashanti Empire, its power continued to expand with his successors, becoming larger than modern Ghana. Administrative innovations by Osei Kwado, a later ruler, led to the expansion of the civil service. The bureaucrats now appointed to its commercial, financial and political posts had to show efficient service; appointments were no longer based on who deserved to inherit the position. Moreover, the Empire had an efficient network of couriers to carry the Asantehene's orders in all directions. By the early nineteenth century Kumasi, the capital city, boasted two-storey buildings and arcades and a population of 40,000. Thomas Bowditch, an English visitor, described the capital in his book, *Mission from Cape Coast Castle to Ashantee*, published in 1819:

> *Four of the principal streets are half a mile long, and from fifty to one hundred yards wide. I observed them building one, and a line was stretched on each side to make it regular. The streets*

> *were all named, and a superior captain in charge of each... What surprised me most...was the discovery that every house had its cloacae [i.e. toilet], besides the common ones for the lower orders without the town. They were generally situated under a small archway in the most retired angle of the building, but not unfrequently upstairs, within a separate room like a small closet... The holes are of a small circumference, but dug to a surprising depth, and boiling water is daily poured down, which effectually prevents the least offence [i.e. odour]. The rubbish and offal of each house was burnt every morning at the back of the street, and they were as nice and cleanly in their dwellings as in their persons.*

However, the British were conquerors and conflicts did break out. The battles between the British and Ashanti became known as the Anglo-Ashanti Wars. One took place between 1823 and 1831, a second between 1863 and 1864, and a third between 1873 and 1874. During this campaign the British destroyed the royal palace. The author of *The Story of the Ashantee Campaign*, published in 1874, Mr Winwood Reade gave a description of that remarkable palace. A prisoner showed him the sights of Kumasi:

> *We went to the king's palace, which consists of many courtyards, each surrounded with alcoves and verandahs, and having two gates or doors, so that each yard was a thoroughfare. These doors were secured by padlocks. An ordinary house has one court-yard; a large house three or four; the king's palace had ten or twelve. But the part of the palace fronting the street was a stone house, Moorish in its style...with a flat roof and a parapet, and suites of apartments on the first floor. It was built by Fanti masons many*

years ago. The rooms upstairs remind me of Wardour Street. Each was a perfect Old Curiosity Shop: books in many languages, Bohemian glass, clocks, silver plate, old furniture, Persian rugs, Kidderminster carpets, pictures and engravings, numberless chests and coffers. A sword bearing the inscription From Queen Victoria to the King of Ashantee. *A copy of the* Times, *17 October 1843. With these were many specimens of Moorish and Ashanti handicraft, gold-studded sandals such as only the king and a few great chiefs may wear, with, strange to say, Arabic writing on the soles; leopard-skin caps lined with yellow velvet and adorned outside with beaten gold like that of Kashmir, and a plume of the same precious metal; saddles of red leather, magnificent canopies or state umbrellas of velvet and satin, baskets or cradles in which Ashanti chiefs are accustomed to be carried on the heads of slaves, with other curious and tasteful things too numerous for me to describe or even catalogue.*

The British eventually overran the Ashanti Empire during the fourth Anglo-Ashanti War, which occurred in 1895–96. They changed the name of the conquered territory to the Gold Coast. After independence in 1957 Dr Kwame Nkrumah, the first president, renamed the country Ghana: the name it has today. He took this name from the ancient West African desert empire described above.

THE DAHOMEY KINGDOM AND THE AMAZONS

Dahomey was located where Benin is today. Their kings were some of the best administrators, wisest tacticians and cruellest tyrants in the African story. Their rulers and people belonged to an ethnic group known as the Fon, part of the Benue-Kwa branch of Niger-Congo speakers. Dahomey was divided into six provinces, each controlled by a royal official. The capital was Abomey. The 12 Royal Palaces of Abomey spread over 108 acres and became a city within a city, with decorated walls and painted bas reliefs. At its peak, the palaces could accommodate 8,000 people. The court was steeped in luxury with sumptuous fabrics and works of metal forged in iron and copper. However, for most of its history Dahomey was under Yoruba imperial rule. Only after shaking off Yoruba domination in the nineteenth century did it become one of the most famous military powers in West Africa. The rulers of Dahomey openly championed and practised the slave trade. Europeans saw it as a "Black Sparta", a fiercely militaristic society bent on conquest, whose soldiers struck fear into their enemies all along the Slave Coast.

A visitor witnessed the tough military drill of Dahomey Amazons led by their general. The king gave a signal, whereupon the women assumed an attitude of combat, arms raised, swords in hand, massed in a line of battle. They charged and returned three times across a construction of thorns in bare feet. Their obstacle was a wall – huge piles of acacia branches bristling with needle-sharp thorns, forming a barricade that stretched nearly 440 yards. The troops rushed it furiously, ignoring the wounds that the two-inch-long thorns inflicted. After scrambling to the top, they mimèd hand-to-hand combat with imaginary defenders, fell back, scaled the thorn wall a second time, then stormed a group of buildings, dragging out a group of cringing 'prisoners'. The bravest troops were presented with belts made from acacia thorns. Proud to show themselves impervious to pain, the women strapped their trophies around their waists. Another of the Dahomey Amazons' training exercises was to kill a maddened bull with their bare hands. The women also wrestled one another and undertook survival training, being sent into the forest for up to nine days with minimal rations.

Dahomey traditions suggest that Agassu, a man of part Yoruba origins, was the founder ruler in the late sixteenth century. He and his fellow founders of the Fon princely states migrated from a place in Tado (in Togo) from the west. Agassu founded a polity centred at Allada, which had a tributary relationship with the Oyo Empire. However, a rival settlement was established south near the coast at Porto Novo, with another rival settlement established north at Abomey. From Abomey came the line of 13 kings of which Dahomey history would be made. It was also the centre of weaving, specializing in a particular fabric that fused bark fibre and cotton. The inhabitants of Abomey were expert producers of this textile; they created quality designs that showed technical excellence. Gangni Hessou, Agassu's rival, would be the first king of this line.

At some point, a satellite state was established at Whydah on the coast west of Porto Novo. Allada, Porto Novo, Abomey and Whydah were princely states, all independent of each other but all tributary to the Oyo Empire. However, Allada and Whydah became slave traders and raided inland for people to enslave. By the 1680s Whydah sold a staggering 1,000 people per month.

Ouegbadja became the ruler of Abomey in 1645. He considered warfare a skilled art and instituted military training; he also adopted the tactic of night attacks and was said to have been the first Fon ruler to own firearms. His authority was enhanced by the collection of poll taxes, which boosted the wealth of the court. Moreover, when someone died their property reverted to the ruler. Much of the revenue went towards the purchase of firearms, of which there was a royal monopoly. Royal power was emphasized by religious ceremonies giving the king a semi-divine status. Public sacrifices were made, which gave the rulers a sacred backing. Finally, it was during the time of Ouegbadja that the name Dahomey was established.

Slavery, Oyo power and King Agadja

Slavery altered Dahomey demographics. Women heavily outnumbered men in the towns – the result of a combination of military losses and the effects of the slave trade. Indeed, the Fon were so badly outnumbered by their enemies that Dahomey's kings were forced to conscript women. The Yoruba alone were about 10 times as numerous as the Fon. These two reasons prompted the creation of the world's only all-female combat force. However, drafting women into the army long term reinforced the demographic difficulties. Moreover, Dahomey faced punitive measures from their overlords, the Oyo Empire. They attacked and ravaged the city of Allada in 1682–83, then again in 1698, when cavalry were sent in.

Agadja became the next ruler of Abomey in 1708. Historians credit him with the 'Dahomean Revolution' – that is, the creation of a unified Dahomey. He was skilled and able, with a magnetic personality and a quick sense of humour. Courteous and magnanimous in victory, Agadja also knew how to strike terror into the hearts of a foe. However, scholars disagree on whether he set out to monopolize the entire slave trade or to stamp it out altogether. In either case, he could have changed the course of history had he succeeded. Agadja also suggested to the British an end to the slave trade, proposing that plantations should be established in Dahomey with British technical manpower.

On the military side, Agadja established a military training scheme for boys. Here pupils were drilled on why they must admire courage and how to endure hardship on the battlefield, obey orders and use guns. Ultimately Agadja was preparing them to expand and conquer the rival Allada princely state further south. In 1724 his troops conquered Allada, and he destroyed and closed the slave ports of Offra and Jakin. At Jakin his forces sacked the European factories, seizing men, goods and cannon. He sent presents to the emperor of Oyo to deceive him into believing that his interests were not in jeopardy. Then, in 1726, the Yorubas sent a cavalry force into the region and destroyed Abomey.

The Abomey army was decimated and the royal palace burned. Agadja took refuge in the forests, eventually coming out of hiding, rallying his people and resuming battle. In 1727 he conquered Whydah. Agadja burned its capital, Sahe, to the ground and took 40 Europeans prisoner. He forced out the slave traders, who fled for their lives, and forbade them to return. The European slave traders decided that there was no future in the slave trade in that region as long as Agadja was alive.

The conflict was not over, however. Further Yoruba cavalry campaigns took place in 1728, 1729 and 1730. The Yorubas managed to conquer Dahomey and produced a treaty that Agadja was forced to accept. His own son, who became the next ruler, was brought to the Yoruba court as a vassal prisoner. With Agadja's position weakened, the slave traders returned; Dahomey soon became the major slave-trading kingdom of the region. Agadja died in 1732, a disappointed man.

In this period Abomey had a gated royal area, surrounded by a 29½ foot wall with six entrances across a moat. Inside the walls lived the royals and the royal craftspeople: smiths, leather workers, potters, weavers, appliqué makers, bas relief makers, calabash engravers, gong players, singers and the Hountondji (the guild of jewellers who designed for the royals).

Capture or Be Captured

We have seen that, had King Agadja succeeded, he would have blocked the transportation of people from Dahomey to the New World. But what caused so many Dahomey rulers to become slave traders? In *The African Slave Trade*, published in 1961, Dr Basil Davidson explains that the people of Dahomey were interested in defending themselves from coastal raiders too – but this was only possible if they could lay hold of adequate supplies of firearms and ammunition. Such items could only be obtained by trade with the coast, and only in exchange for captives. The drastic but inescapable alternatives were thus to enslave others and buy firearms or to risk being captured yourself. This was the inner dynamic of the slaving connection with Europe; it pushed Dahomey, as it did other countries, into wholesale participation in slaving. No single state could safely withstand this combination of slaves and guns. Dahomey, like others, was caught in the slave trade's ruinous chain of cause and effect.

The Amazons came into existence as palace guards in the 1720s. A French enslaver, Jean-Pierre Thibault, who called at the port of Whydah in 1725, described seeing groups of women armed with long poles and acting as police. In 1729 the Amazons made their first documented appearance, helping to recapture the same port after it fell to a surprise Yoruba attack. Later, there were about 600 women in the Dahomeyan army – from the 1760s until the 1840s – at which point King Guezo expanded it to as many as 6,000.

In 1732 Tegbessou became the new ruler of Dahomey. Returning from Yorubaland where he had lived as a hostage, his many brothers opposed him becoming king. His mother prevailed, however, and ensured that he was installed. Tegbessou reorganized the government along Yoruba lines and gave male and female ministers greater responsibility in the management of the kingdom. Oral records were kept mentally by women, known for their good memory of the details. Tegbessou followed his father's policy of attempting to free Dahomey from Yoruba control, but ultimately he too failed. However, under him and his successor Kpeingla (r. 1774–89), Dahomey became *the* centre of the slave trade. In 1750 Tegbessou made a staggering £250,000 in just one year by selling people into slavery.

Through the help of a Brazilian slave trader, King Guezo staged a coup against the previous ruler. He had a strong army, which he improved by relying more heavily upon the Amazons and by purchasing more guns from the Europeans. Amazons appear in his palace bas reliefs. In 1823 Dahomey successfully won independence from the Oyo Empire. Moreover, each year Guezo organized an annual festival in which human sacrifices were offered to the gods. Incidentally, a famous Yoruba princess was enslaved by Dahomey and sold on to Britain, where her name became Sarah Bonetta Forbes. Glele was the next ruler, acceding to the throne in 1858. His bodyguard consisted of 200 women and 500 of the finest males. The Amazons were ranked above the men, and the king sometimes picked his wives from among them. Men that had unruly wives, on the other hand, could give them over to the king for his army. The preferred weapons of the female warriors were short swords and knives, while some carried modern rifles. However, European observers were disdainful of the way the women handled their ancient flintlock muskets, firing from the hip rather than aiming from the shoulder. However, even the French agreed that they 'excelled at hand-to-hand combat'.

King Behanzin was the last important king of Dahomey. He aimed to keep all Europeans out of the interior of his kingdom, making exceptions only in rare cases. Even those permitted to enter were not allowed to bring sextants, surveying instruments or cameras.

The customs service was strict, with visitors required to carry a special passport. Fear of the king's wrath and the vigilance of his secret police prevented corruption of the country's officials.

The Final Chapter

The beginning of the end of the kingdom started in 1890. Dahomey defeated a French expedition and made France pay for the use of a port. Moreover, the Germans had supplied Dahomey with modern rifles; five of them even held high rank in the Dahomey army. Moreover, Behanzin flouted a treaty that had been negotiated between France and his father, the previous ruler, declaring that treaty null and void.

In 1892 the French declared that they would take over the kingdom of Dahomey. They recruited troops from Senegal led by Colonel A.A. Dodds, a soldier of Senegalese and European descent. The Dahomey soldiers fought with considerable bravery, but they were successful only when it came to hand-to-hand combat. Even the Amazons fell dead at the feet of the French machine gunners. The French forces, led by Dodds, seized one of the larger royal palaces; later in the campaign they captured the capital of Abomey. Behanzin then ordered the burning of the city, its palace and its wonderful art treasures, but his throne of beaten gold survived undamaged.

The war fought between 1892 and 1894 proved even more ferocious than the first, comprising 23 separate battles. The female troops were the last to surrender, and even then – at least according to rumour – the survivors took devastating revenge on the French. They covertly substituted themselves for Dahomeyan women and were taken into the enemy stockade. Each allowed herself to be seduced by a French officer, waited for him to fall asleep and then cut his throat with his own bayonet.

On 24 January 1894, with the last remnants of his army destroyed, Behanzin surrendered to the French. Initially he was sent off to France, but was later exiled to Martinique in the Caribbean. The French imposed a puppet ruler, then went on to abolish the Dahomey kingdom in 1900. This marks the period of European colonial rule. It ended in 1960, when Dahomey received independence from France. In 1975 they changed the name of the country to Benin, *not* to be confused with Great Benin in Nigeria.

In his book *Wars of Imperial Conquest in Africa, 1830 to 1914*, published in 1998, military historian Professor Colonel Bruce Vandervort notes that the Dahomey Amazons were the world's *only* all-female combat unit operating in the nineteenth century. The women troops aroused a great deal of interest in Europe. They began as royal bodyguards, but evolved by the late nineteenth century into the Dahomeyan army's elite contingent. Entering combat in the 1840s they became the most warlike and the most feared; and it was they who bore the brunt of fighting in the nineteenth-century Dahomeyan Wars.

THE EARLY HISTORY OF CENTRAL AFRICA

In former times, an important civilization flourished in Central Africa. Its span of power included parts of Libya, Niger, Chad, Nigeria and Cameroon. The ruins of its fifteenth-century capital, Ngazargamu, are in Nigeria. However, colonialism has not been kind to this civilization, causing its heritage to be split across five modern countries. Libya was colonized by the Italians in 1911, following a series of military campaigns against the Ottoman Empire. Parts of Niger were ruled by France in the 1890s; it officially became a French colony in 1922. Chad was conquered by France in 1910, when it was named the Military Territory of Chad. The country was then absorbed into French Equatorial Africa, along with other French colonial possessions.

Cameroon was initially colonized by Germany, under the auspices of Gustav Nachtigal, a German official, who arrived in Duala in July 1884. It became a centre of German operations on the coast, providing a base from which Nachtigal negotiated treaties with local rulers around Duala. He then moved on to other areas in the region and secured further treaties. Bamoun, for example, was an important African civilization in the region. The treaties expanded German control until Cameroon became a German protectorate on 17 August 1884.

Originally a military surgeon, Nachtigal developed a reputation as an explorer. In 1881 he wrote a famous book called *Sahara and Sudan* which detailed his travels across Africa. Wilhelm I of Prussia sent him on a mission to carry gifts to Sheikh Umar, the ruler of Borno in Central Africa. The gifts were to acknowledge the kindness shown by Umar to previous German travellers. Nachtigal set out in 1869 from Tripoli in Ottoman-controlled Libya. Travelling with six men and eight camels, he left an account of his journey and the different parts of Africa that he saw.

Eventually Nachtigal reached Borno, a civilization of Afroasiatic and Nilo-Saharan speakers. He published an etching of a royal knight in quilted armour on horseback, the horse also wearing quilted armour. Eventually, on 6 June 1870, he was received at the palace of Sheikh Umar. In his book Nachtigal described what he saw:

> *It was there that we were announced, and soon after, passing through another vestibule, where some eunuchs and slaves were standing, we entered the audience hall. The latter, of moderate size, seemed still smaller because of a double row of large quadrangular pillars, which tapered a little upwards and offered some rudiments of decoration. From there…we had a view of a part of the room…where the reception was to be held. The floor was covered with carpets, and the walls of grey clay hung with fabrics of various colours and of all designs. A pretty layer of iron of European manufacture, and a roughly carved wooden armchair, with a bench transformed into a bare sofa with a mattress, carpets, and cushions, constituted all the furniture of this little recess.*
>
> **Gustav Nachtigal, *Sahara and Sudan*, 1881,**
> **trans. (to French) Jules Gourdault, trans.**
> **(from the French) Robin Walker**

He then received an audience with the ruler:

> *On the bench sat Sheikh Omar ibn al-Hajj Mohammed el-Amin el-Kanemi with his legs crossed. He wore a simple cloth burnous over a white Borno gar and an immense white turban, very artistically rolled up. In front of it, on the divan, was placed the royal sword; beside him, on a cushion, lay a rifle inlaid with silver, while on the ground yawned two yellow slippers embroidered in the fashion of Tunis. The whole person of the Sheikh breathed extreme cleanliness. He was a man about 50 years of age, of noble height, rather fat, with a white beard, a full face, absolutely black skin, with a good and intelligent air.*

The man with whom Nachitgal had an audience belonged to a lineage of kings dating back over 1,000 years. He went on to see indigenous architecture and interior decoration with an equally long history. Moreover, Sheikh Umar gave presents to Nachtigal, through an intermediary, to take home. The gifts included 'various samples of Sudanese costumes'. They were the exquisite, Borno-made textiles typically worn by the elite: fashions for courtly men and women. These were colourfully and elaborately designed, with intricate embroidery of repeated patterns, geometric shapes and Celtic knots. The materials used were cotton and florette silk. The textiles, now in the Ethnology Museum in Berlin, were products of indigenous technology and artistic design. The civilization that produced this culture was Kanem-Borno, which at the height of its power had controlled parts of Libya, Chad, Niger, Nigeria and Cameroon. Even before the Kanem-Borno era, however, there was an earlier civilization in the region called the Sao culture.

THE BAMOUN KINGDOM

Cameroon is also home to other kingdoms and histories. On 13 April 2024 a new museum opened in Foumban. Called the Museum of the Bamoun Kings, it has 10,000 artefacts that chart a history dating back to 1394. The Bamoun people are part of the Benue-Congo branch of the Niger-Congo family. Nshare Yèn founded their kingdom, which is located in western Cameroon. Counting the founding monarch, 16 kings or *mfon* sat on the throne at Foumban before the Colonial Period. Among them were child rulers, female rulers and military usurpers. The dynasty ruled over the creation of the eight-day week, palace reconstructions, suppressed internal uprisings, an 85-year reign, a 30-minute reign, expansionist military campaigns, internal strife and massacres, and much more.

Resembling something from a theme park in Wakanda, the museum itself is a most outlandish piece of architectural design. The nineteenth ruler, Ibrahim Mbombo Njoya, began the project in 2013; his death in 2021 meant that the building was completed by his son, King Mouhammad-Nabil Mforifoum Mbombo Njoya. Built on a circular plan of 53819⅝ square feet, the museum is in the royal compound of Foumban. The design pays homage to the royal emblem of Bamoun: a two-headed snake, a spider and a double gong. The snake represents strength and power, the giant spider symbolizes work and wisdom, and the gong signifies patriotism and unity. Visitors walk through the double gong-shaped arch as they enter the building. The mouths of the snake are other entrances.

Inside the museum are almost a dozen exhibition spaces. Designed ultimately to hold 12,500 Bamoun artefacts, some items are from the rulers themselves. Vast murals show the history of the ruling dynasty; there are also some statues of the kings. Also preserved are parts of an ancient canoe, the royal headdresses, war trophy costumes, pipes, umbrellas, handbags, beaded stools, thrones, sceptres, weapons, beds, and so on. Rooms devoted to the later kings, some of whom converted to Islam following Hausa influence, have manuscripts in the Bamoun script, along with costumes, royal private chambers, Quranic artefacts, musical instruments, masks and portraits. One room features audiovisual projections on the secret societies of Bamoun culture and their ceremonial costumes and masks. Other rooms showcase Bamoun craftsmanship and artistry.

The museum idea originally came from King Njoya (r. 1889–1931), the seventeenth monarch. He opened the royal treasures to the wider community, breaking with the tradition of exclusivity, but is best remembered today as the creator of the Bamoun script. He knew the Arabic script from his contact with his Fulani and Hausa neighbours, but in 1895 he devised a new writing system of 510 pictographic characters. Several revisions later, this became a syllabary of 83 characters plus 10 numerals. With the help of his scribes, Njoya prepared a book on the history and customs of Bamoun, a religious book, a book on medicine and local pharmacopoeia and more. In addition, he opened 47 schools to teach literacy in Bamoun and founded a printing press that used his new script.

Njoya also built a beautiful new palace. A tourist attraction in modern Cameroon, it is a three-storey structure made of local earth and bricks. Its design fused Bamoun with Hausa and German architectural aesthetics. Originally designed to have functioned as a museum, as well as providing living space, it contained 8,000 manuscripts. Njoya was a patron of beadworkers, brass casters, weavers, dyers and other crafts workers. His palace compound contained 300 looms and six dye pits with different colours, some holding dyes created by Njoya himself. This new palace replaced one that dated back to an eighteenth-century ruler, King Mbouombouo.

King Mbouombouo (r. 1757–1814) was the eleventh king of the dynasty. Remembered as a conqueror, he increased the size of the kingdom 20 times. He conquered more than 48 chieftaincies. Wealth flowed into the kingdom as Bamoun gained control over long-distance trade. People from the conquered territories saw Foubam as a metropolitan magnet of opportunity. Foumban probably held 15,000 to 20,000 inhabitants at this time. The capital was surrounded by a 16⅜ foot wall. In Mbouombouo's royal compound was a vast complex of 100 tall wooden buildings with thatched roofs; it could accommodate between 2,000 and 3,000 people, most of whom were royalty. Each building consisted of a single square room, surmounted by a thatched roof. The lattice walls were made from three layers of palm rib, but assembled and joined together. The king's reception area in the inner courtyard was superbly built. It had a semicircular porch with tall pillars supporting the roof, decorated with paired male and female retainers carved into each column.

INTRODUCING KANEM BORNO

German colonization lasted from mid-1884 to February 1916. The Germans were ultimately forced out of the territory following their defeat by Britain and France in the First World War. The new rulers partitioned the land between Britain and France. The British took one-fifth of the territory, which they administered as part of their Nigerian colony. The remaining portion, at the time referred to as East Cameroon, was under the control of France. During this period of English and French colonization, important new discoveries on the history of Kanem-Borno were made.

Sir Herbert Richmond Palmer was a colonial supervisor for Britain. He studied the languages and literature of the region and became an acknowledged authority. In 1928 he published *Sudanese Memoirs*, a three-volume compilation of African manuscripts from Kanem-Borno and Hausaland. Among the manuscripts he translated is a sixteenth-century chronicle called *The Kanem Wars*. This details, among other things, the military and diplomatic conflicts between Idris Alooma, the brilliant ruler of Kanem-Borno, and his enemies, the Bulala. The book makes interesting reading as it shows the rules by which Africans in this part of the world conducted battle. In it the chronicler observes:

> *The Sultan was an accomplished diplomatist and was conversant with correct procedure and methods of negotiation. God most high had endowed him with knowledge. As has been said before in this book: 'There is no forbidding what God has given. Nor can that be given which God has forbidden.' This maxim Idris, with the wise political instinct which, as we have noted, he was endowed, followed in sending an embassy with a note to the Sultan of the Bulala and his captains and his emirs and his chiefs. The ambassador was Fuski ibn Kilili of the tribe of Kayi. The note ran as follows:- 'If my note reaches you in safety, and you read it at leisure, know that my desire is that you should send to me an upright and sensible man to hear what I have to say about the true reason of our coming here, and return to you.' Such was the tenor of our Sultan's letter to the Bulala. When it reached them and they had read the contents in the presence of their people, they became very angry and positively refused to send anyone. They sent a letter written by Hajj ibn Dili, but sent no representative though they had plenty*

of sensible men to send to us even as we had said to them. The contents of their letter were to the effect that they could not understand our action, in that 'you have burnt our houses on your way, and done evil in our land. You have done it and that is all.' That is what they said. When we saw their letter we were utterly astonished, and saw that their action was that of men puffed up with pride, and that none would return answer like this save people confident in their power and strength over all. Had matters been as they thought and argued and supposed, we should have remained at home in our country. Alas! Alas! The matter was not as they thought.

PREHISTORIC GIRAFFE ETCHING

In the Air Mountains in Niger are prehistoric petroglyphs. Carved between 10,000 and 7000 years ago, as many as 828 surviving images have been found. Most depict animals including cattle, ostriches, antelopes, lions, rhinoceros and camels. Seventeen of the images are inscriptions in Tifinagh, an ancient desert script, but the most notable are petroglyphs of giraffes. One is led by a human figure, capturing a moment of interaction between humans and nature. The larger giraffe is male, 18 feet tall and in the front. The smaller one is female. Engraved side by side on the sandstone's surface, the carving combined several techniques including scraping, smoothing and deep engraving of the outlines. Most significantly, these are the largest known animal petroglyphs in the world.

Moreover, they were technical feats of some accomplishment. In *The World's Largest Rock Art Petroglyph*, the Bradshaw Foundation (www.bradshawfoundation.com) comments as follows:

How were the carvings created? 10,000 years ago there was no metal – this was well before the Bronze Age – so how did the artists carve the lines? They must have used a harder material like flint to carve the softer sandstone of Dabous. The desert sands surrounding the outcrop are covered with numerous chisels of petrified wood, perfect for wearing away grooves and then polishing the surface. This in itself magnifies the significance of Dabous, for its scale and craftsmanship, and therefore the amount of time it must have taken to execute.

Today the Dabous carvings offer a rare glimpse into a world long lost to the desert sands. They remind us that the now barren Sahara was once a green and vibrant landscape, alive with both humans and wildlife.

THE SAO CULTURE

The Sao culture was a civilization that flourished across Cameroon, Niger and Nigeria. In *Kanem-Borno: 1,000 Years of Splendor*, a book about Kanem Borno aimed at children, published in 1995, Philip Koslow wrote: 'Remains of Sao settlements to the southeast of Lake Chad have been traced back to the 4th century B.C.'

Two writers from the University of Ibadan, G.T. Stride and Dr Caroline Ifeka, paint a picture of the Sao culture before 700 CE in *Peoples and Empires of West Africa*, published in 1971. The Sao had significant political and artistic skills. In addition, although they didn't form an empire, they developed city-states with strong local patriotism. Each city dominated and protected its surrounding countryside, governed by a divine ruler within an elaborate hierarchy.

Women held respected positions, with both the Queen Mother and Senior Sister influencing government. The Sao were mainly farmers, but they were also skilled craftsmen, creating household items, tools and religious art from clay and metals. Archaeological finds include burial urns, clay figures and bronze figures of animals and humans. However, the vigour of their power is best demonstrated by their long resistance to Kanem Borno. Moreover, many cultural characteristics of the Sao influenced Kanem Borno.

Archaeologists have found settlements around Dala, in Northern Nigeria, that belonged to the Sao. Hausa records tell of the pre-Islamic worship of Tsumburburai, to whom the priest of this religion made annual sacrifices of black animals in the grove of Jakara. In Dala there was an important shrine to this deity, a sacred tree called Shamuz. In his book *A History of Islam in West Africa*, published in 1962, Professor J. Spencer Trimingham claims that this all belonged to the Sao civilization. An important authority on West Africa, he adds that their ruling class practised matrilineal succession and also had 'walled towns'.

Djado is a promising 'walled town' in the Bilma region of Niger. Built on a mountain, the city is circular and protected by walls. Due to these, some call it the Djado Fortress. The buildings, now in ruined form, are clearly of several storeys. Though an abandoned city, Djado is in good enough shape for archaeologists and other experts to attempt a restoration, although no excavations have so far been attempted. No one seems to know how old the town is, but ages such as 800 or 1,000 years have been advanced. Some commentators report a Kanuri tradition that claims the Sao founded Djado. In addition, a tradition says that the Sao founded other places, such as Tedjerhe in southern Fezzan, the oldest known settlement of the Kaouar. Djado became absorbed by Kanem Borno in the early thirteenth century before becoming independent again. It was probably also a part of Kanem-Borno during the reign of Idris Alooma in the sixteenth century. However, during the eighteenth and nineteenth centuries, as the power of the Borno Empire faltered, the people of the oasis were exposed to Tuareg raids from the desert. As a result the population left and settled in Kaouar. Another explanation of why they abandoned the city might be that cattle herding in the region introduced mosquitoes, causing malaria to spread.

THE KANEM-BORNO EMPIRE

The Kanem-Borno Empire thrived in the areas of southern Libya, eastern Niger, western Chad, northeast Nigeria and Cameroon. The Zaghawa, a Nilo-Saharan people, developed this Kanuri culture after being horse-borne nomads. Its rulers, the Sefuwa, came from the same family, starting in the late eleventh century. The known history of this long-lasting empire spans the early ninth century to the nineteenth.

The early monarchs ruled over Kanem, the eastern Niger and western Chad region. Dugu, the first of their kings, is believed to have lived around 800 CE. The Dynasty, sometimes called the Dugawa, ruled until 1075. This began as a very humble period. Al-Yaqubi, a noted Arab writer of the age, informs us that the Zaghawa of Kanem had no use for towns and instead lived in 'huts made of corn stalks' (quoted in Sir Richmond Palmer, *The Bornu Sahara and Sudan*, 1936).

A century later, the condition of culture had evolved greatly. Al-Muhallabi, writing in 985 CE, recorded that the Zaghawa kingdom had become important among the African kingdoms; it was also populous and could boast of two cities, Manan and Tarazaki. In addition, Al-Muhallabi observed:

Their houses are all of plastered clay, as is also the castle of their king, whom they extol and worship as if he were God Most High. They pretend that the king does not eat any ordinary food. For his sustenance he has a secret body of persons, who take food to his compound, so that no one knows where his food comes from. If it so chances that any of his subjects meet the camel which carries the king's food, that man is at once killed on the spot. The king drinks with certain chosen companions. His drink is made from millet mixed with honey. As clothing, he wears trousers made of thin wool, and over them he is decked out in an upper garment of wool of poor quality, prickly and lousy, with silk over that.

Quoted in Sir Richmond Palmer, *The Bornu Sahara and Sudan*, 1936

For the ordinary people, by contrast, things were much more modest. They wore animal skins and subsisted on their own farming produce, supplemented with meat from their own animals. On their farmlands millet, beans and wheat were cultivated.

However, the Zaghawa were conquerors. They had been the main suppliers of slaves to Egypt and North Africa from this region. The trade brought them constantly developing weapons and accessories for successful conquest, such as big Barbary horses – essential for carrying an armoured knight, the chainmail needed for horse and rider, the harness and saddlery, the swords and shields, and the heavy metal lances. To monopolize such a golden road to wealth and power, and to guard it from rivals to the east and west, was an obvious incentive to empire. The Sao people thus became a target of Zaghawa attacks. Zaghawa nomads came to the Sao lands by migration and settled there. Using trickery, the Zaghawa gradually took over these lands and later absorbed them into their own.

The Zaghawa expanded their territory into the Sahara in the eleventh century. They also took charge of the Muslim community's trading operations in the area. The royal court began to be influenced by Islam; for four years, Queen Hawwa ruled Kanem, becoming the first Islamic monarch. Another reign proved equally brief. In 1075, amid all this confusion, Mai Humé Jilmi seized power. He established the Sefuwa Dynasty and put an end to the Dugawa's rule.

Creating the First Cultural Flowering

Mai Dunama ibn Salma transformed Kanem into a major regional force in the thirteenth century. He fought in the desert, leading 30,000 cavalry and an additional force of infantry. His war machine fought southern Libya's Fezzan region using camels rather than horses. The eastern Bulala, Kanem's main enemies, were crushed. The Hausa cities of Northern Nigeria were pillaged. In his book *Old Africa Rediscovered*, published in 1959, Dr Basil Davidson, a pioneering authority on African history, reconstructs a scene of:

> *Swinging tassels in the dust, harness brasses that glitter against quilted armour, long spears pennoned and pointed, brilliant cavaliers, all the creak and swing and clatter and pomp of an aristocratic army saddled for sack and loot: with the footsore* plebs *in goat-skin, armed with clubs and spears and small hope, trailing out behind.*

Njimi became the new capital. From here, official and cultural contacts were established with the world at large. Trade flourished across the Sahara. From the north came horses, fine metalware, glassware, fabrics and copper. From the west came kola nuts and ivory. From the south came cotton goods. Merchants traded with Tripoli, Fezzan and Egypt. Kanem exported slaves, ivory, ostrich feathers and live animals. Kanemi Muslims established a school in Cairo that gained a considerable reputation. The institution had hostel facilities used by Kanem pilgrims going to or from Mecca or studying at Cairo's Al-Azhar University; they regularly sent money for its upkeep. In her book *A Tropical Dependency*, published in 1905, Lady Lugard commented that 'The thirteenth century would seem to have been a brilliant period'. Sir Herbert Richmond Palmer appeared equally impressed, noting in his *History of the First Twelve Years of the Reign of Mai Idris Alooma*, published in 1926: 'The degree of civilisation achieved by its early chiefs would appear to compare favourably with that of European monarchs of that day.'

However, internal issues were brought to light by the conflict with the Bulala. Dunama II was a strict Muslim, converting many of the conquered peoples to Islam and instituting the Koran as the basis for law. Unfortunately, he went much further. He was determined to destroy Kanuri traditional religion by demonstrating that it was built on mere superstition. As a result, the Bulala made a risky attempt to gain independence from Kanem. The empire expanded its territory because of additional wars. In North East Nigeria, the land of Gaga (Borno) was conquered and taken over by the Kanemi. Henceforth, the Mais were known as Kings of Kanem and Lords of Borno. The Borno people were Afroasiatic speakers.

Examining the management of this enormous area is intriguing. Surrounded by titled officeholders and palace slaves, the ruler lived a ceremonially isolated life. The Queen Mother and the Queen Sister (as opposed to 'Senior Sister' in Sao times), two women who each had their own court and officers, occupied the highest positions in the kingdom, as was the case in many African nations. In theory, the provincial governors in charge of the north, east, south and west were the highest-ranking male dignitaries. Frequently princes of the royal house, they were given responsibility for the administration of distant provinces; each of them surrounded himself with a court and officers that mirrored the central one. There was also an Astronomer Royal and a Reckoner of the Months.

Problems with the Bulala emerged, with battles taking place in the fourteenth and fifteenth centuries, which the Mais lost. When Ali Ghaji was in power, however, the tide of bad luck changed. He established a new capital in Borno to consolidate power rather than risk more losses at the hands of the Bulala. Ali Ghaji also established the city of Ngazargamu, close to the Yobe River, in 1484. Even though it is now in ruins, a sizeable complex of distinctive red-brick construction can still be identified – apparently the Mais' palace. Other red-brick ruins were the homes of the leading persons. An overwhelming rampart, 23 feet in height and approached through five entrances, encircled this central area, covering 6½ square feet. Lastly, Ali Ghaji, like his Songhai contemporary Sonni Ali, achieved world renown. His state, Borno, appears on a Portuguese map of 1489.

At the Height of Power

The sixteenth century was associated with greater town and city life. Some of the towns (at Ali Gajiri, Damasak, Difa, Duji, Gashagar, Wudi and Yo) developed into considerable urban centres, where pottery, weaving, leatherwork and dyeing flourished. Borno leather paid for the importation of European manufactured goods, perfumes, armaments, etc. Great luxury was associated with this period. The emperor's cavalry, according to Leo Africanus, had golden 'stirrups, spurs, bits, and buckles'. Even the ruler's dogs had 'chains of the finest gold' (quoted in Basil Davidson, *A History of West Africa 1000–1800*, 1977).

Mai Idris Alooma (1564–96) was a most successful politician of the period. Mahmud Kati, the great Songhai historian, wrote that: 'The mass of our contemporaries hold that there are four Sultans not counting the supreme Sultan [the Sultan of Constantinople] to wit – the Sultan of Baghdad, the Sultan of Cairo, the Sultan of Borno and the Sultan of Mali' (quoted in Sir Richmond Palmer, *The Bornu Sahara and Sudan*, 1936). His military prowess was outstanding, with Idris's armies being possibly the first in Africa to have muskets. He acquired them from the Turkish Empire. Lady Lugard noted how '[n] orth, south, east, and west he carried his conquering arms', adding that 'To give a list of the many [peoples] that he subdued could only weary the reader'.

Idris reformed and standardized the judiciary by establishing a system of Islamic courts. He himself ruled according to Islamic political theory, taking a stand against, among other things, immorality in the capital. In their book *Medieval Africa: 1250–1800*, published in 2001, Roland Oliver and Anthony Atmore wrote that: 'He presided over a court famous for the high standard of its legal and theological disputations'. Like his Songhai contemporaries Idris was a patron of learning, encouraging scholars from many other African countries to take up residence in Borno. He improved navigation on the Yobe River and commissioned the building of longer, flat-bottomed boats, initially for his navy. For land transportation, Idris imported a far greater number of camels, replacing the dependence on mules, oxen and donkeys. The great Mai was also a builder, constructing new brick mosques in the cities that replaced the older buildings. He also founded a hostel in Mecca for Borno pilgrims. Following the fall of Songhai in 1591, the great Mai became the undisputed champion of the region's Muslims. The empire became the Borno Caliphate. Phillip Koslow, a modern historian, declared that:

> *His contemporary, Elizabeth I of England, a shrewd and strong-willed monarch who gave her name to an age and has been repeatedly celebrated in books and films, could hardly have claimed greater achievements in war, administration or diplomacy.*
>
> **Philip Koslow, *Kanem-Borno: 1,000 Years of Splendor*, 1995**

In the seventeenth century, the Caliphate repelled invaders from all directions by projecting an image of strength to the outside world. The capital, Ngazargamu, exploded into one of the world's biggest cities. Susan Denyer, an architectural scholar, estimates in her book *African Traditional Architecture*, published in 1978, that the city had 'about quarter of a million people' living there by 1658. There were 660 streets in it. As a reflection of town planning, many were broad and rigid. Trees provided shade on both sides of the dendal, or high streets. Religious needs were met by four Friday mosques, each of which could accommodate 12,000 worshippers at a time. These structures must have been constructed on a grand scale.

Dr Davidson has described this as the 'harvest time of Kanem-Bornu civilisation'. He notes that though little is known about the way of life for ordinary people during this period, we 'may well imagine that they made the best of these peaceful years' (Basil Davidson, A *History of West Africa 1000–1800*, 1977). Farmers worked safely in their fields. Travellers and pilgrims used the roads without fear. Towns and villages thrived with increased trade due to security and unified rule. Learning expanded in towns and schools grew in villages.

Towards the End of Kanem Borno History

This tranquillity was challenged in 1667 by two serious invasions. Both the Tuaregs of the desert and the Junkun of Eastern Nigeria were defeated by Mai Ali with success. Both groups raided the capital in search of booty. Dan Marina, a contemporary at the Hausa University of Katsina, composed a poem dedicated to the Borno Caliph:

Ali has triumphed over the heathen [i.e. Junkun],
a matchless triumph in the path of God.
No sultan like him; A Laith among Laiths, ever stout of heart.
Has he not brought us succour? Verily but for him
Our hearts had never ceased from dread of the unbelievers.
Narrow had become to us the earth pressed by the foe,
Till Ali saved our children and their children yet unborn.
O people! Say with one accord 'May God grant
him recompense for our deliverance'.
He drove back to the furthest borders the army of the Junkun,
And God scattered their host disheartened.

Dan Masina, 'Ode – A Poem in Praise of Mai Ali of Borno', quoted in Sir Richmond Palmer, *The Bornu Sahara and Sudan*, 1936

The empire survived the invasions, but towards the end of the seventeenth century the first of a series of great famines occurred.

The terminal decline and break-up of the empire began towards the very end of the eighteenth century, possibly prompted by economic factors. The Caliphate lost control of an important desert trade in salt to the Tuaregs. This disruption of the trade routes caused a series of famines in the southern part of the empire. In 1808 Ngazargamu was taken over by the Fulanis, another group in the area whose power was growing, and in 1812 the capital was destroyed. All of this led to both the decline of the Caliphate and the end of its internal cohesion. The remaining empire was subsequently divided between British, French, Italian and German colonial forces as part of the 'scramble for Africa'.

THE EARLY HISTORY OF ETHIOPIA & ERITREA

Raffaele Rubattino, an Italian entrepreneur, ran a shipping company that sailed on the Mediterranean and the Red Sea. In late 1869 he purchased the Bay of Assab from local rulers on the Red Sea coast. With this acquisition, a tiny piece of Eritrea was now in Italian private hands. However, in 1882 the Italian government took control of the port. Massawa, a historic port city on the Red Sea coast, also in Eritrea, was taken over by the Italians in February 1885. Over the next few years, the Italian government acquired more and more Eritrean land. In 1889 a treaty of friendship, the Treaty of Wuchale, was signed between Ethiopia and Italy. In it Ethiopia recognized Italian control over Eritrea. In any case, Ethiopia's king, Menelik II, had no direct control over Eritrea. He thus had no problem with the Italians exercising control over lands ruled by his rivals. Finally, in 1890, the Colony of Eritrea was officially founded, to remain under Italian rule until 1941.

Following the collapse of Italy during the Second World War, Eritrea came under British administration. In 1951 the country transferred to United Nations supervision, only to become an autonomous part of Ethiopia again in September 1952. However, after the eventual fall of the Derg regime in 1991, Eritrea sought and achieved de facto independence. The key issue that discredited the

Derg regime was the famine 'of biblical proportions' that ravaged Ethiopia in 1984 and 1985. Not only did the publicity around the famine paint this part of Africa as a begging bowl, but it also gave Eritrea the impetus to break away from Ethiopia.

However, the region had a history beyond this. In 1855, Captain Sir Richard Burton visited an East African city called Harar. He described his voyage there in a book called *First footsteps in East Africa, or, An exploration of Harar*, published in 1856.

> *The following pages contain the writer's diary, kept during his march to and from Harar… Harar, moreover, had never been visited, and few are the cities of the world which in the present age, when men hurry about the earth, have not opened their gates to European adventure. The ancient metropolis of a once mighty race, the only permanent settlement in Eastern Africa, the reported seat of Moslem learning, a walled city of stone houses, possessing its independent chief, its peculiar population, its unknown language, and its own coinage, the emporium of the coffee trade, the head-quarters of slavery, the birth-place of the Kat plant, and the great manufactory of cotton-cloths, amply, it appeared, deserved the trouble of exploration.*

The city of Harar in southeastern Ethiopia was founded in 1007 CE. Walls were built around the city between the thirteenth and the sixteenth centuries. In the sixteenth century Harar became the capital of the Adal Sultanate, which ruled over southeastern Ethiopia, Somaliland and northern Somalia. The sultanate's greatest ruler was the Imam Ahmed Gragn. Born around 1506, probably to an ethnic Somali family, Gragn led a jihad against the Ethiopian Empire, whose power was exercised further north. Armed with superior weapons from his allies in the Ottoman Empire, he battled Ethiopia between 1528 and 1543, when he was killed at the Battle of Wayna Daga. A statue of Gragn on horseback, holding his shield, stands in Mogadishu, the capital of Somalia. Some people regard Harar as the fourth holiest city in Islam, after Mecca, Medina and Jerusalem. The city was an early centre for coffee distribution to the outside world; coffee itself originated in a region called Kaffa in southwestern Ethiopia.

There are other examples of heritage from southern Ethiopia. In 2015 an article was published called 'Defensive Walls under Threat: Examining the Status of the Great Medieval Defensive Walls of Dawuro People in Southern Ethiopia'. Written by Zelalem Tesfaye Sirna, the article tells of walls dating to between the sixteenth and the eighteenth centuries CE, constructed by the Dawuro kings of southern Ethiopia. The rulers pursued a common goal of establishing a dependable defence mechanism by building walls and digging ditches. Known as the Great Walls of Dawuro, and to locals as 'kati halala keela', these defensive walls are on average 8½ feet high and 11½ feet wide. The stone walls were erected without joining materials such as masonry and cement. Even more astonishing, however, was the scale of this achievement, with the sum of the rows estimated to be more than 621 miles.

THE DA'AMAT KINGDOM

Yeha in Ethiopia is a ruined capital from an ancient African kingdom. Called the Kingdom of Da'amat, its authority spread over Ethiopia and Eritrea, with some of its remains dating from before 800 BCE. Yeha was agriculturally rich and abundant in wood, stone, minerals and frankincense trees. In his work *Ancient Ethiopia*, published in 1998, Dr David Phillipson reports archaeological speculation that Yeha had a population of 10,000 inhabitants. Who were these people and what were their origins?

The people of Yeha were Afroasiatic speakers, belonging to the branch of languages called Semitic. Semitic languages originated in the Horn of Africa, but then spread into the Middle East. Scholars today classify the language of Yeha as an early form of Ethiopic or Sabaean. Since there were people in Yemen, southern Arabia, who also spoke this language, this led to speculation that the people of Yeha were not Africans but migrants from across the water in Yemen. This is not universally accepted, however, with some archaeologists arguing the exact opposite. They speculate that the people who built the Yemeni civilization were not indigenous Arabs, but rather migrants from the Horn of Africa. Moreover, genuine cultural links between the Yemenis and the Da'amat Kingdom really did exist; they flourished from ancient periods and were symbolized by the Queen of Sheba, a key figure in both lands. This controversy could have continued indefinitely, but new evidence has come to light that may settle the issue.

The ancient Egyptians wrote about the Land of Punt as 'God's Land'. A major voyage was ordered there in the fourteenth century BCE by Pharaoh Hatshepsut. Most writers originally believed that Punt was Somalia. However, when a team from Dartmouth College, New Hampshire, USA, set out to find clarification in 2020, they traced the geographic location of mummified baboons found in Egyptian tombs, formerly thought to have originated in Punt. Led by Nathaniel J. Dominy, the Charles Hansen Professor of Anthropology at Dartmouth College, the team identified Eritrea, Ethiopia or Somalia as the likely place of origin for these creatures. Of the three possible candidates, Ethiopia was the middle choice. The evidence from Pharaoh Hatshepsut's temple walls shows that the people of 'Punt' had a king called Perihu and a queen called Aty. Is there any evidence of monarchy in Yemen dating back to Hatshepsut's time? Since the answer is probably 'no', monarchy in the Da'amat Kingdom probably predates Yemeni culture.

Over a 62 miles distance in and around Yeha, archaeologists found temples, a palace, a throne, water reservoirs, inscriptions, graveyards, exquisite statues, religious artefacts, altars and censers. The inscriptions were in a script variously called Proto-Ethiopic, Himyaritic or Sabaean. What is in a name? The writers who continue to believe that this culture originated in Yemen are likely to call both the Yemeni and the African inscriptions 'Himyaritic' or 'Sabaean'. Those who maintain the culture originated in Africa are likely to refer to both the African and Yemeni inscriptions as 'Proto-Ethiopic', with 'proto' meaning the first version of a creation or invention.

The Great Temple of God Almaqah in Yeha is iconic. A two-storey structure, it is raised on a stepped plinth, 82 feet long and rectangular in plan. The walls consist of huge limestone blocks, up to 9⅞ feet in length, finely dressed and polished with two small windows. Visitors to Ethiopia and Eritrea have written about the Great Temple since the sixteenth century. Near to it archaeologists, some of whom were Germans, excavated the Royal Palace or Administrative Building, which dates from 800 BCE. The German scholars think that the original core building was 5 storeys high, with a central tower of eight storeys; it was 164 feet long and 128 feet wide. In front of the temple was a large stairway that led to a monumental gateway of six entrance pillars.

Artefacts excavated in Yeha reveal that the population included skilled metallurgists, able to make articles from copper alloy: weights and trays to weigh things, monograms to depict individuals' names and a dagger have been found. The non-metallic objects include a seal, used by royals and administrators to sign off documents, and an incense burner, used by priests to burn frankincense in temple rituals.

In Meqaber Ga'ewa stands another temple dedicated to Almaqah. Built before 700 BCE, its altar has an exquisite inscription by the building's founder, King W'rn. Describing himself as 'the victorious king', W'rn also built the Great Temple of Almaqah in Yeha.

At Hawelti, archaeologists found two stone-built temples, ceramic figurines depicting animals and houses, and fragments of statues. Two exquisite statues of a distinguished lady were also found. Of plump build, she is opulently dressed, resembling a queen-mother in the Sudanese civilization of Kush. Seated on a throne, she wears an exquisite, pleated dress and has a royal pectoral around her neck. She also has short, beautiful, tightly curled hair. Who is this Great Woman? Could this be a depiction of the woman who entered legend as the Queen of Sheba? Archaeologists do not yet know.

THE AXUMITE EMPIRE

In the Ethiopia and Eritrea region, power shifted from Yeha to another capital called Axum. The Empire of Axum at its height was considered the third most powerful empire in the world, after those of Persia and Rome. The Empire of Axum controlled the waterway between Africa and Arabia, one of the world's great sea routes of the world. Some of Axum's kings sent armies across the Red Sea to maintain power in Arabia.

By 50 CE Zoscales had become the first of its line of rulers to take the imposing title *Negus Negaste* ('King of Kings'). Some later kings appear on inscriptions. However, beginning in around 270 CE the names and faces of 20 successors, beginning in around 270 CE, are preserved in gold, silver and bronze coins, struck during their lifetimes. There were mints in Axum, and probably also in Adulis and Yemen. Other rulers left behind massive, precisely constructed granite obelisks that still adorn the city. Aligned to the sun, these obelisks were dedicated to Almaqah, the moon deity. Power was probably conferred on these rulers through election rather than inheritance. They headed a confederation of subsidiary, tributary and vassal kings.

The imperial capital was also called Axum. Here archaeologists have excavated ruins of castles, palaces and chateaux of a powerful elite – but no one, strangely enough, has yet found the palace of the emperor. Two of the palace and castle complexes were called Ta'akha Maryam and Enda Semon. Originally built around 100 or 200 CE, they were three- and four-storey structures, approached by monumental stairways. The walls were made of stone, with wooden buttressing, while the window frames consisted of interlocking pieces of timber. Another Axumite ruin is popularly known as the Dungur Chateau. Within the structure was a four-tower castle, surrounding courtyards and a Roman-style heating system.

Axum is adorned by seven giant obelisks. Carved by the Axumites between 300 BCE and 300 CE, their details represent the windows and doorways of several storeys. The largest obelisk, now fallen, is in fact the largest monolith ever made, anywhere in the world. It is 108 feet long, weighs a staggering 520 tons and represents a 13-storey building. The largest standing obelisk is 75 feet tall and represents a nine-storey building. These monolithic towers may have been placed to mark the sites of royal burials and their construction is a remarkable feat; even modern technology would be taxed by the technological problem of moving and erecting such sizeable structures. Loads like these simply cannot be hoisted by the typical tower and hydraulic cranes we are familiar with from modern building sites. These cranes, which are pieces of advanced technology, can generally 'pick' a maximum load of 20 tons. Loads that exceed 50 tons require special cranes. Furthermore, there are few cranes in the world today that would be capable of picking even a 200-ton block, only half the weight of the Fallen Obelisk.

Axum remained the chief power in the region washed by the southern Red Sea until the eighth century. In about 523 CE, merchants from the cities of Axum and Adulis wrote to an Alexandrian merchant; they also had trading links with Kush, Egypt, the Roman provinces, the Mediterranean, Arabia, India, Sri Lanka and China. Axum's merchant vessels were so famous that a Mesopotamian poet used them to describe the progress of a royal caravan: it forged ahead, he said, like one of the ships of Adulis, whose 'prow cuts through the foam of the water as a gambler divides the dust with his hand'. The Axumites traded ivory, gold, rhinoceros horn, hippopotamus hides and teeth, exotic animals, frankincense, emeralds (originally from Nubia) and slaves. These exports paid for the importation of silks, cotton, swords, wine and glass drinking vessels. They also imported metals. Gold and silver were transformed into plates. Gold and bronze were fashioned into statues, some to a towering height of 15 feet. They fashioned weapons of steel, and they also made olive oil.

Through these trading links, foreign influences entered the country. Coins struck in Axum and Adulis show similiarities to those of the Greeks and the Romans, though still bearing African heads. Some coins carry inscriptions in Greek, a language of scholarship in the region. Moreover, possessing golden coinage was an achievement, since few contemporary states anywhere in the world could afford to issue such precious coins. Outside of Axum, only Rome, Persia and the Kushan kingdom in northern India had gold coins.

In 150 CE the *Adulis Inscription* was written. It paints a picture of a diverse, multi-ethnic society brought together under the common law and order of the *Negus Negaste*. The text calls for peace among the nations under the king's rule, combined with freedom of movement, safety along the caravan routes and uninterrupted import and export of goods by land or sea. Among the peoples governed were those 'in the interior of the frankincense country', while the peoples near the sea are given 'instructions to guard the coast'. Unfortunately for modern scholars, the king's name has been lost.

In 183 CE King Gadara exercised imperial ambitions in Yemen on the other side of the Red Sea. His son and successor proved equally dominant in Yemen until 213 CE. King Azbah, a later Axumite king, sent military forces to Yemen and settled troops there. The Strait of Bab-al-Mandeb was one of the three main shipping highways in the ancient world. Ethiopia had some control over it.

Just after 330 CE King Ezana proclaimed Axum to be a Christian state, and it is one of the oldest surviving Christian nations in the world. An inscription of the period recorded a prayer of the *Negus Negaste*:

> *May the Lord of Heaven make strong my kingdom! And as He has this day conquered for me my enemy, may he conquer for me wheresoever I go...(I will rule) the people with righteousness and justice, and will not oppress them.*
>
> **E.A. Wallis Budge, A *History of Ethiopia, Nubia & Abyssinia*, Vol. I, 1928**

A Byzantine writer called Rufinus related (in his *Church History*, 403 or 403 CE) how Christianity spread to the Axumite elites. Rufinus narrates how two Syrian boys, Frumentius and Aedesius, were on a Greco-Roman ship that was attacked as they tried to moor at an Axumite port. Relations between the inhabitants of the port and Greco-Roman sailors had become strained due to earlier abuses of Axumite hospitality. The Axumites sought revenge on all who were kinsfolk of the Greco-Roman merchants, hence their storming of the ship. Once on board, the Axumites killed everybody apart from the two boys, spared because of their young age. Eventually, the two young Syrians were taken to King Ella Amida, Ezana's predecessor. The king saw potential in the boys, making Aedesius his cupbearer and later installing Frumentius as his treasurer and secretary. Frumentius rose to great influence within the country. After Ella Amida's death he was succeeded by Ezana, his young son, and the Queen-Regent invited Frumentius to assist in governing the country until the young king came of age. The Syrian encouraged the spread of Christianity throughout Ethiopia, building churches and encouraging trade. The early coins of Ezana's time show the crescent-and-disc emblem of the old deity Mahrem, but later coins issued just after 330 CE carry the Christian cross with the motto: 'May the country be satisfied'. These were the first coins in the world to carry this Christian design.

Another development attributed to Ezana's reign was the introduction of a new written script – the vocalized Ethiopic. A refinement of the Proto-Ethiopic/Sabaean script of the Yeha period, vocalized Ethiopic influenced the Armenian and Georgian scripts of Eastern Europe. In his book *Aksum: political system, economics and culture, first to fourth century*, published in Volume II of a *General History of Africa*, 1981, the Russian historian Yuri M. Kobishanov noted that:

Soon after its creation, the Ethiopic vocalized script began to influence the scripts of Transcaucasia. D.A. Olderogge suggested that Mesrop Mashtotz used the vocalized Ethiopic script when he invented the Armenian alphabet. Not long before this time (at the end of the fifth century) the Ethiopian script may have been introduced into Armenia by the Syrian bishop Daniel.

Ezana also battled with other nations. Between 335 and 370 CE, he ordered the occupation of Yemen once more. He also led victorious campaigns against Kush, the peoples of Lake Tana and the peoples of the desert. In this way, Ethiopia seized the trade routes linking Egypt and Syria with the countries of the Indian Ocean.

Churches and convents date back to Ezana's time. Axum contained the Cathedral of Saint Mary of Zion, one of the oldest Christian cathedrals on Earth. A priest to the Portuguese king who was sent to lead an official visit to Ethiopia, Francisco Alvarez, saw it and wrote a description in around 1520:

In this town, we found a noble church; it is very large, and has five naves of a good width and of great length, vaulted above, and all the vaults are covered up, and the ceiling and sides are all painted; it also has a choir after our fashion. This church has a very large circuit, paved with flagstones like gravestones, and it has also a large enclosure, and is surrounded by another large enclosure like the wall of a large town or city.

Francisco Alvarez, *A True Relation of the Lands of Prester John of the Indies*, 1526 or 1527, quoted in Graham Hancock, *The Beauty of Historic Ethiopia*, 1996

The description is important because the building surviving today in Axum is a poor seventeenth-century rebuild, only a fraction of the original size.

The achievements of the Axumites were outstanding. They enjoyed far-reaching maritime trade, from the Roman provinces on one hand to China on the other. They minted gold, silver and copper coins, and also had literature and scripts of their own. Their cultural influences spread far and wide. A Persian cleric of the third century CE, known as 'Mani', identified Axum as the third most important state in the world after Persia and Rome.

Emperor Kaleb was an important monarch on the sixth-century world stage. Remembered as a passionate defender of the faith, he commissioned the magnificent chapel of Debre Damo, made of dry stone and timber. According to a visitor to Ethiopia – 'Julian the Magistrate', sent to Axum by Emperor Justinian of Byzantium, and the oldest surviving account of what Julian saw being *The Chronicle* of John Malalas (491–563 CE) – he appeared at the court in magnificent attire consisting of pearl-set, gold-embroidered white linen. Four elephants pulled a gilded wheeled chariot that served as the royal throne and flute music accompanied the proceedings. In later life Kaleb became a monk, devoted to studying the divine word. He was buried in Axum on a nearby hilltop, in a tomb or chapel. However, Kaleb, like previous monarchs, was heavily involved in Yemenite affairs.

In Yemen a civil war erupted between Christians and Israelites. The Axumites were invited to help the Christian effort; Emperor Kaleb responded by sending across 70,000 men and an armada of 150 ships. General Abraha headed the campaign. The Axumites triumphed, but the victorious General had ideas of his own, proclaiming himself ruler of Yemen. Abraha raised a fine cathedral at Sana, containing marble and mosaics and decorated with gold.

Its purpose was to win converts to the Christian faith. However, Abraha's religious zeal was his undoing. He attempted to challenge the religion of the Holy City of Mecca, inflaming the anti-Christians who in turn appealed to the Persian King Chosroes for armed assistance. The Axumites were beaten in 572 CE and Yemen became a territory of the Persians. Edward Gibbon, the venerable classical historian, wondered whether

> *If a Christian power had been maintained in Arabia, Mahomet must have been crushed in his cradle, and Abyssinia would have prevented a revolution which has changed the civil and religious state of the world.*
>
> **Edward Gibbon, *History of the Decline and Fall of the Roman Empire*, Vol. 7, 1811 edition**

A notable king of the seventh century was Emperor Armah. He lived during the period in which Islam came into existence in Arabia, founded by the Arabian prophet Muhammad. Some of the first converts to the new religion fled persecution in Arabia, seeking refuge under Armah. Bilal, one of Islam's founders, came from Axum. In addition, the World Architecture Community has a website called worldarchitecture.org. In a 30 June 2008 article entitled *Islamic Architecture*, the Community states:

> *In 630 C.E. Muhammad's army reconquered the city of Mecca from the Banu Quraish tribe. The holy sanctuary of Ka'ba was rebuilt and re-dedicated to Islam, the reconstruction being carried out before Muhammad's death in 632 C.E. by a shipwrecked Abyssinian carpenter in his native style. This sanctuary was amongst the first major works of Islamic architecture.*

Unfortunately for Axum, however, Yemenites adopted Islam – as did the nomads who lived on Axum's Red Sea coast. So it was that Axum, as a Christian state, found itself surrounded by Islamic states. Their key port of Adulis was destroyed towards the end of the century, effectively barring them from trade with the rest of the world. Axum went into decline. As Gibbon poetically put it:

> *Encompassed on all sides by the enemies of their religion, the Ethiopians slept near a thousand years, forgetful of the world by whom they were forgotten.*
> **Edward Gibbon, *History of the Decline and Fall of the Roman Empire*, Vol. 8, 1811 edition**

In 940 CE Judith, a Falasha conqueror, seized the throne and proclaimed herself Queen. Inspiring dread in many Christian minds, she attacked Axum. Her armies destroyed books, monuments, palaces and churches, killing thousands in the process. Her campaigns ended both the 1,000-year supremacy of the city of Axum and an era of Ethiopian and Eritrean history.

THE CITY OF LALIBELA

The centre of political power in the region moved from Axum in the north to the Lalibela Mountains, 186⅜ miles further south. A new capital had to be established after Queen Judith in 940 CE led Ethiopia's Jews in attacking the city of Axum and leaving it in ruins.

King Yemrehanna Krestos ruled between 1087 and 1127. He is best known today for ordering the construction of his Cave Church and Treasury. Built in the Lalibela Mountains, the region's

Christians developed a tradition of building cave churches. These are traditional monuments built up from the bottom, one brick on top of another, but wholly constructed inside a pre-existing cave. Over time thousands of these types of churches were built. The two Yemrehanna Krestos buildings possess ornate and elaborate wooden ceilings that have attracted much praise. They contain intricate geometric designs. One Ethiopian scholar – Dr Alemseged Beldados quoted in *Restore or Lose Forever – The Urgent Need for the Conservation of Historical Heritage: The Case of Yemrehannä Krestos*, by Department of Archaeology and Heritage Management, Addis Ababa University (2013) – thought they were so good that 'they could be copied by present-day elite Ethiopians in their villas and mansions'. The Yemrehanna Krestos Cave Church is still in use – the oldest church still used by indigenous Africans.

The city of Lalibela, to the south of the Yemrehanna Krestos buildings, has some of the most remarkable churches built anywhere in the world. While churches in Europe rose to the sky, churches here were gouged out of the ground to a depth of around 36 feet. The churches were built between 1180 and 1220 AD during the reign of King Lalibela – although 'built' may be the wrong word; some scholars describe these monuments as 'sculptures' instead. A nineteenth-century manuscript, a photograph of which is reproduced in *African Kingdoms* by Basil Davidson (1967), portrays the emperor with an adze in his hand, chiselling away and carving the buildings. His dream seems to have been the creation of a New Jerusalem in Ethiopia: the region contains a 'River Jordan', a 'Calvary', a 'Mount of Transfiguration', a church called 'Golgotha' and another called 'Bethlehem'. Some think that these churches were built in Lalibela to form a pilgrimage site, after Muslim conquests halted Christian pilgrimages to the Holy Land in the Middle East. Today the city has a local museum that houses royal robes and four royal crowns. They belonged to King Lalibela and others of his dynasty.

A building project of this kind tested the architects' skills to an astonishing degree. In choosing a rough block of stone for the future masterpiece, one had to conceive not only the size of the church's outer walls, but also those parts of the building which would projected from the surface of the wall: the corner pieces of the window frames, the roof guttering and the gargoyles. Fixing these problems later would not be an option. Moreover, one would have to plan the contextual arrangements of the churches; some of their ceilings form the floors outside other churches.

The largest church in Lalibela is the House of the Redeemer of the World. A staggering 110⅝ feet long, 77⅞ feet wide and 37¾ feet deep, it is surrounded by a forest of columns, all carved and sculpted. Amazingly, the outer columns line up with the 28 inner columns showing engineering precision. Internally it has five aisles. Archaeologists have discovered that the windows used to contain coloured glass.

The House of Mary has beautiful painted interiors. Lalibela himself considered it the most beautiful of the churches and held mass there. However, many of the paintings have faded over the last 800 years. The church, 49⅛ feet in lengh, 36 feet wide and 32⅞ feet deep, has swastika-shaped windows; in its courtyard is a deep, square, baptismal pool.

The House of Emmanuel is very rigorously carved on its three floors. Each floor of the church has a different style of windows and it is 60¾ feet long, 41 feet wide and 39⅜ feet deep. As with the other churches, some of its designs are in the classical Axum style, but carved from rock: for example, the square frames and bosses of the doors and windows, the three-level plinth and the horizontal bands of the facade. The church's plan is basilica, with an elevated and vaulted central nave, sanctuary and dome. The top floor has nine rooms.

The House of St George is the most celebrated of the Lalibela churches. Shaped like a concentric cross, the building looks like a four-storey structure from the outside and is more than 39⅜ feet deep.

The other seven churches are almost hidden away and could easily be missed by a visitor. Among these, the House of Golgotha has pointed arch windows, with a tendril-like tracery topped by a cross, like a Maltese cross. The House of Abba Libanos has plain pointed arch windows, combined with cross-shaped openings. The House of Mascal has Romanesque arches and windows of twinned crosses.

Connecting the churches is a complex and bewildering labyrinth of tunnels and narrow passageways, all with offset crypts, grottoes and galleries. Throughout this mysterious settlement, priests and deacons go about their timeless business. The churches are places of prayer and pilgrimage. People from all over Ethiopia and foreign tourists congregate in Lalibela on 7 January each year to celebrate the Ethiopian Christmas.

Ethiopian priest Dr Abba Tewelde Medhin Yosef wrote that the monolithic building tradition must have predated Christianity in the region. Some rock-hewn churches do not have Christian-type decorations. The suspicion is these buildings were carved for some other reason, then later re-dedicated as churches. Consequently, some estimate that the oldest rock-hewn temples were carved before 100 CE. Moreover, Dr Peter Garlake (in *Early Art and Architecture of Africa*, 2002) estimates that the region may have a total of 3,000 rock-cut and cave churches. Continuing to be built into the sixteenth century, these monuments were either sculpted from rock or built from the bottom up in caves.

FROM MOVING CAPITALS TO ADDIS ABABA

In 1270 a new line of kings appeared in Ethiopia. Claiming descent from the pre-Queen Judith dynastic line, legend had it that these kings went back to the Queen of Sheba and the biblical King Solomon. Historians therefore call this dynastic line the Solomonic Dynasty. However, the new line of kings had no fixed capital; each ruler built their own.

Amda Seyon was the ninth king of this reconstituted line, ruling from 1314 to 1344. He was crowned in Axum and became, according to Edward Ullendorff, a British expert on Ethiopia, in his 1966 review of Huntingford's translation of *The Glorious Victories of Amda Seyon, King of Ethiopia*, 'one of the most outstanding Ethiopian kings of any age and a singular figure dominating the Horn of Africa in the fourteenth century'. Most of Seyon's wars were against the Muslim kingdoms to the southeast, where he fought with Zeila and Berbera; he defeated these challengers, one by one. Moreover, Seyon made previously disrupted trade routes safe. These battles substantially expanded Ethiopian territory by gradually incorporating several smaller states. During his reign the clergy compiled the *Kebre Negaste*, a book regarded as the national epic of Ethiopia.

King Zara Yacob reigned from 1434 to 1468. He ascended the throne during a time of internal conflict and external threats, notably from the expanding Muslim Sultanates in the Horn of Africa, and went on to write a treatise on ethics and religious philosophy. Called *The Law of the Kings*, this was a fusion of Christian theology, medieval philosophy and legal principles; it formed the basis of Ethiopian law for five centuries, until 1930. Yacob also wrote religious books: *The Book of Light* and *The Book of Nativity*. In 1441 he sent delegates to the Council of Florence and established ties with the Holy See. He also sent a diplomatic mission to Europe in 1450, asking for artisans. The mission, led by a Sicilian, Pietro Rombulo, reached the court of Alfonso V of Aragon. Yacob received a favourable response from Alfonso V in a letter addressed to 'Zere Jacobo, son of David of the house of Solomon, Ethiopian Emperor, our very dear friend and brother', dated 18 September 1450.

Abba Mika'el was an Ethiopian cleric who probably belonged to Saint Steven of the Abyssinians, a church community in Rome. In 1534 Martin Luther, the founder of Protestantism, met with Mika'el to hold theological discussions. The different meetings between Mika'el and Luther took place at Wittenberg, Germany, between 31 May and 4 July 1534. Since Mika'el could speak some Italian, an interpreter translated between them. They discussed the doctrine of the Trinity and the Last Supper. In addition, the two clerics compared the Lutheran Mass to that used by the Ethiopian Orthodox Church and found that they agreed. Reflecting on this discussion a few years later, Luther claimed that Mika'el declared that the Protestant articles of faith were 'a good creed'.

The empire now faced a grave threat to its survival. The Imam Ahmad Gragn, 'the left-handed', was a powerful Muslim warlord. Driven by religious fervour, he led a jihad into Ethiopia that commenced in 1528 from his city of Harar, capital of the Adal Sultanate. Gragn sought to unite the Muslim Sultanates in the Horn of Africa under his leadership, and was prepared to fight the Christian monarchy of the Solomonic Dynasty. His military tactics were innovative and, often employing firearms, he had well-organized and disciplined forces. His armies decimated Ethiopian strongholds such as the ancient capital of Axum and the fortress of Debre Damo; by 1535 he controlled nearly all the country. However, his conquests were halted when the Ethiopian king gained support from the Portuguese. Gragn died in February 1543 during a battle with the forces of Emperor Geladewos.

Susenyos the Catholic (r. 1607–32), as his name suggests, attempted to spread Roman Catholicism in the country. A distinctive figure, he was described by the Portuguese Jesuit Manuel de Almeida as

> *tall, with the features of a man of quality, large handsome eyes, and an ample and well-groomed beard. He wore a tunic of crimson velvet down to the knee, breeches of the Moorish style, a sash or girdle of many large pieces of fine gold and an outer coat of damask of the same colour, like a Moorish jacket.*
> **Manuel de Almeida, quoted in C.F. Beckingham, and G.W.B. Huntingford, *Some Records of Ethiopia, 1593–1646*, 1954**

Susenyos's style and appearance was one thing; his religious affiliations quite another. His failed attempt at popularizing Catholicism resulted in civil strife. Ultimately he was forced to abdicate in 1632, in favour of his son Facilides.

During this time a great philosopher emerged in Ethiopia called Zera Yacob. The author of an important book called *The Inquiry*, he lived in a town near the original capital of Axum. Some historians think that his work was the first book on modern philosophy to be written anywhere in the world. Yacob lived in a cave as a hermit, visiting only the nearby market to get food, and it was in his cave that he developed his new ideas. Many seem to us surprisingly modern: he believed that reason should be supreme, for example, and that all males and females were created equal. He also argued against slavery, criticized all established religions and believed in a theistic Creator.

In addition Yacob reasoned that the world's order makes that the most rational option to hold. Dag Herbjørnsrud, a Norwegian historian of ideas, suggests:

> *In short: many of the highest ideals of the later European Enlightenment had been conceived and summarised by one man, working in an Ethiopian cave from 1630 to 1632.*
> **Dag Herbjørnsrud, 'The African Enlightenment', essay on aeon.co, 13 December 2017**

Gondar became the new capital of Ethiopia, the first fixed capital for hundreds of years. Founded by King Fasilides in 1635, it had schools, churches, gardens, pools and zoos. While basically a Christian city, it had separate districts for Ethiopia's Jews and Muslims. Gondar is also called 'the Camelot of Africa' because of its 11 castles, the oldest commissioned by Fasilides in 1636. This was the largest and most impressive in the royal enclosure. Consisting of three storeys with round towers at each corner, the roof had a tall tower with views over the surrounding regions. A Yemeni ambassador, Hassan ibn Ahmad al-Haymi, who visited the castle in 1648 or 1649, described it as 'worthy of admiration, and the most beautiful of outstanding wonders' (trans. F.E. Peiser, *Zur geschichte Abessiniens im 17. jahrhundert; der gesandtschaftsbericht des Hasan ben Ahmed El-Haimî*, 1898; trans. into English by Robin Walker). Inside he saw beds from Constantinople, mattresses from India glittering with gold, sofas inlaid with jewellery and gems, and swords from Sennar, inlaid with the choicest pure gold. The courtiers wore gowns of silk brocade embroidered with gold, set with marvellous stones and precious gems. Abdal Kerim, an Indian architect, built the castle, having previously worked on the palace of Susenyos the Catholic at Danqaz. The Royal

Chronicles report that Walda Giyorgis, an Ethiopian architect, built the castles of later rulers in Gondar, Yohannes and Iyasu I, describing him as 'able, intelligent, and of good renown' (trans. Richard Pankhurst, *History Of Ethiopian Towns*, 1982). The contractors were local Ethiopian Jews, particularly the Kayla clan, who traditionally worked as masons, metalsmiths and carpenters.

Empress Mentewab was born in or around 1706. Despite Emperor Iyasu and his grandson, Emperor Iyoas, officially holding power, she was in fact the ruler. Crowned Empress in December 1730, she faced an uprising of nobles only two years later; they laid siege to her castle in Gondar for over two weeks in December 1732. Mentewab defeated another rebellion, led by an ambitious duke, in 1747, then survived a civil war in 1767 between nobles from different parts of the country who disputed their respective share of power. The empress had relatives on both sides of the civil war. During her time distinguished Christian art was produced in the form of churches and illuminated manuscripts. Today her castle in Gondar is a tourist attraction, while another castle and church at Queskam, though in ruins, are powerful reminders of a glorious age. However, the British invaded Ethiopia in 1868 and stole artefacts, many of which came from Gondar and are now in London museums: precious manuscripts, church art, gold and silver treasures and intricate royal crowns. Mentewab's three-tiered golden crown, for example, is in the V & A Museum in London.

After this period, the empire entered the Era of Princes, which lasted from 1784 until 1855. Competing warlords became rulers of different portions of the empire, the most powerful of them coming from the House of Yejju, a region in Wollo. Other regional lords included Kenfu Hailu of Gondar and various rulers of Gojjam, Tigre, Simien and Shewa. The warlords challenged each other over the expansion of territory and to become guardians of the emperors who still nominally ruled in Gondar. However, the monarchy only continued in name because of its sacred character.

Tewodros II began to conquer and dethrone the warlords in 1855. He sought to re-establish a cohesive state for the first time since the eighteenth century. In modernizing the land, he wanted governors and judges to be salaried appointees. The emperor established a professional standing army, rather than depending on the warlords to provide soldiers for his expeditions. He introduced a collection of books in the form of a library, as well as tax codes and a centralized political system, complete with respective administrative districts. During his time, the capital city was moved from Gondar, first to Debre Tabor and later to Magdala. Facing a rebellion in October 1862, Tewodros wrote to Queen Victoria as a fellow Christian, requesting her help with technical support. However, the British official tasked to deliver the letter did not deliver it personally. It was posted, but officials in London ensured that the Queen did not see it. An angry Tewodros ordered the imprisonment of European representatives in Ethiopia, which sparked a diplomatic backlash. The British sent an army of 32,000 troops to attack Ethiopia. On 15 April 1868, as the British troops stormed the citadel of Magdala, Emperor Tewodros committed suicide rather than surrender. The British looted the artefacts that ended up in the London museums.

Yohannes IV, a later ruler, attempted to consolidate central authority and to defend Ethiopia from the encroaching powers of the Ottoman Empire, Sudan and Italy. He battled and repulsed Turko-Egyptian incursions into Eritrea at the Battles of Gundet in 1875 and Gura in 1876. The Ottoman presence continued to menace the area until their power in Egypt was broken by British imperialism. Yohannes IV also faced threats from the Mahdist state in Sudan. His leading general, Ras Alula, successfully fought them at Kufit in

1885, but in 1889 his second battle against the Mahdists did not go well. Yohannes IV himself was fatally wounded after this last battle. However, the Italians gained ground in Eritrea. By late 1869 they controlled the Bay of Assab, and by February 1885 they had acquired Massawa. During the late 1880s the Italians took control of more and more Eritrean land.

Menelik II was the next ruler of Ethiopia. In May 1889 he signed an agreement with the Italians called the *Treaty of Wuchale*, the stated purpose of which was to promote friendship and trade between the two countries. However, the *Treaty of Wuchale* contained a major deception. The Italian version of Article 17 was significantly different to the Amharic translation. It was worded to suggest that Ethiopia was now a protectorate of Italy.

Menelik II denounced the treaty in 1894 when the deception was detected. In response the Italians put 'boots on the ground' in Eritrea and invaded deep into Ethiopian territory. At the Battle of Adwa, on 1 March 1896, the Italian army met its Ethiopian counterpart. The Ethiopian forces quickly surrounded and destroyed the first battalion of Italian General Albertone; the remaining Italian forces were crushed by other Ethiopian troops, who fired rifles, hurled javelins, swirled swords and fought hand to hand. Captured Italians were subsequently released by Ethiopia in exchange for a 10 million lira reparation by the Italian government. The defeated Italians were forced to sign a peace treaty in October 1896, the *Treaty of Addis Ababa*. The victory at Adwa secured Ethiopian sovereignty for another 40 years – although the Italians did keep control of Eritrea.

Emperor Menelik and his third wife, Empress Taitu, founded Addis Ababa in 1886. Originally famous for a mineral spring that attracted the nobility of the empire, leading them to establish a permanent settlement, it also attracted artisans, merchants and foreign visitors. Menelik built his imperial palace there in 1887 and Addis Ababa became the empire's capital two years later. In the early twentieth century things changed rapidly. Bridges and modern roads were built, a postal system was created and telegraph lines were erected. More important still, construction of a railway began. It would ultimately connect Addis Ababa with the Red Sea port of Djibouti. The creation of this transportation and communications infrastructure opened the country to new markets. The capital had its first hotel, modern schools and a hospital, while a state printing press began operations in 1911.

THE EARLY HISTORY OF CONGO & ANGOLA

During the so-called 'Scramble for Africa', several European powers colonized countries in Central Africa. In 1885 Belgium, under King Leopold II, claimed the Congo Free State, which became the Belgian Congo in 1908. France expanded its empire across Central Africa, establishing colonies such as French Equatorial Africa (comprising Chad, the Central African Republic, Congo-Brazzaville and Gabon) between 1900 and 1910. France also controlled Cameroon from 1916, following Germany's defeat in the First World War. Portugal began to colonize Angola in around 1575, although it only became a fully integrated colony under Portuguese rule in 1850. In reality Portuguese control was often limited to coastal areas. Only by the early twentieth century was the interior fully incorporated into the colony, following campaigns against indigenous people and rival European powers.

The Southern Savannah region of today's Democratic Republic of Congo, Angola and surrounding countries was home to Bantu and Nilo-Saharan civilizations. Some of them had important Batwa populations, including the Mangbetu Kingdom, the Luba Empire, the Lunda Commonwealth, the Kuba Kingdom and the Kingdom of Kongo. However, the information that has survived on most of these kingdoms is sketchy. The Kingdom of Kongo has a well-documented history, but we can only offer a thin outline for the others.

THE MANGBETU KINGDOM

The Mangbetu kingdom was in the northeast of the Democratic Republic of Congo, Central Africa. Founded in the second half of the eighteenth century, its population lived at the northern end of the rainforest, close to the upper sources of the Uele River. Elites, mainly from the Mabiti clan, assumed control over other Mangbetu clans and unified them into a kingdom. The kings were of Medje-Lombi ancestry, which is a branch of Nilo-Saharan. They ruled over a multi-ethnic population of other Nilo-Saharans, Bantus and Batwa peoples, maintaining a productive manufacturing sector in which they worked imported copper. Imported south from Darfur, they made exquisite copper ornaments, iron tools of all types and weapons. The people of the Mangbetu kingdom also made knives for throwing, which operated on the principle of a boomerang.

Georg Schweinfurth, a Swiss visitor, entered the Mangbetu kingdom in the late 1860s and wrote a travelogue called *The Heart of Africa*. His work contains etchings of things that Schweinfurth encountered used by the Mangbetu and others in the region: knives, throwing knives, scimitars and daggers, five-stringed harps with ornately decorated necks and resonators, exquisitely carved stools, a gaming board to play *oware* or mancala and gorgeous water bottles. In *The Heart of Africa*, published in 1873, Schweinfurth describes the last in glowing terms:

> *All the vessels and drinking-cups of the Africans in general have the character of urns, being made without handles and being never otherwise than spherical in form; but those of the [Mangbetu] exhibit a manifest improvement, and by having the surface decorated either with some raised symmetrical pattern*

> *(which is especially the case upon their oil vessels) or with some ornamental figures, they afford a firm hold to the hand, and thus make good the lack of handles for lifting them. It is, however, principally upon the water-bottles that the greatest care is bestowed, some of which may fairly be said to rival in symmetry the far-famed examples of Egyptian art.*
>
> **Georg Schweinfurth, The Heart of Africa, Vol. II, trans. Ellen Elizabeth Frewer, 1873**

Surrounding the Mangbetu capital were large, cultivated fields, with orchards of oil palms and other types of trees. In the capital were many large buildings, as well as smaller huts filled with curious objects: animal skins, feathered hats and necklaces, and an armoury consisting of iron spears, piles of knives and hundreds of polished copper lances. Schweinfurth also visited the ruler, King Mbunza, where he saw thousands of subjects at the royal court, including hundreds of nobles and courtiers. Among the king's personal household were musicians, eunuchs, jesters, ballad singers, dancers and bodyguards. A range of musical instruments were played, among them wooden gongs, kettle drums, timbrels, bells, trumpets and horns. In *The Heart of Africa*, Schweinfurth left a powerful description of the architecture of the royal halls:

> *The hall itself was the chief object that attracted my attention. It was at least a hundred feet in length, forty feet high, and fifty broad. It had been quite recently completed, and the fresh bright look of the materials gave it an enlivening aspect, the natural brown polish of the wood-work looking as though it were gleaming with the lustre of new varnish. Close by was a second and more spacious hall, which in height was only surpassed by*

*the loftiest of the surrounding oil-palms; but this, although it had only been erected five years previously, had already begun to show symptoms of decay, and being enclosed on all sides was dark, and therefore less adapted for the gathering at a public spectacle. Considering the part of Africa in which these halls were found, one might truly be justified in calling them wonders of the world; I hardly know, with all our building resources, what material we could have employed, except it were whale-bone, of sufficient lightness and durability to erect structures like these royal halls of Munza, capable of withstanding the tropical storms and hurricanes. The bold arch of the vaulted roof was supported on three long rows of pillars, formed from perfectly straight tree-stems; the countless spars and rafters as well as the other parts of the building being composed entirely of the leaf-stalks of the wine-palm (*Raphia vinifera*). The floor was covered with a dark red clay plaster, as firm and smooth as asphalt. The sides were enclosed by a low breastwork, and the space between this and the arching roof, which at the sides sloped nearly to the ground, allowed light and air to pass into the building.*

Professor Ehret says the Mangbetu royal halls rivalled Japanese temples as the largest wooden structures ever built (*The Civilizations of Africa*, 2nd ed., 2016). Professor V. Tarikhu Farrar points out, in *Precolonial African Material Culture* (2020), that in using raffia palm, the builders made rational and efficient use of every part of the tree. Rope and twine were woven from fibres derived from the leaves while the trunks were made into posts. The fronds were used for roofing and thatch, and the mid-rib of the frond was used to create laths and rafters. Not only were the parts of trees carefully processed, but they also built structures that were comfortable and ecologically sound.

THE LUBA KINGDOM

In the Democratic Republic of Congo, archaeologists discovered a culture that flourished between 600 CE and the eleventh century. Called the Early Kisalian culture, it was located in the Upemba Depression. This was an area of bayous and lakes along the Lualaba River. Crucially, the people spreading this culture spoke early dialects of Luba, a Bantu language. Other populations in the region originally spoke Sabi but, as the culture spread, Sabi-speakers became incorporated into this Luba-speaking Early Kisalian culture. The Luba speakers also reintroduced the practice of male circumcision.

Iron and salt were already abundant in the region. In burials, barbed arrowheads, spearheads, curved knives and hoes have all been discovered. In a burial dating from the eighth to the tenth centuries, axe heads were found. They possessed the curious shape that axes have today, owned by people of high status and authority, indicating that the person with whom it was buried had reached the top of a social hierarchy. Communities near the lakes and bayous built up levees on which they built fishing villages, periodically clearing floating reeds from the different stream channels. Consequently, fish and reeds were available. The reeds were valuable to those involved in mat-making, basketry and thatching. In addition, a new trade product was exploited: copper. Available 186⅜ miles south of the Upemba Depression, copper became associated with wealth, with iron, salt and copper being exported to outside regions. Moreover, in the late first millennium, cross-shaped copper ingots became the currency.

In the twelfth century the culture of the region evolved into Classical Kisalian culture. At Sanga in the Upemba Depression archaeologists found royal burials. Elites were interred with opulent arrays of copper and other grave goods: copper necklaces, bracelets, bells, copper and iron armlets, shell beads, iron pendants, ivory objects and well-decorated vessels in a variety of shapes. Professor Ehret (*The Civilizations of Africa*) calls this the Upemba Kingdom, but suggests that it would not be an exaggeration to give it an even grander name: the First Luba Empire. A word entered Luba vocabulary which translates as 'tribute paid by a subordinate chief', reflecting an hierarchical relationship of emperor to kings of tributary status; this probably existed between the Luba elite and the political entities they subordinated. Ehret suggests that the kings may have legitimated their role by taking credit for the public works activities of building levees and clearing vegetation from the streams. The Upemba Kingdom remained in power until some time before 1450. However, the Classical Kisalian culture discovered by archaeologists appears to have spread its influence even further, extending into Malawi. Moreover, a second kingdom emerged, 186⅜ miles to the north, called the Songye kingdom. It flourished at about the same time as Upemba: that is, 1100 to 1400 CE.

Loom technology had been a part of Niger-Congo culture since the fourth millennium BCE. The skills to make raffia fibre textiles probably spread into Malawi 2,000 years ago; they may also have spread into Zimbabwe at the same time. Since cotton textiles that date from the thirteenth century have been discovered in Zimbabwe, Ehret speculates that cotton technology spread there, and to Malawi, at some point between 2,000 years ago and the thirteenth century.

From 1450 onwards, following the collapse of centralized Upenba power, there was an interregnum of well over a century. The region probably consisted of small states and statelets. According to oral traditions, a new Luba state emerged in around 1585. The royal centres were no longer in the Upemba Depression, but built in the hilly areas to the west. The traditions name 20 rulers of Luba between

1585 and the beginning of Belgian colonization (1885), with oral traditions describing Kongolo and Kalala Ilunga as the first two of 20 kings. However, a novel innovation with this new state was the creation of a secret society known as the Bambudye. Men who wanted power had to join up and to accept the rituals of the organization. Initiates into its sacred knowledge included practitioners from several professions, titleholders, diviners and healers. Moreover, the Bambudye had forums in which to discuss political policies. This meant that the secret society could act as a check on royal power.

The central government consisted of the king and his titleholders. Each king was required to build his own capital, the *kitenta*. On his death his capital became sacred and free from all interference by his successor. It was entrusted to a woman called a *mwadi* and the *twite*, the chief minister of the deceased king. Below the king, the most important functionary was the *twite*; he was also the war leader and the head of an officer corps who acted as a police force. Beneath him was the *inabanza*, the next most important personage who kept the sacred emblems. He was followed by the *sungu*, the next most important of the high officials. Beneath this were the chiefdoms, a group of which was headed by a territorial chief known as a *kilolo*. A chiefdom was created by the joining together of several villages, each headed by a headman. All title holders down to the position of chief claimed a special spiritual power, called *balopwe*. This was acquired through bloodline descent from the lineage of the two founder kings: Kongolo and Kalala Ilunga.

The new Luba state formed the basis of the Luba Empire of the eighteenth and nineteenth centuries. Building the largest state seen in this part of the world, Luba power came to stretch from the Kanyok Kingdom in the west to Lake Tanganyika in the east, and from the Songye state in the north to the Copper

Belt in the south. The state resurrected industries in salt and iron that dated from the earlier kingdom period. Moreover, they regulated control over access to copper. Unreliable trade links connected the Luba Empire in Central Africa to trade from both the Atlantic and the Indian Ocean. Non-Luba men absorbed into the Luba Empire also had to join the Bambudye secret society, if they wanted any kind of power, as noted above. In this way non-Luba men who belonged to the elites maintained some power over their home territories if they could demonstrate their loyalty to Luba power.

Wonderful regalia was a feature of the lives of Luba chiefs and kings. At their investitures they were given stools, staffs of office, bowl stands, cups, headrests and ceremonial weaponry. Decorating these objects were female images, possibly representing the daughters and sisters of kings. Headrests of great beauty protected the elaborate hairdos of their owners while they slept in comfort. Many of these pieces have now made their way into European museums, with the abstract dimensions of these pieces attracting curious attention. Dr R.E.G. Armattoe argues, in *The Golden Age of West African Civilization* (1946), that these pieces show that Africans were producing art with modernist aesthetics centuries before European artists. He seems to be thinking of Pablo Picasso.

Ultimately, the Luba kingdom continued into the late nineteenth century. Not only did it face threats from Arab slave traders, but also from the arrival of European colonialists, by whom it was ultimately overwhelmed. In Luba's case, their nemesis was the Belgians, who seized this part of Africa in 1885, whereupon the people of this kingdom faced genocide at the hands of Belgium's king. In 1908 the surviving Luba became part of the Belgian Congo.

THE LUNDA KINGDOM

The Nkalany Valley of the Upper Kasai River region lies 186⅜ miles to the south and west of the Luba Kingdom. The Lunda speakers, a Bantu-speaking people who exercised power there, spread their influence into parts of three modern countries: Democratic Republic of Congo, northeastern Angola and northwestern Zambia. However, in the fifteenth century this area was home to Tubungu kingdoms, ridden by petty conflict derived from competing royal bloodlines. Even during this period, however, they had a word for 'tribute' – so some petty kings evidently ruled over others and extracted tribute.

In the sixteenth century, however, men descended from Luba chiefs moved into the Lunda region. We do not know if these Luba elites were responsible for the political turmoil that occurred between the petty Lunda kings. Ultimately, they created the Rund Kingdom in the late sixteenth and early seventeenth centuries. An oral tradition may have encapsulated this idea. It recounts how in around 1600 a Luba prince called Chibinda Illunga came south from Luba to marry a Lunda woman of royal heritage. Surviving wooden statues depicting him were a common theme in the art of the Chokwe, a neighbouring ethnic group in the Angola region. They usually portray the prince with an extravagant hairstyle of elite status, a medicine horn as a symbol of his mystical knowledge and a staff, which shows his kingship. Whatever the case may be, the grandson of Chibinda and the Lunda royal woman became the first ruler of the Lunda. The grandson was the first to hold the lofty title 'Mwata Yamvo', meaning 'Lord of the Viper'. No one is sure when the first Mwata Yamvo ruled, but dates such as 1695 have been given. He was the first of 17 or 18 dynasts who held this title before European colonialism swept this kingdom away.

At the base of the Lunda political structure was the village and its surrounding lands. Ruling the villages were a council of elders, supported by a hereditary head man. He had a spiritual role looking after the spiritual wellbeing of the villages due to a direct connection with his ancestors, who founded the village. A group of headmen were ruled over by an elder headman. These elders were grouped into political districts governed by a *cilool*, whose main role was to act as a tax collector. The taxes he collected would be sent to his superior in the capital, who in turn dispatched it to the king.

At the head of this structure was the Lord of the Viper. He had sacred attributes, nominated court officials, had the power to create new titles and could depose officials of all ranks. He presided over a national council of the highest title holders. Assisting him were the headmen of the 15 oldest villages in the land. Also assisting him were a second group of officials: two elite women, who held the titles Perpetual Mother of the Lunda and the Perpetual Aunt, in addition to the crown prince, the war leader and others. All members of this second group lived in the capital. The third and final group, who assisted the king, were the tributary chiefs. They lived in the countryside, but had delegates based in the capital.

By 1680, the Lunda Kingdom controlled an estimated 57,915 square miles. At its height in the nineteenth century it became the Lunda Commonwealth and grew to double the size, reaching around 115,831 square miles. The Lunda extended their influence through southwestern Katanga into Angola and northwestern Zambia. Conquered rulers of foreign lands were kept in charge of their homelands, as long as they adopted Lunda titles of office. Since there was no regular standing army, the kingdom's expansion over large parts of the region was a remarkable achievement. The conquered territories paid their tribute once a year in the dry season. The Lunda system of recognizing the power of the headman's relationship to their ancestral land meant that they retained their status even under Lunda colonial rule.

The Lunda Commonwealth came to an end in the nineteenth century when it was invaded by the Chokwe, armed with firearms. The Chokwe then established their own kingdom, with their own language and customs. Lunda chiefs and masses continued to live in the Lunda heartland, but their power was greatly reduced. However, during the Colonial Period the Lunda heartland was divided between Portuguese-controlled Angola, Belgium's Congo Free State, ruled over by Leopold III, and North-Western Rhodesia, governed by the British. After colonization, these lands became respectively Angola, the Democratic Republic of Congo and Zambia.

THE KUBA KINGDOM

As the Portuguese slave raids spread, so the Bushoongs moved inland from the Atlantic. They enlisted new followers as they moved and headed towards the Congo region. However, fleeing from Europeans was not their only problem. When they settled near the lower Kwango River early in the sixteenth century, their immediate foes were the fierce Jaga warriors – a roaming tribe more interested in raids of disruption than in settling anywhere. They waged war against the fledgling Bushoong state that was forming over a wide area along the Kwango, leaving the Bushoongs with no choice but to flee. Most went along the Sankuru and Kasai rivers; other groups split off from the main body and went in other directions. Oral traditions name Woot as the chief and leader of the main body of the people. During the third quarter of the sixteenth century they made their way into the plain of Iyool in Kasai. As they entered Iyool, the Bieeng, a rival ethnic group, challenged the Bushoongs' authority. Despite conflict, the Bushoongs' move into this territory marks the beginning of the formation of the little state, which became known as Kuba.

The kingdom was located between the Sankuru and Kasai rivers. The Bushoong created a federation of voluntary kindred groups; there were 18 such foundational groups in all, including the Kete and the Batwa. The Bushoongs, in contrast to the previous two ethnic groups, considered themselves to be newcomers. Nevertheless, the Kete and the Batwa offered no opposition to the newcomers and welcomed them. With Woot as king, members of other ethnicities and splinter groups joined the newly forming federation: Mongo, Ilebo, Shoowa, Kel, Kaam, Kayilweeng, Lulua, Luba, Ngeende, Maluk, Pyaang, Ngoombe, Byeeng, Coofa and Mbeengi Ngongo. The total population of the federation at its formation was between 75,000 and 100,000 people, with ethnic Bushoongs making up 80 per cent. However, they arranged the political system in a manner that was welcoming to the voices of the smallest ethnic groups. The outcome of this policy was if the Pende excelled in a particular dance, for example, it would become the national dance of Kuba. Similarly, if the Luba excelled in architecture, they would be the lead builders and planners in Kuba, and so on. In the end many of the ethnic groups were absorbed into the Bakuba, or People of Kuba, becoming a single people and losing their distinct identities and languages. However, conflicts continued between some of the ethnic groups. The Pyaang and Kete captured and destroyed the capital city, for example, while the Bieeng continued to dispute Bushoong power.

Woot was followed by 26 kings during the 342 years of Kuban history, which takes us from 1568 to 1910. Beneath the king in the ruling hierarchy were the linguist, the Prime Minister and the paramount chiefs. There were also administrators who were not members of the State Council, including the first chief of the treasury, chief of the border defences, supervisor-general of tax collection, goods and services, the chief of the King's household and protector of ancestral tombs and regalia, the chief of roads and markets and the collector-general for tributary states.

Shyaam the Great was the single most important figure in Kuba's history. Ascending the throne in around 1630, he set in motion an economic development plan that transformed the nation. Until that point the economy had remained at subsistence level; agriculture, fishing, weaving, mat-making, basketry, woodcarving, carpentry, furniture-making, pottery, iron, coppersmithing and painting were the main economic activities. The king's search for new and better ways of doing things served to break with some long-established traditions. New crops such as maize, sorghum, cassava, tobacco, yams and beans were introduced. There were also new developments in weaving and embroidery, and new art patterns and styles appeared in wood carvings. However, Kuba was not connected to international caravan routes. As a result, trade missions were sent to near and more distant nations in order to establish markets and trading centres. Every occupation apart from agriculture had its professional society or guild. New forms of court etiquette and procedures began, as did the wearing of resplendent regalia. However, the general prosperity created an influx of endless streams of migrating people, attracted to this new land of opportunity.

Under the next two autocrats, Mboong a Leeng and Mbo Mboosh, there was continued relative peace, stability and progress. Together with Shyaam the Great, a 50-year period of development took place that saw Shayaam himself enter legendary status; he became known as the 'lieutenant of God on earth'. However, by the end of Mbo Mboosh's lengthy reign in the 1690s, the people had grown tired of his rule. They persuaded his favourite wife to have Shayaam killed, and she strangled him with a noose. Despite this sticky end, Kuba had reached the zenith of its power. Its capital, Nsheng, had become a vibrant centre of architecture, sculpture, textiles and other decorative arts. When the African American missionary Dr William Sheppard (*Presbyterian Pioneers in Congo*, 1917) visited it in the late nineteenth century, the city held 10,000 people. The royal compound had wide streets laid out at right angles. Professor Donald Crowe, an American mathematician, has analysed the use of symmetry, translation, reflection, rotation and so on in Kuban designs. He found all seven mathematically possible strip patterns in their designs. He also found 12 out of the 19 mathematically possible two-dimensional patterns in their designs ('Geometric Symmetries in African Art', in *Africa Counts*, by Claudia Zaslavsky, 1973).

From the death of Mbo Mboosh in 1695 until the coming of the Europeans in the 1800s, internal strife was a feature. Rebellions and civil strife between royal sons, representing patrilineal interests, and royal nephews, representing matrilineal interests, were sparked by constitutional violations. Other problems were uprisings of different ethnicities, rebelling against centralized power. However, markets for Kuban goods became widespread outside of the country; some even ended up as luxury goods in European countries, where they entered museum collections. This prompted European travellers to enter the country, seeking to learn more about where these luxury textiles came from. Kuba had rigidly banned non-Africans from crossing their borders, but attitudes towards this began to change. First came a lone

Portuguese man looking for trading opportunities, followed by some Germans. The exploration trips up and down the rivers did not alarm anyone; in fact, trading relationships with the Europeans were established and growing in profitability.

Between the years 1835 and 1885 Mbop Mabiinc ma Mbul ruled for one of the longest and most tumultuous reigns in the nation's history. Not only did he not see the Europeans as a threat: he and his immediate successors regarded then as a godsend, able to solve critical problems that the kingdom was facing. The Portuguese offered to buy the captured rebels, such sales helping to replenish a drained treasury. In addition, these sales might bring peace to the country and put an end to civil strife. However, selling malcontents into slavery did not bring this about – nor did it end the conflicts between members of the ruling house.

The general upheaval after the Berlin Conference of 1885 made it easy for Europeans to enter and spread all over the country. The missionaries and traders allied themselves with opposing chieftains and opposing royal factions. Putting puppets on the throne of a dying Kuba was the next goal. In 1902 Kot a Pe became the last precolonial ruler of Kuba, but he was to be king in name only: the real power behind him was the Belgians. Ultimately Kuba became part of the Belgian Congo. We give the last word to Professor Leo Frobenius, who visited the region in 1906. He described it in his book *Histoire de la civilisation africaine*, published in 1936:

> *I found still, villages of which the principal streets were bordered on each side, for leagues, with rows of palm trees and of which the houses, decorated each one in charming fashion, were works of art as well. No man who did not carry sumptuous arms of iron or of copper, with inlaid blades and handles covered with*

serpent skin. Everywhere velvet and silken stuffs. Every cup, each pipe, each spoon was an object of art perfectly worthy to be compared to the creations of the Roman European style.
Leo Frobenius, trans. in English and quoted in W.E.B. DuBois, *The World and Africa*, 1946

THE KONGO KINGDOM

The Kingdom of Kongo was a Bantu-speaking culture that flourished in the region of northern Angola and western Congo. In the fifteenth and sixteenth centuries its population consisted of two or three million people spread across six administrative provinces and several dependencies. The provinces were Mbamba, Mbata, Mpangu, Mpemba, Nsundi and Soyo. Among the dependencies were Matari, Wando, Wembo and the province of Ambundu. Mbanza Kongo, the capital city, was in Mpemba province. Mbamba was the military stronghold from which the kingdom could field 400,000 soldiers.

The village, ruled by a dynastic chief, was Kongo's smallest political unit. Above the village were the districts, headed either by royally appointed officials or by provincial governors. All titleholders bore the title of *mani* (lord), followed by the name of their province, district or their function. The Mani Kongo, the king, was perched at the top of the structure. The government's income came from taxation and labour. Tribute was paid in raffia cloth, ivory, hides, slaves and tolls. Brightly coloured *nzimbu* shells were the currency. These came from the island of Loanda and were mined and graded into size by women; the size dictated the relative value of each shell. The courts, both royal and provincial, had officials, pages, musicians and soldiers. Taxes were paid once yearly at a ceremony in front of the royal palace. All territorial officials would come and bring their produce from their locality. Additionally, they would reaffirm their oath of allegiance to the Mani Kongo.

In an earlier age, however, Kongo may have ruled a vast empire. The Mani Kongo in the sixteenth century still held regal titles that hinted at these vanished glories. The Mani Kongo once ruled Kongo, Loango, Kakongo, Ngoyo, the Zaïre River region, the Ambundu, Angola, Aquisima, Musuru, Matamba, Mulilu, Musuku, Anzico, Pangu-Alumbu and other territories. The region covered stretches as far north as modern Gabon and as far south as into Angola. In other words, the empire covered a vast region of 115,831 square miles. The Kikongo language is spoken the length of the coast as far north as Ogooué, from Stanley Pool to the Ocean. In the interior it is spoken as far as the territory of the Bateke; it is also spoken as far east as the Kwango River. By the late first and early second millennium period there is evidence of copper mining and manufacture, ironsmithing, ivory trading and cloth manufacture, including bark and raffia textiles.

The Portuguese made official contact with Kongo in 1485, when envoys were exchanged between the two countries. The Portuguese left four Christian missionaries at the Kongo court and four Mpinda nobles accompanied the Portuguese sailors on their return voyage to Portugal. The Portuguese missionaries in Kongo experienced a well-organized political system with taxes and rates. There was a brilliant court and an excellent civil service. The state constructed roads, imposed tolls, supported a large army and had a monetary system of shells. The Kongo kingdom even had a few satellite states, for example Ndongo in present-day Angola.

In April 1491, on the return of the Portuguese, the Mani Soyo was baptized a Christian by the Portuguese missionaries, taking the Portuguese name Dom Manuel. Months later the Mani Kongo received the Portuguese in Mbanza Kongo, laying on a celebration of music and dance for them. At this display the Kongo nobles carried ironwood swords and shields, while lower orders carried bows and arrows. The king himself was seated on a throne inlaid with ivory; he was raised on a platform. Trumpeters with instruments of ivory repeated their composition 12 times, symbolizing the 12 generations of kings since the founding of the Kongo kingdom. The Mani Kongo became a Christian during this gathering, taking the name Dom Joao I. However, it was only then the Portuguese learned the real reason for the quick conversion; the kingdom was on the point of civil war. Several peoples were rebelling against the central power and Mani Kongo was about to help his son Affonso put down the revolt. Naturally he wanted Portuguese aid, not least the skill of their musket-using mercenaries. It is hardly surprising that they won the day and returned to the capital in triumph. The Mani Kongo settled the Portuguese in a part of the city not far from his own palace out of gratitude. The co-existence had begun.

Professor Chancellor Williams (*The Destruction of Black Civilization*, 1971, 1987), however, interprets the Christianization of the Kongo as a cynical plot to Europeanize the country. Kongolese kings and nobles received European names on being baptized; they had their children educated in Portugal and paid allegiance to the Roman pope. By 1512 the Portuguese *Regimento* appeared. Issued by their king, Manuel, it contained an outline for their Kongolese policy. The document begins with the assertion that all Catholic kings are brothers. It therefore follows that Manuel will help his brother, the king of Kongo, to build Christianity in the kingdom. Moreover, the Portuguese ambassador is to act as an advisor to the Kongolese king in reforming the Kongo court along Christian lines. In particular, the

Kongolese should receive European titles, carry European emblems and adopt Portuguese courtly etiquette. In addition, the Kongolese should pay for the Christianization programme by exporting copper, ivory and slaves to Portugal. Professor Williams says it was the first detailed blueprint for the conquest of the African mind by acculturation via Christianity, his body through slavery and his country by conquest.

However, from Portuguese documents written at the time, we learn that the capital Mbanza Kongo was advantageously situated on the highest mountain in the country. This provided a natural defence and gave a panoramic view of the kingdom. One source (Filippo Pigafetta, *History of the Kingdom of Kongo*, 1591) estimated its population to be over 100,000 people. The king, Nzinga a Kuwu, raised thick walls, one mile in circumference, around his palace and the royal houses. An area of similar size was reserved for the Portuguese; this was also walled. The doors of aristocratic homes faced the walls of the church, as did the homes of the Portuguese. Outside of the enclosures stood numerous buildings owned by various lords. Apparently, it was not possible to determine the size of the town because all the countryside was filled with palaces and rural houses. The habitation of each lord was a walled village. Another source (cited by Alan Scholefield, *The Dark Kingdoms*, 1975) adds that the royal enclosure had several gates guarded by soldiers and trumpeters. One source (cited by Georges Balandier, *Daily Life in the Kingdom of the Kongo*, 1968) gave the population of Mbanza Soyo, the capital of the Soyo province, as 30,000 people.

An abundance of agricultural products was grown in Kongo. Among them were crops of bananas, cauliflowers, coconuts, cola, citrus fruits, cucumbers, palms of various varieties including date palms, pineapples, plantains, rice, watermelons, yams and many others. Other grains were imported from Egypt by an overland route. In addition, other agricultural produce of American origin was imported via the Portuguese. Built on their agricultural industries, the Kongolese produced oil, wine, vinegar and bread. From wild palms they made mats, baskets and other articles for everyday use. Furthermore, their houses were typically made of tightly interlaced palm branches, divided into convenient rooms; the roofs were thatched. The impression conveyed by these buildings was more akin to that of weaving or basket-making than of building in the traditional sense. The Kikongo word *tunga* means to build and to weave. Ornamental wooden palisades surrounded these habitations and mats covered the floors. However, the most revered profession in Kongo was that of the ironsmith. They were responsible for forging knives, weapons, axes and hoes. They also made bracelets using the lost wax technique.

Pigafetta, Dapper (*Description de l'Afrique*, 1668), and Ogilby (*Africa*, 1670) – three European authors of the time – tell us about the intricate crafts made by the people who lived in eastern Kongo and nearby Kuba. They manufactured various textiles, including damasks, sarcenets, satins, taffeta, cloth of tissue and velvet – cut and uncut. The palm tree leaves used to make the yarn created fine and even threads. The products were light and waterproof. Many such treasures are still to be found in European museums. Professor Frobenius, the pioneering German Africanist, highlighted the importance of these collections in his book *Histoire de la civilisation africaine*, published in 1936:

> *And what they told – those old captains, those chiefs of expeditions, the D'Elbées, the De Marchais, the Pigafettas and all the others, what they told is true. It can be verified. In the old*

royal Kunstkammer of Dresden, in the Weydmann collection of Ulm, in many another European 'curiosity cabinets' one still finds collections of objects from West Africa dating from that epoch: wonderful plush-velvets, of an extreme softness, made from the tenderest leaves of a certain banana tree; stuffs, soft and pliant, brilliant and delicate as silks, woven with well-prepared raffia fibre, ceremonial javelins – their blades to the very points inlaid with the finest copper, bows so graceful, and ornamented so beautifully that they would do honour to any museum of arms whatsoever; calabashes decorated with the most perfect taste; sculpture in ivory and wood, the workmanship of which reveals skill and style.

Leo Frobenius, trans. Anna Melissa Graves, *Africa, the Wonder and the Glory*, 1942

Affonso I, a Christianized son, succeeded Dom João I in 1506. However, Mpanzu a Kitima, his non-Christian brother, vigorously opposed him. Prince Mpanzu occupied the capital with the support of the Mani Kabunga, the traditional priest, and forces of nearly 200,000 men. They viewed the Christian influence as a threat to their power. However, Affonso triumphed despite inferior numbers of perhaps 10,000 soldiers and 100 Christians, both Kongolese and Portuguese. He attributed his victory to a holy miracle and thus strengthened his desire to spread Christianity in the land.

In a letter, he requested that King Manuel of Portugal send priests and technicians to spread Christianity further. Schools were established in which students were instructed in Portuguese and Christianity. Affonso also helped bring more Kongo students to Portugal, and he himself studied Portuguese laws. The Portuguese sent him a collection of these in five great volumes. Affonso wanted to create a Renaissance-style Christian state, such as then existed in Europe. Eventually local scribes could communicate in Latin, Portuguese and Kikongo. By 1516 one source (Rui d'Aguiar, vicar of the kingdom of Kongo, writing in 1516, quoted in Georges Balandier, *Daily Life in the Kingdom of the Kongo*, 1968) reports that the capital had 1,000 students studying grammar, humanities and aspects of the faith. Schools for girls had also been established, directed by the sister of the king. Finally, Affonso built churches. By the close of the century the capital had six churches.

However, the relationship between Kongo and Portugal soured. In 1508 the first slaves from Kongo were sent as presents to King Manuel to pay for the Christianization programme. The Portuguese workers sent to Kongo in return failed to deliver on the work that was agreed. Nor was it long before their enslaving activities and abuses of Kongolese women got out of hand. To begin with, priests were not only among the leading slave traders, but they also owned slave ships to carry the 'black cargoes' to distant lands. Priests also had harems of African girls, some containing as many as 20 each. These abuses prompted a series of letters from Affonso I to the Portuguese court. More than 20 of Affonso's letters to King Manuel and his successor, King John III, have survived. One such letter was dated 6 June 1526:

> *There are many traders in all corners of the country. They bring ruin to the country. Every day people are enslaved and kidnapped, even nobles, even members of the king's own family.*
> **Quoted in Jan Vansina, *Kingdoms of the Savanna*, 1966**

The pleas fell on deaf ears and enslaving continued. Moreover, Affonso sent a gift of silver to Portugal in the 1520s. This convinced the Portuguese that silver mines existed within Kongo territory, despite Affonso's assertions to the contrary.

In 1556 a major crisis ensued. Slave-trading factions, supported by the vassal king of Ndongo, to the south, engaged in war with the Kongolese king's forces. Both sides were aided and abetted by rival Portuguese parties, with the Ndongo and the slave dealers emerging triumphant. Their country became independent of Kongo overlordship. A second problem for Kongo arose in 1569. The Jaga, a semi-barbarian slave-trading horde, invaded from lands to the east. In Kongo they caused a sudden and unprecedented breakdown of social order, leading to a famine and a six-year economic collapse. With the help of some of the Portuguese, Kongo expelled this element. The Portuguese had other ideas, however. Beginning in 1575, they launched a series of wars to capture Ndongo which lasted for over a century. They must have believed that Ndongo contained silver mines.

Kongo made some sort of recovery during this period and entered the seventeenth century with most of its institutions and infrastructure intact. Moreover, it developed a newly created messenger system using runners. Marathoners were established at different posts along the main communication routes, able quickly to relay messages from the capital and court to the distant provinces.

However, in Ndongo the Portuguese army commander-in-chief instituted a new policy of repression. After 1608 Bento Cardoso devised a system in which every Ndongo notable would be owned by a Portuguese official and was responsible for delivering a certain quantity of slaves to the Portuguese. Should the Ndongo notable fail to do so, he too would be enslaved. Over a hundred notables were enslaved in a single year. Moreover, the Portuguese killed a further hundred of them. War dragged on for years, but the Portuguese were forced to sue for peace.

In 1622 Ann Nzinga, the Ndongo royal sister, attended a peace conference with the Portuguese convened in the coastal city of Luanda. She demanded firstly that the Portuguese evacuate Kabasa, the Ndongo capital; secondly, that the Portuguese wage war on the Jaga; thirdly, that all Ndongo notables who had become vassals of the Portuguese must return to their former loyalty to the Ndongo crown. In return, Nzinga promised to hand over Portuguese prisoners of war. The provisions of the treaty were designed to end all fighting in the region, but unfortunately the Portuguese breached it almost immediately by invading Kongo.

In 1623 Ann Nzinga officially became the Ngola, the male title 'king' and the basis of the modern name 'Angola'. In this capacity she made the regional alliances necessary to fight the Portuguese. Ndongo was declared a free country the following year and all slaves entering the country were legally declared to be free. By 1629 her forces and allies captured Matamba, the neighbouring state to the east. This too was declared a free country.

In 1641 Garcia II, a vigorous king, emerged in Kongo. He made alliances with the Dutch to fight Portuguese aggression. His death in 1661 brought the great era of Kongolese culture to an end. In Ndongo, the death of Ann Nzinga in 1663 marked a turning point. Her extraordinary and brilliant reign had only delayed the inevitable. Towards the end of the seventeenth century, both Kongo and the combined states of Ndongo and Matamba fell victim to European predator activities, with executions, treachery, robbery and violence becoming the order of the day.

THE EARLY HISTORY OF SOUTHERN AFRICA

Mozambique, South Africa and Zimbabwe were colonized by the European powers of Portugal, Holland and Britain. The Portuguese established coastal trading posts in Mozambique in the sixteenth century, but expanded control over the interior in the nineteenth century. Portugal maintained dominance until 1975. The Dutch began the colonization of South Africa in 1652, establishing a colony at the Cape of Good Hope. However, in the mid-nineteenth century control shifted to the British. They solidified their presence in the country, establishing a settler colony and eventually uniting the region into the Union of South Africa in 1910. Zimbabwe, formerly known as Southern Rhodesia, was colonized by the British in the late nineteenth century, driven by Cecil Rhodes and the British South Africa Company. It was formally incorporated into the British Empire in 1923.

In 1869 a strange book with an intriguing title appeared: *The Ruined Cities of Zulu Land*. Its author was Hugh Mulleneux Walmsley, a British military man who had joined the semi-mercenary Ottoman force known as the 'Bashi Bazouks', or 'crazy heads'. Colonel Walmsley was keen to explain his reasons for writing this unusual book:

> *No one ever reads prefaces now-a-days; why, therefore, should I write one? may be fairly asked. Simply, I reply, to tell the reader that the tale imperfectly related in these volumes is not a mere work of fiction. It is based on a document sent to me by my brother, to whom I have dedicated this work, and who has for many years been a resident of the frontiers of Zulu Land.*

The book narrates the adventures of two individuals: Captain Hughes and another individual known simply as 'the missionary'. Inspired by a taste for adventure, they are on the hunt for the ruined cities of Zulu Land. In Chapter 10 the two men make a breakthrough. Colonel Walmsley narrates what happened:

> *'Gold, cedars and now the ruins: we have found all,' muttered the missionary, as, yielding the point, he strode onward, once more sinking into reverie. There rose right in front of them two massive ruins of pyramidical form, which must at one time have been of great height. Even now, broken and fallen as they were, the solid bases only remaining, they were noble and imposing. Part had come tumbling down, in one jumbled mass, into the bed of the river, while the dwarf acacia and palm were shooting up among the stones, breaking and disjointing them. The two gazed long and silently at these vast mounds, the very memory of whose builders had passed away. Awe-struck and surprised, they sat down by the stream, and, without exchanging a word, drank of the clear water. Their clothes torn, hands and faces bleeding from the exertions made in forcing their way through the bush, their skin tanned to a deep mahogany colour, there they stood at last among the ruined cities of a lost race… Overshadowing the fallen blocks of stone, the date-tree and palmyra waved their fan-like*

leaves. Dense masses of powerful creepers crept up the ruins, rending the solid masonry; and the seeds of the trees dropping year by year had produced a rapid undergrowth, those which had once been valuable fruit-trees having degenerated into wild ones. Chaos had, in a word, re-appeared where once trade and prosperity, order and regularity reigned... It was no easy task; for the accumulation of fallen masonry, and the dense growth of the brush, rendered it often necessary for the onward path to be cleared by the use of the knife. The whole mass appeared at one time to have been encircled by a wall, now fallen, the entrances to which could be distinctly traced, and this confirmed the report which had been gathered by the missionaries of Santa Lucia Bay. Slowly the two men forced their way towards the vast ruined mound they were striving to gain, often stumbling and falling among the loose stones and treacherous creepers. A crowd of half-fallen passages led away to right and left, terminating in what appeared to be a courtyard, in which were the remains of pillars of stone. 'There has once been carved work on these pillars, Hughes,' said the missionary, as they paused, breathless with their exertions, before a mighty column. 'The action of ages has worn it away.' 'And what is more singular,' replied Hughes, who now seemed as much interested in the ruins as his comrade, 'no mortar of any kind appears to have been used, the massive stones fitting into one another exactly.'

However, despite Colonel Walmsley's protestations in the preface, his 1869 book was a work of fiction. Nevertheless, inexplicably, majestic stone ruins of a great age were discovered – only these were in Zimbabwe, not in Zululand. Karl Mauch, a German prospector, found them fully two years after this fictional book came out. In getting to the site, Mauch had to cut through vegetation which had to be 'cleared by the use of the knife'. Strangely enough, the real ruin did have two stone towers in its design and a circular wall. Stranger still, the real ruin really was built with a drystone wall technique in which 'no mortar of any kind appears to have been used, the massive stones fitting into one another exactly'. The Great Zimbabwe ruin consists of a hilltop castle, called the Acropolis, and a walled city, called the Temple.

In the 1930s stone structures were discovered in South Africa. The Blaauboschkraal stone ruins have become a provincial heritage site in the country's Mpumalanga province. According to Professors Roland Oliver and Brian Fagan, authors of a classic book on African history, *Africa in the Iron Age* (1975), ancient stone buildings 'widely occur' in Transvaal and Orange Free State of South Africa. A good example is the Uitkomst culture in the Transvaal, which 'had roots in the first millennium A.D'. Moreover, Oliver and Fagan believe that it 'could well be that the elements of the practice" of stone architecture 'were introduced into South Africa from Rhodesia'. There are similarities between the plans of the South African ruins and the plans of West African buildings, such as the *tata* or forts in the Mossi kingdoms. The similarities indicate that the South African ruins were forts, which would give them the same function as the buildings in Zimbabwe.

IN THE LAND OF THE ZULU

The Mtetwa Paramountcy was a southern African state that arose in the eighteenth century. They were Bantu speakers who flourished south of Delagoa Bay and inland in eastern southern

Africa. The Paramountcy consisted of roughly 30 Nguni chiefdoms, lineages and clans. Dingiswayo was its most distinguished ruler, reigning from c. 1760 to 1817. Under his rule the Mtetwa rose to prominence, assimilating nearby chiefdoms to strengthen their power. They allied with the Tsonga to the north, for example, and began trading ivory with the Portuguese in Mozambique. About 1811 the Buthelezi and several other Nguni groups, including the then marginal Zulu clan, were also integrated. The country was a confederacy in which the Mtetwa clan predominated. However, in 1817 Dingiswayo was killed in a battle with the Ndwandwe. Shaka, a former lieutenant in the Mtetwa army, assumed leadership of the entire Mtetwa Paramountcy. He had been mentored by the late Dingiswayo.

Under Shaka, the Mtetwa Paramountcy became the Zulu kingdom and evolved into a highly militarized state. Men conscripted into his armies were segregated from the rest of Zulu society and trained as a standing army called the *amabutho*; they had to remain in service until their thirties. Shaka introduced new battle techniques, methods of training and tough discipline regimes. In addition, long-throwing javelins were discarded in exchange for the more effective short-stabbing spears called assegais. The troops were forbidden to marry or to wear shoes – the latter prohibition meaning that the men's feet would be tough, enabling them to run swiftly and feel little pain. Mr Henry Fynn travelled through the Zulu state with a party of Europeans in 1824. His diaries describe, among other things, a war dance drill of the Zulu army:

> *On entering the great cattle kraal we found drawn up within it about 80,000 natives in their war attire... It was a most exciting scene, surprising to us, who could not have imagined that a*

nation termed 'savages' could be so disciplined and kept in order. Regiments of girls, headed by officers of her sex, then entered the centre of the arena to the number of 8,000–10,000, each holding a slight staff in her hand. They joined in the dance, which continued for about two hours.

Henry Fynn, 'The Diary' in *The Diary of Henry Francis Fynn*, ed. James Stuart and D. McK. Malcolm, 2nd Ed., 1950

A 'kraal' was originally an Afrikaans word for an enclosure for cattle or other livestock, surrounded by a fence or wall of circular plan. Unfortunately, the same word entered the literature to describe a traditional Nguni house form. Sharing the domed shape and size of igloos, the Nguni homes were made of rope, lattice, thatch and wooden strips. Shaka's original capital was on the banks of the Mhodi, a small tributary of the Mkhumbane River in the Babanango district. He called it KwaBulawayo, meaning 'at the place of the murder'. As his kingdom grew, however, he built a second and far larger KwaBulawayo, with a royal household of about 1,400 domed dwellings, in the Mhlathuze valley. In his diaries Henry Fynn described the seraglio. This was the royal district for women of the harem:

The seraglio of the Zulu king consists of the upper part of the royal kraal and measures about 300 yards in length by 200 in breadth. It is separated from the main or lower portion of the kraal by a neat fence of closely plaited brushwood, five feet in height. The area cut off by the fence is subdivided by similar fences into compartments for the different divisions of the household, and these subdivisions are such as to give the whole appearance of being an intricate labyrinth. In each compartment there are neatly finished hearts, the insides being of the neatest workmanship. The sticks are worked so closely together as to be of themselves nearly watertight. The spaces between the huts are levelled and kept constantly clean. Every compartment is named according to its use, or the division of the household who occupy it.

Henry Fynn, 'Historical Introduction' in *The Diary of Henry Francis Fynn*, ed. James Stuart and D. McK. Malcolm, 2nd Ed., 1950

A.T. Bryant, an authority on Zulu history and culture, wrote that:

the untutored Zulu has succeeded in evolving one of the cosiest, safest and best ventilated types of habitation ever conceived by primitive man. An even temperature is preserved at all times by the thick layer of thatch covering, not only the roof, but also the walls, which keeps the internal atmosphere cool in the intense heat of noonday and warm in the cold of winter and night. Has any simpler and equally effective scheme of central-heating ever been devised?

A.T. Bryant, *The Zulu People*, 1948, reprint 1970

While Bryant has described the positives of Zulu domed dwellings correctly, it is a shame that he used terms such as 'untutored' and 'primitive'. He knew better. This same author also wrote a book on Zulu medicine for the benefit of Western medical practitioners. In it he concluded:

In spite of such blind empiricism, it cannot be denied that the native doctor does sometimes work a cure, sometimes quite a startling cure, where the efforts of European physicians have proved utterly unavailing.

A.T. Bryant, *Zulu Medicine and Medicine-Men*, originally printed in *Annals of the Natal Government Museum*, Vol. II, Part 1, 1909

How did the people in the seraglio and royal areas conduct themselves? Fynn comments favourably upon this in the 'Historical Introduction' to his diary, noting: 'As a matter of fact, in no place in Europe is greater decorum, order and etiquette observed than in these seraglios and their various departments'. Moreover, he was much impressed by the apparel of the women in the seraglio, observing:

Such costumes were superb, and far beyond anything the reader would imagine after taking into consideration the apparent absence of articles which would seem to be necessary for creating grand effects.

Henry Fynn, 'Historical Introduction' in *The Diary of Henry Francis Fynn*, ed. James Stuart and D. McK. Malcolm, 2nd Ed., 1950

Moreover, Shaka had various buildings reserved for his own private use. In some of them, he had meals; in another he dressed; in another he slept; and in yet another he gave audiences. Other buildings were used for storing his provisions. What typically did Shaka eat? Fynn's 'Historical Introduction' gives us an answer:

His meals generally consisted of stewed beef or mutton, potatoes, beans, a pudding made of Guinea corn flour, mixed with rich soup, beer, plantains and sugar cane, when in season. All the food was cleanly cooked by his female attendants, and served up in wooden dishes of curious workmanship.

In April 1818 the Zulu kingdom survived an assault by the Ndwandwe, a rival kingdom, at the Battle of Gqokli Hill. However, in 1820 the Ndwandwe were defeated by Shaka at the Battle of Mhlatuze River, which destroyed the Ndwandwe alliance. Despite this, remnant forces of the defeated Ndwande began a murderous campaign against other Nguni people; it wreaked havoc, consisting of a marauding army of broken and defeated men. The death toll has never been satisfactorily determined, but the campaign almost depopulated the whole region, with some Nguni fleeing as far north as Tanzania and Malawi. By 1822 Shaka's forces had conquered an empire encompassing around 80,000 square miles, covering the area from Pongola to the Tugela River.

Shaka's strategy for expansion was brutal but effective. Once a regional kingdom had been conquered, he replaced the king with an *induna* (meaning 'general') who was directly answerable to Shaka. Those who quickly accepted Shaka's overlordship could be made *indunas* who served him. Those who refused to submit to his authority were killed, along with their families. Consequently, Shaka's conquests left behind a trail of cruelty and destruction. Some estimate that nearly a million people were killed or left homeless by his wars. Famine and chaos followed, with the destruction of herds and crops between the Limpopo and the Gariep River.

The word Zulu means 'heaven' in English and their country is called KwaZulu, the 'place of Zulu'. The Zulu themselves believe that the land, like the rain, belongs to no one; it is simply there for all to share. However, this philosophy was not shared by the Europeans who entered South Africa at the Cape with van Rieebeck in 1652.

With them came the notion of private ownership of the land, sparking vigorous disagreements between Africans and Europeans. Van Rieebeck's party met the indigenous Khoi and San people at the Cape. Soon they were to meet the Xhosa. By the time of Shaka, the British had pushed on into Natal, where they sought profits and land. Shaka had acquiesced in the establishment of British trading and missionary posts while trying to protect the Zulu from the fate of the Xhosa and other southern ethnic groups that had been pacified by wars with the Europeans. Zulu would not be pacified, nor would it submit to European rule.

Mzilikazi was the son of a chief under the paramount king of the Ndwandwe. When his father was killed, he took over the kingdom but switched sides. He and his people showed loyalty to Shaka and Heeven moved his people to the capital, KwaBulawayo. Shaka allowed him the exceptional privilege of forming his own regiment and retaining hereditary and military control over it. However, this was to prove a mistake. Mzilikazi defied Shaka after a raid on another kingdom. His regiment seized goods there, but refused to bring the spoil to Shaka. Mzilikazi refused to back down, but eventually had to flee with all his people from Zulu territory. By 1825 Mzilikazi was leading his people across the great plains and hills of South Africa in search of a homeland; they were ultimately to become the Ndebele nation. Mzilikazi led them north into Zimbabwe, where they encountered and defeated the Shona. The Ndebele created an even larger empire than the Zulus did, their rule encompassing large parts of the highveld and modern-day Zimbabwe. Today Zimbabwe has a majority Shona population and a minority Ndebele population.

However, in 1828 Shaka was assassinated by two of his brothers and one of his closest friends. His brother and assassin, Dingane, became the new king of Zulu. J.R. Mackenzie described his royal buildings as follows:

> *The king's kraal are of enormous dimensions, and are several in number. Panda, for example, has one kraal, the central enclosure of which is nearly a mile in diameter... The vast central enclosure is used almost exclusively as a parade ground, where the king can review his troops.*
>
> **J.R. Mackenzie quoted in *Indlu: The Domed Dwelling of the Zulu, in Shelter in Africa*, ed. Paul Oliver, 1971**

King Dingane took a forceful position against the intrusions of Europeans into Zulu territory. He met the leaders of the Boer farmers, who had begun to move into the interior to escape British domination, and warned them against violating Zulu territory. When a Boer intruder refused to adhere to one of his decrees, he was killed. The Boers, who had previously battled the British and other Africans at the Cape, promptly declared war on the Zulu. On 16 September 1838 the army of Dingane met the Boer army at Blood River. They were to carry the day, with the Zulu nation losing more than 3,000 soldiers. In 1840 a younger royal brother, with Boer support, overthrew Dingane in a royal coup to become King Mpande.

In his 32 years on the throne, Mpande neither threatened the Boers nor participated in any effort to keep them from expanding. Essentially a puppet, he sold out the birthright and traditions of the ancestors. During this time many new *indunas* chose non-Zulu names and even adopted non-Zulu cultural practices. Facing both British and Boer intruders on his borders, Mpande tried not to alienate either party. In 1843 he surrendered all the territory between the

Buffalo and Tugela River, now forming Klip River county, to the British. Together with other colonies the British already controlled, it became the Colony of Natal. In 1854 he granted the Boers in northern KwaZulu Natal a deed of cession for an area between Zululand and the Transvaal Republic. This ultimately became the Republic of Utrecht.

Cetshwayo became the next king on 1 September 1873. As was customary, he created a new capital for the nation, this time called 'Ulundi', meaning the high place. However, Cetshwayo faced critical threats from the Boers and the British during his reign. In 1875 Boers flooded across into Zululand, claiming land south of the Pongola River as well as attempting to tax Zulu homesteads in the northwest. Several thousand troops were sent to the border and the Boers eventually retreated. The arrival in March 1877 of Sir Bartle Frere, the High Commissioner for Southern Africa, brought a new threat to Zulu independence. He was convinced the British could prevent an independent Zulu nation if they acted quickly to curb the power of Cetshwayo. Frere duly picked a fight in the belief that the British, armed with guns and cannons, could easily defeat the Zulu army who depended on Shakarian war strategies from 50 years before. In addition, when a Zulu *induna* killed his wife in a domestic dispute that could have been dealt with under Zulu law, the British demanded that the case be tried under their law. In December 1878 the British presented Cetshwayo with an ultimatum: hand over this *induna* for trial in the British courts or face the consequences. The Zulus refused.

Led by Viscount Chelmsford, the British invaded KwaZulu on 10 and 11 January 1879. Half of the 14,000 troops that invaded were Africans, under the control of the British. There were many skirmishes. Caught by surprise, the Zulu battled Colonel Pearson's column at Nyeazane River and were badly beaten. They then engaged the British column, led by Colonel Wood, in an inconclusive battle near Hlobane Mountain. It was at the Battle of Isandlwana that the tide turned. The Zulu army met the British and their African allies in the foothills of Isandlwana Mountain, striking with lightning speed and taking the battle to the enemy. Using assegais, or hardwood spears tipped with iron, they cut their foes to pieces. Fifty-five British soldiers and 300 Africans fighting alongside them survived. The British had never before suffered such a defeat at African hands.

However, the Zulu celebrations were short lived. Five months later the British organized another campaign against them, this time armed with Gatlin guns. They reached the Zulu capital of Ulundi at the end of June and prepared for a final assault against Cetshwayo. They burned the city and, after a few months of conflict, the British had gained enough power in the region to govern KwaZulu. By the end of 1879 the land was firmly under British rule. Eventually, in 1910, it became part of the Union of South Africa.

BIRTH OF MINING IN ESWATINI

In **1964** a haematite mine (a type of iron ore) was found in Eswatini (Swaziland). It was discovered at Bomvu Ridge in the Ngwenya mountain range. Professor Raymond Dart, a scholar at the University of Witwatersrand in Johannesburg, made a scholarly study of the site. His team discovered a large cache of ancient mining tools, as well as tunnels and adits, or horizontal passages leading into a mine. Over time as many as 300,000 artefacts were recovered, including thousands of stone-made mining tools. Adrian Boshier, one of the archaeologists on the site, estimated the date of the mine to be 43,200 years ago. Because of the very early date, it is likely that these miners did not speak languages related to the six or so main civilizational groups that we described elsewhere. Archaeologists believe that the ancient miners were digging for specularite, a type of haematite. The theory is that the prehistoric miners were using specularite as a cosmetic dye.

EVOLUTION OF SOUTHERN AFRICAN CULTURE

South Central African villages were thriving during the Iron Age. These communities, usually covering one acre or more, were situated close to deep soils, most likely to engage in agriculture. Pottery, pieces of bone and evidence of homes have been found by archaeologists. Evidence of hunting wild game can be seen in the bone fragments, which also typically reveal evidence of domesticated cattle in later-dated sites. The sticks and mud homes had thatched roofs and were held up by a central pole. They had hardened floors.

Evidence of the oldest known iron-using communities in southern Africa was discovered by J. Desmond Clark, the former director of the Rhodes-Livingston Museum. Dr Clark conducted systematic excavations in the early 1950s at two sites in Zambia, Lusu and Machili, concluding that iron was used in villages in parts of south-central Africa 2,000 years ago. Sites in the northeast Transvaal, near Phalaborwa, were excavated by another archaeologist, N.J. van der Merwe, beginning in 1965. From as early as the eighth century CE to the nineteenth century, van der Merwe discovered plentiful evidence of iron and copper mining shafts and furnaces.

Ziwa and Leopard's Kopje, two southern African sites connected to gold mining, were excavated by other archaeologists. A unique pottery style from the fourth, ninth and tenth centuries CE flourished at Ziwa. An early pottery style known as Leopard's Kopje I was found at Leopard's Kopje, and is once more connected to gold-mining operations. The eighth and ninth centuries were when this pottery was made. According to Professors Oliver and Fagan in *Africa in the Iron Age*, the Ziwa date from the fourth century was probably not correct. They thus deduce that between the eighth and tenth centuries the groups that produced the Ziwa and Leopard's Kopje I pottery also engaged in gold mining.

At Leopard's Kopje evidence of a new culture was discovered, associated with a new style of pottery (Leopard's Kopje II). The new culture, dating back to the tenth and eleventh centuries, emerged in southwest Zimbabwe and the northern part of South Africa. Bambandyanalo, in South Africa, is the best-known site belonging to this culture. The Leopard's Kopje II villages were built near rocky hills and were enclosed by rough stone walling. The culture produced clay figurines of women, domestic animals and cattle. The human figurines depict features typical of Khoisan women, showing that the Khoisan were a powerful element within this culture. Furthermore, the culture was strongly pastoral, with cattle becoming the currency. Finally, evidence of trade links to the Indian Ocean has been discovered. Among the artefacts recovered were glass beads, thought to have come from Indian Ocean trade with East Africa.

A Roman coin dating from the first century CE was discovered in an abandoned mine. From the second century BCE to the sixth century CE, additional coins from Persia, Rome and Greek-ruled Egypt have been found in Pemba, on the East African coast. The existence of a culture in the Zambesi region is implied by the fact that life there is inextricably linked to life along the coast. Archaeologists in the Zambesi region have found three pole and *daga* structures, constructed on a stone podium, and dry-stone walling, created during the first two-thirds of the first millennium CE. The Acropolis in Great Zimbabwe either itself originated during these eras or the stone masonry tradition that produced it is that old.

Ancient stone structures are common in South Africa's Transvaal and Orange Free State. The Transvaal's Uitkomst Culture, which dates to the first millennium AD, is a prime example. There are hundreds of stone-built forts around the Johannesburg area, and it is possible that this area was already a regional capital judging by the overwhelming amount of evidence. A limestone-brick capital site was discovered at Manikwene, close to Mozambique's East African coast. According to carbon dates, the court was at its height between approximately 1150 and 1600. Among the items discovered there were iron gongs, a representation of royal power.

GOLD WORKING IN SOUTHERN AFRICA

In 1998, the African American scholar Professor Charles Finch penned a significant book about ancient African technology and science called *The Star of Deep Beginnings*. In it he noted that ancient gold mines in Zimbabwe have been found which are more than 4,000 feet in length and 150 feet deep. The amount of extraction work completed is attested to by the large number of adits driven into the hillsides. It is estimated that the ancients extracted over 43 million tons of gold ore from the entire area. The ore yielded nearly 700 tons of pure gold, which at 1998 gold prices would be valued at over $7.5 billion.

Ian D. Colvin made an equally astonishing observation many years ago:

The bygone miners must have been industrious beyond belief, since they worked in rock so obdurate that the same sort of reef is nowadays blasted with dynamite, and yet they removed many million tons of ore. It is a practical testimony to their skill that the modern engineers follow to this day the lines of their ancient workings.

Ian D. Colvin, 'Zimbabwe's Ruins of Mystery', in *Wonders of the Past*, Vol. 2, ed. Sir J.A. Hammerton, 1937

The southern African goldsmiths used tools to burnish gold to increase the shine, such as beating hammers, and stamps to imprint designs directly onto golden objects. They engaged in techniques such as gold wire drawing, beating gold into thin sheets and plating other metals with gold. They also manufactured gold ornaments and jewellery. Iron and bronze were plated with sheets of gold, beaten to a remarkable thinness. Beaten gold covered headrests, furniture, statues, battleaxes and even arrowheads. Gold wiring was drawn to create different gauges of thickness. Gold chain links were also created. At its thinnest, gold thread was woven into cloth. Elite members of the courts wore rich silk, damask, satin and gold and silk garments, some of which were decorated with woven gold roses on silk.

THE GREAT ZIMBABWE

Great Zimbabwe is a significant ruined city in modern Zimbabwe. Its impressive stone ruins, which span roughly three square miles and consist of 12 buildings, resemble a megalithic fortress. Some of the walls are 17 feet thick and 35 feet high; they are made of granite bricks that lock together without the need for mortar. Crushed granite cement was used to build their floors, while dadoes and drains were everywhere. With 18,000 residents, some archaeologists believe more, the city was as big as medieval London at its height in the fourteenth century CE. The Shona *Zimba Oye*, which translates as 'Great Revered House', is the source of the name Zimbabwe. Shona was the Bantu language of the builders.

Historians have traditionally divided the most notable parts of the ruins into the 'Temple', famous for its conical tower in the lower valley, and the 'Acropolis', the turreted castle structure on the overlooking hill. The Acropolis may have first been built in around 1085. The Temple may have been built some centuries later, in around 1335 CE. Mr J. Theodore Bent, an English scholar, was an early excavator of the site, working there in 1891. Clearly overwhelmed by the experience, Bent described the 'labyrinthine character of the interior'. Referring to the Temple, he observed:

> *Entering from the northern portal, we at once plunge into its intricacies. The great and astounding feature is the long narrow passage leading direct from the main entrance to the sacred enclosure, so narrow in parts that two people cannot walk abreast, while on either side of you rise the stupendous walls, thirty feet in height, and built with such evenness of courses and symmetry that as a specimen of the dry builder's art it is without a parallel.*
> **J. Theodore Bent, *The Ruined Cities of Mashonaland*, 3rd Edition, 1902**

The use of dry-stone walling and crushed granite cement proved to be an excellent choice. It is vindicated by the fact that many of its walls still stand; elsewhere, cemented masonry has succumbed to the passage of time. Reconstructing the early history of this city has been difficult, however, as Bent clearly explained:

> *Vainly one tries to realise what it must have been like in the days before ruin fell upon it, with its tortuous and well-guarded approaches, its walls bristling with monoliths and round towers, its temple decorated with tall, weird-looking birds, its huge decorated bowls, and in the innermost recesses its busy gold-producing furnace. What was this life like?*
>
> **Bent, *The Ruined Cities of Mashonaland***

The cottages within the walls and elsewhere were circular in shape with thatched roofs. Their walls, 12 to 18 inches thick, were made of *daga*, a clay and gravel mixture used to build walls. The cottages' intricate designs and opulent construction, which required a lot of labour and materials, also demonstrate a high level of technical skill and virtuosity. They produced effects that almost resembled sculpture. In actuality, the *daga* structures in the ruins were structural achievements, on a par with the masonry walls. However, at their core, they are merely advancements and improvements upon customs that were nearly universal in the cultures of this region and era. Regardless of the expense of labour or materials, both exhibit a concern for appearance and ostentation.

Just outside the Temple, European treasure hunters found a trove of goods in 1902. The variety and quantity of the goods were astounding. Fifty pounds of iron hoes, golden beads, a vast amount of coiled wire made of bronze, copper, gold and iron (some twisted into bracelets), copper jewellery, iron gongs, stone moulds for copper ingots and a lot of ivory. All of these were locally made. In addition there were goods of foreign origin: a Persian bowl, a Chinese celadon, a Syrian glass, an iron spoon, iron lamp stands, copper chains, bronze hawk bells, glass beads, cowrie shells and a coral chain. What were these goods doing there? Were they tribute received by the ruler of Great Zimbabwe?

THE MUNHUMUTAPA EMPIRE

An empire began to take shape in the twelfth and thirteenth centuries. In southern Africa, it was the first. Professors Oliver and Fagan (*Africa in the Iron Age*) agree that the empire unified numerous territories, including the Ziwa culture, Leopard's Kopje I and Leopard's Kopje II, and controlled the region's trade. They imported glass beads, produced more metal items and exported ivory and gold to the Indian Ocean by controlling access to the gold-producing areas. Its capital was Zimbabwe. By 1085 the Shona built the mighty stone castle on the hilltop. Known today as the Acropolis, this structure gave a panoramic view of the vast plateau. In the valley below, they built the first stone walls of the Temple. Larger and more substantial houses were also built. Finally, archaeologists have discovered spindle whorls, clear evidence of a textile industry. What was the name of this empire? Later sources called it Munhumutapa.

Traditionally the first ruler of this empire is known as Mutota; another early ruler is called Matope. Each took the imposing title of Mutapa i.e. Emperor. Before the imperial rule of the Mutapas, the kings were simply rulers of Great Zimbabwe. One of these was remembered as Chimubatamatosi. Historians usually place all these men in the fifteenth century, but this is a weak interpretation of the traditions. Dr Stan Mudenge, author of *Political History of*

Munhumutapa c. 1400–1902 (1988), pointed out that there is dearth of precise dating in the history of the Mutapa Empire that lasts from its founding until roughly 1490. Six Mutapas are said to have succeeded before 1490, but their names appear to be a telescoped version of reality. The accomplishments frequently attributed to such mythical individuals as Mutota and Matope might reflect state-formation processes aided by several other, as yet unidentified, Mutapa rulers. As a result we assign the twelfth or thirteenth century to Mutota. Furthermore, we place Chimubatamatosi after 1085, but at an even earlier time. According to one traditional tale, Mutota was a prince of Great Zimbabwe. To obtain a trustworthy supply of salt, he then led an army that conquered the Shangwe region and entered Dande. Before he died Mutota also established control over the Guruuswa lands.

The greatest of the early conquerors was a successor named Matope, who overran Tonga and Tavara in a series of campaigns. He also took control of the kingdom of Barwe. Economic considerations seem to have been paramount. Swahili traders used to sail to the mouth of the Zambezi. Six leagues upstream was the town of King Mongalo, where the Swahili hired almadias, or bark canoes, to carry their merchandise along the channel to a trading bazaar. This was in a large village in Tonga country. Here Swahili and Shona traders met and exchanged goods. In the interior, another famous trading centre was in the land of the Mambara, where large quantities of copper were traded. The overland trade route with Sofala through Manyika had its own bazaars. In addition to these, trade was facilitated by individual Swahilis who travelled throughout the land selling their merchandise. Matope, in imposing a political empire over this network, offered the peace and security that allowed the gold and ivory trade to flourish. The next important phase in the growth of the Mutapa Empire was the inclusion of the lands of Uteve and Manyika.

At Mapungubwe in South Africa, which may have served as an imperial religious centre, gold ornaments were discovered, interred with significant figures. This site has characteristics of a trading capital; cattle and trade goods were discovered in abundance. A golden rhinoceros, a wooden bowl and a staff covered in sheets of beaten gold were found in one of the graves. Chinese celadon dishes dating from the fourteenth century were also discovered, along with golden necklaces.

Ingombe Illede in Zambia was home to a trading community that specialized in copper production. Gold was also buried there with significant figures. There are unquestionably Zimbabwe-style ruins at both locations, according to Oliver and Fagan (*Africa in the Iron Age*). Since there are stone-built forts in the Johannesburg region, Ingombe Illede and Manikwene, we conclude that the Mutapas held sway from Ingombe Illede in Zambia to Johannesburg in South Africa. The empire ruled as far east as Manikwene, near to the coast of the Indian Ocean. It was already one of the largest empires in mediaeval Africa.

Zimbabwe was at its most prosperous and prestigious between 1350 and 1450. After a devastating fire around 1350, a large portion of the capital was rebuilt in a new and much improved masonry style. Regular coursing and dressed stones were used to construct the walls. Although the walls themselves most likely appeared as they do today, it is important to keep in mind that there would have been homes both inside and outside of *daga*. During this time, additional courts were established in Ruanga, Nhunguza, Lekkerwater and Chipadze. They were constructed of stone, just as Great Zimbabwe was. They also contained the same mix of luxury products and locally produced goods. Cattle continued to be an important part of their economies. Professors Oliver and Atmore tell us that:

> *It looks very much as if they were the provincial outposts of a Great Zimbabwe kingdom that was expanding its territory northwards during this period.*
> **Roland Oliver and Anthony Atmore,**
> ***Medieval Africa: 1250–1800*, 2001**

However, from the period of the Mutapa Mutota, Great Zimbabwe ceased to be the administrative capital of the region. The new capital of Munhumutapa was at Mount Fura, much further north. Great Zimbabwe held significance as a cultural and religious centre. Portuguese sources from the seventeenth-century describe the new capital, but it was then in ruins. Manuel de Faria e Sousa, a seventeenth century Portuguese historian and poet, wrote: 'In the mountain…near Masapa are seen the ruins of stately buildings supposed to be palaces and castles' (quoted in David Randall-Maciver, *Mediæval Rhodesia*, 1969, original 1906). What did the palace look like before ruin came? An eighteenth-century geography book says:

> *The inside consists of a great variety of sumptuous apartments, spacious and lofty halls, all adorned with a magnificent cotton tapestry, the manufacture of the country. The floors, ceilings, beams and rafters are all either gilt or plated with gold curiously wrought, as are also the chairs of state, tables, benches &c. The candle-sticks and branches are made of ivory inlaid with gold, and hang from the ceiling*

by chains of the same metal, or of silver gilt. The plates, dishes and bowls belonging to the emperor's table are made of a sort of porcelain, curiously wrought on the edges with springs of gold resembling those of coral. In short, so rich and magnificent is this palace, that it may be said to vie with that which distinguishes a monarch of the east.

George Henry Millar, *The New and Universal System of Geography: Being a Complete History and Description of the Whole World*, 1782

The region's currency was X-shaped ingots. These are a regional development of cross-shaped ingots used in other Bantu lands. The empire received valuable imports such as fine Indian textiles, Persian glazed wares, celadon and Ming porcelain, and glass. The empire produced opulent items such as jewellery and ornaments made of copper and gold to cover this cost.

The Portuguese sailed to this region in about 1499. Their sources provide useful data on the Mutapa Empire. Father Antonio Gomes, a Portuguese Jesuit priest who was in Munhumutapa in the 1630s, for example, tells us that the people dress in various ways:

At court and Zimboôe [sic] *of the Kings their grandees wear cloths of rich silk, damask, satin, gold and silk cloth; these are three widths of satin, each width four* covados *[8¾ feet], each sewn to the next, sometimes with gold lace in between, trimmed on two sides, like a carpet, with a gold and silk fringe, sewn in place with a two fingers' wide ribbon, woven with gold roses on silk – a very well made thing manufactured by the [people] themselves… These cloths are worn from the waist down the right side trailing along the floor and the left just down to the knee. Others dress in cotton cloth with coloured stripes, black being their favourite colour. Of all the women, the Mocranga* [sic] *are the ones who dress best, the cloth coming down to one* palmo *above the feet; that part of the leg showing is covered with bright copper bands. At some other places where they do not have so much cloth, the men wear skins, one in front, one at the back, and the women dress in a very short cloth and those who do not have one wear a piece of threshed bark that becomes cinnamon coloured and is as soft as cloth and woven by nature as if it were cloth. In other places the men wear skins and the women a little net made of coloured beads and nothing else… Elephant hunters and their wives dress in the stomachs of the animals they kill, very nice grey cloth which, divided in two, is enough for two people and is so soft that it feels like satin.*

Quoted in S.I.G. Mudenge, *A Political History of Munhumutapa c. 1400–1902*, 1988

The Mutapa had a standing army of 100,000 men, but he could mobilize 300,000 should the need arise. In addition, he had 5,000 or 6,000 Amazons. The empire of Munhumutapa, while not militaristic in character, possessed a strong military structure, able to defend itself and to enforce authority over a vast area. This is demonstrated by the fact that houses of ordinary people needed no doors, because 'They say that houses are built with doors for fear of thieves and malefactors, from whom it is the king's duty to protect his people, and above all the poor'. Putting of doors at the entrance of houses was a privilege granted by the Mutapa to a few nobles.

Agriculture, pastoral pursuits, trade, mining, hunting, tribute, taxes, gifts, crafts and industries were the sources of the imperial court's wealth. Agriculture was the main economic activity. Pastoralism, particularly with regard to cattle, was the second source of economic power. Gold remained important for trading purposes. The Portuguese claimed that by observing vegetation and soil types, the Shona could determine where gold could be found. According to Portuguese sources, hunting elephants led to the annual slaughter of between 4,000 and 5,000 animals, yielding from 9842 to 24,605 tons of meat. Tariffs and tolls were levied and collected from international traders. In addition to the above sources of income, the Mutapas received presents from traders as well as from their subjects who visited their royal courts. Textiles were an important craft industry. Threads of imported cloth were woven together with locally produced cotton to produce cloths of rich silk, damask and satin laced with gold. Finally, boat building increased as more *almadias* (bark canoes) were needed to carry trade goods up and down the river. Tribute, taxation, judicial fees and presents were other sources of royal income.

What did they do with the money? Most of this went to the Mutapa and his immediate family, but some of it also went to a form of social security. According to Bocarro, a Portuguese chronicler:

> *The Mutapa show great charity to the blind and maimed, for these are called the king's poor, and have land and revenues for their subsistence, and when they wish to pass through the kingdoms, wherever they come, food and drinks are given to them at the public cost as long as they remain there, and when they leave that place to go to another they are provided with what is necessary for their journey, and a guide, and someone to carry their wallet to the next village. In every place where they come there is the same obligation, under*

penalty that those who fail therein shall be punished by the king.

Antonio Bocarro, Decade 13 of *History of India*, 1635, quoted in S.I.G. Mudenge, *A Political History of Munhumutapa c. 1400–1902*, 1988

However, the Portuguese role in this land was controversial. Portuguese Jesuits attempted to convert people to Christianity, in which they had some success. On 15 March 1561 a Portuguese missionary was killed, creating a whodunnit in the area. Bad relationships developed between Munhumutapa and Portugal as a result. Other Jesuits in Portugal lobbied their government for more interventionist policies in Munhumutapa, with many now advocating evangelization through 'sword and fire'. A chief motive for Portugal was to seize 'the abundance of the wealth' in Munhumutapa. In the 1580s, through naivety on the empire's part, they allowed the Portuguese to establish marketplaces at Masapa, Ruhanje and Bukutu. Commercial intercourse between the Portuguese and the Mutapa thus increased considerably.

By 1589 the throne had passed to a new ruler: Gatsi Rusere. During his reign of approximately 34 years, a large portion of the empire was to collapse due to civil war and rebellions. In 1625 Kapararidze succeeded to the throne of a greatly diminished Munhumutapa. His ascent to power was not without controversy, as many believed that the rival Mavhura family should have inherited the throne. The *prazo* system, which the Portuguese instituted during his reign, saw large amounts of land distributed to individual Portuguese officials. The rival, Mavhura, grew close to the Portuguese Dominicans in the meantime. This development alarmed the emperor, who took action to stop it in its tracks.

He gave the order to kill the Portuguese ambassador on 17 November 1628. The Portuguese raised an army when Tete and Sena learned of the ambassador's death. Meanwhile Mavhura was proclaimed the legitimate Mutapa by other anti-Kapararidze forces. However, he and his allies were met with Kapararidze's army at Masapa. The Mutapa lost the battle and had to retreat with significant casualties. Mavhura-Portuguese troops overran and pillaged the imperial Zimbabwe. At a small church devoted to Our Lady of the Rosary, the victorious party celebrated a victory mass. In May 1629 Mavhura was crowned Emperor of Munhumutapa.

However, the Portuguese required the new ruler to sign a treaty of vassalage to the Portuguese crown. The treaty made it clear that (i) he received the throne in the name of the King of Portugal; (ii) the Portuguese were to be allowed complete freedom to convert all to Christianity; (iii) all the Swahili were to be expelled from his dominions within one year; (iv) Portuguese ambassadors were to be allowed to enter his Zimbabwe in full armour and to speak to him seated on a chair without clapping their hands; (v) he was to treat all other Portuguese as if they were ambassadors; (vi) he was to consult with the Captain of Masapa on matters of war and peace; (vii) he was to search and reveal the existence of silver mines. Finally, (viii), he was to allow Tete to annex the surrounding lands for the Portuguese crown. Moreover, Mavhura, his queen and four or five nobles were baptized by the Portuguese. Mavhura was given the name Dom Filippe and his Queen that of Dona Giovanna.

The Treaty of 1629 represented the death of the Munhumutapa Empire. Through the rest of the seventeenth century, the

Portuguese gained control over more and more land. With this control came increased political power and the spread of mass enslavement. Compounding the problem for Munhumutapa, the Portuguese enslaved not only ordinary people, but also sons and daughters of the nobility.

THE EARLY HISTORY OF EAST AFRICA

The German East Africa Company colonized Tanzania in 1885. At the end of the First World War control of this territory was given to Britain following a League of Nations mandate. The British also colonized Zanzibar in 1890, Uganda in 1894 and Kenya in 1895. Both Uganda and Kenya became part of the British East Africa Protectorate. Portugal had a long-standing presence in East Africa, having exercised sporadic control of Mozambique, off and on, since 1498. However, it was not until the late nineteenth century that Portugal formally established a structured colonial presence. In 1890, following pressure from other European powers during the 'Scramble for Africa', Portugal officially declared Mozambique to be a colony.

During this period, archaeologists and other specialists began to survey the land under their control. They began to turn up evidence of Bantu achievements in East Africa. Professor Louis Leakey, a Cambridge-educated British archaeologist, heard news of an old, stone-built site in Tanzania, now in ruins, at a place called Engaruka. He contributed a paper on his survey to a colonial journal called *Tanganyika Notes and Records*. In it Leakey explained: 'I received the news that Mr Wetherell had "discovered" a large ruined city at Engaruka'. This news had prompted Leakey to do a preliminary survey, from which he concluded:

I estimate that there are about six thousand three hundred houses in the main city on the scree slopes…and that there are about five hundred houses in the valley ruins, where burials are far commoner than houses. The population figure was probably between thirty and forty thousand and I think this may be an under-estimate. There is a vast mesh of stone walls and terraces in the valley ruins which I take to be connected in some way with cultivation and irrigation, but this is not proved. Should these on future examination proved to be house areas also then the size of the city was very much larger.

L.S.B. Leakey, 'Preliminary Report on Examination of the Engaruka Ruins', *Tanganyika Notes and Records*, No. 1, March 1936

Maurice Henry Dorman, another Cambridge-educated scholar, went on to have a distinguished career as a colonial administrator in Malta and Sierra Leone. He too submitted an article on an East African discovery to *Tanganyika Notes and Records*, this time beginning the survey of a ruined city on the Tanzanian coast. However, his description makes a serious error. Instead of describing it as an *African* fort, he refers to the structure as an *Arab* fort.

When I landed at Kilwa Kisiwani for the first time it was at night; since sunset we had been silently drifting down the long dark reaches of mangrove past Songomanara…until at last we drew into the shore and were aware of the mass of Kisiwani Fort dwarfing our dhow. When we left next morning it was an unforgettable picture, its walls alight with the rising sun.

> *The old Arab fort is the most impressive of all the buildings. It stands pugnaciously facing the harbour mouth; seaward its walls are in ruins: two bastions with the half of a tower still stand and in places the old crenellated battlements are visible. The glory of the fort is its wooden gate: its silver-grey lintel and doorposts are boldly carved with a kind of* fleur de lys *and Tudor Rose – the lintel bears a date plaque flanked by two large conventionalized flowers. Through the gate a broad passageway leads into a small inner courtyard with rooms on all sides, some of them are two storeys. It is still possible to climb across the gateway up a small flight of stairs and on to the original battlements and towers.*
>
> **M.H. Dorman, 'The Kilwa Civilization and the Kilwa Ruins', *Tanganyika Notes and Records*, No. 6, December 1938**

This building is today known as the Husuni Kubwa. In addition, Dorman came across the ruins of the Great Mosque of Kilwa. Both buildings are discussed further in the section on Swahili antiquities below.

> *The large mosque is one of the best preserved of all the ruins. Its roof, cut up into cupolas and small barrel vaults, presents a grotesque and undignified appearance from the outside. Inside, from hexagonal pillars spring simple pointed arches, giving the impression of a groined roof, and on the arches rest the small domes or cupolas; its proportions resemble more than anything the crypt of a cathedral.*
>
> **Dorman, 'The Kilwa Civilization and the Kilwa Ruins'**

THE BUNYORO-KITARA KINGDOM

Robert Felkin was a member of the Anthropological Institute of Great Britain and Ireland and a corresponding fellow of the Berlin Anthropological Society. With some background in medicine, he made two voyages to Central and East Africa to compile a study on childbirth there. His first journey, which took place between 1878 and 1880, was to the Kingdom of Bunyoro-Kitara, now part of the Central East African country of Uganda. His second journey ('all round Africa') was from 1880 to 1881. On 9 January 1884 Felkin gave a lecture on his findings to the Edinburgh Obstetrical Society in a paper called 'Notes on Labour in Central Africa'. He wrote:

> *So far as I know, Uganda is the only country in Central Africa where abdominal section is practised with the hope of saving both mother and child... It was performed in 1879 at Kahura.*

However, this wasn't just exceptional for Central Africa – it was exceptional for the whole world! Even in Europe caesarean sections performed in 1879 had a 100 per cent death rate for the mother. Surgeons performed the operation only to save the child. Felkin continued:

> *The patient was a fine, healthy-looking young woman of about twenty years of age. This was her first pregnancy. I was not permitted to examine her, and only entered the hut just as the operation was about to begin. The woman lay upon an inclined bed, the head of which was placed against the side of the hut. She was liberally supplied with banana wine, and was in a state of semi-intoxication. She was perfectly naked. A band of mbugu or*

> *bark cloth fastened her thorax to the bed, another band of cloth fastened down her thighs, and a man held her ankles. Another man, standing on her right side, steadied her abdomen… The operator stood, as I entered the hut, on her left side, holding his knife aloft with his right hand and muttering an incantation. This being done, he washed his hands and the patient's abdomen, first with banana wine and then with water.*

Alcohol was thus used as an anaesthetic for the mother. It also had antiseptic and sterilizing properties. What happened next?

> *Then…he proceeded to make a rapid cut in the middle line, commencing a little above the pubes, and ending just below the umbilicus. The whole abdominal wall and part of the uterine wall were severed by this incision, and…a few bleeding-points in the abdominal wall were touched with a red-hot iron by an assistant. The operator next rapidly finished the incision in the uterine wall; his assistant held the abdominal walls apart with both hands, and as soon as the uterine wall was divided he hooked it up also with two fingers. The child was next rapidly removed, and given to another assistant after the cord had been cut, and then the operator, dropping his knife, seized the contracting uterus with both hands and gave it a squeeze or two. He next put his right hand into the uterine cavity through the incision, and with two or three fingers dilated the cervix uteri from within outwards. He then cleared the uterus of clots and the placenta, which had by this time become detached, removing it through the abdominal wound. His assistant endeavoured, but not very successfully, to prevent the escape of the intestines through the wound. The red-hot iron was next used to check some further*

> *haemorrhage from the abdominal wound, but I noticed that it was very sparingly applied.*

Cautery iron is important to prevent bleeding, but it was important to use it sparingly. This reduced the patient's exposure to skin damage and scarification. Felkin continued:

> *All this time the chief 'surgeon' was keeping up firm pressure on the uterus, which he continued to do till it was firmly contracted. No sutures were put into the uterine wall. The assistant who had held the abdominal walls now slipped his hands to each extremity of the wound, and a porous grass mat was placed over the wound and secured there. The bands which fastened the woman down were cut, and she was gently turned to the edge of the bed, and then over into the arms of assistants, so that the fluid in the abdominal cavity could drain away on to the floor. She was then replaced in her former position, and the mat having been removed, the edges of the wound, i.e., the peritoneum, were brought into close apposition, seven thin iron spikes, well polished, like acupressure needles, being used for the purpose, and fastened by string made from bark cloth… A paste prepared by chewing two different roots and spitting the pulp into a bowl was then thickly plastered over the wound, a banana leaf warmed over the fire being placed on the top of that, and, finally, a firm bandage of…cloth completed the operation. Until the pins were placed in position the patient had uttered no cry, and an hour after the operation she appeared to be quite comfortable. Her temperature, as far as I know, never rose above 99° F, except on the second night after the operation, when it was 101° F, her pulse being 108.*

So far, so good. The patient was comfortable one hour after the operation, but did get a temperature the following night. Felkin concluded this part of the story:

> *The child was placed to the breast two hours after the operation, but for ten days the woman had a very scanty supply of milk, and the child was mostly suckled by a friend. The wound was dressed on the third morning, and one pin was then removed. Three more were removed on the fifth day, and the rest on the sixth. At each dressing fresh pulp was applied, and a little pus which had formed was removed by a sponge formed of pulp. A firm bandage was applied after each dressing. Eleven days after the operation the wound was entirely healed, and the woman seemed quite comfortable. The uterine discharge was healthy. This was all I saw of the case, as I left on the eleventh day. The child had a slight wound on the right shoulder; this was dressed with pulp, and healed in four days.*

Mother and child were doing well eleven days after the operation. The surgical team were clearly skilled, efficient and well-practised, carrying out a routine operation with unhurried skill.

In 1959 J.N.P. Davies contributed an article to the journal *Medical History* entitled 'The Development of "Scientific" Medicine in the African Kingdom of Bunyoro-Kitara'. He was *not* particularly impressed by the fact that the Bunyoro-Kitara inoculated their citizens against smallpox, noting only that 'Variolation against smallpox was certainly practised, but this was a widespread feature of African medicine'. In other words, so many other African nations traditionally practised this that Bunyoro-Kitara deserved no special credit. However, Davies did observe that:

Both in the case of preventive inoculation against syphilis and in the caesarean section with its meticulous technique we seem to see the evidence of analytic minds at work, capable of observing over long periods and possibly capable of experimenting.

One key question that Felkin and Davies did not ask was: what do we know about the civilization capable of such advanced and efficient surgery?

The Kitara kingdom, a Bantu-speaking people, flourished in the western Great Lakes area. Emerging in around 1100 CE, it was the most powerful state in the region. Its rulers have since taken on the status of legend; Ugandans today recount an era of myth when a dynasty of demigods ruled. Supposedly the founders of Kitara, these legendary rulers are called the Bachwezi. Coming from a foreign or a mystical place, legend has it that they brought advanced knowledge of agriculture, technology and governance. Endowed with spiritual and material knowledge, the Bachwezi could even control the weather! Some believe the extent of the Kitara kingdom in the era of the Bachwezi extended into parts of Uganda, Rwanda and Tanzania. Control of cattle, iron production and salt were key sources of wealth. However, in the early fifteenth century this kingdom fell apart, leaving a two-generation interregnum. Historians do not know what brought about the collapse of this Great Age. However, archaeologists have found tangible evidence of this culture: the Bigo Bya Mugenyi.

Following Kitara's collapse, many aspiring princes spread far south and established new dynasties. Some made themselves rulers over previously existing tiny kingdoms while others founded new states. Into this vacuum came an intrusive Luo clan from Pabungu, known as the Bito, who successfully claimed the Kitara leadership.

In the late fifteenth century the Bito began a successor state to Kitara called Bunyoro. In addition, they claimed descent from the legendary Bachwezi.

In the sixteenth century Bunyoro, the successor state, ruled over western, central and southeastern Uganda. Within their territories were iron-producing centres. Moreover, they controlled the salt-producing sites of the western rift. The Bito kings granted landed estates to leading provincial chiefs, required in turn to maintain houses at the Bunyoro capital. Ruling an empire, the Bito kings claimed tribute from smaller states to the south and east. In addition, they launched great cattle raids as far south as Rwanda. Cattle continued to be a marker of wealth. Royalty owned massive herds, cattle captured in war were redistributed and court fines were paid in cattle. Holding regular markets, bark cloth and banana flour were available from the then tiny tributary state of Buganda. Dried fish was available from several lakeside areas while sorghum and sesame came from the southwestern grasslands.

Between 1640 and 1800 the Bunyoro kingdom remained the mightiest regional power, with smaller subordinate kingdoms to the south still recognizing their overlordship. But they faced upstarts, even from one of their former tributary states. The biggest challenge came from the increasing power of the Kingdom of Buganda to the east; its centre was along the northwestern shores of Lake Nyanza. However, through further military expansions, Buganda became a force to be reckoned with in the late seventeenth and eighteenth centuries.

The Bunyoro kingdom was eventually colonized by the British. During the 'Scramble for Africa', Uganda fell under British jurisdiction. In July 1890 an agreement was made in which Great Britain received the entire region north of Lake Victoria. The British claimed the region as its protectorate in 1894.

On 15 May 1909, during the beginning of the British Colonial Period, the *Uganda Official Gazette* featured a report on the discovery of a site of archaeological interest. The District Commissioner, Masaka, reported of the existence of a fortified camp known by locals as Bigo, meaning 'Forts', or Bigo bya Mugenyi, meaning 'The Stranger's Forts'. What had actually been discovered?

The fortifications consist of an outer rampart and ditch extending over 2¾ miles in length, the flanks resting on the Rivers Katonga and Kachinga. The interior works, which are built on the summit of a low hill in the centre of the position, consist of a central work, rampart and ditch, with two adjoining works on the eastern face. The rear face is formed by the Katonga, which at this point is some 1,000 yards broad and unfordable... There arc also two small outlying forts lying some six and four miles west and east of Biggo.

H.R. Wallis, *The Handbook of Uganda*, 2nd Ed., 1920

It was not unique, however. Edward James Wayland, the first president of the Geological Survey of Uganda, observes:

Similar ancient forts have been reported in Uganda and contiguous territory, one on the Kagera River at Kyaka and another in Bunyoro, found by Mr D.N. Stafford... The earthworks referred to by Mr Wright...may yet be others.

E.J. Wayland, 'Notes on the Biggo Bya Mugenyi: Some Ancient Earthworks in Northern Buddu', *Uganda Journal*, No. 2, 1934

Archaeologists have since dated the *Bigo bya Mugenyi* dates to between 1300 and 1500 CE. Moreover, there are other important large earthwork sites: Kibengo and Munsa. Because of this, John E.G. Sutton, a former Director of the British Institute in East Africa, has suggested the three large earthwork sites – Kibengo and Munsa, as well as Bigo – were three different capitals. He therefore concludes that Kitara may not have been a single kingdom with one line of kings, as previously visualized. Instead he proposes that it was probably a confederation.

BIRTH OF ANIMAL HUSBANDRY

In Kenya, people domesticated cattle 15,000 years ago. This important discovery was announced in the *New York Times* in 1980 by Professor Charles Nelson, an anthropologist at the University of Massachusetts. He led an archaeological team that had found teeth and cattle bones spread over a limited area, suggesting that the animals were not wild. (Had they been wild, the remains would have been scattered over a larger area.) Consequently, this reveals human activity in controlling the movement of the cattle. The remains were found on three sites in the Lukenya Hill district of the Kenyan Highlands.

THE HAYA IRON SMELTERS

Al-Idrissi, the twelfth-century Moorish geographer who worked at a court in Sicily and author of *The Book of Roger*, says that East Africans traded iron on the Indian Ocean. The metal was of a superior quality and was used to make the famous Damascus Blades of the Middle Ages. This trade proved profitable, and its proceeds have been linked to the early development of the Kenyan city of Malindi. Other towns that depended on the iron trade were Mombasa, Quelimane and Chindi. Professor Charles Finch (*The Star of Deep Beginnings*) has also identified the superior iron described by Al-Idrissi as steel. Evidence discovered in 1978 has shown that East Africans had been making steel for more than 1,500 years, fully 600 years before Al-Idrissi documented the trade. Two American academics from Brown University, Peter Schmidt, Professor of Anthropology, and Donald H. Avery, Professor of Engineering, found that Africans living on the western shores of Lake Victoria had produced carbon steel. They made the steel in preheated forced draught furnaces, a method more technologically sophisticated than any developed in Europe until the mid-nineteenth century.

Schmidt and Avery found 13 ancient iron furnaces in the Lake Victoria region of Tanzania. The furnaces made use of blowpipes and bellows to inject oxygen into the base of the furnace, which saved fuel. When smelting steel, it is important to keep the temperature above 2102°F to melt the impurities and to separate the iron from the ore. It is also important to keep the temperature below 2804°F, the melting point of iron. The metallurgists of this region worked with temperatures of around 2642°F.

BIRTH OF EAST AFRICAN SHIPPING

East Africa was a key player in the Indian Ocean trade. With a shipping tradition going back 2,000 years, sailors from the region traded on the high seas. They sold locally made products and products from Munhumutapa for thousands of miles across the ocean. East African sailors travelled to Oman, India, China and Cambodia. In 1414 the ruler of Malindi in Kenya even shipped a giraffe to the Chinese emperor as a gift.

East African ships could carry up to 69 tons of merchandise. Their hulls were made of wooden planks, sewn together using ropes. An ancient Greek sailing book, written 2,000 years ago, describes these same East African ships, held together using ropes. Some ships had square or rectangular-shaped sails made of huge woven mats; others used triangular sails made of cotton. On the walls of the royal palace of Kilwa and the Great Mosque, archaeologists have found graffiti sketches showing both types of ships.

Steel was the main product traded by the East Africans. Moreover, the Swahilis minted their own coins of copper and silver; archaeologists have discovered these twelfth-century coins in northern Australia. On 22 August 2013 the *Daily Mail* published an article titled 'How 900-year old African coins found in Australia may finally solve the mystery of who arrived Down Under first'. It also raised the question of how they got there. It may well be that Swahili sailors visited these lands 600 years before Captain Cook.

THE SWAHILI CONFEDERATION

The Swahili states were major cities that flourished on the East African coast between the ninth and the sixteenth centuries. Well known for their tasteful and sophisticated architecture, some were even mentioned by the English poet John Milton in *Paradise Lost*. The Swahili mosques have been compared to 'grand medieval cathedrals of Europe' in a Time Life documentary, while Lamu, one of their cities, was considered 'as sophisticated as medieval Venice'. Moreover, the region 'was the setting for the legendary adventures of Sinbad and the Arabian Nights'. Even in ruin, these sites are deservedly major tourist attractions in Kenya and Tanzania. On the East African coast, from Somalia to Mozambique, archaeologists discovered the remains of 400 settlements. These were cities, towns and grand burial sites for a Bantu civilization. The major city-states were Mogadishu and Brava in Somalia, Lamu, Mombasa and Malindi in Kenya, Kilwa and Mafia on islands just off the coast of Tanzania, the islands of Pemba and Zanzibar and finally Sofala in Mozambique.

The Swahili culture flourished due to its important role in the Indian Ocean trade. When merchant ships arrived at their ports, the authorities charged fees and taxes. However, patterns of trade between Asia and East Africa were influenced by the seasonal winds of the monsoon. Beginning in November, the northeast monsoon reached its peak strength in January. From India and the Persian Gulf, it blew towards and along East Africa's coast. The monsoon produced a current that travelled south to Lamu, Kenya, along the East African coast, while the winds reliably carried ships even further south to Kilwa in Tanzania. Arab and Asian sailors generally traded in the Gulf and Red Sea at the start of the season, when they accumulated cargo. They would then set sail and convey their cargo to markets in East Africa. In April the southwest monsoon started, establishing a strong northerly current that would flow up the Somali coast towards India by June or July. When the monsoon was strong enough, the dhows usually headed for Asia from East Africa.

Of course, not all the merchant shipping came from the Arab or Asian worlds. East African ships also sailed the Indian Ocean, drawing on a 2,000-year shipping tradition. Like the Arab sailors, East African mariners used the monsoon winds, this time for sailing to and from Asia. Just as Arab sailors stopped off in East Africa between January and June, in between the monsoons, African mariners stopped off in Asia between July and November for the same reason.

Some historians used to claim that the East African culture was partly, if not entirely, of Arab or Persian origin; they believed that it was established by merchant sailors from these distant lands. However, visitors to the coast such as Ibn Hordadbeh, a Persian geographer and bureaucrat of the ninth century, writing in 886 CE, wrote: 'whoever goes to the land of the Zanj, surely catches the itch' (quoted in Basil Davidson, *Old Africa Rediscovered*, 1959). East Africans were then called Zanj, the basis of the modern name Zanzibar. The great Venetian traveller Marco Polo, writing in the thirteenth century, describes the Zanzibari as being quite black, giant statured, and large limbed, with large eyes, flat noses and very full lips. The celebrated traveller Ibn Battuta, who visited the coast in 1331, described the more northerly people of the coast as Berbers, 'a people of the Blacks' and the more southerly people, whom he calls Zanj, as being 'of very black complexion' (*Travels in Asia and Africa*, trans. and ed. Said Hamdung & Noël King, *Ibn Battuta in Black Africa*, 1993). Both the Zanj and the Berbers of the coast were Bantu-speaking. However, while the masses of coastal people remained Africans, intermarriage between local Swahili elites and elites originating in Persia was a very common occurrence throughout the Swahili Golden Age.

The Zanj traded ivory with India and China, with the traffic passing through Oman. In China and India ivory was used to make royal chairs and dagger handles, as well as chess pieces. It is possible that some of these products came from Great Zimbabwe, especially the ivory and gold. Ambergris (a perfume made from whales) and rhino-horn, used for medicinal purposes, were also exported from the coast, the latter proving popular in Far Eastern markets. Another important product for trading was timber; mangrove-poles were sold to the building industries of Oman and Persia. Finally, the Zanj traded steel on the Indian Ocean as noted above.

As the cities developed, mosques and graveyards became the focal points around which the houses were grouped. As the towns became larger and the graveyards filled up, new mosques and graveyards were built, followed by new houses grouped around them. Between 800 and 1000 CE Shanga and Manda became major cities, consisting of between 15,000 and 18,000 people. Professor Christopher Ehret wrote, in *The Civilizations of Africa* (2016), that they were far larger than any contemporary town in Europe north of the Pyrenees. The houses themselves were grouped close together; narrow walkways separated them to accommodate donkey traffic. In the fourteenth and fifteenth centuries pillar tombs were built. These structures, a uniquely Swahili construction, consisted of tall pillars, inlaid with Chinese porcelain bowls and connected to one end of a tomb.

Ibn Battuta's book *Travels in Asia and Africa*, which draws upon his explorations of 1331, contains an interesting account of Swahili cuisine from the Somali city of Mogadishu:

> *The judge took my hand and we came to that house which is near the shaikh's house. And it was bedded out and set up*

with what is necessary. Then he came with food from the shaikh's house. With him was one of his ministers who was in charge of guests. He said, 'Maulana says peace be unto you and he says to you, you are most welcome'. Then he put down the food and we ate. Their food is rice cooked with ghee, placed on a large wooden dish. They put on top dishes of kushan *– this is the relish, of chicken and meat and fish and vegetables. They cook banana before it is ripe in fresh milk and they put it on a dish, and they put sour milk in a dish [i.e. yogurt] with pickled lemon on it and bunches of pickled chillies, vinegared and salted, and green ginger and mangoes. These are like apples and they have a stone, and when they ripen they are very sweet and are eaten like fruit. But before they ripen they are bitter like lemons and they pickle them in vinegar. When they eat a ball of rice, they eat after it something from these salted and vinegared foods.*

Ibn Battuta, *Travels in Asia and Africa*, quoted in Said Hamdun and Noël King, *Ibn Battuta in Black Africa*, 1994

Days later Battuta visited the Tanzanian city of Kilwa:

We spent a night on the island of Mombasa, *and then set sail for Kilwa, the principal city on the coast the greater part of whose inhabitants are Zanj of very black complexion. They have tattoo marks on their faces... A merchant told me that a fortnight's sail beyond Kilwa lies Sofala, where powdered gold is bought from a place a month's journey inland... Kilwa is one of the most beautiful and well-constructed cities in the world. The whole of it is elegantly built.*

The opulence evident at Kilwa was found all along the coast at numerous sites, including Kua, Songo Mnara, Mombasa and Malindi. Their palaces and town houses contained the striking pottery of Nishapur and Sultanabad, the celadon of Song China, Ming ornaments and bowls of great elaboration, beads and precious stones of India, artefacts and figurines in ivory and gold, jewellery of copper and jade, and carpets of the Middle East and Mecca. The trading networks paid for the construction of world-class architecture all along the coast. Grander houses had stone-built benches outside, designed for receiving guests; exquisite brass bosses adorned the double front doors, framed by wooden floral designs. There were art deco-inspired decorations on the walls and doorways inside. The houses, between one and five storeys in height, possessed indoor toilets, bathrooms, bedrooms and rooms for entertaining. Beds, chairs, children's cots, kitchenware and tableware from city life are among the exquisite pieces of reconstructed furniture in Kenyan museums.

Swahili is the most widely spoken language in Africa. Some ancient manuscripts, over 4,000 years of age, are preserved at the University of Dar es Salaam at their Institute of Kiswahili Research. There are collections totalling over 600 manuscripts in Zanzibari Museums, Archives and Antiquities departments, while other Swahili manuscripts are held in Germany and in London. The oldest surviving Swahili manuscripts date from the seventeenth century, but the poetry tradition is much older than that. The quality of Swahili poetry has been ranked with the poetry traditions of Turkey, Iran and India. A fourteenth- or fifteenth-century poetry cycle tells the story of Fumo Liyongo, a Swahili hero, and his struggle with the Sultan of Pate, off the coast of Kenya. The Sultan viewed the poet as a potential usurper to his throne while Liyongo believed that he was the rightful heir to the kingdom. The Swahili Epics, or *tendi*, are often 5,000 quatrains or more in length, the longest known *tendi* being 45,000 quatrains long.

However, this splendid culture came to an unfortunate end. Early in the sixteenth century the Portuguese sent their fleets and armies into this region, causing great ruin. In 1502 Vasco da Gama returned to the coast, accompanied by a score of ships from home. He threatened to burn Kilwa unless its ruler acknowledged the supremacy of the king of Portugal and agreed to pay yearly tribute in gold. Other Portuguese forces did the same. Meeting with resistance, the Portuguese went on to storm, burn and destroy. They wrecked Kilwa, Mombasa, Zeila, Brava and several other coastal cities.

In 1938 Maurice Henry Dorman published his survey ('The Kilwa Civilization and the Kilwa Ruins', in *Tanganyika Notes and Records*, No. 6, December 1938) on the ruins of Husuni Kubwa, the royal palace of Kilwa. No one now knows what the building was originally called, but archaeologists today call it the 'Husuni Kubwa', the Swahili for 'Large Fort'. Located a mile away from the rest of the city, it was built on a breezy cliff overlooking Kilwa harbour. A monumental stairway connected the harbour to the top of the cliff and the palace entrance.

The white South African architect, Dr Peter Garlake, surveyed the building in 1962. He found that it contained over one hundred rooms, including a reception hall, galleries, courtyards and terraces. The palace was constructed in around 1300 and its walls were covered with a silky smooth white finish. Parts of the structure were two storeys in height. The king and court sat in an audience court which looked like a theatre. On both sides of this theatre oil lamps burned. One part of the palace, entirely secluded, was probably a private area for the ruler's wives and children. Behind the palace were 38 warehouse rooms, used for storing merchandise; these rooms were secure and had no windows. Garlake also found a major surprise: the palace had an octagonal-shaped swimming pool!

A FINAL WORD

Our knowledge of African history has come a long way since the late nineteenth century. In Volume 1 of his book *The Voice of Africa*, published in 1913, Professor Leo Frobenius quoted a German newspaper of 1891 which describes Africa as follows:

> *'If the soil of Africa is turned up to-day by the colonist's ploughshare, no ancient weapon will lie in the furrow; if the virgin soil be cut by a canal, its excavation will reveal no ancient tomb, and if the axe effects a clearance in the primeval forests, it will nowhere ring upon the foundations of an old-world palace. Africa is poorer in recorded history than can be imagined.'*
> **Extract from an article in an 1891 'Berlin newspaper', Leo Frobenius, *The Voice of Africa*, Vol. I, trans. Rudolf Blind, 1913**

Among the German people who read these comments, how many would ever have believed that a library would be discovered at Qasr Ibrim with medieval manuscripts in eight different languages: Meroïtic, Old Nubian, Coptic, Greek Creole, Greek, Latin, Arabic and Turkish? Who would have thought that a visitor to a Sudanese city would be tripping over ruins of marble and porcelain before scaling the six-storey tower of the palace? Who would have believed that walls in Nigeria would be featured in the *Guinness*

Book of Records as the largest construction ever made before the mechanical era?

In *The Voice of Africa* Professor Frobenius addressed some of the German newspaper misinformation by citing evidence from Mangbetu, Kuba, Lunda and Bunyoro:

> *Thus the Berlin journal! I cut this passage out that night with my scissors by the light of the midnight oil in my tiny study. My thoughts were profoundly stirred, and I put it away. I turned to my friendly bookshelves and allowed King Munsa's court as pictured by Schweinfurth, Wissmann's descriptions of the troubles in the Bassonge towns, Pogge on Muata Jamvo and the English explorers' sketches of the ceremonials of the sovereigns of Uganda to unroll themselves before my eyes.*

We have seen that eyewitnesses described caesarean sections performed in Bunyoro, an indigenous writing system in Igboland, industrial-scale metallurgy in Mossi and agricultural water-wheels in Sudan. Archaeologists have found evidence of the world's oldest mining in Eswatini, the world's oldest iron working in Nigeria and the world's oldest cotton making in Sudan.

Moreover, we have seen West African stone ruins in Dhar-Tichitt dating back to 2000 BCE. Stone ruins have been found in Zimbabwe, Mozambique and South Africa. The Great Mosque of Djenné, a glory of Sudanic architecture, began life as an eleventh-century palace. Other architectural splendours are the palaces in Hausaland, such as the Gidan Rumfa, the Royal Palace at Kano. The 700,000 manuscripts believed to have survived in Timbuktu contain astronomical, medical, mathematical and climatological content. The bronze and ivory pieces from the Nri state, Benin and Yorubaland are among the finest examples of medieval art and craft in the world. Alongside them are the exquisite textiles from Nupe and Borno, now held by museums in London, Liverpool, Berlin and elsewhere. Glass was made at Ife, with glass windows featuring in the castle of the Ghanaian emperor, in the city of Gao, in the Lalibela churches and the Nubian cathedrals. In East Africa the ruins of splendid ghost towns appear all along the coast from Somalia, through Kenya and Tanzania, down to Mozambique: stone houses, palaces, grand tombs, wells, madrasas and mosques. The royal palace of Gedi, for example, has ruins of 54 rooms, 11 courtyards, seven burial areas and six double cubical toilets. In the Horn of Africa are temples, obelisks, castles, chateaux, inscriptions, statues, monograms and coins. Moreover, this region participated in the early history of Judaism, Christianity, Islam and Rationalism. It is also the home of coffee. Finally, we have the heritage of ancient Sudan and Egypt: pyramids, temples, inscriptions, fine art, jewellery and monumental sculpture. Despite misinformation to the contrary, this heritage belongs to Africa.

What has been presented here is an overview of what is presently known about African history. Our knowledge will grow when Africa has been as thoroughly excavated as Asia or Europe. In his book *The Star of Deep Beginnings*, published in 1988, the American academic Professor Charles Finch acknowledged how much more remained to discover. As he pointed out:

> *Fewer than 10% of the known archaeological sites on the continent have even been surveyed, let alone excavated. Archaeologically, Africa is still largely* terra incognita… At

last report, there are supposed to be one million mounds in the northern Sudan that have never been touched by the spade! The Meroitic city of Naga is said to be so large that it may take 70 years to excavate.

We are still only at the start.

A FINAL WORD

ANCIENT KINGS & LEADERS

This section lists key African leaders from selected regions and empires discussed in this book. It cannot hope to be exhaustive but provides an overview, and reminds us that the origins of peoples and leaders stretch far back into the mists of time, often with roots in mythical pasts.

ANCIENT AFRICAN LEADERS

Please note that due to incomplete or conflicting records, dates are approximate. Where dates of rule overlap, rulers either ruled jointly or ruled in opposition to one another. There may also be differences in spellings between different sources. It has unfortunately not been possible to include rulers for every kingdom or empire mentioned in the book. This list focuses on rulers of those civilizations which can be more easily traced through history.

CARTHAGE (*c.* 814–308 BCE)

Dido (or Elissa, founder of Carthage, mythological) *c.* 814 BCE

Hannonid Dynasty (*c.* 580–550 BCE)

Hanno I	*c.* 580–556 BCE
Malchus	*c.* 556–550 BCE

Magonid Dynasty (*c.* 550–340 BCE)

Mago I	*c.* 550–530 BCE	Hannibal I	440–406 BCE
Hasdrubal I	*c.* 530–510 BCE	Himilc. II	406–396 BCE
Hamilcar I	*c.* 510–480 BCE	Mago II	396–375 BCE
Hanno II	*c.* 480–440 BCE	Mago III	375–344 BCE
Himilc. I	460–410 BCE	Hanno III	344–340 BCE

Second Hannonid Dynasty (*c.* 340–308 BCE)

Hanno I	340–337 BCE	Hamilcar II	330–309 BCE
Gisco	337–330 BCE	Bomilcar	309–308 BCE

Carthage became a republic in 308 BCE

WEST AFRICA: MALI EMPIRE (*c.* 1235–1610)

Sundiata Keita	*c.* 1235–1255	Camba Keita	*c.* 1360
Uli Keita	*c.* 1255–1270	Mari Jata Keita II	*c.* 1360–1374
Wati Keita	*c.* 1270–1274	Musa Keita II	*c.* 1374–1387
Khalifa Keita	*c.* 1274–1275	Maghan Keita II	*c.* 1387–1389
Abubakari Keita I	*c.* 1275–1285	Sandaki	*c.* 1389–1390
Sakura	*c.* 1285–1300	Maghan Keita III	*c.* 1390–1404
Gao Keita	*c.* 1300–1305	Musa Keita III	*c.* 1404–1440
Mohammed ibn Gao Keita	*c.* 1305–1312	Uli Keita II	*c.* 1460–1480/81
Mansa Musa Keita I	*c.* 1312–1337	Mahmoud Keita II	*c.* 1480 or 1481–1496
Maghan Keita I	*c.* 1337–1341	Mahmoud Keita III	*c.* 1496–1559
Suleiman Keita (with his wife, Kassi)	*c.* 1341–1360	unknown mansa	*c.* 1559–1590
		Mahmoud Keita IV	*c.* 1590–1610

NIGERIA: BENIN (1440–1914)

Ewuare the Great	1440–1473	Ozolua	1483–1504
Ezoti	1473; 14 days	Esigie	1504–1550
Olua	1473–1480	Orhogbua	1550–1578

Ehengbuda	1578–1606	Akenzua I	1713–1735
Ohuan	1606–1641	Eresoyen	1735–1750
Ohenzae	1641–1661	Akengbuda	1750–1804
Akenzae	1661–1669	Obanosa	1804–1816
Akengboi	1669–1675	Ogbebo (for 8 months)	1816
Ahenkpaye	1675–1684	Osemwende	1816–1848
Akengbedo	1684–1689	Adolo	1848–1888
Oroghene	1689–1700	Ovonramwen N'Ogbaise	1888–1914
Ewuakpe	1700–1712		
Ozuere	1712–1713		

CENTRAL AFRICA: BAMOUN KINGDOM (1394–1931)

Nchare Yen	1394–1418	Koutou	1682–1757
Ngoupou	1418–1461	Mbouombouo	1757–1814
Monjou	1461–1498	Ngbetnkom	1814–1817
Mengap	1498–1519	Mbeikuo	1817–1818
Ngouh I	1519–1544	Ngouhouo	1818–1865
Fifen	1544–1568	Ngoungoure (for 30 minutes; only female ruler of Bamoun Kingdom)	1865
Ngouh II	1568–1590		
Ngapna	1590–1629		
Ngouloure	1629–1682	Nsangou	1865–1884, 1884–1889

The Bamoun Kingdom was incorporated into Kamerun, part of the German Empire, on 14 July, 1884.

Ibrahim Njoya	1889–1914

Incorporated into French Cameroun in 1914. Independent in 1960.

ETHIOPIA AND ERITREA

Axum Kingdom

Few dates are available for rulers of the Axum Kingdom but the length of rules have been recorded and *selected* leaders are listed here.

Arwe (mythological)	Ruled for 400 years in 18th century BCE
Angabo (mythological)	Ruled for 200 years in 14th century BCE
Gedur I (presumed mythological)	Ruled for 100 years in 12th century BCE
Sebado (p. mythological)	Ruled for 500 years in 11th century BCE
Kawnsaya (p. mythological)	Ruled for 1 year in 10th century BCE
Makeda, possibly Queen of Sheba (p. mythological)	Ruled for 50 years in 10th century BCE
Menelik I (p. mythological)	Ruled for 24–29 years in 10th century BCE
Handadyu I	Ruled for 1–8 years in 10th century BCE
Tomai	Ruled for 15 years in 10th century BCE
Aweda	Ruled for 11 years in 10th century BCE

Many subsequent leaders ruled for varying or unknown periods until the following selected leaders – ones attested not just in the regnal lists:

Zoscales (or King of Kings)	1st century CE
GDRT (or Gadarat)	Early 3rd century CE
DBH (or Azaba)	R. for unknown
Sembrouthes	R. for unknown
DTWNS (or Datawnas)	R. for unknown
Endubis	c. 295–310 CE
Aphilas	c. 310–320? CE
Ousanas	c. 320?–330? CE
Wazeba	c. 330? CE
Ahyawa (r. with her son, Ezana)	c. 330s CE

Subsequent Christian monarchs included:

Ezana	mid-340s–380
Ouazebas	late 4th century
Eon	early 5th century
MHDYS (or Mehadeyis)	c. 430
Ebana	middle 5th century
Nezool (or Nezana)	later 5th century
Ousas (or Ousanas II)	early 6th century
Kaleb	510s–late 530s
Israel	c. 550 or 570s
Wazena	550s and 560s
WʿZB (or Waʿzeb)	6th century
Gersem	c. 580
Ioel (or Joel)	c. 600
Hataz (or Hethasas)	c. 590/620
Armah	late 6th/early 7th century
Najashi	614–630
Dil Na'od	905–915

Emperors of Ethiopia

Yekuno Amlak	1270–1285
Yagbe'u Seyon	1285–1294
Senfa Ared IV	1294–1295
Hezba Asgad	1295–1296
Qedma Asgad	1296–1297
Jan Asgad	1297–1298
Saba Asgad	1298–1299
Wedem Arad	1299–1314
Amda Seyon I	1314–1344
Newaya Krestos	1344–1372
Newaya Maryam	1372–1382
Dawit I	1382–1413
Tewodros I	1413–1414
Yeshaq I	1414–1429
Andreyas	1429–1430
Takla Maryam	1430–1433
Sarwe Iyasus	1433–1433
Amda Iyasus	1433–1434
Zara Yaqob	1434–1468
Baeda Maryam I	1468–1478
Eskender	1478–1494
Amda Seyon II	1494–1494
Na'od	1494–1508
Dawit II (Libne Dengel)	1508–1540
Gelawdewos	1540–1559
Menas	1559–1563
Sarsa Dengel	1563–1597
Yaqob	1597–1603
Za Dengel	1603–1604
Susenyos I	1606–1632
Fasilides	1632–1667
Yohannes I	1667–1682

Iyasu I	1682–1706
Yeshaq Iyasu	1685–1685
Tekle Haymanot I	1706–1708
Amda Seyon	1707–1707
Tewoflos	1708–1711
Nebahne Yohannes	1709–1710
Yostos	1711–1716
Dawit III	1716–1721
Bakaffa	1721–1730
Iyasu II	1730–1755
Hezqeyas	1736–1737
Iyoas I	1755–1769
Yohannes II	1769–1769
Tekle Haymanot II	1769–1770
Susenyos II	1770–1770
Salomon II	1777–1779
Tekle Giyorgis I	1779–1800
Iyasu III	1784–1788
Iyasu	1787–1788
Baeda Maryam	1787–1788
Tekle Haymanot	1788–1789
Hezqeyas	1789–1794
Baeda Maryam II	1795–1795
Salomon III	1796–1799
Yonas	1797–1798
Demetros	1799–1801
Egwale Seyon	1801–1818
Iyoas II	1818–1821
Gigar	1821–1830
Baeda Maryam III	1826–1826
Iyasu IV	1830–1832
Gebre Krestos	1832–1832
Sahle Dengel	1832–1855
Egwale Anbesa	1832–1832
Yohannes III	1840–1851
Tewodros II	1855–1868
Tekle Giyorgis II	1868–1871
Yohannes IV	1871–1889
Menelik II	1889–1913
Lij Iyasu	1913–1916
Zewditu	1916–1930
Haile Selassie	1930–1974

CONGO: LUBA KINGDOM (*c.* 1585–1889)

Kongolo	*c.* 1585–1620
Kalala Ilunga	*c.* 1620–1640
Kasongo Mwine Kibanza	*c.* 1640–1650
Ngoi Sanza	*c.* 1650–1670
Kasongo Kabundulu	*c.* 1670–1685
Kumwimba	*c.* 1685–1700
Kasongo Bonswe	*c.* 1700–1715
Mwine Kombe Dai	*c.* 1715–1740

Kadilo c. 1740–1742
Kekenya c. 1742–1749
Kaumbo c. 1749–1769
Muketo c. 1769–1780
Ilunga Sunga c. 1780–1809
Kasongo Mukaya c. 1800–1809?
Kumwimba Ngombe c. 1809–1837
Ndai Mujinga c. 1837
Ilunga Kabale c. 1837–1864
Muloba c. 1864–1865
Kitamba c. 1865–1869
Kasongo a Kalombo c. 1869–1886
Nday a Mande c. 1886–1889

Here the kingdom was divided into the two royal lineages of Kasongo and Kabonga

SOUTHERN AFRICA: MUTAPA KINGDOM (*c.* 1430–1760)

Nyatsimba Mutota	c. 1430–1450
Matope Nyanhehwe Nebedza	c. 1450–1480
Mavura Maobwe	1480
Nyahuma Mukombero	1480–1490
Mavhuramhande	1490–1494
Chikuyo Chisamarengu	1494–1530
Neshangwe Munembire	c. 1530–1550
Chivere Nyasoro	c. 1550–1560
Negomo Chirisamhuru	1560–1589
Gatsi Rusere	1589–1623
Nyambo Kapararidze	1623–1629

Mutapa became part of the Portuguese Empire in 1629.

Mavura Mhande Felipe	1629–1652

Siti Kazurukamusapa	1652–1663

Mutapa became part of the Rozvi Empire in 1663.

Kamharapasu Mukombwe	1663–1692
Nyakambira	1692–1694

Mutapa again became part of the Portuguese Empire in 1694.

Nyamhande	1694–1707
Nyenyedzi Zenda	1707–1711
Baroma Mugwagwa	1711–1712

Mutapa again became part of the Rozvi Empire in 1712.

Samatambira Nyamhandu I	1712–1723

Mutapa gained independence. from Rozvi Empire in 1720.

Samatambira Nyamhandu I	1723–1735
Nyatsusu	1735–1740
Dehwe Mapunzaguta	1740–1759

Mutapa largely collapsed during the civil war in 1760.

SOUTHERN AFRICA: ZULU KINGOM (*c.* 1627–1879)

Zulu I kaMalandela	*c.* 1627–1709
Nkosinkulu kaZulu I	*c.* 1709?–?

Ntombela kaNkosinkulu	Dates unknown
Zulu II kaNtombela	Dates unknown
Gumade kaZulu	Dates unknown
Phunga kaGumede	c. 1657–1727
Mageba kaGumede	c. 1727–1745
Ndaba kaMageba	c. 1745–1763
Jama kaNdaba	c. 1763–1781
Mkabayi kaJama (regent)	c. 1781–1787
Senzangakhona kaJama	c. 1787–1816
Sigujana kaSenzangakhona	c. 1816
Shaka kaSenzangakhona	c. 1816–1828
Dingane kaSenzangakhona	c. 1828–1840
Mpande kaSenzangakhona	c. 1840–1872
Cetshwayo kaSenzangakhona	c. 1872–1879

Zulu became part of the British Empire in 1887.

EAST AFRICA: BACHWEZI KINGDOM (*c.* 1090–1485)

Kogyere I Rusija-Miryango (empress)	1090–1120
Kogyere II (empress)	1120–1130
Kyomya I kya Isiimbwa	1130–1140
Mugarra I	1140–1150
Ndahura I kya Rubumbi	1150–1160
Mulindwa	1160–1170
Wamara Bbala Bwigunda	1170–1200
Kyomya II Rurema	1200–1210
Kagoro	1210–1220
Kakara-ka-Shagama	1220–1250

Njunaki Kamaranga (empress)	1250–1280
Shagama-rwa-Njunaki	1280–1300
Wahaiguru Rukuba-Ntondo	1300–1310
Kateboha	1310–1330
Nyakahuma (queen regnant)	1330–1375
Kirobozi	1375–1400
Mugarra II wa Kirobozi	1400–1420
Buyonga bwa Kirobozi	1420–1430
Kyomya III	1430–1460
Nkome	1460–1485

The Bachwezi dynasty ended when the Babiito or Bito Dynasty formed Bunyoro-Kitara, which they rule to this day.

ANCIENT EGYPTIAN PHARAOHS

There is dispute about the dates and position of pharaohs within dynasties due to several historical sources being incomplete or inconsistent. This list aims to provide an overview, but is not exhaustive and dates are approximate. There may also be differences in name spellings between different sources. The throne name is given first, followed by the personal name.

ANCIENT EGYPTIAN DEITIES

Ancient Egyptian gods and goddesses were responsible for maat (divine order or stability), and different deities represented different natural forces, such as Ra the Sun God. After the Egyptian state was first founded in around 3100 BCE, pharaohs claimed to be divine representatives and successors of these gods. Some of the significant gods and goddesses and their significant responsibilities are listed here.

Amun/Amen/Amen-Ra	Creation
Atem/Tem	Creation, the sun
Ra	The sun
Isis	The afterlife, fertility, magic
Osiris	Death and resurrection, agriculture
Hathor	The sky, the sun, motherhood
Horus	Kingship, the sky
Set	Storms, violence, deserts
Maat	Truth and justice, she personifies *maat*
Anubis	The dead, the underworld

PREDYNASTIC AND EARLY DYNASTIC PERIODS (*c.* 3000–2686 BCE)

First Dynasty (*c.* 3150–2890 BCE)

The first dynasty begins at the unification of Upper and Lower Egypt.

Narmer (Menes/M'na?)	c. 3150 BCE
Aha (Teti)	c. 3125 BCE
Djer (Itej)	54 years
Djet (Ita)	10 years
Merneith (possibly the first female Egyptian pharaoh)	c. 2950 BCE
Khasti (Den)	42 years
Merybiap (Adjib)	10 years

Semerkhet (Iry)	8.5 years
Qa'a (Qebeh)	34 years
Sneferka	*c.* 2900 BCE
Horus-Ba (Horus Bird)	*c.* 2900 BCE

Second Dynasty (*c.* 2890–2686 BCE)

Little is known about the second dynasty of Egypt.

Hetepsekhemwy (Nebtyhotep)	15 years
Nebra	14 years
Nynetjer (Banetjer)	43–45 years
Ba	unknown
Weneg-Nebty	*c.* 2740 BCE
Wadjenes (Wadj-sen)	*c.* 2740 BCE
Nubnefer	unknown
Senedj	*c.* 47 years
Peribsen (Seth-Peribsen)	unknown
Sekhemib (Sekhemib-Perenmaat)	*c.* 2720 BCE
Neferkara I	25 years
Neferkasokkar	8 years
Horus Sa	unknown
Hudejefa (real name missing)	11 years
Khasekhemwy (Bebty)	18 years

OLD KINGDOM (*c.* 2686–2181 BCE)

Third Dynasty (*c.* 2686–2613 BCE)

The third dynasty was the first dynasty of the Old Kingdom. Its capital was at Memphis.

Djoser (Netjerikhet)	c. 2650 BCE
Sekhemkhet (Djoser-Teti)	2649–2643 BCE
Nebka? (Sanakht)	c. 2650 BCE
Qahedjet (Huni?)	unknown
Khaba (Huni?)	2643–2637 BCE
Huni	2637–2613 BCE

Fourth Dynasty (*c.* 2613–2498 BCE)

The fourth dynasty is sometimes known as the 'golden age' of Egypt's Old Kingdom.

Snefru (Nebmaat)	2613–2589 BCE
Khufu, or Cheops (Medjedu)	2589–2566 BCE
Djedefre (Kheper)	2566–2558 BCE
Khafre (Userib)	2558–2532 BCE
Menkaure (Kakhet)	2532–2503 BCE
Shepseskaf (Shepeskhet)	2503–2498 BCE

Fifth Dynasty (*c.* 2498–2345 BCE)

There is some doubt over the succession of pharaohs in the fifth dynasty, especially Shepseskare.

Userkaf	2496/8–2491 BCE
Sahure	2490–2477 BCE
Neferirkare-Kakai	2477–2467 BCE
Neferefre (Izi)	2460–2458 BCE
Shepseskare (Netjeruser)	few months between 2458 and 2445 BCE
Niuserre (Ini)	2445–2422 BCE
Menkauhor (Kaiu)	2422–2414 BCE

Djedkare (Isesi)	2414–2375 BCE
Unis (Wenis)	2375–2345 BCE

Sixth Dynasty (*c.* 2345–2181 BCE)

Teti	2345–2333 BCE
Userkare	2333–2332 BCE
Meryre (Pepi I)	2332–2283 BCE
Merenre I (Nemtyemsaf I)	2283–2278 BCE
Neferkare (Pepi II)	2278–2183 BCE
Merenre II (Nemtyemsaf II)	2183 or 2184 BCE
Netjerkare (Siptah I) or Nitocris	2182–2179 BCE

FIRST INTERMEDIATE PERIOD (*c.* 2181–2040 BCE)

Seventh and Eighth Dynasties (*c.* 2181–2160 BCE)

There is little evidence on this period in ancient Egyptian history.

Menkare	*c.* 2181 BCE
Neferkare II	unknown
Neferkare III (Neby)	unknown
Djedkare (Shemai)	unknown
Neferkare IV (Khendu)	unknown
Merenhor	unknown
Sneferka (Neferkamin I)	unknown
Nikare	unknown
Neferkare V (Tereru)	unknown
Neferkahor	unknown
Neferkare VI (Peiseneb)	unknown to 2171 BCE
Neferkamin (Anu)	*c.* 2170 BCE

Qakare (Ibi)	2175–2171 BCE
Neferkaure	2167–2163 BCE
Neferkauhor (Khuwihapi)	2163–2161 BCE
Neferiirkkare (Pepi)	2161–2160 BCE

Ninth Dynasty (*c.* 2160–2130 BCE)

There is little evidence on this period in ancient Egyptian history which is why many of the periods of rule are unknown.

Maryibre (Khety I)	2160 BCE to unknown
Name unknown	unknown
Naferkare VII	unknown
Seneh (Setut)	unknown

The following pharaohs and their dates of rule are unknown or widely unconfirmed.

Tenth Dynasty (*c.* 2130–2040 BCE)

Rulers in the Tenth dynasty were based in Lower Egypt.

Meryhathor	2130 BCE to unknown
Neferkare VIII	2130–2040 BCE
Wahkare (Khety III)	unknown
Merykare	unknown to 2040 BCE
Name unknown	unknown

Eleventh Dynasty (*c.* 2134–1991 BCE)

Rulers in the eleventh dynasty were based in Upper Egypt.

Intef the Elder	unknown

Tepia (Mentuhotep I)	unknown to 2133 BCE
Sehertawy (Intef I)	2133–2117 BCE
Wahankh (Intef II)	2117–2068 BCE
Nakhtnebtepefer (Intef III)	2068–2060/40 BCE

MIDDLE KINGDOM (*c.* 2040–1802 BCE)

Eleventh Dynasty Continued (*c.* 2134–1991 BCE)

This period is usually known as the beginning of the Middle Kingdom.

Nebhepetre (Mentuhotep II)	2060–2040 BCE as king of Upper Egypt, 2040–2009 BCE as King of Upper and Lower Egypt
Sankhkare (Mentuhotep III)	2009–1997 BCE
Nebtawyre (Mentuhotep IV)	1997–1991 BCE

Twelfth Dynasty (*c.* 1991–1802 BCE)

The twelfth dynasty was one of the most stable prior to the New Kingdom, and is often thought to be the peak of the Middle Kingdom.

Sehetepibre (Amenemhat I)	1991–1962 BCE
Kheperkare (Senusret I / Sesostris I)	1971–1926 BCE
Nubkaure (Amenemhat II)	1929–1895 BCE
Khakheperre (Senusret II / Sesostris II)	1898–1878 BCE
Khakaure (Senusret III / Sesostris III)	1878–1839 BCE
Nimaatre (Amenemhat III)	1860–1815 BCE
Maakherure (Amenemhat IV)	1815–1807 BCE
Sobekkare (Sobekneferu/Nefrusobek)	1807–1802 BCE

SECOND INTERMEDIATE PERIOD (*c.* 1802–1550 BCE)

Thirteenth Dynasty (*c.* 1802–*c.* 1649 BCE)

There is some ambiguity on the periods of rule of the thirteenth dynasty, but it is marked by a period of several short rules. This dynasty is often combined with the eleventh, twelfth and fourteenth dynasties under the Middle Kingdom.

Sekhemre Khutawy (Sobekhotep I)	1802–1800 BCE
Mehibtawy Sekhemkare (Amenemhat Sonbef)	1800–1796 BCE
Nerikare (Sobek)	1796 BCE
Sekhemkare (Amenemhat V)	1796–1793 BCE
Ameny Qemau	1795–1792 BCE
Hotepibre (Qemau Siharnedjheritef)	1792–1790 BCE
Lufni	1790–1788 BCE
Seankhibre (Amenemhat VI)	1788–1785 BCE
Semenkare (Nebnuni)	1785–1783 BCE
Sehetepibre (Sewesekhtawy)	1783–1781 BCE
Sewadijkare I	1781 BCE
Nedjemibre (Amenemhat V)	1780 BCE
Khaankhre (Sobekhotep)	1780–1777 BCE
Renseneb	1777 BCE
Awybre (Hor)	1777–1775 BCE
Sekhemrekhutawy Khabaw	1775–1772 BCE
Djedkheperew	1772–1770 BCE
Sebkay	unknown
Sedjefakare (Kay Amenemhat)	1769–1766 BCE
Khutawyre (Wegaf)	c. 1767 BCE
Userkare (Khendjer)	c. 1765 BCE
Smenkhkare (Imyremeshaw)	started in 1759 BCE

Sehetepkare (Intef IV)	*c.* 10 years
Meribre (Seth)	ended in 1749 BCE
Sekhemresewadjtawy (Sobekhotep III)	1755–1751 BCE
Khasekhemre (Neferhotep I)	1751–1740 BCE
Menwadjre (Sihathor)	1739 BCE
Khaneferre (Sobekhotep IV)	1740–1730 BCE
Merhotepre (Sobekhotep V)	1730 BCE
Knahotepre (Sobekhotep VI)	*c.* 1725 BCE
Wahibre (Ibiau)	1725–1714 BCE
Merneferre (Ay I)	1714–1691 BCE
Merhotepre (Ini)	1691–1689 BCE
Sankhenre (Sewadjtu)	1675–1672 BCE
Mersekhemre (Ined)	1672–1669 BCE
Sewadjkare II (Hori)	*c.* 5 years
Merkawre (Sobekhotep VII)	1664–1663 BCE
Seven kings (names unknown)	1663–? BCE

Note: the remaining pharaohs of the thirteenth dynasty are not listed here as they are either unknown or there is a lot of ambiguity about when they ruled.

Fourteenth Dynasty (*c.* 1805/1710–1650 BCE)

Rulers in the fourteenth dynasty were based at Avaris, the capital of this dynasty.

Sekhaenre (Yakbim)	1805–1780 BCE
Nubwoserre (Ya'ammu)	1780–1770 BCE
Khawoserre (Qareh)	1770–1745 BCE
Aahotepre ('Ammu)	1760–1745 BCE
Maaibre (Sheshi)	1745–1705 BCE

Aasehre (Nehesy)	*c.* 1705 BCE
Khakherewre	unknown
Nebefawre	*c.* 1704 BCE
Sehebre	1704–1699 BCE
Merdjefare	*c.* 1699 BCE

Note: the remaining pharaohs of the fourteenth dynasty are not listed here as they are either unknown or there is a lot of ambiguity about when they ruled.

Fifteenth Dynasty (*c.* 1650–1544 BCE)

The fifteenth dynasty was founded by Salitas and covered a large part of the Nile region.

Salitas	*c.* 1650 BCE
Semqen	1649 BCE to unknown
'Aper-'Anat	unknown
Sakir-Har	unknown
Seuserenre (Khyan)	*c.* 30 to 35 years
Nebkhepeshre (Apepi)	1590 BCE?
Nakhtyre (Khamudi)	1555–1544 BCE

Sixteenth Dynasty (*c.* 1650–1580 BCE)

Rulers in the sixteenth dynasty were based at Thebes, the capital of this dynasty. The name and date of rule of the first pharaoh is unknown.

Sekhemresementawy (Djehuti)	3 years
Sekhemresemeusertawy (Sobekhotep VIII)	16 years
Sekhemresankhtawy (Neferhotep III)	1 year
Seankhenre (Mentuhotepi)	less than a year

Sewadjenre (Nebiryraw)	26 years
Neferkare (?) (Nebiryraw II)	*c*. 1600 BCE
Semenre	*c*. 1600 BCE
Seuserenre (Bebiankh)	12 years
Djedhotepre (Dedumose I)	*c*. 1588–1582 BCE
Djedneferre (Dedumose II)	*c*. 1588–1582 BCE
Djedankhre (Montensaf)	*c*. 1590 BCE
Merankhre (Mentuhotep VI)	*c*. 1585 BCE
Seneferibre (Senusret IV)	unknown
Sekhemre (Shedwast)	unknown

Seventeenth Dynasty (*c.* 1650–1550 BCE)

Rulers in the seventeenth dynasty ruled Upper Egypt.

Sekhemrewahkhaw (Rahotep)	*c*. 1620 BCE
Sekhemre Wadjkhaw (Sobekemsaf I)	*c*. 7 years
Sekhemre Shedtawy (Sobekemsaf II)	unknown to *c*. 1573 BCE
Sekhemre-Wepmaat (Intef V)	*c*. 1573–1571 BCE
Nubkheperre (Intef VI)	*c*. 1571–1565 BCE
Sekhemre-Heruhirmaat (Intef VII)	late 1560s BCE
Senakhtenre (Ahmose)	*c*. 1558 BCE
Seqenenre (Tao I)	1558–1554 BCE
Wadkheperre (Kamose)	1554–1549 BCE

NEW KINGDOM (*c.* 1550–1077 BCE)

Eighteenth Dynasty (*c.* 1550–1292 BCE)

The first dynasty of Egypt's New Kingdom marked the beginning of ancient Egypt's highest power and expansion.

Nebpehtire (Ahmose I)	c. 1550–1525 BCE
Djeserkare (Amenhotep I)	1541–1520 BCE
Aakheperkare (Thutmose I)	1520–1492 BCE
Aakheperenre (Thutmose II)	1492–1479 BCE
Maatkare (Hatshepsut)	1479–1458 BCE
Menkheperre (Thutmose III)	1458–1425 BCE
Aakheperrure (Amenhotep II)	1425–1400 BCE
Menkheperure (Thutmose IV)	1400–1390 BCE
Nebmaatre 'the Magnificent' (Amehotep III)	1390–1352 BCE
Neferkheperure Waenre (Amenhotep IV)	1352–1336 BCE
Ankhkheperure (Smenkhkare)	1335–1334 BCE
Ankhkheperure mery Neferkheperure (Neferneferuaten III)	1334–1332 BCE
Nebkheperure (Tutankhamun)	1332–1324 BCE
Kheperkheperure (Aya II)	1324–1320 BCE
Djeserkheperure Setpenre (Haremheb)	1320–1292 BCE

Nineteenth Dynasty (*c.* 1550–1292 BCE)

The nineteenth dynasty is also known as the Ramessid dynasty as it includes Ramesses II, one of the most famous and influential Egyptian pharaohs.

Menpehtire (Ramesses I)	1292–1290 BCE
Menmaatre (Seti I)	1290–1279 BCE
Usermaatre Setpenre 'the Great', 'Ozymandias' (Ramesses II)	1279–1213 BCE
Banenre (Merneptah)	1213–1203 BCE
Menmire Setpenre (Amenmesse)	1203–1200 BCE
Userkheperure (Seti II)	1203–1197 BCE

Sekhaenre (Merenptah Siptah)	1197–1191 BCE
Satre Merenamun (Tawosret)	1191–1190 BCE

Twentieth Dynasty (*c.* 1190–1077 BCE)

This, the third dynasty of the New Kingdom, is generally thought to mark the start of the decline of ancient Egypt.

Userkhaure (Setnakht)	1190–1186 BCE
Usermaatre Meryamun (Ramesses III)	1186–1155 BCE
Heqamaatre Setpenamun (Ramesses IV)	1155–1149 BCE
Heqamaatre Setpenamun (Ramesses IV)	1155–1149 BCE
Usermaatre Sekheperenre (Ramesses V)	1149–1145 BCE
Nebmaatre Meryamun (Ramesses VI)	1145–1137 BCE
Usermaatre Setpenre Meryamun (Ramesses VII)	1137–1130 BCE
Usermaatre Akhenamun (Ramesses VIII)	1130–1129 BCE
Neferkare Setpenre (Ramesses IX)	1128–1111 BCE
Khepermaatre Setpenptah (Ramesses X)	1111–1107 BCE
Menmaatre Setpenptah (Ramesses XI)	1107–1077 BCE

Twenty-first Dynasty (*c.* 1077–943 BCE)

Rulers in the twenty-first dynasty were based at Tanis and mainly governed Lower Egypt.

Hedjkheperre-Setpenre (Nesbanadjed I)	1077–1051 BCE
Neferkare (Amenemnisu)	1051–1047 BCE
Aakkheperre (Pasebakhenniut I)	1047–1001 BCE
Usermaatre (Amenemope)	1001–992 BCE
Aakheperre Setepenre (Osorkon the Elder)	992–986 BCE
Netjerikheperre-Setpenamun (Siamun)	986–967 BCE
Titkheperure (Pasebakhenniut II)	967–943 BCE

Twenty-second Dynasty (*c.* 943–728 BCE)

Sometimes called the Bubastite dynasty. Its pharaohs came from Libya.

Hedjkheneperre Setpenre (Sheshonq I)	943–922 BCE
Sekhemkheperre Setepenre (Osorkon I)	922–887 BCE
Heqakheperre Setepenre (Sheshonq II)	887–885 BCE
Tutkheperre (Sheshonq Llb)	c. the 880s BCE
Hedjkheperre Setepenre (Takelot I Meriamun)	885–872 BCE
Usermaatre Setpenre (Sheshonq III)	837–798 BCE
Hedjkheperre Setepenre (Sheshonq IV)	798–785 BCE
Usermaatre Setpenre (Pami Meriamun)	785–778 BCE
Aakheperre (Sheshonq V)	778–740 BCE
Usermaatre (Osorkon IV)	740–720 BCE

Twenty-third and Twenty-fourth Dynasties (*c.* 837–720 BCE)

These dynasties were led mainly by Libyans and mainly ruled Upper Egypt.

Hedjkheperre Setpenre (Takelot II)	837–813 BCE
Usermaatre Setpenamun (Meriamun Pedubaste I)	826–801 BCE
Usermaatre Meryamun (Sheshonq VI)	801–795 BCE
Usermaatre Setpenamun (Osorkon III)	795–767 BCE
Usermaatre-Setpenamun (Takelot III)	773–765 BCE
Usermaatre-Setpenamun (Meriamun Rudamun)	765–762 BCE
Shepsesre (Tefnakhte)	732–725 BCE
Wahkare (Bakenrenef)	725–720 BCE

Twenty-fifth Dynasty (*c.* 744–656 BCE)

Also known as the Kushite period, the twenty-fifth dynasty follows the Nubian invasions.

Piankhy (Piye)	744–714 BCE
Djedkaure (Shebitkku)	714–705 BCE
Neferkare (Shabaka)	705–690 BCE
Khuinefertemre (Taharqa)	690–664 BCE

LATE PERIOD (*c.* 664–332 BCE)

Twenty-sixth Dynasty (*c.* 664 – 525 BCE)

Also known as the Saite period, the twenty-sixth dynasty was the last native period before the Persian invasion in 525 BCE.

Wahibre (Psamtik I)	664–610 BCE
Wehemibre (Necho II)	610–595 BCE
Neferibre (Psamtik II)	595–589 BCE
Haaibre (Apreis)	589–570 BCE
Khemibre (Amasis II)	570–526 BCE
Ankhkaenre (Psamtik III)	526–525 BCE

Twenty-seventh Dynasty (*c.* 525–404 BCE)

The twenty-seventh dynasty is also known as the First Egyptian Satrapy and was ruled by the Persian Achaemenids.

Mesutre (Cambyses II)	525–1 July 522 BCE
Seteture (Darius I)	522–November 486 BCE
Kheshayarusha (Xerxes I)	November 486–December 465 BCE

Artabanus of Persia	465–464 BCE
Arutakhshashas (Artaxerxes I)	464–424 BCE
Ochus (Darius II)	July 423–March 404 BCE

Twenty-eighth Dynasty (*c.* 404–398 BCE)

The twenty-eighth dynasty consisted of a single pharaoh.

Amunirdisu (Amyrtaeus)	404–398 BCE

Twenty-ninth Dynasty (*c.* 398–380 BCE)

The twenty-ninth dynasty was founded following the overthrow of Amyrtaeus.

Baenre Merynatjeru (Nepherites I)	398–393 BCE
Khnemmaatre Setepenkhnemu (Hakor)	*c.* 392–391 BCE
Userre Setepenptah (Psammuthis)	*c.* 391 BCE
Khnemmaatre Setepenkhnemu (Hakor)	*c.* 390–379 BCE
Nepherites II	*c.* 379 BCE

Thirtieth Dynasty (*c.* 379–340 BCE)

The thirtieth dynasty is thought to be the final native dynasty of ancient Egypt.

Kheperkare (Nectanebo I)	*c.* 379–361 BCE
Irimaatenre (Teos)	*c.* 361–359 BCE
Snedjemibre Setepenanhur (Nectanebo II)	*c.* 359–340 BCE

Thirty-first Dynasty (*c.* 340–332 BCE)

The thirty-first dynasty is also known as the Second Egyptian Satrapy and was ruled by the Persian Achaemenids.

Ochus (Artaxerxes III)	*c*. 340–338 BCE
Arses (Artaxerxes IV)	338–336 BCE
Darius III	336–332 BCE

MACEDONIAN/ARGEAD DYNASTY (*c*. 332–309 BCE)

Alexander the Great conquered Persia and Egypt in 332 BCE.

Setpenre Meryamun (Alexander III of Macedon 'the Great')	332–323 BCE
Setpenre Meryamun (Philip Arrhidaeus)	323–317 BCE
Khaibre Setepenamun (Alexander IV)	317–309 BCE

PTOLEMAIC DYNASTY (*c*. 305–30 BCE)

The Ptolemaic dynasty in Egypt was the last dynasty of ancient Egypt before it became a province of Rome.

Ptolemy I Soter	305–282 BCE
Ptolemy II Philadelphos	284–246 BCE
Arsinoe II	*c*. 277–270 BCE
Ptolemy III Euergetes	246–222 BCE
Berenice II	244/243–222 BCE
Ptolemy IV Philopater	222–204 BCE
Arsinoe III	220–204 BCE
Ptolemy V Epiphanes	204–180 BCE
Cleopatra I	193–176 BCE
Ptolemy VI Philometor	180–164, 163–145 BCE

Cleopatra II	175–164 BCE, 163–127 BCE and 124–116 BCE
Ptolemy VIII Physcon	171–163 BCE, 144–131 BCE and 127–116 BCE
Ptolemy VII Neos Philopator	145–144 BCE
Cleopatra III	142–131 BCE, 127–107 BCE
Ptolemy Memphites	113 BCE
Ptolemy IX Soter	116–110 BCE
Cleopatra IV	116–115 BCE
Ptolemy X Alexander	110–109 BCE
Berenice III	81–80 BCE
Ptolemy XI Alexander	80 BCE
Ptolemy XII Auletes	80–58 BCE, 55–51 BCE
Cleopatra V Tryphaena	79–68 BCE
Cleopatra VI	58–57 BCE
Berenice IV	58–55 BCE
Cleopatra VII	52–30 BCE
Ptolemy XIII Theos Philopator	51–47 BCE
Arsinoe IV	48–47 BCE
Ptolemy XIV Philopator	47–44 BCE
Ptolemy XV Caesar	44–30 BCE

In 30 BCE, Egypt became a province of the Roman Empire.